Flipping the Birdie

S. L. WOEPPEL

RIVER GROVE
BOOKS

Published by River Grove Books
Austin, TX
www.rivergrovebooks.com

Distributed by River Grove Books

Design and composition by Greenleaf Book Group and Kimberly Lance
Cover design by Greenleaf Book Group and Kimberly Lance

Publisher's Cataloging-in-Publication data is available.

Print ISBN: 978-1-63299-877-4

eBook ISBN: 978-1-63299-878-1

First Edition

For Jeremy

1

"I'M GONNA WAIT FOR the fire department."

"You've got to be kidding me," I replied, staring at the drunken base-ball fan in front of me. He wore an imitation team jersey with the number sixty-nine, which maybe fit him last season, but not so much anymore. It was well shy of touching his belt, providing me an all-too-personal view of his beer-filled belly.

"You want the Chicago Fire Department to drive a truck out here, prop a ladder," I said, looking around, "who knows where, and send firefighters up to *carry you down* on their backs? Rather than be saved by someone who is fully capable of doing it right now and in fact trained and employed to do so?"

He smiled, his body swaying after what was probably several hours of guzzling beer. "I don't need no saving by a girl." Then he belched. Loudly. In my face.

"Fucking typical," I muttered as I turned away.

He belched a few more times. "Aftershocks," he laughed, losing his balance only to catch himself against the stadium grandstand lights that rose high above Wrigley Field.

How the hell did this guy even get up here? I wondered, as he gazed out over the stadium of sports fans. He smiled like he had all the time in the world, like he wasn't holding up a Major League Baseball game that was being televised live. Did he not hear that the fans, who had admittedly cheered him on at first, now were growing angry as an official game delay ensued well beyond the novelty of his stunt?

"Just let me get you out of here, yeah?" I asked in my nicest voice, the one that apparently didn't sound as nice to everyone else.

"Hell no." He patted his belly as though it contained something precious instead of High Life and stadium dogs. "I got the best seat in the house, right here."

I swore under my breath. "Guess we're waiting for the fire department. They have nothing better to do anyway."

My sarcasm didn't register.

Chicago Fire was going to love this. I pulled my phone out and hit my direct line to the fire chief. Superfan stared at me half-dazed, his eyes traveling up my jeans and pausing at my T-shirt. Reaching my face, the upper half of which was obscured by a simple black mask, he took in my death glare, cleared his throat, and looked away.

I willed my anger to settle as I waited for the chief to answer my call.

"Winston," came a gruff voice over the line.

"Hey, I'm at the stadium. We've got a code asshole." I raised my voice on the last word for the benefit of my companion. The "nice voice" wasn't working anyway.

"Bullshit. It's the first seventy-degree Saturday of the year—we're spread thin." Shuffling papers sounded in the background. "Just take care of it."

"He's refusing my assistance," I argued, staring out at the crowd that was beginning to stand and stomp their feet. "You know my hands are tied. The new law states that if he's not in immediate danger, I need his permission to—"

"I know what the law says," Winston replied. I could hear his utter distaste for me, the echo of his words that this was no job for a woman. Today was another reason for him to push for replacing me. "You know how much manpower this is going to take? Isn't this *your* job? Figure it out. I'm not wasting time on this."

I winced because he was right. But I was stuck.

"My hands are tied," I repeated, looking over at Superfan. "Shit, I'll call you back."

I hung up as Superfan staggered, the cardboard signs he had clasped under his arm slipping from his grasp and hitting the deck before sliding down the pitched rooftop.

"Oops," he said as they sailed over the seats below in the early summer breeze, landing softly in midfield. *Hey Chicago* and *What do you say?* stared up at us. He looked down and grimaced, appearing to suddenly realize his potential fate from this height, and swayed again.

If he were to fall, even slip a little, I could legally intervene, catch him, get him down from there, and this would be over. If I intervened before that, no doubt my "bruised-ego complaint file" would grow, and I was on strict instruction to *be nice.*

I willed his feet to step closer to the edge.

But instead, he shakily lowered himself to the steel rooftop and took a seat.

With a huff, I sat down next to him. Groans and boos made their way up from the stands.

"Yeah, yeah," I mumbled.

The faint chant of *Push them off, push them off* didn't seem to reach his sloppy brain, as he held true to the belief that his masculinity could better withstand the negative press coverage—and the large fine that was likely to come—more than the idea of being rescued by me, a city-employed *female* superhero. Problem was, I wasn't sure my already shaky reputation could handle another public fail.

So we waited. In the meantime, the press made their way closer, cameras and boom mics in hand, maneuvering to find a good angle from below us. The mood in the stadium was turning hostile.

"You know," I said as I gazed into the stands, "for a minute, years ago, I naively thought being a 'superhero' would offer me some magical ego boost. That I'd be adored or even just appreciated by my city. That I'd be saving lives on a daily basis. But in reality, it's a good job about three or four days out of the year, the days I can actually do some good, make a difference. The rest are increasingly like this—a shit show." I turned toward my half-passed-out rooftop companion. "I should thank you for your part in curing me of my childish delusions."

He had no reply.

If I were Chief Winston, I'd disregard the rules and take care of the situation. Ask for forgiveness instead of permission. But Winston had backup, people who would support his decision.

I didn't. Mine was more of a solo operation.

I decided to try another tactic.

"Should we go get some beer at Stinky's Bar?" I asked with all the pep I could muster. "They have the best pretzels in the city."

"Is it true what they say about you?" Superfan slurred as he tried to stand and failed, still oblivious to the jeers and profanity rising from the crowd.

If he asked what seemed to be the question of the year, I might pick him up and throw him off the roof myself, aiming him right where Sanchez had hit an epic double last week.

"Can you actually crush my penis with your vagina?"

I rolled my eyes so far back they almost hurt, but I didn't respond. This conversation was nothing new to me in recent months. Someone on TV had mentioned something about female supers and the strength of our vaginas. As the strongest female super on record, they specifically noted mine.

Funny that questioning a male super's ability to control their sex organs wasn't a topic of discussion. It was only powered women who couldn't wield the strength of their vaginas, apparently. Yeah, like that's ever been a thing.

"We don't have to worry about *you* finding out, do we? I can, however, crush your balls with my pinky toe, so I recommend you show a little respect."

He sneered.

"I have better things I could be doing, asshole."

"Wow." He whistled. "Is it that time of the month? Should you even be working right now?"

I got right in his face, immediately regretting my proximity to his breath. "You've got real shit for brains, don't you? I recommend you keep your foul trap shut before I push you right off this little perch myself."

I could see the wheels turning. Slowly, but turning nonetheless. He opened his mouth to speak.

I cut him off before he could even start. "You know what you are? You're the embodiment of whisky dick. Your whole person right now screams flaccid, useless, tiny, fumbling pecker."

Yeah, so maybe this wasn't me being *nice*.

"You're a crazy bitch. I don't need you here. I've got it all under control."

"I see that," I said, getting to my feet and trying to ignore the frustration emanating from the stands. "You're a real problem solver." Why was I even engaging? This wasn't part of my training. I was trained to take it silently and just do the job. But when my job turned into pecker-sitting . . .

And why were the chants directed toward me now? I'd heard this particular ditty a few times before and had chosen to ignore it. But it seemed to have legs today. *Fly away, Bird! There's no trophy for third. Fly away, Bird. You're as useless as a turd.*

See, I was known as the Chicago Bird, with powers of strength and speed and outfitted with a handy little jet pack developed at the Jet Propulsion Lab. I was technically the third most physically powered hero in the world, and the only woman in the top twenty. The rhyme was clever, no?

Though, let's be honest—despite the value I brought to my city, be it saving lives or, on most days, just lifting heavy shit for other city departments, I've never been valuable to the people of my city. I was ignored or mocked by the press, unappreciated, underpaid, hamstrung by city council, and blamed for messes that were not my doing, like this one.

"So, Bird, could you crush a whole car with just your va . . . *burp* . . . gina?"

"You kiss your dog with that mouth?"

"Sure do."

"Poor dog."

"Whatever, you're just pissed cause you can't get no man to get you off."

I exhaled slowly, working to keep my cool while letting the daydream play out in my mind. I grab Whisky-Dick by the balls and toss him, one-handed, far out into the middle of Wrigley Field. His toddler-like screams accompany him all the way down, as the eyes of everyone in the stadium follow, brows up and mouths agape. He lands like a water balloon, his beer belly bursting open on second base, the endless supply of beer rising like a glorious fountain, filling all the empty cups of the angry baseball fans. They'd rise up and cheer. Fists pumping. Awe on their faces. Chanting my name. "Bird. Bird. Bird."

It was a good daydream.

———

"YOU LEFT HIM THERE." Harold Thompson, mayor extraordinaire and my boss, chastised me while delivering a punitive glare . . . again. "You are paid to help people out of sticky situations, even if they get there of their own stupidity. You are not paid to berate them with what I can only call *highly* explicit profanity that is now all over social media and the news. Did you have any idea there was a boom mic right behind you?"

"No. But I can't—"

"Wait," he said, his hand flying up. "I'm not done. Are you aware that there's a viral video of you flying off in your jet pack and leaving a helpless citizen to fend for himself? How does that make us look?"

"You're kidding. Helpless citizen?" I shot back from my chair on the other side of his desk, my boot-clad feet resting atop the hundred-year-old oak surface.

"The truth is what the media prints, not what actually happened. Your actions reflect on all of us. Look, Bird, I'm constantly going to bat for you with this job. You know I value you, but you've got to meet me halfway."

"He was sexually harassing me!" I raised my voice, staring down his warm brown eyes shining with equal parts pity and anger.

"He was a drunken idiot. He has no power."

"Oh, I get it. I'm just supposed to deal, right? Take it with my mouth shut? I'm a joke, and I'm supposed to let it be that way, not defend myself? Besides, this guy didn't even want to be saved. He demanded the fire department."

"Birdie," he sighed, using my actual name, indicating we were shifting from boss/employee into the zone of work friend. "You're not a joke. You've always just heard the negative and chosen to ignore everything else."

"Whatever. I should have shocked him with the news that today's fire department is 35 percent female."

Thompson dropped his head and shook it slowly, as if he didn't know what to do with me. Welcome to the club. I didn't know what to do with me either.

"Birdie, your role as our muni-hero—"

"Muni-hero?" I interrupted, raising my eyebrow.

"I'm testing it out."

"Well, consider the test a fail."

"Hmm." He considered it. "Your role as our CityJack."

"Nope," I replied quickly.

"CityJack, like a jack of all trades—"

"Master of none—I get it. Still no."

"Whatever. My point is your job includes gaining the trust of the people of this city. Things were fine enough for a while, but you're slipping."

I snapped my head up. "I have more saves than anyone in the union. I work twenty-four hours a day. I cover the city *by myself*, not to mention all my calls out of town—"

"And you've got the lawsuits to prove it."

I sighed and took my feet to the floor, leaning in. "It's all crap. None of it is valid."

"Bird." Back to boss. "Fifteen years ago, the world was still figuring out what to do with people like you. Hundreds of supers were coming out of the woodwork—the rest of society panicked a bit. Evolution had somehow sped up overnight. The goal defaulted to getting control over the science of it all. Yes, mistakes were made. Then the goal shifted to finding gainful employment for supers, a purpose to utilize their talents quietly. But you know all this. And you know society's changing now; the fear is subsiding. Supers are being celebrated for their differences instead of living on the perimeter. And the aldermen of this city want a face, a representative of the city—like New York's got."

"I see. So after being told to be quiet, hide in the shadows for ten years, not draw attention, not talk to the press, I'm suddenly supposed to be the perfect mascot, because now it reflects well on you? I'm supposed to just change overnight? Forget the past?"

"Do you *like* your job, Birdie?"

I furrowed my brow. "What kind of question is that? Do *you* like your job?"

"I do," he responded without hesitation and then waited for my reply. "It's a serious question."

"It's a stupid question. Of course I like my job. I'm a superhero, for God's sake. Who wouldn't want this job? It's got shit hours, shit pay, a less-than-adoring fan base, and zero vacation time. What's not to love?"

The truth was, I had loved the job, once. But now I wasn't sure if I loved it, or if it was just all there was to me.

Thompson walked out from behind his desk, looking very mayorly in his fitted light-blue suit that complemented his dark skin and bald head. "Do you even like people?"

In the moment, I couldn't think of a single person I liked. Maybe RuPaul, because he'd always been as unapologetic about his identity as I wanted to be.

"Thompson, I love this city. I grew up here. Haven't I proved that every day for the last ten years? I'm out there getting people out of sticky situations, as you say. What are you getting at?"

"Are you seeing anyone, Birdie? Dating?"

I laughed. "Yeah, the entire city of Chicago. When would I have time to date?"

"The job requires that you be on call twenty-four seven, not that you need to go out and find work to do twenty-four seven. A lot of the calls you respond to could be left to the police and fire."

"That's a waste of resources."

"That's government."

I might have laughed if I wasn't so pissed off.

"You throw yourself into this work at the exclusion of everything else." He met my eyes and didn't look away.

"I don't need anything else. There's nothing else out there for me. Whatever chances I once had at a normal life were snuffed out when I became a super."

He smiled kindly. "It doesn't have to be that way. Maybe if you change your outlook . . ."

I sat up straight again. "Since when do mayoral duties include psychiatry?"

"Well, it's just that this last lawsuit flagged our insurance."

"What does that mean?"

"It means your litigation load is too high. It's been steadily rising, having very much to do with your off-color commentary during jobs. And you've been flagged."

"The lawsuits are proportional to my saves," I stated confidently, not sure if that was true or not.

"They're not, Bird. Our insurance premium on you is more than your salary and mine combined. You are now considered," he paused to give air quotes, "an elevated risk."

This was bad, very bad. Anytime they wanted to get rid of a super, they began quoting insurance rates and property damage. The truth was, I prevented damage more than I ever caused it, but that wasn't a factor in the models. If we were liked, no one cared about the insurance. They just paid. If we were less than popular, as I seemed to be more and more, it suddenly became a topic of concern and grounds for release.

The last thing I needed was to get sent back to the "minors," which was how we supers referred to small-town heroing, where the jobs were about finding lost farm animals and hanging bunting from the courthouse for the Fourth of July.

"And you told them to shove their risk profile, right, Mayor? I have a perfect record in people safety—nothing beyond a few bumps and scratches."

He frowned. "Your record on customer dissatisfaction is off the charts. Their models have you at exceptional risk."

"What happened to elevated?"

"I was being nice."

"What the hell is customer satisfaction? They're alive, aren't they? What does my personality have to do with anything?"

"Look, I don't completely disagree with you, but your attitude doesn't scream hero, and city council is breathing down my neck to get a more people-pleasing face on the operation. Someone who kisses babies and waves from a Corvette during parades."

"No one's ever asked me to be in a parade," I argued.

"And why do you think that is?"

He had to be kidding with this. I stood. "From day one, you have told me to hide in the shadows. City fucking council told me I'm no different than any other city worker. Don't talk to press; don't get friendly with citizens. So I did it, and earned myself a reputation as a bitch when I was just following orders." I shrugged. "You reap what you sow, Mayor."

"Well, now we need our female hero to be out there more, in a better light. And you need to be visible. Happier."

"I am happy."

"Come on, Bird. You know you've got a bad attitude."

I opened my mouth to argue but didn't, because I did have a bad attitude, particularly the last few years. But what did they expect? The job was not all that exciting most days, but the saves I made were quickly pushed aside to focus on a "brush-off" or off-color comment I gave. I was a deemed a bitch by the press because I didn't talk to them; I didn't talk to anyone. Lately, a bitch was all I was. Now too many people in the city wanted me gone—replaced by a "friendly super."

"Fine. I'll be better. Is that all?" I grabbed my black mask off his desk, securing it over my eyes as I made my way to the door.

"Not so fast."

Dammit. So close.

"You're going to use some of that vacation time you've accrued. All of it, in fact. Take some time to get happy."

I spun around. "That's like ten weeks!"

"Eleven."

"And what exactly am I supposed to do for eleven weeks?"

"Therapy," he said, stone-faced.

I tipped my head slightly, waiting for the punch line. "Wait, seriously?"

"It's the only option if you want to keep the job. I pulled some strings and got you set up with someone I know outside the city, someone who may actually help you, instead of some government shrink."

"What about the city? My job?"

"We're bringing in James from his Indianapolis internship, and we still have our police and fire. If anything big happens, I've got Milwaukee and Des Moines on call."

"Sounds like everything is arranged, then," I said sarcastically.

"Bird, this is for your own good."

I huffed. I couldn't recall a time when anyone did something for my own good. I wasn't even sure what my own good was anymore.

"Take this time," his voice softened again. "Get yourself a life outside of the job. When you come back—"

"If I come back, you mean."

"*When* you come back, your job will be waiting. And James will be here for a while, to help ease you back in."

James the Juggernaut? Jimmy the Jughead was more like it. He was a kid, and his powers were big but not honed. He was a calamity waiting to happen. And I was the one with exceptional risk?

"This is a suspension, then?"

"I don't think of it that way. But things have to change. We need you to be mentally healthy. This job isn't suited to someone who is miserable. It just isn't. You're a public figure. You've got to learn to let these comments roll off your back. Remember," he said, pointing at me, "with great po—"

"Don't! Please don't say it." I turned and walked out, mumbling along with his booming voice behind me. "With great power comes great fucking responsibility. Got it."

2

DOCTOR MARLY EVANS LIVED in a town called Grove, a little beach community north of Chicago. According to Thompson, she was the best psychiatrist in the state, her alternative methods highly effective. I'd make the forty-five-mile trip twice a week to see her. Which was fine; I had nothing else to fill my time. Plus, I could run the forty-five miles in about ninety seconds easy.

I'd been there once before, on a call—a couple of dogs trapped on the ice a few hundred yards into Lake Michigan. When flying out there on my jet pack proved to panic the dogs too much to catch, I resorted to swimming out to them. I was a powerful swimmer, and I could break through the ice well enough to get to the dogs quickly, but I'd caught a nasty case of hypothermia in the process. I'm resilient, but still very much human.

Grove was a far cry from the city, the energy slower and more relaxed. Moving through the streets, I thought it kind of resembled an old Ray-Ban ad, teeming with beachcombers when the weather was warm, while only locals remained during the winter months.

I stood out in my jeans, road boots, and baseball cap. Most people didn't recognize me without my mask, and even more wouldn't care much if they did, but I hated getting stopped, so I did my best to not draw attention.

I walked through a group of twentysomethings drinking on a restaurant patio, the men in linen shirts and shades, the women in summer dresses and strappy sandals. The stores spilled out to the sidewalks, and I glanced at the swimsuits, dresses, and colorful trinkets as I walked past. But I didn't stop; I had no use for such things.

Walking through the restaurant's sidewalk seating, I was surrounded by groups of laughing friends and families taking a break from the beach to fill their bellies. My brain wandered, and I imagined that, in another life, I'd have lived here. Maybe I would have had a handsome husband who worked in one of these shops. He'd be kind and funny—not a super, just tan and fit. And I'd be polite and less foul-mouthed. Well, a bit anyway.

We'd walk through the streets together and sip wine at a cafe while picking actors to play the tourists who walked past. We'd people-watch from under a sun umbrella, like the couple currently across the street deep in conversation at their café table. He wouldn't even realize when his hand rested on my bare leg, his thumb absently caressing the skin.

"You all right?"

A woman's voice broke me out of my trance. I'd stalled in the middle of the sidewalk and zoned out.

Shit. I glanced at the woman before I gathered myself and started to walk away.

"You look familiar. Do we know each other?" she called after me.

"Nope," I said without turning back, making my way to the address in my email.

—

DOCTOR EVANS'S OFFICE was located off the main street of Grove's downtown in an old Victorian home painted the same color as the yellow daffodils that grew in the front yard, with bright white trim that made the house hard to miss. Her name was displayed on a sign out front, along with an optometrist, a chiropractor, a massage therapist, and an accountant. I opened the white picket gate into a vast, immaculately maintained yard with summer buds starting to push past the maturing spring growth. It looked the same now as I imagined it had

one hundred years ago, with a massive porch, shutters, and ornamenta-
tion at the peaks. A small group of women were drinking wine off in the
corner of the wraparound porch, each dressed in shorts or dresses with
pastel sweaters to protect them from the early June breeze. They looked
like a bunch of fucking ice-cream cones.

One of the women smiled as I took the stairs to the porch. I flattened
my lips and tipped my head in response but didn't stop. The scene was
a little unnerving, a little too familiar. Because this could have been my
mother's house. Her yard. Her life. She was so meticulous about presentation, the flowers in the windowsills, the perfectly mowed grass thick
and satiated.

*I stared at myself in the mirror. "This is my favorite," I said to my mother
as she eyed the purple dress, a knee-length halter with a small flair at the
waist.*

*Mother shook her head, her perfectly curled hair swaying gracefully
with the movement. She caressed my shoulder in examination.*

"Too much swimming, dear," she said. "The boys prefer a lithe girl."

She held up a sparkly silver dress with capped sleeves and low back.

*"You'll look more feminine in this one," she said. "A lady only ever
displays one feature. Arms, legs, cleavage, or back. You have a lovely back.
But you really should pick more feminine hobbies."*

*I smiled. I liked the dress. I liked my arms. And I liked my hobbies. But
I didn't tell Mother any of that.*

These women could have been part of her social circle, all sitting
cross-legged and sipping from their wine glasses. The youngest woman,
maybe seventeen, looked about as bored as I remembered feeling when
surrounded by a group of my mother's friends.

It felt good to clash with the scene of it now—it felt appropriate.
Because I wasn't one of these women, not anymore. I never really had
been.

I looked for a doorbell but found nothing.

"You can go in. They only lock it after hours," one of the women called cheerfully as she took a sip of her wine. Her blonde hair was pinned up neatly, her dress the color of a sprouting green at the first hint of spring. Her friends laughed at something, eyeing me without turning in my direction.

"Thanks," I muttered, then stepped inside. The large foyer was original, the woodwork gleaming. The various offices were listed similarly to the sign in the yard but on a wooden plaque that was created to mirror the original oak in the home. Doctor Marly Evans's office was on the second floor. I started up the creaky stairs and walked down the hallway until I came upon an open door with a little sign outside that read *Please knock up to five minutes before appointment time.* I was about seven minutes early, but the door was open, so I stepped inside. The room was small, with two additional doors that were closed. A loveseat sat against the wall and a tiny refrigerator with a clear door showcased various beverages, including one lone Fanta orange soda. I made a mental note to grab it on the way out.

I took a seat and reminded myself I was there to secure my job, my life. I needed to get back to it. I'd do whatever was needed to get my identity back. That was all there was for me, after all. I'd cooperate and share—with as positive an attitude as I could muster. I stood quickly when one of the internal doors opened and a man appeared. He had his back to me, his voice speaking to someone inside, his hand tightly gripping the door handle.

"This was a waste of time. I appreciate your commitment to her health, but she's my responsibility, and I don't need instruction from anyone."

A woman inside responded to what he'd said, though I couldn't make out her words. He mumbled something under his breath and stepped outside the door. Catching sight of me, he stopped. We stared at each other, and I was struck dumb.

He was six foot plus, with ruffled medium-brown hair, dark jeans, and a fitted T-shirt that showcased a hard, flat chest and generous biceps that I could only assume came from living a physical life and not from a gym.

It was a subtle difference, but one women recognized. One I recognized, anyway. As he stood there, I looked him up and down.

I probably should have felt bad for openly checking him out, for wondering where his chest sat on a scale of bare baby bottom to full bear, but I didn't. I guessed somewhere perfectly in the middle. I'd never see him again, so why not?

He furrowed his brow as I appraised him, his perfect face morphing from displeased to angry.

"You'll want to put inappropriate staring on your list of fucked-up shit to discuss with the good doctor," he said, not taking his dry glare from my face.

"Excuse me?" I said, resisting the urge to take a step back. I wasn't embarrassed to get caught checking him out, only a little surprised at myself for doing so since I couldn't remember the last time I'd bothered to take the time to appreciate any man's physique. "You'd better make your apology now—my appointment starts in four minutes."

He smirked and leaned down to grab *my* bottle of Fanta from the fridge before he started toward the door, not glancing back.

"Repressed fucking asshole," I muttered as he reached it, a momentary pause in his step a clear sign that he'd heard me.

When I turned around, there was a small woman standing there, her hair set into a perfect bun atop her head, a few curls breaking free, her face half-amused, half-something else.

"You must be Birdie," she said, as though my reputation had proceeded me.

"How'd you know?" I asked sarcastically, and she smiled, inviting me to enter her office with a sway of her arm.

"Would you like something to drink?"

I declined, still wishing I'd grabbed the Fanta first, and she closed the door behind us.

She was small, but she had that air of confidence that said, *Don't try to outsmart me; you'll fail,* and I wondered about the balls on that guy to

argue with her. Her cream dress screamed stylish professional as it illu-
minated her dark skin.

"Who was that guy out there?" I asked.

She raised her eyebrow.

"He's suffering from a serious case of asshole."

She frowned, hiding a smile. "I'm sorry about that. I'll speak to him."

"Is he a patient of yours?"

"Why don't you have a seat, Birdie?" She gestured toward two classic
wingback armchairs that sat across from each other, a small table between
them with water and tissues.

I took a moment to situate myself and didn't speak as she did the same.

"This is your first experience with therapy?" she finally said.

"No, but I wouldn't call it therapy per se." The words came out more
disgruntled than I'd intended.

She gave me a warm smile, like a mother to a sad kid. "It wasn't a good
experience, I take it?"

"It was fine," I said, looking out the window to the landscaping
outside. Budding roses lined the interior of the fence, and there was a
Juliet balcony outside the French doors. "Nice office."

She nodded. "I think so. Grove is probably a change of pace from
the city?"

I cleared my throat, uncomfortable with the lingering silence that
often accompanied small talk. "It is."

"How about you tell me a little about yourself?"

"Don't you already know why I'm here?" I asked, not eager to explain
the reasons.

"Well, yes. I was given a little info, and I do have access to social media.
But I'd love to hear from you. I find that most of that other information is
pretty useless in the scheme of things."

"In this case, it's pretty accurate. I'm angry and short-tempered. But
I'm good at my job, and no one's ever gotten hurt. No one who didn't
deserve it, anyway."

She smiled. "Humor me."

I sighed, leaning back a little dramatically. "I grew up in Chicago. Pretty typical. The abilities came on gradually, starting when I was about seventeen and fully developed by twenty."

"How was that time for you? Through that development?"

"Ha. Yeah . . . not great." An understatement.

She nodded. "How was it on your family? How did they react to the changes?"

"So we're really just jumping in, huh?" I said with an awkward laugh while she sat quietly waiting. "Okay. My dad died before it happened, and my mom freaked."

"Are you close?"

"With my mother? No."

"Why is that?"

I resituated myself in the chair. "What? No small talk to develop a rapport, gain my trust?"

"Do you want small talk to develop a rapport, Birdie?"

Nope. I didn't. "She changed when I changed. Our relationship changed."

"Her perception of having a daughter changed, then? Her plans for your life? I can see how that would be difficult for a mother."

I huffed. "She called the government. Yeah, it was *real* hard for *her.* She found out her sweet, docile, obedient daughter, who she dressed up like a doll, could bench a car, so she had me committed."

"How old were you then?"

"Eighteen."

The sheer relief on my mother's face when three men escorted me from our home to a government facility for supers—that was the image that always came to mind when I thought of her now.

Doctor Evans nodded, looking at me like I'd say more. But that was it. I'd just told her my life story in sixty seconds. I couldn't think of anything else to say. There wasn't much left.

"Tell me a little about the final in a series of incidents that led you here. Tell me about the stadium."

"The guy was verbally assaulting me, and I defended myself."

She didn't reply—her body language said I wasn't done yet.

"He was an asshole."

"Just like the man in the entry was an asshole?" she asked me.

"Who?"

"The man you spoke to before you came into my office, the one you called a . . . what was it? A repressed asshole?"

"A repressed *fucking* asshole."

"That's right. Do you often have these feelings toward men you just met?"

"What feelings?"

"Do you feel most men are assholes?"

"No. Most *people*."

She smiled weakly, like I was sadly funny. "Birdie, I'd like you to think of me not so much as a psychiatrist and more as a life coach."

"You're not a shrink?"

"No, I am. I'm also a certified life coach. With some of my clients, I like to mix things up. As part of this process, I think you might benefit from a mix of disciplines. I'm going to assign you some activities to get yourself out of your comfort zone, so you can get to know yourself."

"That sounds great," I replied, not bothering to hide the sarcasm. "But I think I know myself pretty well." I uncrossed my legs just to cross them on the other side.

"First, I'd like you to refrain from using your abilities for the duration of our time together."

"Is that a joke?"

"No. And it's just for the duration of your vacation."

"You mean my suspension."

"Semantics. But yes."

"Why?"

"It's clear that you primarily identify yourself with being a super. Tell me, Birdie, what are your interests outside of work? Do you go out with girlfriends? Date?"

Silence.

"Book club?"

I uncrossed my legs and sat back in my seat, my hands on the armrests. Not this again. "I don't want all that stuff." I just needed my powers. And my job.

"Be that as it may, I often ask my clients to do things like this. It's a way to detach from their primary identity marker. It's a tool for self-exploration, that's all."

"What if I'm needed, to help?"

"Mayor Thompson has told me your obligations are being taken care of. Now, if you happen by a life-or-death situation, I won't ask you to ignore it, but I'm sure you can otherwise handle the assignment. You'll be inclined to cheat, but I implore you not to. Not if you want to get something out of this time we have together."

I shook my head in resignation. I wanted to scream. Another person trying to ground me. The story of my life.

I could refuse. But refusing to cooperate wasn't likely to get me back to work. Knowing I had little choice if I wanted to keep my job, I said, "Okay, I guess I can start tomorrow."

"No, Birdie. Starting now."

—

SITTING ON THE FRONT STEPS outside of Doctor Evans's office, my gaze targeted my boots. They didn't look very different from any other boots, although they were a bit bulky at the sole. You could only really get away with them stylistically if worn with jeans; hence the uniform. But they cost about sixty-five hundred dollars a pair, given they were made with the same stuff they used to build jet tires, and the job paid for one pair a year. I went through about three pairs a year with the time I spent patrolling. I'm not bulletproof, and my feet required shoes that could handle my speed.

I stared at them and wondered what the hell to do with myself now. I looked through the contacts on my phone. My favorite take-out places. My mother. Jace. It was a short list. I clicked on Jace and opened our text stream, where his last text from a week ago stared at me. It was a meme of me giving a nasty look to someone with the word *Superbitch* above my head. His words underneath, **Embrace the Superbitch!** Jace loved to give me shit about my terrible press. He thought I needed to joke about it, lighten up. Even play into it. But as the most beloved super in the world, it was an easy outlook for him. I typed out: **See the latest? I'm off duty. No more Superbitch.**

I then slipped the phone back into my pocket and went back to staring at my boots, wondering if I should buy another pair of shoes, like from the department store.

"Everything okay?"

I looked up to see the spring-green lady from the wine club. Assuming I was blocking her path, I scooted to the side. "Sorry," I said.

"Don't apologize," she said, smiling. "No law against relaxing on the stairs."

She leaned against the post at the base of the steps. She was younger than I'd originally thought. Eyeing my feet, she said, "Killer boots. You military or something?"

"Or something," I mumbled as I stood and then stepped down to her level. I had about six inches on her, but if anyone was looking at us together, she'd be the first person they'd see. Flawless skin, bright green eyes, light blonde hair, and a warm smile. "Do you know where I can get a taxi?" The words were foreign on my lips.

"Oh well, most places in town are walking distance. We do have a couple pedicabs, if you don't feel like walking."

"I have to get back to the city, actually."

"Oh." She forced a smile, and I absently tapped my foot. I'd already done more talking today than I normally did in a week, and I just wanted to be back at my apartment, or out running and pushing my body to its limits. "If you search Surdeen's Taxi Service, ask for Hank. He should be able to help you out."

I nodded and stepped away. Reaching the little picket gateway, I did a quick search on my phone and found the number. As the phone rang, I considered saying fuck it and running home to burn off the restlessness that was inside me. I didn't want to be here in this posh town for one more second, with these people on vacation with their families and dogs. Cheerful people.

As I pulled the phone from my ear, ready to hang up, a woman answered. When I asked for a ride to the city, she replied that it would be an hour before Hank could get there. Feeling my frustration boil, I said, "Fine," and she informed me he'd give me a call when he was on his way.

As I slipped my phone into my pocket, I felt my eyes well up. *Shit, what is this?* I couldn't even remember the last time I'd cried. But as I touched my eyes, that seemed to be exactly what was happening.

I didn't think crying was bad—I just wasn't a crier. I was a moper, a binger of sugar, but not a crier. Yet here I was—after possibly losing my job; after one shrink session where I was stripped of my only source of power; after a decade of being a solitary person who avoided human interaction—swallowing back my tears all because I couldn't get a ride and I was stuck in this little town for God knows how long.

The first tear fell as I stared down at the gate without opening it, uncertain where I'd go once I walked through it.

"Hey," green dress called from behind me. She approached slowly. "You want to get a drink with me?"

"What?" I turned. She stood there with an anticipatory smile.

"Oh. Yeah, no," I replied in confusion. Her brows rose, and she laughed out loud. I wasn't sure if I'd said something funny or if I was just laughable to her. I pushed my errant tears away with my thumbs.

She watched me as I mentally sorted through what was happening. I didn't have a job to do, didn't have anyone to call for a ride. I couldn't rely on the only thing I did have, my abilities. I was stuck where I was, like everyone else. And tears, on top of it all.

"Well, how about some company?" she said, her wedge sandals sounding against the pavement as she linked her arm though mine to step through the gate.

Get yourself together, I thought, my tears drying on my cheeks. *For fuck's sake, you're a super. You don't cry.* Except I wasn't a super anymore, not for the next eleven weeks anyway. I just had to prove my sanity, clean up my act, and get my job back.

"No. Thanks, though," I said absently. Yet I didn't make an effort to move away from her as she led me down the street.

"There's this place I'd like to show you."

"Listen," I said and stopped walking. "I really appreciate it. But I'm okay. Just needed a moment, you know?"

"Do I ever. I have one of those weekly."

"I do need to get back to the city." I removed my arm from hers and stepped back. I pulled my phone out like I knew someone to call, but green dress didn't move.

"I'm Evelyn—Evie to most folks. I'm a good listener. And," she said as she held her hand up when I tried to speak, "if you don't feel like talking, I can pretty much carry on a conversation alone. It's one of my many talents." Her face was imploring, as though she needed me to come with her. Like she'd be failing if she couldn't make me feel better.

And because I really had absolutely nothing else to do, I finally said, "Where are we going exactly?"

"You'll see."

3

WE LEFT THE SUNNY MAIN street and entered what felt like, with its exposed plumbing, brick walls, and stale smell, a seedy Chicago nightclub. A few day drinkers were scattered at the tables surrounding an open dance floor, their eyes observing us as we came in. A man wearing a T-shirt with a dancing cartoon bear appeared to greet us, and Evie spoke to him as I took in the long bar along the back wall, the bartender, also in a bear T-shirt, and swinging doors that led to what I assumed was the kitchen.

"Follow me, ladies," the greeter said as he turned to guide us through the tables. But instead of leading us to a table, we followed him through an open door next to a sign with a finger pointing that read *7 days since last axident*, the seven in the shape of an axe. Evie laughed when she saw it, then turned to me and smiled.

"Ready?" she asked.

I once again considered turning around and walking in the other direction.

"Okay, ladies, I'll put you in this second lane," Bear T-Shirt said, and we started down what looked a lot like a short row of horse stables. When we arrived at our stall, the greeter stopped us. "I'm Cole. I'll be your *axepert* today. Have either of you thrown axe before?"

"What?" I said, tearing my face from the big wooden target. "Wait, what?"

"I'm going to assume that's a no," Cole said as Evie leaned in and whispered, "I've always wanted to try it."

"Rules are simple," Cole began, as I stared at his well-manicured beard. "Rule number one—two-drink maximum while axe throwing. Rule number two—always stay behind the yellow line—I'll retrieve the axes for you. Rule number three—don't touch the axe until it's your time to throw. And rule number four—have fun, responsibly." Cole then demonstrated the correct throwing technique, and I stared at him, half listening, wondering aloud, "What am I doing here?"

"Oh come on, it'll be fun. We can just have a drink and work out our anger."

"I don't have anger," I said through gritted teeth, so Cole couldn't see that I was barely paying attention to him.

"*Okaaay*," Evie replied. "You can watch me work out my anger, and you can just throw an axe. See? Fun."

I sighed. Again, it wasn't like I had anything better to do.

The woman I'd noticed from behind the bar slipped inside and asked, "Would you ladies like a drink?"

"I'll take a glass of white wine," Evie replied, and Cole smiled at her.

"Pilsner, please," I said. I wasn't much of a drinker, mostly because it didn't do much for me, and drinking alone wasn't a good look on me.

Evie scoffed. "It's not even four o'clock yet. Wine is better."

I would have laughed if it hadn't reminded me so much of my mother, who, as long as she drank the right things at the right time of the day, could be continuously drunk without any social backlash. I pushed the thought away and nodded, not sure why I had agreed to any of this. Maybe because I'd cried in front of Evie earlier and so now drinking and throwing axes with her seemed to be the logical next step?

Five minutes later, I was standing with a beer, watching Evie in her pretty summer dress and wedge sandals, with her perfectly coiffed hair, handing her glass of wine to Cole as he replaced it with an axe.

"Wow, it's heavier than it looks," she said.

"I get that a lot," Cole replied with amusement, and I couldn't help but bark a small laugh.

Evie eagerly gripped the handle just as Cole had instructed. She threw with all her might, a catlike growl leaving her mouth as she heaved it forward. It bounced off the wood and hit the floor with a thud.

"Not too bad," Cole said. "Good force; try again."

Evie took the second axe, and this time it stuck lightly to the edge of the board, completely out of the bullseye, and she squealed in delight.

She turned to me, and her glee faded at what I assumed was my bored expression. "Want to try?"

"Yep." I stood from where I leaned against the wall, beer in hand, and walked to the line. I grabbed the axe from Cole just as he started to speak and, with one hand, sent it straight for the center bullseye, where it remained.

I turned back to Evie, who stood slack-jawed. "Wow, you're a natural."

I took the next axe from Cole and did the same thing again, the clang of the metal on metal sounding through the room.

"Nice," Evie said, whistling. "Not a drop spilt."

Meeting her eye, I smiled a real smile, and it felt a bit foreign. "Again?"

We threw several more rounds. Evie eventually got the hang of it, hitting somewhere near the bullseye most times she threw. By the end of it, I found that I was almost enjoying myself, even laughing when she did a little breakdance whenever she hit anywhere on the board.

"Imagine all the people that've done you wrong as you throw the axe," Evie implored.

And I did. Winston, Jimmy, Mayor Thompson, my ex, my mother. A bit dark, but I felt . . . well, I felt just a little less by the end of it.

An hour in and still no taxi notification. I wasn't quite as annoyed by this as I expected to be, and I let Evie pull me over to the main bar for another round. We found a seat in a red linoleum booth. She was close to a bottle of wine in at this point, if you included the porch wine, and was feeling quite loquacious.

"Okay, Birdie, tell me everything."

"About what?" I said, as I slid over the deep cracks in the booth's padded seat.

"About you, of course. Why you are in Grove, of all places, alone and," she whisper-shouted the next part, "crying."

"One of those days, I guess." I waved her off. But she was like a dog with a bone.

"Come on, Birdie, I'll start. I moved here about a year ago. I live in a lakeside cottage for now, one of the cute ones on the beach. I work there, cleaning the cottages, which my brother owns. I wasn't always a maid. I went to school for public relations. Had a good job, too, at a sports marketing firm. But a few years ago, I quit."

"Why?" I asked, because as long as she talked, I didn't have to.

She smiled. "Life got in the way."

"You're too young for that," I said.

"Ha! I'm thirty."

"Oh." She seemed much younger than me, like early twenties. Maybe because she was so cheery and perfect—and small compared to my 5'10" frame.

"Sometimes I feel eighty," she said, and I couldn't imagine her ever feeling that way. Thirty-year-olds always said that dumb shit when we had no idea.

She took another sip of wine. "You were seeing Evans?" she again whisper-shouted across the table as someone turned up the music. "Don't be embarrassed. I think everyone in town has seen her at some point. I saw her after I first moved. I still do here and there."

What could this woman need a shrink for? I imagined her kind of problems only centered around her mother and wedding planning.

When I didn't offer more information, she filled the empty space. "You married?"

I smirked knowingly. Here it was. "No."

"Boyfriend? Girlfriend?"

"No and no."

"No one? Not even a booty call?"

I shook my head, covering my mouth with my beer.

"I'm divorced," she said with a shrug. "Well, sort of divorced. It's complicated. I'm still in love with him. We want to work things out. It's just hard."

So it was the end of marriage as opposed to the beginning of one. He'd probably had a side piece. She was too busy planning social outings and the perfect future for their children, and he strayed. Although, that didn't feel quite right. Yes, Evie seemed, at least outwardly, to be everything I kind of resented. But there was also something else there. I considered asking her for more information. But what I really wanted was to get up and leave after the beer. I'd let her talk until then.

When I didn't respond, a look of anxiety passed over her face, and she shifted in her seat. She was carrying this conversation. I almost felt a little bad for her. "Was that some kind of book club you were at before? On the porch?"

She smiled, relieved. "Oh, no. I finished an appointment and got caught up with those women. They're planning the big summer festival in town. I meandered over to say hello and they offered me a glass of sparkling wine, so I took them up on it. I don't know a lot of people in town yet. But I'm pretty sure I'm not right for the committee. Though they didn't ask me to join or anything."

I couldn't think of anything worse than joining a wine club that masqueraded as a committee to plan events. And I couldn't think of anything else to say to this woman who obviously didn't share my opinion.

Then she brightened. "Should we take a shot?"

"Look, Evie, thanks for the invitation." I pulled some cash out of my pocket. "But I really need to find my way back to Chicago."

"Oh come on, stay. Please. The truth is, I asked you to hang because when I saw you, you looked like I feel."

"Like shit."

She shrugged. "A bit unhappy."

"The story of my life."

I looked at my nonexistent watch, but before I could decline, she wiggled in her seat with a happy squeal as a new song started over the speakers, even louder than before.

She jumped up and out of the booth and began dancing. "Come on, Birdie, dance with me!" she called out. I remained in my seat, jarred, my mouth open. "It's Lizzo! You can't *not* dance."

"I can, actually."

She grabbed my hand and pulled me into the center of the dance floor where we stood alone. Then she closed her eyes and started swaying with her whole body. And I thought, *This woman could be just a little bit nuts.*

She started moving our hands, while I remained stiff as a board, wishing I was wearing my mask. This was antithetical to everything I was. This was making a scene, and I wanted to hide.

But there was something about the way she didn't stop, didn't look around as she danced, didn't care who was watching—didn't even consider the impact—that kind of floored me.

The idea of being a spectacle for just a minute in front of a dozen half-drunk people in a dark club in a tiny town in the middle of the day, in this place I wasn't expecting to ever return to, was slightly appealing, and I thought, *Why not? What else have I got to do?*

The answer was absolutely nothing.

I pulled my hands away from Evie and walked to the bar. "Vodka, please," I called over the music. A shot glass appeared in front of me. I took it and then asked for two more. The young bartender looked at me warily but followed my instruction. I rarely drank, but I needed a little liquid courage to get through the next five minutes.

I walked back to Evie. She squealed again and continued shaking her ass as Lizzo crooned about body positivity.

I let myself start to move, swaying and bouncing and forgetting, letting the vodka push away all my ingrained instincts that said I needed to be someone else, someone who looked on and watched life happen but didn't get involved.

One song melted into another, and we didn't stop. The bartender obliged us with dance-floor lights, and a few patrons joined us here and there as one song played after another. We danced together like we'd been friends forever. I didn't hate it.

Finally, we found ourselves back in our booth, laughing, a little drunk, and sweaty.

"I got suspended," I yelled over the music.

"What?" she yelled back, downing one of the bottles of water the bartender had left for us.

"I got suspended. From my job. I have a bad attitude. I work all the time, so now I'm not sure what to do with myself all summer. Seeing Doctor Evans is mandatory." These five consecutive sentences were more than I'd voluntarily said to anyone in . . . well, a very long time.

"Shit. I'm sorry."

I shrugged and hiccupped. Then her eyes lit up, and I considered running away.

"What?"

"Stay with me this summer!"

"What? No. That's not what I meant—"

"I know. But it would be perfect! I have a spare room. You can help me clean the cottages. Most days, it's just a few hours, and it'll be twice as fast if there's two of us. Then we can hang at the beach."

"I can't." My voice felt slurred, but I couldn't tell because the whole room had started to wobble.

"Birdie, I live on Lake Michigan. Who doesn't want to spend the summer at the beach?"

She was insane. She didn't know me. "No. Really. I have stuff I need to do."

"You just said you don't have work, or a boyfriend. So, why not?"

She got me there. "What am I supposed to do all summer, huh? Sit around in pretty dresses, drinking wine and harassing strangers?"

Shit, that was mean. I needed to do something about my lack of word filter.

Her eyes went wide, and she made no effort to hold back her laughter. "I like you, Birdie."

Was this what it was like to be without the weight of responsibility, of always being careful who is watching?

"Aiden!" she squealed. This girl should have been assigned her own noise ordinance. She stood as well as she could in the booth and waved, calling out, "Aiden!" a few more times.

I turned and stalled on the vision of a man walking in our direction. A tall, broad, *familiar* man.

"Shit," I muttered.

Evie threw me a side glance. She slid over in the booth, patting the seat next to her. The man sat down and leaned in to kiss her cheek.

"Evie," he said, eyeing the glass of wine in front of her. "This isn't the first glass, huh?"

She shrugged and glanced at me. His gaze followed. I lifted my hand to my face in an effort to hide, realizing I still was holding a full shot of vodka. *How'd that get there?*

"This is my new friend, Birdie. Birdie, this is Aiden."

His eyes narrowed, and his gaze felt icy.

Damn, he was even more beautiful under the veil of alcohol, all defined jaw and scruff and dark eyes and corded forearms . . . fuck, I was doing it again.

For a moment, I thought he'd call me out, but too quickly he cleared his throat, returning his attention to Evie. Maybe he didn't remember seeing me just a few . . . shit, what time was it? I looked at my phone—5:00 p.m. We'd been here for three hours! I probably missed my ride. I checked my missed calls but found none.

"Evie, you picking up psych patients now?"

Seriously? "And you were there for gardening advice?" I tossed out.

"Wait, you two know each other?"

"No," we both answered at the same time, his gaze lingering on my face, utter distain emanating.

"Evie," he said, finally relieving me of his glare, "it's time to go."

"You're leaving already? *Staaay*, have a drink with us," she replied.

"I've got somewhere to be, and you've had enough. You shouldn't be here." He said the last part with a tone of tenderness none of his prior words conveyed, and I wondered what the story was there. "Time to go."

I bristled. Who was he to tell her what to do? "Ha. Okay, Dad," I offered from across the table. He closed his eyes like my presence pained him. Evie giggled.

"Evie," he scolded. "Please. You've had your fun."

"Correction. I'm having fun. And you are ruining it." If it were me, I'd have kicked his ass out already, but Evie's well of patience was apparently much deeper than mine. "Stay and hang with us. Birdie was about to spill the deets on her love life."

I was?

He side-eyed me. "I'm afraid I have no interest in that conversation."

Seriously? Who was this guy? I glared and downed the shot of vodka that sat in front of me, daring him to say something. His horrified expression was exactly the response I was going for.

"Evie, call me when you need a ride. Please."

She laughed. "Yes, Dad."

"Jeez, no wonder you left him." The words were out before I could stop myself. Maybe my tolerance wasn't as high as it once was.

Aiden turned his strong, angry jaw toward me, and I hated myself for noticing again how incredibly sexy the angles of it were. He stood, departing as quickly as he'd arrived, while Evie failed to control her laughter.

"Jesus. Is he always like that?" I asked her, watching him as he stopped to speak with the bartender, no doubt cutting us off.

She nodded, a bit calmer, and said, "Pretty much."

"And you're still in love with him?" I asked, unable to keep the mortification from my voice.

"Gross!" she spit out. "He's my brother."

"He's . . . um . . . oh." I glared at the bar where he stood very close to the pretty bartender. She leaned in to hear him and smiled.

"Oh," I repeated. "He's very . . ."

"What?" she asked with an evil grin.

"He's very . . ."

Shut up, Birdie. Shut up before you say anything more.

"He's a bit rough around the edges?—I hear that a lot. That, and he's gorgeous, moody, and completely un-datable."

"That's not what I was going to say."

She grinned. "Well, he's also very single, just like you."

"What? No. I'm very, very uninterested. I'm the opposite of interested, so please don't give that another thought. Besides, you just said he's un-datable." A lot like me.

"That's what other people say," she clarified with a shrug. "He's just protective. Shall we get another drink? Maybe someplace else?"

I checked my phone, buying time.

"I wasn't kidding before, you know. I like you, Birdie, and you have nothing to do this summer. I could use some help with the cleaning. And we'd have a blast."

"Huh?" Oh yeah, her invitation.

The bartender arrived in her bear tee, informing Evie she was cut off. As they playfully argued, I snuck a peak at the beautiful jerk before he exited. He saw me, and I gave him the bird followed by a very grown-up version of sticking out my tongue.

And he smiled. Like I was some kind of kid who'd learned her first curse word.

I huffed and returned my attention to Evie as she was shot down one final time. She shrugged it off. "We're going to need some apps, then."

"You got it," the bartender agreed and was off.

"Stay the summer," Evie repeated.

"That's insane. We don't know each other. Plus, you'll be sick of my ass within the first seventy-two hours, I promise."

She laughed again, undeterred. "Good. It's settled then."

4

I BURROWED UNDER THE covers as the light hit my eyes, realizing that nothing felt right—the lumpy cushions, the smell of detergent that wasn't my spring scent, too much weight in the blanket. This wasn't my bed.

I sat up quickly, alert, my head spinning. I was on a couch, a soft, cream-colored one that matched the light beachy palette of the room. A TV hung on the wall in front of me, two matching chairs on either side of the couch. My eyes focused on the coffee table—reclaimed wood with lines of color in the grooves. I'd never seen anything quite like it. Where the fuck was I? And why didn't I remember anything after finishing a plate of nachos at . . . a bar . . . with a stranger? Evie. I closed my eyes and pinched my brows, the headache receding slightly.

"You stalking me?" The deep voice came from behind me, and I swiveled to see a familiar man behind a kitchen island filling a glass of orange juice. I stared at him, dumbfounded, as he lifted the glass to his mouth and drank the whole thing before setting it down and refilling it, his eyes never leaving mine.

My mouth hung open in shock as I took in his sexy bedhead and the stubble lining his jaw.

I looked away, not having any words, and pulled back the blanket to find myself fully dressed from yesterday, the stench of stale beer and yesterday's drama lingering. I pressed my eyes closed, hoping this was all a dream, that I'd open them and be home. No such luck.

How in the world did I get here?

I touched my hair and found the strands mostly pulled from the ponytail and ratted into what my mother called my bird's nest. I tried to tame it as I stood up from the couch, the dizziness briefly threatening my ability to stay upright. I took a breath and turned to find that infuriatingly attractive man had diverted his attention to the stove. I watched his muscles through his T-shirt as he shook a pan and returned it to the burner. The smell of bacon assaulted my senses in the best way. My stomach growled loudly as I watched his back working.

Then he stepped to the side and pulled another glass from the pale-blue cupboard, filling it in silence, never giving me his attention. I stood there like an idiot, having no clue what to say or do. And where were my boots?

He walked around the island toward me, and I got a better look at the scrub-style pants that hung low on his lean hips. He held out the glass to me.

"Did we . . . ?" I managed to squeak out.

He smirked, and I took a drink of the cold juice, desperate to soothe my cottonmouth. A million thoughts went through my head. God, I hoped I didn't have sex with this beautiful specimen of a man last night. But if I did, go me, right? It must have been amazing, and I couldn't even remember it.

His smirk morphed into disapproval. "You really shouldn't drink like that, you know?" His tone was contrite, almost annoyed.

"What business is it of yours?" I replied before I finished the glass, wishing I had more, just to have something to do other than stare at the man in front of me who was staring back, his eyes leaving my face to take in the state of me. I could only imagine what he saw, how disheveled and pitiful I appeared.

Then I realized that my state of dress and placement on the couch likely ruled out any fun in the sheets. *Damn.*

"It's my business when my sister is involved." He took the glass from me, his hand grazing my fingers, making my head swim, and made his way back to the kitchen. "You don't seem too bad off this morning, considering the volume of alcohol you consumed."

"I uh . . . I don't really get hungover," I said, and he looked down his nose at me. "Fast metabolism. Lucky that way, I guess."

"Evie isn't so lucky." His disapproval was clear.

Shit, Evie.

"She okay?"

"She will be."

I nodded. She wasn't my responsibility. She was a grown woman. And it had been her idea. I walked back to the sofa and started to fold my blanket in the silence that hung like a thick fog. "Is this your place?"

"Sure is," he started, not bothering to look at me. "Imagine my surprise when I woke up to find a stranger in *my* living room, sleeping on *my* couch, without *my* permission."

By his tone, he wasn't pleased with the development. Imagine that.

How *had* I ended up on *his* couch? Had I blacked out? That wasn't like me. That hadn't happened to me since . . . never. Flashbacks of shots and beers and well . . . more shots entered my brain. At least Evie had stuck with the wine.

"You don't know how I got here?"

"Why would I know that? We don't know each other."

Damn, he was angry in the morning. Sharp, angry ticking jaw and intense eyes.

"Right, well, I'll get out of your hair, then." I fluffed the couch, trying to erase any evidence of my unwanted visit. When I looked up, I saw my boots had been placed neatly by the front door. "Can I use your bathroom first?"

He gestured to the hallway without looking my way. "First door."

I moved quickly and locked the door behind me with a deep exhale. God, he had the kind of eyes that made you forget to breathe—deep and haunting, the kind that attracted pretty virgins or sweet bakers with tragic pasts. I was neither, just a sad cat lady without a cat.

Yesterday was the first day I hadn't worked in years. Yesterday was . . . jeez, it was a disaster. It was stupid. It was reckless. Yesterday was . . . fun.

Evie was fun. She'd helped me forget about everything bad for a minute or two. It was the first fun I'd had in as long as I could remember.

I peed and washed my face and underarms with wet toilet paper, not wanting to use the towel as evidence of my visit. I tied my tangles back into a frazzled ponytail and stole some toothpaste, using my finger to remove the taste of last night's bad decisions.

After a fortifying breath, I stepped out to find a very hungover Evie waiting for me. She smiled painfully, as though any movement hurt, then grabbed my hand and pulled me further down the hallway.

"I should probably go," I said as we entered a dark bedroom, long heavy curtains drawn over the windows.

"Don't let that ogre scare you off," Evie said, dropping my hand and crawling back into the bed's indent. "We'll have breakfast as soon as my head stops melting inside my skull."

I closed the door to the lovely guest room. Even in the dim light, I could make out the light linens and wicker furniture. "You live with him?"

"No," she said, half groaning and muffled as she pressed her face into her pillow. "My place is next door, but Aiden's doing some work on it, so I'm staying here for a few days."

"Oh," I replied, sneaking over to the window and peering out. Evie groaned behind me as the light assaulted us. The window turned out to be French doors that opened to a tiny side patio, encased by a small railing. On the patio was a single wicker chair. And beyond the patio to the left was another cottage, very similar to this one by the looks of it, and to the right was sand for fifty yards until it disappeared under the lapping waves of Lake Michigan.

"Holy shit. This view!" I said, looking back at Evie.

She lifted her head and squinted at me. "How are you not dying right now? You drank like an entire bottle of vodka by yourself."

I winced and let the shade close. "Lucky genetics."

"Do you even have a headache?" she whined.

I lifted a shoulder and made a face of apology. "I have a fast metabolism."

"Bitch," she muttered, and I smiled because she was funny and I felt a strange affection for her after she was so kind to me yesterday.

"Don't worry about Aiden—my place will be ready today."

I moved closer to sit next to her. "I really appreciate you letting me crash here. I'll get out of your hair as soon as possible."

She sat up and quickly regretted it. "What are you talking about? Wait. You don't remember our conversation, do you?"

"There may be some gaps in my memory."

She grinned with her eyes half-closed. "We decided that you're staying with me."

"We did? I am?"

She nodded. "We agreed you'd stay the summer. You know, since you have therapy here and don't have a car. You said you had nothing else to do. That you needed to get away."

"I said that?" I wouldn't have said something like that.

"Yes. We shook on it."

"How?" I started but paused. I was going to argue that staying here for the summer was a ridiculous idea and absolutely out of the question. But something stopped me. Maybe it was the view of the lake. Maybe the seclusion of the cottage. Maybe it was Evie, who, after last night, felt easy to me, just the right amount of eccentric.

I thought about the prospect of going home versus the idea of staying with her for the summer on the lake, where I could forget the whole reason I wasn't working. I wasn't the Chicago Bird anymore, at least not now. I no longer had to play by those rules, right? Here, I could be someone else. No one would ever have to know.

"You really want me here? I mean, I'm a bit of a mess, as you can see."

"Yes," she said with a pained smile. "Please. I need someone to distract me from my own drama this summer. I need girl time and you, my friend, are a hoot."

"I am?"

"Yep."

"What exactly happened last night?" I asked, though the scenes were slowly coming back to me.

She lay back on the bed, her forearm over her eyes. "Drinking. Singing. Secret telling. Proclamations of lifelong friendship between strangers. The regular stuff." She removed her arms to say the next part. "I also don't usually drink like that, by the way. In fact, never. You caught me on a weird day. Or I caught you, I guess." A hint of a smile emerged. "It *was* really fun, though. I haven't had that much fun in a long time."

More flashes of the evening emerged. A game of darts with some bar regulars. Singing loudly with a band. My arm around Evie as we walked through town and down the beach to the front porch of this little house. Laughing on said front porch, and then nothing. Except the strange feeling of being tucked in to sleep. I shook my head to clear it.

"We're a bit old for this type of behavior, don't you think?" I said.

"Well, yeah, but I've never engaged in binge drinking before, so maybe I'm just late to the game. Once was definitely enough, though."

"Sorry you're feeling bad," I offered. "I think I had fun too."

She laughed, then winced in pain. "I *know* you did."

I smiled and lay back on the bed next to Evie, a stranger I'd met yesterday who just opened her home to me for the summer. A pang of guilt came up for not telling her about my job, about who I was. But then again, I wasn't that person, not for eleven weeks. I wasn't the Chicago Bird—I was just Birdie Bowden—so there was nothing to tell.

"But you have to promise me something," Evie said with a groan.

"What's that?"

"Promise we're never drinking alcohol again. Deal?"

I laughed, the feeling a little bit foreign. "Deal."

5

SUPERS RARELY WORE SPANDEX. There were a few who took to the whole flashy superhero thing—even a few capes among us. Some supers embraced the public life, making themselves household names. They were the baby-kissers, the serial celebrity-daters, the beautiful ones. The rest of us were about as famous as the local weatherman in a mask.

My uniform since day one consisted of a tight brown braid that stopped midway down my back, Goodyear-designed boots, a specially designed pair of jeans with lots of stretch, and a T-shirt branded with the word *Chicago*, the skyline below and a bird above. I added the simple black eye mask to maintain a level of anonymity, which seemed necessary in the beginning, but proved useless when it became clear no one cared who I was outside the job anymore.

I exited the elevator on the top floor of my residential high-rise, head hung like a sad sap. I walked through the hallway, past strangers behind closed doors, toward my small studio with its personal roof access for quick departures.

I'd left Evie sleeping it off with no intention of returning. As I'd sat on that little patio, Evie asleep inside, I realized there was no way I could stay there. I didn't know these people. Evie was nice and all, but her brother hated me. Well, okay, so I had been a tiny bit rude to him. But he was a total ass. In any case, I needed to lie low until my suspension was over and I could get back to work—concentrating, in the meantime, on figuring out who it was they wanted me to be in order to keep my job.

I dug my key out of my pocket and looked up, halting at the sight of someone standing at my door. "Shit. Jace, you can't sneak up on a person."

"I wasn't. I was just standing here. You're jumpy," he said, his pity-filled green eyes telling me he had seen the news. "How you holding up?"

I shook my head. "I'm not. I'm suspended."

"Seriously?" He stepped closer and pulled me in. I welcomed the feeling of his hard chest and familiar scent. "That's fucked, Benji. I'm sorry."

I closed my eyes and sighed at *Benji*. Jace never called me by my real name. Instead, it was always some variation of a pet name traditionally reserved for old ladies or dogs.

"Whatever," I said, pulling back.

He held my shoulders. "Want me to hang out a while?"

"Don't you need to be in New York?"

"I've got a few hours." He smiled as he followed me into my apartment, his presence too large for the four-hundred-square-foot space. "I have two junior supers now. Plus, I figured you could use one of our old talks together, like in the facility days."

"You know, I've been missing the old days . . . of being institutionalized," I quipped, knowing Jace was the reason I'd gotten through my time there shortly after my powers had materialized. We'd bonded over the fact that our families hadn't known what to do with us and sent us to a government facility whose goal was "to ensure we weren't a danger to ourselves and society."

"I do miss it in a way, oddly enough," I said.

"You're joking," he said as he plopped down on my twin bed, the only place to sit aside from a floral loveseat I'd picked up secondhand. His large, perfectly fit body and angular Clark Kent face never did look right in my drab apartment.

"It was fucked up, for sure," I said, opening the fridge. I pushed aside the week-old Chinese takeout and grabbed a water and a beer that had probably been there since the last time Jace visited. "But there was something to being hidden away, not having to figure anything out for yourself, you know? Everyone else fumbling about, figuring out our lives, where we fit in the world—it took the pressure off us figuring it out ourselves."

I handed him the beer, and he sat up.

"What's going on with you, Betty?"

"I'm not sure I've ever figured anything out for myself. Not since before the powers, and maybe not even then. I mean, I was a normal college freshman. I had friends. My boyfriend had proposed. Then everything changed. We were taken away, studied, tracked, and put back in the world with parameters. We were supers. I never got to decide who I was. I just became . . . this."

"Is this how we're explaining your sudden social media explosion?"

I shrugged. "Maybe?"

"Bertrude," he said, tapping his bottle to my water, "I like who you are, just the way you are." He smiled at his own Darcy reference. "I want you to be happy." He took a sip and grimaced. "Hell, woman, how old is this?"

I shrugged, and he took another pull. Another grimace. "We can't blame everything on that time in our lives, B. Believe me, I've tried. Many years of being in this life has taught me one thing."

"What's that?"

"Everything past the age of thirty is our own fault."

"You're thirty-two."

"Yes, and I spent the five years before thirty figuring shit out so I could be free of it by the time I turned thirty."

"Did it work?"

He stood, walked into the kitchen, and turned the bottle upside down over the sink. "Jury's still out."

Remember when I said most of us were nothing like the comics and movies? Well, Jace was the exception. Jace was the most powerful super there was, the closest thing to Superman you'd find, yet far from invincible and not as fast as me.

"Now, I could use some Oreos and *Drag Race*," he said, rummaging through my cabinets.

RuPaul's Drag Race and sugar binges were what got us through the facility days. We often tagged important events in our lives by a RuPaul timeline. Jace was watching season two when we'd met and started a sexual relationship, season three when it'd ended. Season four was when I started the job in Chicago and Jace had told me he preferred men to women, but also that it wasn't *completely* my fault. Season seven was when he very publicly saved the mayor's life, season eight when he took the mask off, and season nine when he'd said he didn't think he would ever be in a real committed relationship given his hero responsibilities. And now, season fourteen would forever be the year I got fired . . . suspended . . . whatever.

"I know they're here somewhere," Jace muttered from the kitchen.

I didn't bother pointing him in the right direction. I just smiled as I watched him search, his body taking up most of the space in my kitchen.

We'd had a brief friends-with-benefits situation in our early twenties, when all we'd had was each other, but ours was never meant to be romantic love, just best friendship. So that's what it became. I went through a phase back then, eager to find love through sex, with supers and non-supers alike. But alas, it didn't work, and I'd gone without any friends or benefits for some time now.

In fact, I was so used to being alone that the few visits I got with Jace each year were almost hard to stomach. He pulled months of pent-up human interaction out of me in a night, and it always left me on empty emotionally. Tonight, I wanted to wallow in my public ridicule alone.

But I could never send him away.

"Yes!" he called from the kitchen, having found what he was looking for. "What? No milk?"

"Sorry. Should I go get some?"

"Nah, it's fine. You got creamer?"

I made an *eww* face and sat back in my love seat as he returned to the bed and ripped open the package of Oreos. "Okay, B, spill it."

I leaned over for a cookie. "Apparently, I have a bad attitude." I stuffed it in my mouth. "Who knew?"

He snickered, but his gaze melted into pity when he caught my glare. "Whatever. It's fine. I guess I probably do."

"Like I said, you're not happy."

"Thanks, Captain Obvious. Why would I be happy about this?"

"No, B, you're not *happy*. With your life."

I considered it. *When was the last time I even stopped to consider whether I was happy?*

"Do you still like it?" I asked. "The job? The saving, I mean."

His brows creased, like the question was ludicrous. "Yeah, it's the fucking best. Why, you don't?"

My head tilted back to stare at the ceiling that still showed water damage from a leak two years prior that I hadn't bothered to fix. "I don't know. I guess I do, but it's just . . . New York loves you. You have a presence that people are drawn to . . . and trust. You're a huge part of the reason supers are more accepted now. You paved the way with how good you are, with your city, the press. I'm . . ."

"What?"

I didn't know what.

"Benny." He came to the edge of the bed, feet on the floor, and leaned in. "We've been friends a long time. And you were great in the sack, if I remember correctly." I shook my head but laughed. "But you aren't the easiest person to get to know."

That's what happens when you live your life under the thumb of everyone else, being told who you are, how to be—when you're left to hide in the shadows while the world figures out if your mere existence is okay or not.

"I know," I said morosely.

He was up in a flash and sitting next to me. His arm curled around my back, and I rested my head on his shoulder. "I'm going to be brutally honest here. Don't get mad at me."

I looked up, unsure I wanted to hear this. "Go ahead."

"You are the most closed-off person I've ever met."

I pulled away. "I am not!"

He smiled with a hint of pity. "For example . . . I've seen the stack of novels in your closet, and I've snuck a peak at your e-reader."

"So," I said defensively.

"So you're a romantic, but you'd never know it. You love stories about strong men, grand gestures, hearts on a string, dirty talk in the bedroom. Stories about friendship and family. None of these things anyone would ever guess about you, including me. You don't ask for any of that. You project aloofness, like you prefer to be alone. You've left everything behind to be *the Chicago Bird*," he said with jazz hands.

I knew the truth of his words. "I'm good on my own. Who cares what I read? What does that have to do with anything?"

He squeezed me a little. "You're not built to be alone. You're too amazing not to share yourself." He kissed the top of my head chastely. "You're stuck in here. You're going to have to get unstuck if you want to move forward, to find happiness in what you do or in something else. Get out of *this* apartment."

Get unstuck, huh? Evie came back to my mind. "A woman invited me to stay at her beach house up in Grove for the summer."

"What? Who is this woman? Can I come?"

"I met her yesterday, after therapy."

Jace pulled away from me. "Therapy? Let's back this train up. Explain."

"Mandated therapy. Doc told me I couldn't use my powers for the summer. I was fucked up about it after the session. This woman, Evie, saw my mini breakdown. We ended up throwing axes, which led to alcohol, which led to dancing and singing and a bunch of other nonsense. I slept on her *very* attractive brother's couch, and Evie asked if I wanted to stay at her perfect little cottage on the lake in exchange for helping her clean the other cottages her brother rents out. Then I came home."

Jace shook his head quickly, trying to catch up with me. "Shit. You've had a day."

"Yep."

"This Evie . . . you just hung out with a random stranger? Who is she? Who are *you*? Wait, do you have a *friend* now?" he teased.

I considered it. "I know. The thing is, I think I had fun. And I can't remember—"

Jace stood up. "Get your shit packed."

"What?"

"You are going to stay with this Evie person. You are going to have a fun summer. You are totally going to have a fling with the hot brother—I don't want to hear another word about it."

"I can't," I said.

"Why?"

We stared at each other while I tried to come up with a good reason. Then he released a slow grin before something occurred to him and it disappeared.

"Wait. If you can't use your powers, how'd you get home this morning?"

Oops.

6

OKAY, SO I CHEATED . . . again. I had to get back to Grove, and a cab all the way up there was at least a day's paycheck. I reasoned that the brief use of my powers was necessary in preparation for my non-super-powered summer. Fact is, the more I thought about not using my powers, the more I accepted the idea. The expectations were gone, and it felt like a weight had been lifted. Evie wouldn't ask me to show her what I could do. I didn't have to tell anyone who I was. I was someone else completely, pretending to be normal before I returned to who I really was.

I showed up on Evie's patio later that afternoon. With my bag containing my Bird uniform—not that I'd planned to use it—some clothes, my e-reader, and toiletries, I knocked lightly on the patio door.

The door opened to a sleepy-looking Evie.

"You came back!" she whispered excitedly as she placed her hand to her head. "My place is done, and Aiden went to town for a date or something, so we have time before I have to get out of bed."

I followed her inside her room, leaving the door open a bit to let some fresh air in. "A date?"

She sat on the bed this time, instead of burying herself in it. Seemed like progress. "The daughter of a professor at the community college. She's asked him like a dozen times, and he finally gave in. You should have seen him before he left, all grouchy and hilarious."

"Oh." I didn't like the stupid twist in my stomach at this news. I didn't care if the asshole had a date. He could come back married with a baby, for all I cared. "I'll make you something to eat. Eggs okay?"

"Ugh, no. Wait, yes. No. I don't know. I'm hungry but the idea of food is . . . blah." She mimed vomiting.

"Cute," I replied. "I'll keep it simple. I'm not a chef, but I can scramble some eggs and use a toaster."

I walked into Aiden's kitchen to find the fridge fully stocked and orderly. Of course it was, because he was a grown-up. Evie and I were misbehaving children in his eyes.

To drive the point home, I found his kitchen to be annoyingly neat. The utensil drawers were clearly organized, with spatulas and wooden spoons in the first drawer, separated by serving spoons next to a potato masher and a lemon-lime squeezer. Tongs, a pizza cutter, and taco holders were neatly situated next to those little corn-cob pokers. The silverware was one matching set, each utensil perfectly tucked into its space. His pans were next to pans, pots next to pots. It was so different than my own kitchen drawers. On the rare occasion I actually cooked, I had to look through two or three drawers to find what I needed.

Evie ate slowly, starting with dry toast and moving on to nibble on the eggs. She downed some ginger ale, then pushed the plate aside, stood, and went to rummage through the kitchen. She returned with a half-eaten package of chocolate chip cookies she'd located above the refrigerator.

"What? These are easier on the stomach," she said, stone-faced. I just smiled and grabbed a few. And for the first time in a long time, I didn't want to be anywhere but where I was.

—

EVIE'S HOUSE WAS A SMALL cottage in a long line of a dozen that Aiden owned and rented out to beachcombers. They were all single-story, two-bedroom, one-bath Craftsman-style with great views. They were also conveniently close to downtown, within walking distance for typical humans, which I was for the summer. Evie's was painted pale blue on the outside, while Aiden's was white. Both had little front porches set back behind a sandy dune of Lake Michigan.

This time, I got the guest room, a near carbon-copy of the room Evie had been in last night, but with more feminine touches, including a pale-blue floral pattern on the bedspread, warm light-gray walls, and the world's fluffiest rug. I placed my underclothes, jeans, and T-shirts in the dresser. I put my uniform in the bottom drawer.

The rest of the cottage had pictures of Evie's parents, Aiden, and several of her with an attractive man who I assumed was the ex/not ex. Just being in her space made me realize how cold and lifeless my own home was.

Since Evie was still struggling with our choices from the night before, I volunteered to turn over one of the cottages after a late checkout. She gave me a checklist, and I headed out to get started. I could have cleaned this place in a few minutes, and while I was tempted, I resisted the urge. It's not like I had anywhere else to be, so why not go slow?

I was finishing up the bathroom, scrubbing the floor on my hands and knees, when someone came in the front door. Assuming it was Evie checking on me, I called out, "In here," and continued scrubbing.

"This is a good look for you," came a deep voice behind me.

I glanced up and immediately regretted it. Looming handsomely was Aiden, looking down at me in my oldest pair of jeans and a T-shirt of Evie's that was too small for me, my ass crack clearly on display.

I stood up as he perused the bathroom and then, with equal attention, me.

"This work suits you, I think," he mused, his eyes lingering a little too long on the exposed skin below my shirt.

I followed him out of the bathroom, rubber gloves and all. "What's that mean?"

Was he always trying to be an asshole? Aiden the Asshole. That would be his super name, and his power would be making women dumbstruck by his flawless smirk.

"Means exactly what it sounds like," he said as he examined the kitchen.

"It's clean."

He nodded and proceeded to walk through the rest of the house silently, checking for dust or some other violation. He wouldn't find it. I'd been meticulous.

"What do we have here?" He bent down next to the window and picked up what appeared to be nothing, a piece of string maybe.

"You've got to be kidding me."

His brows rose. "If you expect to get free housing for the summer, you need to clean . . . well."

I was going to kill him. Literally murder him in his sleep. It would be like destroying a priceless work of art. Rather, he was Helen of fucking Troy and I'd be doing humanity a favor if I killed him before his beauty started a war.

"I'm not sure it's any of your business. I'm staying with Evie. It doesn't even concern you."

"These cottages are mine. Everything here concerns me."

"Oh." My comebacks were brilliant.

"My sister works here, so she stays without rent. You, on the other hand, do not."

"Right." I considered telling him off and just leaving. I didn't need this crap. But the truth was, I already liked it here better than Chicago. More air, water, a chance to be someone else. More space and anonymity. The idea of returning to my sterile box in the sky, as opposed to Evie's lovely guest room, made me bite my tongue.

I gritted my teeth and cleared the snark from my voice. "I'm sorry, sir. Rest assured, I'll not let it happen again." I stepped closer to him and held my hand out, waiting.

His gaze didn't leave mine and his arrogant smirk fell away to something else I couldn't read but made my stomach ache, and I resisted the urge to look away. He stared down from a good five inches above me, his eyes dark, his mouth parted on an exhale. He faltered, his gaze dropping to my mouth before it went back to my forehead, steeling his expression. He grabbed my hand, and I felt the callouses of his palms, his fingers long and large, his knuckles a bit oversized. With the other hand, he placed the string in my palm and cleared his expression. "See that it doesn't."

He moved to walk away, and I couldn't stop myself. "I take it the date didn't go well?"

He slowed but didn't turn before he walked out the door and closed it behind him. I smirked, vowing never again to let Aiden get one over on me.

I dropped the string on the floor and went back to work.

7

THE NEXT MORNING, Evie and I sipped our coffee and grazed on pastries while the morning news droned on in the background. I was relaxed, having slept better last night than I had in years. She was looking at the calendar and apologizing for how heavy the workload was going to be today. We had to turn over nine of the twelve rentable cottages.

"Thank God you're helping me," she said. "I'm definitely going to pay you."

"No, you are not."

"It's going to take all day."

"It's fine. I have nowhere to be."

"You don't need to spend your vacation working every day and not getting paid for it."

"Evie, it's fine. I want to do it. I kind of enjoyed yesterday."

She gave me a weird look. "You need help."

"That's exactly what I'm here for."

She looked sheepish. "Sorry, I didn't mean—"

I laughed and waved my hand. "I just meant that the work distracts my mind from all the nonsense in my life. It's nice. And now that I know what the cleaning consists of, I'll move a little faster."

Then a familiar sound from the TV stole my attention. I stood up to get a closer look, Evie following. There was Thompson, front and center outside the state building, microphones in his face. I grabbed the remote and turned the volume up.

". . . taking a little well-deserved sabbatical. Jimmy will be watching out for our city in the meantime. I and the council have placed a lot of trust in Jimmy, and he's done some great work in our neighboring cities. We're excited to welcome him to Chicago."

Then, there was Jimmy standing next to him, where I had never once stood.

"I'm so happy to be serving the Windy City, the Second City. And rest assured, under my watch, it will never need to be a Third City."

Thompson cringed at his reference to the Great Fire that burned most of the city over a century ago. The kid needed a lesson in tact. This was the guy who was supposed to calm fears and gain trust better than me?

"You a fan of the supers?" Evie asked, and I jumped at her proximity.

"No," I answered quickly. She stared at me curiously before looking back at the TV.

"He's cute."

"He's too young," I said without thought.

"Oh, right—you work with the city; you probably know him."

I grunted. "We've met."

"What happened to the other one, the lady hero they had before?"

"Not sure," I responded as Thompson presented Jimmy's short history as something admirable, something that qualified him, when it was anything but.

"I wish we had a real lady super, like the female version of the super in New York. You know, the one who looks like Captain America and Thor's love child."

My hackles went up. "You mean like the one we do have."

"Well, yeah," she responded, not sensing my ruffled feathers, "but like one who really flaunts it. You know—one we can look up to and emulate. Someone with a little attitude, like a lady Iron Man or something."

"The Chicago Bird has a record of twenty-seven saves last year alone," I said.

"Oh my God, is she your friend? Sorry. I just meant that she's like a ghost hero—you never see or hear from her. She's got a shitty reputation, wears that terrible mask. Does she even have PR? I don't know. I mean, what's she really like?"

I wanted to argue that she was strong and powerful and someone who was all those things Evie said she wished the city had. But I couldn't, because she was right. The Chicago Bird was a ghost.

"She's pretty much like she seems," I mumbled. "Let's get rolling on these cottages."

—

WALKING INTO THE LAST COTTAGE of the day, we both groaned. It was a doozy.

"Well, someone had some fun in here," I winced. The microwave hung open, obliterated from some kind of food explosion. The sunset painting had spots on it, wine maybe. No dishes had been washed, and the house was so full of sand we could have used a shovel to remove it.

"Ugh. Come on, people," Evie groaned as we entered.

We got to work, and I got lost in Evie's voice in the background, as she talked more than she was silent. But I welcomed it. She kept my mind off Chicago, the city council, Jimmy the Jughead, and what kind of trouble he was going to find himself in because he acted before he thought. I hoped that whatever it was, it was nothing that couldn't be undone.

"I'm so glad you're here, Birdie," she said as she removed her head from behind the open microwave door, tossing her rubber gloves into the sink.

I smiled. "I'm not doing the bathroom."

"I wasn't going to ask that," she said.

"Weren't you?"

"Okay, maybe I was, but I hate doing bathrooms."

"I did the last eight—this one's yours."

She huffed and walked down the hall, spray bottle and rags in hand.

"We might just want to burn this one down and start over," she called from the door, and I laughed.

"*Eww*, gross! I'm going to need more Clorox!" she continued. "Like six bottles maybe."

Her head popped out of the bathroom. "I'm actually out. Could you go get some more?"

"Gladly," I said and set the window cleaner aside.

"It's in Aiden's workshop, in the back. It's that big outbuilding in the trees behind the cottages."

I'd seen the building. "Okay, be right back."

I dropped my rags on the end table and walked behind the cottages to the enormous green shed that sat behind a row of skyrocket juniper and birch trees lining the area behind the cottages, hiding the building from the obvious view of the guests.

The oversized door squeaked as I pulled it open and stepped inside, letting it close behind me. Looking around, I saw no cleaning supplies, but something much more interesting.

It was full of furniture—a few tables, chairs, a bed frame. An oversized chair made of exposed knotted wood sat next to where I stood. The natural gaps in the wood were filled with color, giving it the appearance of a deep blue river flowing. It was smooth to the touch and the most beautiful contrast of color and wood I'd ever seen.

My eyes darted all over the shed, trying to find similar styles. There was so much, but from what I could see, nothing was quite like this chair.

I sat down and leaned back. As I ran my hands along the sculpted arms of the chair, the blue dissolving into green at the ends, it was heaven. I closed my eyes, picturing myself sitting in front of Evie's cottage, an old woman with a book in hand, enjoying the lake breeze and summer sun on my face, all in this perfect chair.

"You break it, you buy it."

I opened my eyes to find Aiden walking around the corner, coming to stand a few feet away at a nearby table, where he began clamping a piece of wood. I stood up, watching him adjust the vise until the piece was snug.

"Sorry. It looked finished."

"It is," he replied without looking my way.

"Did you make it?"

"I did," he said and moved to the other side of the table, glancing at me before returning his attention to whatever it was he was doing.

"It's beautiful. Everything in here is amazing. Like really amazing."

He grunted, clamping the wood from the other side.

"How did you get the color in there? It looks so natural—it reminds me of driftwood," I said, once again eyeing the lines of the chair.

Aiden stopped what he was doing. "It's eighteen hundred dollars."

I jerked my head back to his. "Really? I mean, it certainly looks like it could sell for that much. How long did it take you to make it?"

"A week."

"It's perfect," I whispered as I looked at it once again, getting lost in the lines. "I hope it goes to a good home."

"Do you need something?" he said, suddenly standing in front of the worktable, closer to me, and bending to pick up a bucket. "Or do you just make a habit of trespassing?"

I stepped back. "Right." Guess he still hadn't warmed up to me one bit. "I'm looking for cleaning supplies."

He turned away without another glance in my direction. "Other side of the shed. Walk around from the outside."

"Okay. Sorry, I didn't mean to intrude on your solitary man time," I said, not feeling sorry at all. But I wanted to stay here for the summer, and I wouldn't make it if Aiden continued to look at me with this level of contempt. "Have I done something major to make you dislike me?" I blurted out. "I mean, other than that first encounter."

He took a rag from his pocket and wiped his face. "I don't know you well enough to feel any way about you. And I don't plan on it. You're Evie's guest. I'll stay out of your way; you stay out of mine."

"I think it's going to be impossible for us to completely avoid each other," I said, and he grunted. "How about I'll try to stay out of your way more than in it, out of your workshop, and in exchange, you try to be a tolerable human being, instead of a tactless tyrant?"

"Excuse me?" he said, finally giving me his full attention.

"You are being an ogre. I don't believe it's warranted," I told him, but then thought back to my own behavior when we first met. "You caught me on a bad day, okay? I was rude, but I'm trying to be nice . . . or at least civil, because I'm staying at your place, even though I *am* working to pay my way. Maybe just cut me some slack?"

He stared at me, his cheek twitching. I was waiting for him to step up, yell at me, tell me to get lost. But he turned and walked back to his table, and I assumed the conversation was over. I was about to turn and walk away when he said, "Why do I get the feeling that you've never been nice?"

My shoulders lifted and fell. "I can be nice."

"Hmm. I'm not sure you can."

"What's that supposed to mean?"

"Give it a try and say something nice. Now. Say something nice to me. About me."

What? That's weird. "Okay. You have an awesome sister."

He huffed. "Try again."

"Your cottages are quite lovely."

"True. But that's too easy and not so much about me personally." He smiled. "You can't do it, can you?"

"Why do *I* have to say it? You say something nice to me first. How about you apologize for being so rude before?"

"Fine." He dusted his hands off on the rag and set it down before rounding the table, coming to stand in front of me. "I'm sorry you took my sister out and got her so drunk she was sick for two days. She's . . . fragile. If you're going to spend time with her, you need to leave your bad habits at home. Apology accepted?"

"That wasn't . . . it wasn't . . . I didn't . . . I wasn't paying attention, okay." I paused, getting the sense that he really was simply concerned for his sister. I couldn't totally hate him for that, so I relented. "She's an adult and can make her own decisions. That said, it won't happen again on my watch."

"Good," he said, waiting for me to leave.

"Something nice about me," I reminded him, unmoving, my body highly aware of how close he stood.

He nodded, pushing his hands into his jeans as through he needed to contain them. His eyes went dark, his mouth too close to my own as he leaned in. I held my breath and my pulse picked up. There was something about his directness, his lack of tact or propriety, that excited me, made me eager to hear what he'd say next. What I initially took as rude seemed more like complete and total honesty, unpackaged and unfiltered. My job always had me so focused on keeping my mouth shut, on maintaining public niceties. Come to think of it, so had my mother. And so had . . . But I didn't want to think of them right then. In any case, no one wanted to hear what I had to say, and no one spoke to me honestly. Aiden's blatancy—his inability to smother his thoughts in false fluff— clearly garnered a reaction from a part of me that hadn't reacted to much in several years. Aiden Anders was just the right amount of asshole, and I was apparently thrilled by it. My mother would be shocked.

"You have the most gorgeous plumber's crack I've ever seen."

My jaw went slack, and he laughed. I failed to contain my blush. "Ugh." I struggled for words, and he was still laughing. "Seriously?"

"What?" He threw his hands out. "That was nice."

I glowered at him. "Fine. Good. Glad we're friends now," I said, before walking out the door, not giving him a chance to respond.

———

I HADN'T HEARD FROM THOMPSON. Part of me had expected a call with some kind of emergency. Not getting the call was messing with my head. Was I that easily replaceable? Despite settling into a routine with Evie, my unknown future kept me on edge. A part of me wanted to put my mask on and head back to the city, follow Jimmy around like some kind of babysitter. But that was going backward, and I was here to move forward, to find out something about myself that wasn't wrapped up in being the Chicago Bird. I was here for Birdie, whoever that was anymore.

I leaned back in one of the two Adirondack chairs that adorned every cottage's front porch, knowing now that they were created in the shop behind the trees.

"Your brother hates me," I said.

"What?" Evie replied from the chair opposite mine, glass of tea in hand, a bowl of popcorn between us, our stomachs content from the pork tacos we'd whipped up. "No, he doesn't."

"I'm pretty sure he prefers I not be here."

She sat back and took a sip. "Well, Aiden's always been a bit strange with people."

"He hates them?"

She laughed. "No. And he doesn't hate you. He's just . . . slow to trust. What did he say?"

I thought about our last meeting. "It's not so much what he says. It's his general air of superiority, like I'm an irritating fly at his picnic."

She smiled before her expression turned serious. "Well, Aiden has always been blunt about everything. Mom was always patient about it, but it got him in trouble a lot as a kid, especially in school. He's not capable of subtlety, and he's not afraid to say exactly what comes to mind, no matter the topic—kind of like someone else I've recently met?"

I raised my brows and pointed at myself in question, and she chuckled. "Also, serious ego on my brother. But he's not usually so obvious about it." She scrunched her face. "I think this might be all my fault."

"How so?"

"The day I met you, I'd asked Aiden to see Doctor Evans with me because he's over-the-top protective. I left the appointment early so they could talk alone—I waited outside and chatted with that group. I'm assuming Evans discussed with him ways to be protective that weren't so smothering, or something like that. I'm not sure what all was said between them, but he came out pissed and left me there, and then I found you and proceeded to get very drunk, and well . . ."

So that's what Aiden was doing with Evans. That's why he walked out ready for a fight.

What was my excuse?

"What business of it is his, your life?"

She tapped her glass with her fingernails. "He worries."

"That's sweet, but it's still none of his business. You're an adult."

"Well, I'm not supposed to drink that much."

"No one is, Evie. Still doesn't give him the right—"

"I'm in remission," she blurted.

I sat up.

"Breast cancer. I was diagnosed a few years ago, and I've been in remission a while, but he worries about me and my health."

"Evie. I'm sorry."

"Why? Don't be. The thing is, Birdie, I'm tired of being treated like a cancer patient and a child. I'm better. I want to live a normal life. I've been staying home and not putting anything but healthy food in my body. I'm still living like a cancer patient. I feel like you are exactly what I need to get back to living a real life." She grabbed a handful of popcorn and filled her mouth.

Was I corrupting this sweet woman? "Me?"

"Yeah," she said, swallowing the popcorn. "Seems to me we are both looking for something. We can help each other."

The instinct to argue was squashed by the realization that she wasn't wrong. I needed a life, and maybe with her, for eleven weeks, I could have a semblance of one.

"Why *did* you kidnap me, anyway?"

She laughed. "I didn't kidnap you."

"Debatable."

She shook her head like I was ridiculous and took a sip of her tea. "You want to know why I approached you?"

I shrugged.

"I don't have girlfriends. No friends, really. A long battle with cancer and moving away does that."

I raised my brow, waiting for more.

"When I saw you, I decided we were going to be friends."

"Oh my God, you really did kidnap me." We both smiled. "Shit, Evie. Between the two of us, I thought you were the one that had it all figured out."

"Ha! Nope, the opposite is true. This is going to be an interesting summer." She leaned in for more popcorn. She tossed a kernel into her mouth, but it missed her face entirely and fell to the porch floor. "Maybe he likes you."

"Who?" When it hit me, I guffawed. "Yeah, right." A man like Aiden would never be interested in someone like me. I knew that from experience, and I was perfectly fine with it.

"Why not? You're hot and single. He's hot and single. It makes sense."

"Have you not been listening to a word I'm saying? He *hates* me. And we're not children on the playground."

She shrugged, tucked her feet under her, and snuggled deeper into her chair. "I'll talk to him."

"Oh God, please don't. The last thing I need is him thinking I complained to you that he was mean. I'll just make myself scarce." Or push his buttons for fun.

"You don't need to do that."

"Please don't say anything."

She shrugged. "I think you should meet my ex."

"What? *No!*"

After a moment of confusion, she burst out laughing, nearly spilling her tea all over herself. "Not like *that*—I meant platonically. Like just meet him."

My face reddened. "Why?"

She was still laughing. "He'd like you. He was always trying to get me to call my girlfriends, but they disappeared when I needed them. Or maybe I pushed them away. Anyway, he'd like you. And we're still trying to work things out."

"Why'd you break up?"

"He cheated."

"And you want him back?"

"Technically, yes, he did cheat. But there's a lot more to it."

I gave her a scolding look.

"I mean, if I'm being totally honest, the man withstood more from me than any person should have to. When he finally did cheat, he was heartbroken and told me about it immediately."

"That doesn't make it okay."

"I know," she said quietly. "But cancer wreaks havoc on the body and the mind. Especially when you have both your breasts removed at the age of twenty-seven."

I hated that I glanced at her chest. But she puffed up and beamed. "New boobs. They look good, right? Don't feel like the old ones, but you can't have everything, I guess."

Suddenly, Evie was maybe the strongest person I'd ever met.

"I struggled with the removal," she continued. "I'd taken being female for granted. Losing my hair, then my breasts, was a blow. I didn't handle it well. And even though I didn't cheat, what I did to him was arguably worse. I wanted him for myself but wouldn't let him have me. I made him feel bad for not loving me when it was *me* who didn't love me. I think I knew I was doing it, but I didn't care. He stayed anyway, was loyal and took care of me, never asking for anything for himself."

"It was his choice to cheat," I said.

She shrugged like it wasn't cut-and-dried. "I wanted out. I was tired of seeing him every day, knowing I was hurting him. I had nothing to give anymore—no job, no body, no sex drive, no joy. I was wallowing. I told him it was over. He left and came back the next morning and confessed what happened."

"Oh."

"I was relieved. It let me off the hook a bit. Maybe it wasn't completely my fault, the death of our relationship. Anyway, that was it." She shook her head, as though shaking back tears. "In the end, I was the one who pushed him away. I didn't feel like a woman, didn't want to be touched. I didn't hear him when he said I was as beautiful now as ever. That he loved me with or without *real* breasts."

"He left, though, so he didn't really mean it."

She quirked her head, a brief look of pity crossing her brow. This was her sad story, but she pitied me. "It was me, Birdie, not him. I was trying to come to terms with the new me. I couldn't see myself as a sexual person anymore, and I projected that onto my husband. I was angry at life, and I made it his fault. There's only so much rejection a person can take." She set her empty glass down. "I filed for divorce. Used his mistake as an excuse to end things for real."

"And then what?"

"Then . . . well, I came here to help my brother and maybe gain a little perspective. I've been here ever since."

"Wow," I said, unsure what to follow up with.

"It took a lot of time with Doctor Evans to get to where I am now. But I'm comfortable with myself. Truth is, though, I miss him. He hates himself for what happened, and he adores me. But . . ."

"But what?"

"I really miss him. But it's not fair for me to ask him back if I can't move forward without baggage, you know?"

"You should call him. Start making new memories. Take the next leap. It may just come naturally."

"We talk or text every day. He wants to come here. I want him to. I'm just scared it will all fall apart." Then she smiled mischievously. "I still think my brother likes you."

"Ugh." I threw some popcorn at her. "No."

"He was engaged once, you know."

"Really?" I didn't like to think of Aiden engaged. "I mean, I can't imagine that."

"He used to have some fancy job in Texas, where we're from. Still has it, actually. Anyway, that's where he met her. They were both workaholics and she was exactly how you might expect—nice, smart, beautiful."

"What happened?"

"She left him."

"Because he's a grumpy bastard?" I asked.

She laughed, then her face was serious. "Because he didn't love her."

"Oh."

"Aiden's always had trouble with relationships. I think he loves more deeply than most, but so far that only extends to family. I'm sure that feels lonely. Maybe that's what makes him grumpy."

Maybe the asshole and I did have something in common. "Is that you or him talking?"

Her face wasn't joking anymore. "He really is the best brother. He's the best man I've ever known. He's just . . . he gives up on strangers easily, or they give up on him."

Well, if my past experiences hadn't sealed my disinterest in Aiden Anders, this little tidbit, *he gives up easily*, was enough to do it.

"Well, I never!" The words rang out from the reception booth on the other side of Aiden's cottage. A fiftysomething woman in a beachy dress stalked across the sand, past Aiden's cabin, and stopped in front of us. "Do you work here?"

"Yes," Evie said, standing up. "Is there a problem?"

"That man at the reception desk was the brashest, rudest person I've ever come across. I've half a mind to post our entire exchange online," she said with a huff. We all looked back to see Aiden exit the reception booth and walk purposefully into his cottage without a glance in our direction.

Before Evie could say anything, the woman continued. "I'm staying in cottage four. I heard that the owner made some of the furniture in the cabins. I asked him . . . ugh. It's one thing to decline business, but only a brute would insult a potential patron."

"Tell me what the problem is exactly. Is there something wrong with your cabin furniture?" Evie asked. She stepped into the sun, looking unfazed as she tied her loose blonde hair into a messy bun atop her head.

"Well, no. I popped in to inquire about some work I had in mind for him, and he shut me down. I described exactly what I wanted, and he went into a tirade questioning my taste and my commitment to the environment. I'm on the board of the conservation society," she declared. "No one is more committed than me."

"Your request wouldn't happen to be making some kind of wooden yard gnome?"

She stood up straight. "God, no. I wanted him to make a replica of my Terrance, carved from wood."

"Terrance?" I asked.

"My Cashmere Lop."

Evie and I looked at each other for explanation.

"My rabbit," she clarified with annoyance.

Evie's hand went to her mouth in a clear attempt to hide her smile. "Ma'am, I do apologize, but Aiden, my brother, has a horrible fear of rabbits—he was attacked by one as a child. Unfortunately, he has an irrational reaction anytime anyone mentions rabbits or bunnies, or any furry woodland creature, really."

"Oh my. A bunny attacked him, you say?"

Evie nodded. "It was rabid—it escaped from the house a few doors down from ours."

The woman's eyes said she was gauging the truth of the story, but she eventually seemed to accept it. "Well, that's no reason for rudeness. He said I was an abomination to the environment, something about trees being used for function only, and not frivolous decoration. He was quite offensive."

"I do apologize, ma'am. Do you think, in this instance, we could let this one slide, on account of a young boy nearly being mauled to death by a rabid rabbit?"

This couldn't be true, but Evie delivered the speech with such poise.

"Would a half-price night at the cottage do the job?"

She huffed. "I'll consider it, but an apology would go a lot further."

"I don't think you want that. He's a crier, an ugly one."

Her face twisted in disgust. "Well, I never." She shook her head and stomped down the sand.

Once out of earshot, Evie looked back to me and tilted her head.

I smiled. "You are so full of shit."

She shrugged.

"What was that all about?"

"Aiden has an aversion to making what he calls 'crap'—he only makes functional items. He gets asked weekly to make some kind of lawn ornament or Nativity scene or a bald eagle or something."

"So?"

"So, he can't seem to keep his mouth shut about it. He must have gone off on her. Poor woman."

"Poor Terrance," I added.

We burst out laughing, and I sat back in my chair as I imagined all the ways I could torture him with this information later on.

8

"**BIRDIE.**" **DOCTOR EVANS'S** voice was clear and bright as she held her office door open for me.

I stepped in and found my seat, trying to clamp down the growing anxiety. Should I tell her I failed my first assignment on day one? I didn't want to say anything that would sabotage her opinion of me, yet I sensed she could read me easily. I wasn't a good liar.

"So," she started as she sat across from me, a light smile resting on her warm face. I wondered if they practiced that in school. "How have the last few days been? Any questions about our first visit together? Questions about future visits?"

"I do have one. Am I right in assuming you hold my future in your hands?"

"How do you mean?"

"Are you talking to my boss? Telling him about our sessions? Is it up to you if I get my job back?"

She smiled with a hint of humor and said, "I will not be sharing any of what we discuss with anyone outside this room." I felt the tension ease from my shoulders, but she continued. "I will, however, be submitting a written psychological assessment at the close of our sessions, without personal detail. Your employer may use it to inform their future decisions regarding your employment."

"Right. Do I need to pass a test or something? Because I need this job. It's not like there's much else out there for me."

"There's no test. Birdie, I don't anticipate that I will find you unfit for any work based on our sessions. That's not really what this is about. Try not to worry. Let this process play out, and keep an open mind. Everyone has something to work through. You're ahead of the game just by being here. Whatever we work through, know it's nothing that should make you afraid." She reached forward to grab her notebook. "And I disagree."

"Disagree?"

"That there's nothing else out there for you. If you didn't have this job, there are others. The world holds many options for an intelligent young woman."

"I'm a super. This is what we do. It's the only job I've ever had."

She smiled. "Is there a gifted person like you that doesn't have a job similar to yours? I mean, since your abilities include strength and speed, what other jobs could you have that also utilize those same attributes?"

"Other jobs?"

"Think about it," she said, then moved on. "What have you been up to the last few days?"

"I met this woman who invited me to stay here in Grove and clean vacation cottages in exchange for a place to stay. I figured it's easier to be close for the appointments with you, and my apartment is so small and boring and maybe . . . I don't know . . ." I was rambling. "I said I'd do it."

"You're staying at the Anders cottages?" Her head tipped in interest.

I panicked a minute. Would she disapprove of that decision? "I did the last couple nights. I just thought . . . but I'm not sure I'm going to stay long. I didn't tell her who I am, and if she finds out, she might get pissed. And her brother hates me."

"Why?"

"Why does he hate me? Hell if I know—"

"No," Doctor Evans interrupted. "Why do you think Evie would be angry if she found out about your job, your abilities?"

"Oh, right. She's also your patient."

"Small town," she replied. "Did she say something that would indicate she'd be unhappy with your job?"

I shrugged, looking away. "No. It's just my experience."

"Tell me more about that."

"It's not that complicated. People don't stick around me long, except Jace, and that's because he's a super too. I'm too much for most people."

"Did someone tell you that or is that your own observation?"

I thought back. "Both," I said without emotion. "Any friends and family I had faded into the background when I went into the facility and disappeared when I got out."

"You mentioned your mother last time we talked. Is that whom you're referring to?"

I shrugged.

"Do you talk to your mother?"

"Rarely. Like I said, we're not close."

"Tell me about her."

I took a calming breath, steeling myself for this conversation. I knew we'd eventually end up here.

"She's embarrassed by me. My job . . . my powers." My mind conjured up a familiar image—a memory I reminded myself of often, particularly when I thought of reaching out to her.

"Hey, sweetie," came my mother's voice on the other end of the line, as I gripped the phone. "How are you doing?"

My tears were coming in waves, but I tried to keep them from impacting my voice, knowing she'd tell me sobbing like a toddler wasn't ladylike. "I'm okay," I lied, feeling a loneliness and fear I couldn't explain since being in this place, this . . . facility. It had been nearly three months since I'd entered the "government training program for enhanced individuals."

"Good girl."

"Mom?"

"Hmmm?"

"Some of the other residents are going home to their families for the holidays. Maybe you could come pick me up for a few days?"

"Oh, sweetie. I'm not sure that's a good idea."

"Mom, I'd like really to come home, please."

"Sweetie, I'm so sorry. You know Aunt Samantha's coming for the holidays, and she's staying in your room. We've got your cousins sleeping downstairs. If I'd known earlier you wanted to come home . . . but now, well, it's just not possible. Maybe next year."

"Next year?" I replied, grasping the phone even more tightly, hearing a distinctive crack.

"Let's wait until you're better, huh? You don't want the family knowing about your condition."

"I'm not sick," I argued, but I felt the room tip a little bit. *"So I'm not getting better."*

"Listen, there's someone at the door. I'll call you back soon."

"Birdie?" Doctor Evans said, her voice sharp. "Where did you go?"

I pulled myself out of my cloud and cleared my throat. "Sorry."

"You were telling me about your mother."

"Right. She just didn't know what to do with me once I developed powers."

"Were you close before that?"

"I mean, I thought so at the time, but considering what happened after . . . Once Nick and I ended things, we didn't really have anything connecting us."

"Nick?"

"My fiancé."

She blinked, but her expression didn't shift. "Was that before or after you developed your powers?"

"Engaged before. Our parents basically arranged it."

"Were you in love?"

I shrugged. "I suppose. It's hard to remember that part now."

"And how did that end?"

I almost laughed. "Badly."

"Birdie, when was the last time you tried to connect with someone new?"

I shrugged. "It's been years, I guess. I dated for a while. Guys were too intimidated or embarrassed by me for it to turn into anything. Men want a woman who fits an ideal. That's not me. I accepted it."

"Have you dated men with abilities like yours?"

"A couple, but it's the same for them. I'm still more physically powerful."

"And friendships?"

"I'm a novelty, entertainment for people. I'm not interested in being anyone's party trick."

"Birdie, what made you accept the invitation from Evie?"

"It just kind of . . . happened. As directed, I'm not a super this summer, so I was interested in being someone else for a while. Also, she's very . . . persuasive."

Evans smiled and wrote a few notes in her pad. I imagined words like *sad*, *pathetic*, or *lost cause* filling the page. I felt the truth of those words. Living my life was one thing; saying it out loud was a whole other—

"Birdie, I'd like you to try dating."

That snapped me out of my internal dialogue. "*What?*"

"I'd like you to date," she repeated, "while you are here in Grove."

"Why?"

She set her notebook on the table between us and clasped her hands on her crossed knee. "Dating is a great way to get to know others and, in turn, yourself. You don't need to date seriously. The idea is to get out of your routine. You've done that to some extent by deciding to stay here in Grove, but that could end up being just another routine. Doing this, you'll be forced to converse, talk about yourself, engage in new activities with other people."

My blood was warming, my face reddening. I didn't date for a reason. "What kind of activities?"

She leaned back, satisfied. "Anything—hiking, boating, book clubs. Fine dining. Conversation. Anything you want. And there are always festivals in town and plenty of activities for tourists in the summer."

"And this will help me how?" I preferred cleaning with Evie, who did most of the talking, and sitting on her porch at night with or without conversation.

"At this point, we're just looking to open up your world a bit."

I couldn't argue that I was closed off. But I wasn't sure *opening up* was such a good idea. I didn't have a good track record with any of this. A flash of Aiden's face came to mind, and I stuffed it away. "I don't think this is a good idea. What are the other options?"

"How are we doing with the abstaining—from the use of your abilities, I mean?"

This woman didn't miss a beat. "I messed up once, but it's been smooth sailing since then."

"Great." She stood and pulled a piece of paper from her notebook, handing it to me. "Here."

"What's this?"

"A list of popular local dating sites."

"You're actually serious?"

"I am."

"What if I say no?"

"Are you saying no?"

Fuck. "I'm not interested in dating. I prefer the single life. There's nothing wrong with that."

"No, there isn't. But is this a life you actively chose, or one you've boxed yourself into?"

"It's the life I have. What difference does it make?"

After a slow blink, she continued. "This isn't about you finding a forever partner. It's about being open to possibilities. I believe the actions that led to your suspension are the result of living a life you aren't necessarily happy with but feel trapped by."

"Wow, and after only two visits, you have me all figured out."

Shit. That filter.

But Doctor Evans only chuckled. "Do you want to improve things in your life, Birdie?"

Mostly, I just wanted my job and identity back. "Fine."

—

RETURNING FROM MY APPOINTMENT with Doctor Evans, I was deep in thought about this dating experiment, wondering what would be the best way to get out of doing it at all. Suddenly a text popped up from Jace with a new GIF of me, my face the definition of defensive humiliation. The words above, *No! My Vagina Won't Crush Your Penis.* It was the third one of this variety he'd sent me.

I typed back, **Thanks for this.**

No problem, Becks, he replied.

I'd been humiliated by the early ones, then angry. With this one, I just felt numb. Jace wanted me to laugh at myself. But I'd been dealing with comments like this for years. This was the just the latest in a long line of sexually charged insults meant to bring me down a peg. I wasn't there yet.

Pulling my eyes from my phone, I was surprised to find a stranger standing on the porch of our cottage, duffel bag in hand.

"Hello," the man said as I approached. He was tall and lean, with an intellectual handsomeness, dark-rimmed glasses, black hair, and two days of stubble.

"Can I help you? Are you looking to check in?"

"No, ma'am," he said with a large smile. "I'm here to see Evie. You must be Birdie?"

"That's right. And you are?"

Another smile. "Right. Sorry." He held out his hand. "I'm Yash."

I stared. Was I supposed to know him? He did look a little familiar.

"The ex-husband," he said with a hint of embarrassment.

"Oh, Yash. Of course." I wasn't sure if Evie had ever mentioned his name. He was just the ex. And he was here. His hand was still out, so I stepped up and shook it, fully recognizing him from Evie's photos. "Evie's probably still asleep. We were up a little late last night. She didn't tell me you were coming."

"Well, she did invite me like . . . ," he said, moving his duffel from one hand to the other, his free hand clenching and unclenching in obvious anxiety, "only ten hours ago."

"You didn't waste any time, did you?"

He stepped aside so I could open the door. "I had my bag packed. Been waiting for this call for some time."

I paused, my hand on the doorknob, struck by his confession. "That's very sweet."

He smiled again, but sadly this time. "I guess that must sound pretty desperate."

I stepped inside, inviting him to follow me. Based on the conversation I'd had with Evie last night, I figured he could be the one to wake her. "Her room is on the left."

"Thanks, Birdie," he said looking down and straightening his shirt, then running his hands through his hair. "Do I look okay?"

I grinned, happy for Evie. "Very handsome."

He beamed. "It was very nice to meet you. Evie has talked about you nonstop for a week now. She was very excited for us to meet."

"And then she missed the whole thing!"

He laughed, slightly wild-eyed, before he walked down the hall to her room, slowly pushing open the door and entering.

—

I TURNED OVER TWO COTTAGES that afternoon on my own, allowing Yash and Evie time alone together. Lizzo sounding in my earbuds, I scrubbed the large bathtub in cottage seven, the only one with a beautifully updated and oversized clawfoot tub. I found a bit of grime lining the back feet of the tub. It was nearly impossible to reach from below, so without even thinking, I lifted one edge of the tub with one hand to wipe the legs underneath before moving to the other side to do the same.

"Evie!" the voice reached my ears as I heard the front door close, footsteps on the hardwood. "Evie!"

"Shit," I swore, pulling the earbuds from my ears.

"Evie," Aiden's voice called again, closer.

Quickly realizing I was about to get caught, I stepped back from the tub and it slipped from my hand, falling hard to the floor.

"Fuck!" I muttered as I heard a loud crack and looked down to see the ornate tile under the tub had shattered under the force. "Fuck, fuck, fuckity fuck."

I made my way to the door and came face-to-face with the chest of Aiden Anders.

"What was that?" he said, looking over my shoulder.

"What was what?" I asked innocently, blocking his entry to the bathroom with my body.

"Move," he demanded, so close I could feel his warm breath on my face. He smelled good, a bit like his woodshop, the dust on his shoulder evidence that he'd spent his afternoon there. I didn't move and neither did he. His eyes were on mine, then slowly moved to my lips before moving lower. I wore the same ill-fitting clothes I'd worn last time he saw me cleaning, but I felt naked under his scrutiny.

"No," I finally said bringing his eyes back to mine.

"No?"

I shook my head without breaking eye contact.

"Did you break something?" His tone was firm and forceful, half-mad, half-gloating.

My brow creased, and my voice came out a little winded. "Of course not. I just dropped the scrub brush. It knocked over some stuff. I'll just get it cleaned up."

He didn't move, his eyes on my lips again. "You're really shit at this job," he said, breaking my trance as I licked my lips inches from his. He cleared his throat. "Whatever you broke better be fixed by tomorrow's reservation."

Irritation crept up my spine. "I didn't break anything. And I thought we were being nice now."

"You're an employee. And not a very good one."

"Fuck you."

"Now, that's not a very *nice* thing to say."

"You started it."

"Your playground tête-à-tête is impressive as always, Miss Bowden."

"Ditto, Mr. Anders."

His eyelids were hooded, his breath heavy. For a second, I thought he might kiss me, as he leaned in even closer. But he quickly pulled back and turned away.

"Dammit," he swore, his hand tugging through his hair as he walked out, slamming the door behind him.

—

RETURNING TO EVIE'S cabin in the late afternoon, I found Evie and Yash sitting on the couch, deep in conversation, their hands entwined tightly, her eyes rimmed with tears—good ones, I hoped.

"Hey, guys," I said as I entered, heading straight for my room. "I'll just change and head out for a while."

I quickly showered and changed into jeans and a T-shirt. The broken tile was hidden under the tub in the corner. I wondered if I could get by with not telling them it was broken. Evie would find it eventually and tell Aiden. He'd know it was me. He'd be pissed. Maybe I would have told him myself if it wouldn't have outed me as a super. I decided I'd try to find a replacement tile—maybe they had extra ones somewhere—and fix it before anyone noticed.

"Birdie?" Evie's voice pulled me from my thoughts. I was sitting on the side of the bed, lacing my boots.

"Hey," I said as she entered, leaving the door open behind her. "How are you?"

"I'm good." She grinned and took a seat next to me, her eyes wet but alight. "He's going to stay here. He's already talked to the vet in town that's retiring in a few years and he's going to start working there, maybe take over the practice eventually."

"He's a vet?"

She smiled and nodded. "Yep. Pretty perfect, huh?"

"You don't plan on moving back to Texas?"

"We still have a lot of work to do. I want to be better. I *will* be better. Him too. We think a fresh start in a new place will be good for us."

I smiled and pulled away the hair that stuck to her wet cheek. "I'm very happy for you."

"I wish you could find your own Yash," she said, and I shrugged.

"I'm good on my own. I told you that." I'd said the words a hundred times. But suddenly, it didn't feel true. Maybe it never had. And for a moment, I wished . . . maybe if things were different. If I weren't a super . . .

Would I still be with Nick? Would we be married? Children? Living in the suburbs? Would my life be everything my mother had wanted and more? Probably yes, though it was hard to imagine now. When I met Nick at my sweet sixteen party, in my mother's pick of sparkling dress with capped sleeves and low back, I knew she had planned it all out. Nick's father and my father had started their company together. Nick would take over eventually. And after my father had died, my mother lost her own future, so she immersed herself in planning mine.

He'd asked me to dance and spoke with a confidence that no eighteen-year-old should have had. He kissed me and told me I was the prettiest girl he'd ever seen. He asked if he could stay in touch with me when he went back to boarding school, and I said yes. He was cocky and popular, and he liked me.

"He'll take care of you," Mother had said, "just as your father took care of us. And you'll have children to keep your days full." That was enough for Mother, so it was enough for me.

After high school, when I told Nick that I wasn't sure I wanted children, he smiled and said it was okay, that we had plenty of time until that stage of our lives. Then he proposed, and we never brought it up again.

But things quickly changed. Despite my inactivity and growing appetite late in high school, I continued to get leaner, stronger, my body sometimes ravenous for food. A few weeks into college, I returned to the physical activity I'd previously given up, eager to find a way to expel the nervous energy that kept me awake at night. But I found it harder to burn out, getting faster and faster until people would stop and stare as I ran past. I started running at night, my body unable to rest until I did.

Everything was becoming easier physically. It came on so gradually that I barely noticed until I started testing my body: lifting things, moving things.

I grew afraid. I'd heard the news of people exhibiting strange and random abilities and what was happening to them. They were disappearing to government facilities for study, torn away from family and friends.

I decided to hide it. I ran only in the darkest hours of the night, and I did it in the outskirts of town where no one was watching. When I found myself in Wisconsin in the middle of the night a few minutes after I'd started my run, I broke down and cried all the way back to my dorm. I cried for days and then weeks. I stopped going to class. I saw less and less of my friends. I stopped seeing anyone but my fiancé and my mother, both of whom thought I just wasn't handling the stress of college well.

When I couldn't take it any longer, I told Nick everything. And everything changed.

"We're going to Aiden's for dinner. Come with us?" Evie said, pulling me from the past.

"What? Oh. No, thanks. I'm going to grab something in town," I said, quickly returning to finish up my laces.

"In Texas, we had family dinners every Friday. Yash, Aiden, and my mom. Mom and Aiden did most of the cooking. It was the one night a week we reserved for one another. It's Friday, so we're renewing the tradition. You must come."

"Evie, I'm not family."

She looked me in the eye. "Doesn't feel that way to me," she said, and I reared back a bit, feeling pressure in my eyes. "Besides, you must meet Yash officially. You're coming."

9

"**YOU SEEM NERVOUS,**" Yash said as we walked across the sand to Aiden's cottage.

"Let's just say Aiden isn't my biggest fan," I replied, feeling both dread and eagerness at the promise of seeing him, having no idea how he'd react to my presence.

Yash patted my shoulder and said, "Aiden isn't a fan of anyone but himself. He'll get over it."

"Were you two close?"

"Ha," Evie spat as she caught up with us on Aiden's porch, having stopped to grab a plate of cookies from the kitchen. "A bromance for the ages!"

"Really?"

Yash and Evie chuckled at my obvious shock.

"Yash was Aiden's friend first," Evie said, "his best and only. He wasn't too happy when we started dating, especially considering Yash was in college and I was in high school."

"Aiden upset? I can't imagine," I said in jest, before turning around to see Aiden standing at the open door, his scowl at seeing me quickly replaced by a face of elation at seeing Yash. I was both horrified for myself and impressed with the level of affection he had for his friend. I wouldn't have thought him capable of it.

Bro-hugs and back pats followed. Aiden leaned to give Evie a kiss on the cheek, his eyes finding mine as he pulled away.

"Bowden," he said.

"Anders," I replied with a smirk, and before he turned away, I could have sworn he was hiding a smile. Would it be like this all summer with us, so hot and cold?

"Thanks for taking care of the cleaning today, Birdie," Evie said as she pulled me to the couch I'd woken up on only a week before. Yash handed us each a glass of wine, and we smiled our thanks before he joined Aiden in the kitchen.

"They are so different. I wouldn't have pegged them as best friends," I said quietly. "Yash seems so easy, so . . . friendly, and Aiden, well—"

"Yeah, but they balance each other. They're pretty adorable together." We watched them puttering around the kitchen, their conversation boisterous enough to drown ours out. It was quite the merry reunion.

"You feeling good about everything?" I asked softly, turning back to Evie, who continued to watch the men.

"I'm glad he wants to stay here," she whispered.

"So, I'm getting a new roommate, then?" I asked, keeping my voice low as well.

"Oh no, he's going to get a place in town—we'll take things slow for a while. But enough about us—how was the session with Doctor Evans this morning?"

I proceeded to tell Evie about the dating thing, immediately realizing I shouldn't have.

"No!" she squealed. "You're kidding. That's freaking classic! Yash, Aiden, did you hear this? Evans is making Birdie date. She even gave her a list of recommended sites!"

"That's something," Yash said, smiling at his wife from the kitchen. Ex-wife. Whatever they were. Aiden glanced over, unaffected by the statement.

"I'm sorry," Evie continued, "but the Doc is like late forties and has been married forever. And she's giving you dating instructions. It's unconventional, but also on brand for her."

I groaned and placed a pillow over my face to suffocate myself.

I heard laugher and, when I pulled the pillow away, Evie was in my face.

"Okay, whatcha got?"

I pulled the paper from my pocket. "It says *Grove meet and greet.*"

"That's not really the right scene for you. It's a bunch of middle-aged desperados."

I scoffed. "You mean like me?"

"You're not middle-aged!"

"I'm thirty-one. About time to adopt my first cat."

"Still no. Let's go with this one," she said and pointed to the third item on the list.

"Grovel?"

"It's a local site for anyone in the area for the summer. It's for summer flings or hooking up."

"It's called Grovel."

"It's funny. It's meta."

"Is it?"

"It's not a good idea." This came from the kitchen. They were the first words directed at me outside of a frosty hello.

"No one asked you," Evie called.

"Why?" I asked at the same time.

When he didn't say more, Yash chimed in, eyeing his friend. "It's fine. Like anything, just make sure you go someplace public."

"How would you know?" Evie inquired.

He shrugged and said, "I'm guessing."

"It's mostly good people. Horny, but harmless," Evie added.

"How do *you* know?" Yash asked from the kitchen.

"Friends," she said. When we all waited for more, she reluctantly continued. "I went on a few dates this year. Nothing came of it, obviously." Yash watched her from the kitchen, a look of pure longing on his kind face.

They were a fascinating couple to observe. She was silly and adorable, a live wire. He seemed thoughtful and grounded. Practical.

"We need to set up a profile," she said, winking at me.

Yash strolled over to top off our wine glasses, which were still mostly full, leaning down to kiss Evie on the forehead before standing and giving her a charming wink.

"So, Birdie," he started, his gaze snagging on Evie until he finally looked my way, "is this a quest for love?"

"Ugh, no way. I don't believe in that stuff. I mean, I do for you guys," I corrected myself quickly, and they both laughed. "It's just not for me. This is an assignment that I have to do to get a job. The same job I already have. Had. Have. Never mind."

Yash grinned. "That's the strangest job requirement I've ever heard. If you want, Evie and I can go with you to wherever you go for the date. Make sure the guy's behaving. Have a signal if you want assistance with a getaway," he said. He looked at Evie again.

"That's very kind, but I'm not too concerned." It was so natural, I thought, a man's instinct to protect the woman he cared for, to demonstrate his ability and willingness to do it. In this instance, even extending to the woman's friend. But I didn't need protection, and I'd learned over the years that it was clearly one of my biggest defects as a datable woman.

Evie smiled at Yash. "You're so cute. But these days, ladies tend to be pretty up-front if the date isn't working instead of making excuses to run and hide."

"That's not what I meant. I was just—"

"That's very sweet, Yash," I offered. "I appreciate it."

We both laughed as he went back to the kitchen.

"Adorable, misguided chivalry," Evie whispered as she sank into the couch and opened Aiden's laptop, popping in the web address. I used the opportunity to glance at Aiden working quietly in the kitchen. His muscles weren't overly huge, but I could see them distinctly moving under his thin T-shirt as he used the kitchen knife. His stomach was flat, and his jeans hung low, and I wondered if his abs were as I imagined. Defined just enough, and naturally bronze with a light trickling of hair. I tried to look for imperfections in Aiden so I could focus on them. His hair was too long, and his nose was a bit large. His jaw wasn't perfectly symmetrical. But he wore these imperfections well—perfectly, really. Good thing he was such an ass, otherwise I was bound to fall for him, like all the other lonely women he wasn't interested in. His bad attitude would help me stop dreaming about him hovering over me . . . oh shit, nope, that made it worse. Who was I kidding? I was attracted to all sides of Aiden Anders, particularly his inability to blend in to the world around him.

I realized he was staring right at me as I had gotten lost in my head watching him. His gaze held mine, intense and a little dark.

"Hello? Earth to Birdie."

"What?" I tore my eyes from a smoldering Aiden and turned to face Evie.

"What are you looking for in a partner?" she asked.

"I'm not. I mean, I don't want a partner, just a date. A bone to throw Doctor Evans."

She dropped her shoulders and glared at me. "Sure, but if you *did* want a partner, what would he be like?"

"Hot," I quipped, and Yash laughed. "I don't know. I haven't given it much thought. I'm just doing what I have to do to get my job back."

Evie shook her head, still waiting for my answer.

"Fine. I guess I want someone who isn't bound by tradition."

"*Okaaay* . . . elaborate please?"

"I mean, someone who doesn't have preconceived notions about what they're looking for. Someone . . . open-minded. Someone who doesn't feel threatened by me or my job. Someone imaginary."

"Any deal-breakers? Tall, short? Funny, rich, athletic? Would you date a bald guy?" she asked, her nose in the computer.

"Doesn't matter."

"College educated?"

"I dropped out after a semester," I said as she typed, implying no preference. "Employed would be good, I suppose."

"And what is it you do for a job, exactly?" Aiden piped up from the kitchen, looking up from chopping something as he waited for the answer. "You never mentioned. I mean, you do work here now. Maybe I should do a background check."

I glared at him, unable to tell if he was messing with me. I tried to divert. "I just mean I work a lot, and the guys I've met are kind of bothered by it. Oh, and if you want to give me a paycheck, I'll answer your questions. Until then . . ."

"My PR job in Texas was demanding," Evie spoke as she continued typing, "before I had to quit, anyway. But we were *both* busy. Ambition shouldn't be a deal-breaker. You're just dating the wrong guys."

"You didn't answer the question, Bowden," Aiden said, amused by my deflection.

"Aiden," Evie chastised, "leave her alone. She's my friend. I've already vouched for her."

I stared at Aiden with my best *she told you* expression. He shook his head with annoyance and maybe a little amusement.

"Okay, back to it, Birdie. What are your nonnegotiables in a date?" Evie asked, and I pulled my eyes from Aiden.

"I don't know. I guess I don't have any. If I'm asking him to be open-minded, I guess I should be too. If there's something there, we'll just know it. Isn't that how it's supposed to work?"

"Wow, that's kind of beautiful," Evie said, and I glanced back to the kitchen to see Aiden listening to our conversation intently. He turned away with a frown when I caught him looking.

"But I'm not putting that," Evie said, "so let's make something up, shall we?"

Not thirty minutes later, I was officially on a dating app, and Evie was eagerly showing me all the options of men available to me. I'd never bought a car, but it felt a bit like what I'd imagined buying one would be like. Sedan or sport. Teacher or contractor. I had no use for either. Then, just before we sat down to dinner with everyone else, she downloaded the app on my phone and gave it back to me, telling me to peruse some more on my own. I tucked it away without opening the app, knowing I'd probably just go with the first person who reached out to me, if anyone did.

"Birdie, tell us how a person comes to a position of being forced to date by her therapist?"

"Yash!" Evie scolded gently, her face propped in her hands. The four of us sat around a small picnic table behind Aiden's cottage, finishing the heirloom-tomato pasta Aiden had prepared. It was glorious, and now I'd have to add amazing cook to the list of his annoying attributes.

"It's none of your business!" Evie added, before sitting up straighter. "Though I am kind of curious to know more myself."

Yash looked at me and, wiggling his brows, said, "Come on, tell us something juicy. I need more gossip in my life."

"Sure, Yash," I said, "right after you share the details of your love life."

He cleared his throat, uncomfortable, and I felt bad for blurting that out, given his and Evie's nebulous status. He lowered his wineglass and leaned the slightest way in my direction while looking at Evie. "I've only ever been in love with one person, and I have been since I was twenty. But life is fucking hard, and when it got really hard, I fell apart and did something that was totally stupid. It meant nothing to me, but it changed my life completely. I take full ownership of it. And I'll spend the rest of my life groveling at her feet if it means I get another chance to make her happy."

The table was silent.

"Geez, man, overshare much?" Aiden chided. Evie and I laughed, but looking at Evie, I could see Yash's words had affected her. Who could blame her? He was obviously beyond smitten and not afraid to tell the world.

I'm not sure what compelled me—maybe Yash inspired me, or maybe I couldn't keep everything hidden forever—but I opened my mouth. "Not much to tell, really. Evans thinks dating, putting myself out there," I said with air quotes, "will solve my problems at work. But what she doesn't know is that I'm un-datable. Sometimes life slots you in somewhere. The normal life of everyone else no longer fits. I am what I am."

Evie and Yash watched me, their faces exuding something between empathy and pity. Maybe I'd said too much.

I chanced a look at Aiden, and he held my gaze, his lip quirking with a hint of a smile. "Fitting is overrated," he said.

My face heated, and I turned away before he could see me smile, his words burrowing somewhere inside me.

"I think you fit right here," Evie said, "perfectly."

Yash nodded in agreement.

"Thanks," I said and smiled, feeling a little bit like I did fit—for now. For just a little while.

"Oh, Aiden, did the couple in cottage eight ask you about the towels?" Evie asked as she refilled her water glass.

"What couple? What towels?"

"Oh my God. So earlier today, someone called reception, and it rang through to me. They asked for an extra eighteen towels."

"What the hell for?" Aiden asked.

"I don't know, but I know it's just the two of them in there, and that's a very specific number."

"Maybe they're making a fort?" I offered.

Evie and Yash laughed, and Aiden cracked a smile and said, "Or a bit of Rapunzel role-play?"

"*Eww*," Evie said, throwing a cherry tomato from her plate at her brother. "What about that group last year? The one with the costumes?"

"What?" I said.

Yash laughed. "I remember when you told me this one."

"Tell me," I insisted.

"There was a large group," Aiden started, setting his fork down and clearing his throat. "Was here early last September, when the water's warmest. Anyway, one person checked in and took the key. An hour later, Evie and I came out and found the person who rented the cottage, along with nine or ten others, all decked out in these elaborate Renaissance costumes. The men had sixteenth- or seventeenth-century soldier gear—armor, swords and sheaths, large wooden shields. One woman was a soldier, and the rest of the women were in these peasant-style dresses, with this intricately braided hair—looked like it took hours to do."

Aiden's face was relaxed as he told the story, but also as animated as I'd ever seen it. I wondered if this was the real Aiden, what he was like when I wasn't pissing him off.

"Anyway," he continued, "they were all acting out this very rehearsed cosplay scene on the beach, Old English speech and all—something about a betrayal and saving a maiden and," glancing to Evie for affirmation, "someone's paternity, if I remember correctly."

"That's amazing. What did you do?"

"What do you mean?" Aiden replied. "We sat down on the beach and watched the show."

I laughed. "And did it inspire you to want to become a LARPer?"

"Not exactly," he responded and took a drink from his bottle, his eyes on me. "The show contained swordplay and a few damsels in distress and such. But it ultimately ended with some kind of ritual suicide."

"Wait, what?"

"In the scene, I mean. It ended not with someone winning the sword fight, but with ten people flailing around in the lake, chanting, ultimately pretending to drown in some kind of messed up Shakespearean tragedy. I might have been worried if any of them had stayed underwater for more than a second or two. But they were too busy making excessive death sounds."

Evie started making said death noises, her hands on her throat, her other hand coming to her brow in a fainting motion. "It didn't quite match up with a water death, but it was entertaining just the same. Anyway, then they all just walked back out, went back to the cottage to change clothes, had a bit of a party, and then left," Evie added.

Aiden glanced around the table as everyone enjoyed a laugh, his eyes finally landing back on me.

"That's hilarious," I said to him. "How do they rank on the guest scale, best to worst?"

Aiden shrugged. "They didn't break anything. I appreciate people who live authentically," he said, and I wondered what that would be like—to live authentically, not caring about the opinions of others.

He leaned in, his attention directly on me. Goose bumps erupted over my body as he said, "They're coming back this year. Stick around, and you'll get to experience it for yourself."

10

HIDING MY ABILITIES WORKED well enough for a few days, but it quickly became an itch I couldn't scratch. I hated it. I wanted to move faster; I wanted to feel my body strain. There were times I felt I might burst at the seams.

I could have cheated. I mean no one would have known, right? Evans wouldn't be the wiser. But maybe I needed to get something out of this time with Evans. Something had to change. Pushing my limits was my way of releasing the day's stresses, emptying the tank, forgetting that I was going home to an empty apartment. Maybe I needed to find new ways to cope.

And maybe there was no hope for a happily ever after, but maybe, by putting myself out there, I could find something to sustain me, get me through the days. I just had no idea what that might look like.

And that's what I kept telling myself as I prepared for my date with Sarge. We'd found each other on Grovel. Also from Chicago, he seemed excited about meeting me. I looked around the sports bar, ten minutes past our meeting time. Maybe he'd seen me and bolted? Evie had tried to get me to ditch my signature jeans and tee, but I refused to entertain the floral dress she brought out of her closet.

Suddenly, a hand was waving at me across the bar and Sarge stepped up to my high top. "Hey. Birdie, right?"

"Hi, Sarge," I said and stood, hesitating. Were we supposed to shake hands? Air kiss, hug? Or just stare at each other blankly, like we were doing now?

"It's nice to meet you," he said, a smile coming to his face. I offered one in return. Sarge had buzzed hair and wore cargo shorts and a gym tee that covered his bulging muscles. His chest was bigger than mine. He was obviously into his body, which wasn't necessarily a bad thing, but . . .

"You live in Chicago?" he asked.

"I do. West Loop."

"Nice. I live in Old Town."

I nodded. "You're here for the summer?"

"I am. I come and work at the gym, doing personal training. Most of my clients are only here for the summer, so I run a boot camp and then one-on-ones during that time. You should come by sometime."

"Are you saying I need to work out?" I quipped, trying to seem . . . I don't know, funny maybe.

"Everyone needs to work out, Birdie," he said with seriousness, and I had the urge to correct him but didn't. His eyes traveled over me. And while I certainly wasn't bulging with muscles, my body was clearly strong. "You look like you take care of yourself."

"Thanks," *I think.* "I'm not much for gyms. This is my first summer here. Any other recommendations to fill my free time?"

"Hell yeah. They have these warrior games on the beach at the end of summer, you could train for those. They do a half marathon after the fourth, too. Oh, and—"

"Anything that doesn't involve exercise?"

Gyms did nothing for me—lifting weights was like lifting feathers, and the track was a baby step. I needed to run faster than any treadmill could go, lift concrete and steel—not barbells. I couldn't do any of that with anyone but Jace. Otherwise, I'd be a spectacle. I cringed at the thought, my mother's disappointment flashing in my head.

Sarge looked confused. "I host an arm-wrestling tournament. It doesn't technically require training, but it would help. We don't have a lot of women who participate, but there are usually a few that give it a shot. I'd do a women's division, but there's not enough participation, so the women just compete against the men. They're always out in the first round. You've got some nice lady guns on you though. You could enter, probably make it past the skinny guys who only sign up for the free beer."

Lady guns?

"Ever dated anyone stronger than you?" I couldn't help it. This wasn't going anywhere.

"You mean a man?" he said, obviously confused by the question.

"Not necessarily." I sipped my water. "Would you ever date a woman who could out-bench you?"

"That's not likely." He laughed.

"Let's try it. Now. Arm wrestle?"

"Seriously?"

"Sure," I replied. "Why not?"

"Because you're not a match for me, that's why."

I pursed my lips, unsure if he was a horse's ass or if it was me who'd led the conversation to a point where he'd inevitably say the wrong thing and I could leave.

"I don't think we're a match romantically, Sarge. Shall we cut our losses?"

He looked confused. "Why? Because I don't want to arm wrestle you? I don't want to hurt anyone."

"I'm sorry. It was nice to meet you."

He shrugged. "Okay. Whatever."

I gathered my things and walked out, leaving Sarge to wonder how this date had turned south so quickly. I'd known, going in, that it was a mistake. I'd worked to bring out any weakness, turn him off as fast as possible, make what was bound to happen, happen as quickly as possible. I'd done it before.

I strolled back to the cottage, wondering why I couldn't just enjoy a date, the company of another person—why I couldn't even get through a single night without sabotaging something. But I knew the answer. And just as if I willed her to do it, my phone sounded and I looked to see the word *Mother* flash on the screen. She only called me a few times a year, usually around Christmas and on my birthday. I considered ignoring it, but maybe she'd heard of me being suspended. Or she needed something. Either way, our calls never lasted more than five minutes, so I figured I'd get it over with.

"Hello, Mother."

"Birdie, dear."

"That's me."

"How are you? I heard you aren't working right now."

"Yep."

"I'm sorry to hear that."

Silence.

"Okay, so, I was wondering if you had some free time, if you wanted to come down to Georgia." Mom had moved back down south where she was from as soon as I got the hero job in Chicago. I wanted to think it was a coincidence.

"Wasn't planning on it."

"Oh." She almost sounded disappointed. "Well, maybe I could come up for a few days? I'd get a hotel? We could see a show or something?"

"I'm not in Chicago. I'm staying outside the city for a while."

"Really?" Her voice perked up. "Where at?"

"I'm at a cottage on the lake, just taking some R&R."

"Oh . . . well, that's great, dear. You're due a vacation. Are . . . are you there alone or with a . . . friend?"

She wanted to know if I found a man to marry me.

"No, Mother, just a solo trip."

"Do you want company?" she asked, her voice exuding an almost hopeful tone. Before I could process that she had just asked three times to see me, she said, "Never mind, dear. I hope you enjoy your time off. Let me know if you need some company or a change of scenery."

"Yeah. Okay," I said. "Talk later, then." I hung up, thankful it was over, happy she didn't push to come out. Our relationship was broken, and as much as we wanted to pretend it wasn't, it was beyond repair. But my mother had always wanted to deny things that were right in her face.

"I think you can work it out. You just need to remember why you fell in love in the first place."

"No, Mother. It's over."

She fidgeted over the tilapia in front of her. "Nick's parents will be so disappointed."

Relieved was more like it. Ever since they'd found out about me, they pushed him to end it. Eventually, after I got out of the facility, he came around to their side. "I suppose we'll cancel the hall, then," she said to herself.

"I got the job for the city. I'll be the first one in Chicago."

"Oh. That's nice, dear," she muttered, not looking at me. She took a drink of her wine.

"You still thinking of going back to Georgia to live with Aunt Samantha?"

She nodded. "Ever since your father . . . well, you don't really need me around anymore."

"You should go," I said. "It's where you've always wanted to be anyway."

She looked at me then, her eyes sad. "All right, dear."

"Go that well, huh?"

I turned around to see Aiden sitting on his porch. I'd been so in my head, I hadn't even noticed him.

"You had a date, right?" He eyed me up and down, and I was instantly on edge. "A short one, it seems."

"Yep. I failed," I spit, throwing my arms out, one boot in each hand as I walked barefoot through the sand. "Like this is a surprise to anyone. And no, I didn't dress up and I'm not wearing makeup. I knew it was a dead end before it ever happened."

He mumbled something.

"What did you say?" I bristled, gearing up for a fight.

He stood from his lounger, taking something out of his mouth that looked like straw and throwing it to the ground.

"I said, his loss."

"Oh." *That was um . . . that was nice.* "Thanks?"

He watched the sun, deep in the horizon. "Did you at least get to eat?"

"No," I said, shuffling my feet. He glanced down at my feet, and I resisted the urge to say something rude—a clear defense mechanism, as Doctor Evans had explained so kindly.

"I got a couple steaks coming up to room temp. Want one?"

"Do I want a steak?"

His expression said *keep up, Bowden,* saying nothing of the fact that he'd just asked me to eat with him like that was normal and not a one-eighty from his previous attitude toward me.

"That's what I said."

"I do want a steak," I replied, my tension from the date and my mother deflating. "I'm starved, actually. I'll just run home and be back in a few."

"Ready in twenty." He turned and went into his house.

And I stood there, dumbfounded, wondering what had gotten into the asshole next door.

——

MY REFLECTION STARED BACK at me, telling me it didn't matter what I wore because this wasn't a date.

Obviously.

In fact, if it were a date, I wouldn't go. I clearly couldn't handle dating.

I changed into the pair of cream-colored linen shorts Evie had left on my dresser with a note that said *'tis the season.* They were a little too short, but they felt nice in the heat and paired well with my plain sky-blue tee. I looked over the mascara and lip gloss she'd left next to the shorts and told myself, again, this wasn't a date. Aiden Anders wasn't interested in me. And I was certainly not interested in sleeping with him. Or him. I wasn't interested in him. "I'm not," I said aloud to my reflection.

But I could see the tiny tug at the corner of my lip. "You're so full of shit," my reflection seemed to be saying back.

I stepped out of the house with one swipe of lip gloss I'd thrown on so quickly I could pretend I hadn't and walked the few paces to Aiden's with my face toward the ground, mind preparing, anxiety rising.

It's not a damn date. It's just extra food. Calm yourself.

I walked behind the cottage where the smells of the grill were coming from and waited on the bench of the teak picnic table. I occupied myself with my phone, scrolling the local news feed because I'd learned long ago that social media wasn't for me.

Aiden walked out with two beers in hand, pretending he hadn't just checked out my bare legs. "So, what happened?"

"Thanks," I said, taking one of the beers from him before he walked to the grill and opened it, heat pouring off. I stared at his back, his thin T-shirt clinging to his shoulders, wondering if I'd ever been so enthralled just watching another human.

"So?"

"Huh?" Man, I was smooth.

"What happened on the date?" He flipped two steaks and tossed a basket of vegetables, his eyes on the food.

"Nothing, really."

"Was he an asshole?" he asked, closing the grill and turning to me, his jaw tight.

I was mesmerized by the ticking of the muscle. He should probably wear a night guard with all that jaw clenching he was fond of doing.

"You're asking me if *he* was an asshole?"

"I am," he said, not catching or just ignoring my implication.

"No. He was just . . . not for me."

He nodded and silence stretched.

"The truth is . . . I think I sabotaged it before it even began."

"Probably for the best." He took a pull from his bottle, and I did the same.

"I mean, he *was* kind of an ass."

He was quiet, waiting for me to continue.

"Not to me, just in general," I muttered, eager to change the subject from my lack of dating ability. "How long have you lived here and run this place?"

He crossed his arms at his chest and looked at the cottages. "My father owned the place. He left it to me."

"Not you and Evie?"

"Evie has a different father."

"Oh." She hadn't mentioned that. "Did you want to be a cottage manager? I mean, before your father gifted it to you?"

"No. But I came here in the summers as a kid, worked the place. I liked it. Guess it's in the blood."

"You're a local, then?"

"Not really. I hadn't been back since high school before the old man died over a year ago."

"I'm sorry for your loss." The words came out stiffly. It was what people said.

He watched me, intently. I sensed a blush rising under his observation. Most people would pull back, embarrassed once they realized they were staring at someone. I wasn't sure if Aiden Anders was capable of the emotion, and it made him all the more interesting for it; because he just continued his examination, as through working out a puzzle of some kind.

"What about you, Birdie?"

There was a tiny, and pathetic, thrill that went through me when he said my first name for the first time.

"What *about* me?"

"What's your story? How did you end up here in Grove, sleeping in the cottage next to mine?"

It sounded suggestive. Or maybe I simply wanted it to be. "I'm taking a break from real life."

"And what did real life consist of?" he asked as he stalked closer to me, his eyes unwavering. Did he not understand that staring like this was seriously unnerving? Stopping in front of me, he picked up the plates in front of me and turned back to the grill.

I exhaled the breath I was unconsciously holding and looked down. "Nothing interesting."

"Try me."

What had I told Evie? I needed to be consistent.

"Let's just say life is more interesting here than it was there. My job at the city is pretty solitary. I needed a break."

"No husband looking for you? Boyfriend?"

"Ha. Uh, no."

He threw a steak on my plate and plopped it in front of me. "Good. Let this rest a minute."

He set his own steak across from me and began dishing out grilled vegetables, first on my plate, then his. Next he disappeared into the house and returned with two waters and a few napkins.

I watched Aiden while he chewed his steak, his mouth working the meat. Questions filtered through my head as we sat without conversation. *Where did you learn to cook? Why did you ask me to eat with you? Are you sleeping with anyone? Would you be interested in sex with me?* But Aiden seemed to be enjoying his meal, having forgotten that I was sitting across from him. So I ate my dinner, sneaking looks at him whenever he wasn't watching me.

"Do you like kids?" I said and quickly cringed.

His eyes found mine across the table. Oh. Hello there. "What?"

"Kids. Do you like them?" Okay, so I'd googled conversation starters before I'd left the house for my date and this had stood out as about the worst question to ask, so naturally it was the only one I could remember in the moment of extended silence.

His eyes went back to his plate. He stabbed a morsel and brought it to his mouth, chewing before he answered. "Maybe. I teach a shop class at the local high school once a week."

"Really?"

His brows crinkled in confusion. "Is that hard to believe?"

I finally pulled my gaze away. "No, it's just, you don't strike me as a teacher."

"Well, it's shop, so." He gave a little eye roll, and I couldn't help but smile. "You like kids?"

"I don't not like them."

He chortled. "That's the answer people who don't want kids give."

"Maybe."

"So you don't want kids?"

"Is there something wrong with that?" I asked, unable to hide my need to sabotage even a non-date conversation.

He pressed his lips together, then said, "Nope. Just making conversation. One that you"—he said, pointing his fork at me—"started."

"Right." I wiped my sweaty hands on my shorts. "I don't like to do things just because I can."

"And why is that?"

"It's limiting, staying in one's lane, don't you think?" But wasn't that exactly what I did, the way I lived my life—staying in my lane?

He rolled his shoulders back and stretched his arms behind him, having finished his dinner. "It could be. Having kids seems a bigger consideration than that, I guess."

"Not for me. Just because I'm a woman, I should want kids? Just because I can crush a pen—" I paused, realizing what I almost said.

"Crush a what?"

"Nothing—I just know myself."

He watched me, unbothered by the eye contact that, to me, felt increasingly intimate.

"Why are you suddenly being nice to me? A day ago, you didn't want me here."

"Who said I've changed my mind?"

"Oh." I considered getting up and walking away. I didn't want to be anyplace I wasn't welcome. But the food was really quite good, and I wanted to finish it. And my brain seemed to be experiencing some sort of whiplash on repeat, needing to sabotage one moment and wanting to stay under his gaze the next.

"Evie," he said with affection. "She likes you."

"Okay," I replied, unsure of what that had to do with anything.

"She doesn't have a lot of friends. She can be a lot to some people. Too often, they don't give her a chance. But she's my sister, and she's a pretty amazing person. She has a way with strays," he said with a small smile, like it was more of a joke than an insult.

"You're very blunt."

He placed his napkin on the table. "So I've been told."

More silence passed, and I felt the awkwardness return. Of course Evie had asked him to be nice to me. This was his way of telling me I was allowed to be her friend but not to expect him to follow suit. Was he waiting for me to finish so I'd go home and he could get on with his night?

"Your parents name you Birdie?"

Okay, we were still talking. "Bernadette, actually, but my father called me his little bird when I was young. Eventually that became Birdie."

"Where is he?"

"He died when I was fifteen."

He nodded silently.

"You finish what you were making in your man cave the other day?"

"Man cave?"

"Your woodshop."

He smiled and leaned in. "Plenty of women do woodworking, Bernadette. Don't be so sexist."

I laughed lightly. "Touché."

It was the first time in a long time I'd heard anyone use my full name. I liked the way it sounded, the way his mouth caressed the syllables.

"I'll just wait until you go to sleep, then go sit in that perfect chair you made and pretend it's mine. It was very impressive—I wish I had a talent like that."

"I also teach adults basic woodworking skills," he offered. "Just finished a spring class at the community college. Another one in the fall."

"Are you inviting me to join your class, Aiden?"

"You do seem to have an affinity for my wood."

I stared. A million quips came to mind, but I was too shocked at what I thought was a joke to reply.

He smiled, unable to hold it back.

"Ha-ha," I said, but I couldn't help the smile that took over my face at the sight of his, broad and beautiful and something I could get lost in.

"Occupational hazard."

"I bet. I would love to watch you make something, make sure you're not just buying things and pawning them off as your own."

He leaned in, elbows on the table, and said, "How about I make you a tiny birdhouse? I'll make a little lock for the door and a little key for me to hold on to. I can put you inside when you grate on my nerves. Let you out only when it suits me."

I felt a rush somewhere totally unexpected, and my head seemed to spin a little. Was that . . . sexual? Surely not, but . . . I leaned in, because this—giving it right back—I could do. *This* was familiar territory.

"I'm guessing you make a lot of birdhouses. Oh, and those little forest creatures that everyone has in their lawns here. They really are quite lovely, Aiden. I do hope you sell them online. That way I can order a few squirrels and bunnies for my patio in Chicago."

He shook his head slowly, looking half-stern, half-amused. "You heard about that, huh?"

"I heard you have a real passion for carving cute furry creatures."

He laughed. "It is amazing how many folks like their woodland creatures carved out of chunks of wood. People make good money doing it."

"People being you? Exactly how many chipmunks have you carved?"

"None," he stated, running a hand through his hair. "Shut up and finish your steak."

I took a bite, feeling his eyes on me as I chewed, oddly exhilarated by the conversation. I wasn't sure if it was entirely friendly or not, but I'd take it, because talking to him made me feel more invigorated than I could remember feeling in a very long time.

"This is amazing, by the way. Can't remember the last time I had steak this good."

"You've been a city girl for too long."

"Maybe," I said with a smile and swallowed my last bite. "You teach anything else at the college?"

"Sex ed."

"No." My mouth fell open. "Really?"

He stood and grabbed my now-empty plate. "You're too easy."

I narrowed my eyes at him while he gathered the rest of the dishes and made his way into his cottage.

"Later, Bernadette."

I couldn't let it end this way, my non-date with Aiden Anders.

"Aiden?" I called as he opened the door. He looked back, waiting for me to say something.

I hesitated, wanting him to know I was choosing my words carefully. "I just wanted . . . I'd just really like a bunny rabbit. Maybe a Cashmere Lop?"

He let a quiet chuckle slip. "Go home, city girl. Dinner's over."

11

MY MOTHER FIRST GAVE ME a Jane Austen book when I was thirteen, and I promptly got hooked, devouring romance on the regular. Whether it was a jealous duke, a ruined reputation, enemies to lovers, a dangerous mobster, or a threatening ex, the man always shows up to protect, to save the day. And even when the heroine saves herself, he still shows up to protect. It's how he loves her. But what if, like me, you don't need anyone to protect you, since there is almost nothing that can threaten you? What if *you* are better suited to protect *him*?

I'll tell you what happens. He doesn't want you anymore because you're emasculating. I should know—I've lived it.

I lay in bed after my non-date with Aiden, fearing the little bonfire burning inside me. It was laughable, really, me with a crush. How long had it been? I thought that part of me had been sufficiently suffocated. It was his looks, sure, but mostly how he carried himself. It was his lack of self-doubt, his utter confidence in who he was, irrespective of what others thought of him.

I had no idea how he felt toward me anymore. Maybe attraction. Maybe absolutely nothing.

I let myself wonder if he could be more, if his seriously inflated ego was just the ticket to handle my strength. But I reminded myself he'd been nice for the sake of his sister. He was a man who, if he even wanted a relationship, could have his pick of women. He'd never pick someone like me, not once he knew the truth.

I needed to put this fire out. I would not read into something that wasn't there, as much as a part of me ached for it. My future was set. I needed to get happy in that. That's why I was here, seeing Doctor Evans. I wasn't here to change anything, not in the long run. I wasn't here to regress into a relationship that was bound for failure. I'd just end up back where I started.

So when I woke at dawn the next morning, staring at the ceiling, unable to stop thinking about his perfect, smug face, I reminded myself it wasn't real. I felt like that girl in grade school the boys only pretended to like as a joke. *Ugh.* I was too old for this shit. Thirty-one and pining. It was pathetic.

I stood, giving up on sleep, and shuffled in my fuzzy slippers to the kitchen. I started the coffee and stared at it for a while as it brewed, then walked to the window, taking in the pink and blue hues peeking over the horizon of the lake. The job usually kept me up late at night, so I wasn't one to see much of sunrises. I stepped onto the porch and took in the view. It's always the simple things that make me realize how out of touch I'd been with the natural world.

As I stood watching, a figure came into view. Squinting against the glare, I recognized Aiden, strolling along the beach, picking up trash. He wore shorts and nothing else. And if I was impressed by the sunrise, it had nothing on this man.

He made his way to the parking lot down by the beach, where a large dumpster sat next to a recycling bin, and began sorting. He was too far away for me to enjoy the movement of his muscles the way I wanted, so I tore my gaze back to the sunrise, telling myself to snap out of it.

I stepped inside and filled my coffee mug, then came back out and settled into the porch chair, gazing in the direction of the sunrise, enjoying the cool air before the heat settled in.

"Got any for me?"

I jumped with a gasp, spilling scalding coffee everywhere.

"Fuck," I uttered, brushing the liquid away from my bare legs.

"Oh shit." Aiden leaped over the side railing with zero effort before realizing there wasn't anything for him to do.

"It's fine," I said.

"I'm fucking sorry about that. I didn't mean to scare you. I thought you saw me on the beach. Is it burning?"

I finally looked at him and saw the hard set of his lips, the look of regret on his face. He was actually concerned. I mentally swooned a little.

"It wasn't that hot. It's fine."

"You sure?" His gaze snagged on my bare legs—my sleep shorts left little to the imagination. "Can I get you anything? Towel? Ice cubes?"

Feeling a little empowered as he continued to stare at my legs, I said, "You can get me a new cup of coffee."

A grin emerged, and he held out his hand. "Hand it over," he said, and I did, careful not to touch his hand for fear of losing my sanity. He disappeared inside Evie's cottage.

I leaned back and took stock of myself, my long hair in a messy ponytail, my face unwashed from the morning sleep. I hadn't brushed my teeth yet.

The door opened, and he stepped out with two mugs, handing me one, his eyes staying above the neckline this time. "What was left in your cup looked pretty black, so I assume that's how you take it?" He took a seat on Evie's lounger. "Sorry again."

He was staying. I tried and failed to keep my heart from fluttering. "Thanks. And stop apologizing."

"Enjoy it. They are words you'll likely never hear from me again."

I placed my hand over my heart. "Is this special treatment from Aiden Anders? What did I do to deserve this dispensation?"

He rolled his eyes, and his lips tilted in amusement as he wrapped his hands around his mug and looked out at the lake.

We didn't say anything for a while. He'd put on a shirt, thank goodness, but his tan legs were on view, golden hair covering hard muscles. I allowed myself a brief examination before returning my gaze to the lake.

"How often do you do that? Pick up trash, I mean?"

He grunted. "Most days."

"Yeah?"

"Believe me, I wish I didn't have to. People are fucking savages."

"Is it that bad?"

"Not always. Today it was."

The waves were large this morning after last night's rain. They drove high onto the clean sand, pulling it back into the depths without the extra trash that Aiden had cleared.

"Maybe you're not *always* an asshole."

He looked at me, considering my words. "I wouldn't count on it."

I hid my smile behind my mug. "Evie was telling me you're from Texas."

"I am."

"You moved here just for the cottages?" It wasn't really a question, and he didn't respond. "Were you close with your dad?"

"No. This is the only place he and I ever saw each other."

"Will you stay then and keep the cottages? Run the place?"

He looked thoughtful, like it was a question he'd struggled with. "I've been modernizing the cottages, but my plan has always been to sell them and move back to Texas."

"Hmmm." I sipped my coffee. "But you have a woodshop set up and you teach at least two classes and pick up trash daily?"

He didn't respond, but I could see his mind working it over.

"Isn't it time for you to get to work?" he asked, raising an eyebrow.

I cleared my throat. "Checkout isn't until eleven, sir."

His eyes flashed, and he cleared his throat. "You're doing a decent job, you and Evie. Not a complaint in sight."

"Did anyone help Evie before I got here? Did you?"

"God no."

"Why?"

He crinkled his brow, like the answer was obvious. "It's woman's work."

My mouth dropped open, and he tried to keep a straight face, but the smirk emerged anyway, slowly turning into a low laugh.

"You're a real shit, Aiden Anders, you know that?"

"So you've said. Before Evie came, I did it alone, then we worked together for months. But since you arrived, I've been off the hook. It was the part of the deal we struck to let you stay."

"Seriously? You pretend my presence is such a burden, but really it frees up your time at no additional cost to you."

He shrugged, not denying it. "It got me back to the woodshop."

"I can't believe you. Maybe Evie and I will take a break, and you can clean the cottages today," I offered.

"Hard pass. I've got orders to fill."

"Fine, but only because I wouldn't want to deprive the world of your creations—your *talent*."

His grin grew wider. "See, now *that* was nice. Well done."

I rolled my eyes.

"Truth is, Evie could do whatever she wants. She's good at everything, the little perfectionist. She had a good corporate PR job before she got sick, but right now, she wants to be here, doing this." He sat forward, turning his body to face mine. "I won't let her do it forever. Question is, why are you here?"

His eyes were close, and his intent gaze had me squirming.

"I told you, I was forced to use my stored vacation."

"Okay, but why here? Why live with my sister? I assume you're still getting a paycheck, so why work here doing this?" His tone turned direct, and I shrugged, feeling like he could see right through me. "What are you hiding from?"

"I didn't have anything else to do," I confessed. "She offered. And she's fun and seems to not hate me. I don't have a lot of people in my life since I work all the time."

The truth of the words sunk in. How pathetic, a woman in her early thirties with no friends, no family, mooching off a complete stranger. "I thought you were on board—"

"It's fine," he interrupted. "I'm not trying to get rid of you. Not yet anyway." He winked.

I grinned, uncrossing my legs and sitting up, needing to move. "I'll do my best to stay on your good side. For now anyway."

He chuckled softly. "Maybe I *was* a bit hard on you when you arrived. It wasn't you."

"No? You're that way with every new visitor?"

He leaned back in the chair, his gaze back on the lake. "I just . . . I have a general aversion to beautiful women."

I choked on my coffee and sputtered, leaning forward in a coughing fit, my face turning cherry red. Then Aiden was there, patting my back. "You okay?"

"Mm-hm," I squeezed through coughs. When I finally got my breath, I wasn't sure what to say. *Did he just call me beautiful?* "Coffee went down the wrong tube."

"I gathered," he said with humor, and I felt my skin continue to flame with embarrassment.

I cleared my throat. "Why do you have an aversion to women? Broken heart?"

"Nah, it's more an aversion to people in general, I guess. Though my mother would say I was born with a broken heart."

I finished my coffee but didn't dare move, happy to sit next to him where I could sneak looks and wonder what was going on in his head, what his mother had meant with those words. "What were you doing before you got here?"

He stood up, and I thought he might leave, but he stopped and put his hand out. "Warm-up?"

I handed him my mug. "Always."

Returning a few moments later, he handed me a fresh cup, and I held it close, blowing on the top before taking a sip. He leaned against the railing in front of me. "I was an environmental engineer."

"Oh? What does an environmental engineer do exactly?"

He grinned and crossed one ankle over the other, giving me his full attention. "A lot of things, but I worked on new recycling technologies."

I nodded and smiled, finally understanding a little bit about Aiden. "Anything I'd know?"

"I built a plant that extracts vanadium and other rare minerals from oil production waste, then neutralizes the waste for safe disposal."

"Oh, sure. You mean the stuff they make in Wakanda. Captain America's shield."

He smiled. "That's vibranium. This is vanadium. The key difference being one is a real substance and one is not. And I don't make it; I extract it. But you're not far off, because it's used to make steel lighter and stronger."

"And all this time I thought you were just a dumb, tyrant asshole."

He shook his head with another grin. "Two out of three ain't bad."

More butterflies erupted in my stomach. "That's what you'll go back to?"

The humor faded from his face. "I should have been back weeks ago. I finished up the bulk of renovations a while back, enough to sell the cottages anyway. I told myself I'd go back when I was done. They were supposed to be sold by now."

"I can't believe you haven't had offers. This place is a dream."

"Haven't listed it yet."

I smiled. He loved the place, couldn't let it go.

"You do seem to be settling in here with your woodshop, your tourists, and the teaching. Did you quit your job?"

"I took a longer leave, for now."

"They must really like you."

"I'm co-owner." He stood straight and stepped out onto the sand before looking back at me. "I don't know what I'll do."

"Well, what is the deciding factor?"

"I didn't know at first."

My heart sped up, though I couldn't pinpoint exactly why. "And now?"

He grinned. "Now things are getting interesting."

I swallowed, silenced by his words and his intent stare as he said them.

His smile got bigger. "Have a good day, Bernadette. Thanks for the coffee." He set his mug on the railing and left me gaping on the front porch.

12

EVIE AND I CLEANED THREE cottages that morning. Very often, we turned on music and sang at the top of our lungs, or we just talked. I may have talked more in the last two weeks than I had in the last decade, even though Evie still did most of the talking.

"I don't know," she said as she sprayed the fridge, her face hidden inside while she wiped it out. "It's like I know he loves me, and I love him. But I just can't bring myself to go back to what we were before. I don't want anyone else, and I don't want to lose him, but something still isn't right."

"Obviously—you want to spend the summer with me."

Her head popped out. "True."

"I don't know, Evie. Once trust is lost, it's hard to rebuild. That may be the only thing making you feel like something isn't right. Give it some more time, maybe." I picked up the remaining cups and plates in the living room and went into the kitchen. The cottage renters had seemingly used every dish and left them scattered around the place. I held a chipped mug in my hand, observing the freshly exposed ceramic. "I hope you don't give these people the damage deposit back."

"But I do trust him. And I take responsibility for my part in all this. I don't know . . . he's always been in my life. Since high school. I've always fallen back on him. And that's been perfect. He's been perfect. But since I've been on my own, I sort of want to be perfect myself—I'm not sure I could have recovered emotionally if we'd stayed together. He was too easy to rely on, too there." She shook her head. "It's crazy to say that, isn't it?"

She closed the fridge and opened the freezer above it. "My God, what is this ooze?"

I peeked inside from behind her. "Looks like Jell-O. Jell-O shots, I'd guess."

"Ugh. It's so not okay for adults to purposefully make Jell-O shots for any event."

"You needed to pick yourself up," I said, returning to the living room to gather pillows and blankets from the floor. *Jesus, how many people slept here last night?* "But as long as he was there, you didn't have to do it yourself."

She pulled her head out of the freezer. "Oh my God, yes! How did you do that? Evans must be rubbing off on you. But this doesn't help me understand why I can't take the plunge. I mean, I'm better. He's pined for me long enough. What's stopping me? He's fucking amazing, and he won't wait around forever."

I stuffed the blankets into the laundry bin, then turned to face her. "Maybe it's not about him or your ability to trust. Maybe you aren't fully standing yet. Maybe there's more to do."

She paused her work, looking thoughtfully confused. "So if I take him back too soon, I'll fall back into old patterns—get too comfortable—and I won't push myself?"

We stared at each other.

"He probably thinks he's doing the right thing by supporting you even in your own complacency. Tell him you need a push."

"Fucking hell." She leaned back and heaved a sigh. "We are blowing my mind right now."

I smiled and made an explosion sound as my hands mimed my head exploding.

"I'm going to tell him. Do you think he'll hate me?"

"No, he could never. He's stupid over you. He'll be happy to know it's not about him exactly. He'll know how he can adjust. He'll be relieved."

"I hope so. OMG. You are a genius, Birdie."

I laughed as I threw pillowcases in the rolling laundry bin and stacked the naked pillows on top. They smelled funky and would need to be washed too. Evie closed the freezer, her hands reaching above it and feeling around. "I could have sworn we left extra sponges up here last time."

In the next instant I was standing next to Evie, my hand above her head, catching a falling kitchen knife before it could connect with her scalp.

She took a step backward and looked up, seeing my hand. "Did that almost—"

I nodded.

"Did you just . . . ?"

"Yes. Please don't hate me."

"You were just—" She turned and pointed to the living room. "And then you were—" she said, pointing to where I stood.

This wasn't something I was used to, telling people about me, having a friend find out. I didn't want her to find out this way. I'd been lying to her, hiding myself, something I'd told myself I'd never do.

"That's why you're here, why you were familiar. I saw the video of you at the . . ." She fell quiet, except she kept saying "huh" as she pieced it all together in her mind.

I placed the knife in the sink and stepped back, bracing for what came next. Was she was going to kick me out?

"You didn't say anything."

I frowned. "Are you very mad?"

She thought a moment before she threw her rag at me. "Damn right I'm mad. We could have finished cleaning this place hours ago!"

—

"YOU CAN'T USE YOUR ABILITIES. Like at all?"

"Not supposed to," I said as we sat on the couch, Evie absorbing the information I'd inadvertently shared. She was handling it well, without an ounce of fear.

"I was wondering how you got to Chicago and back so fast with your stuff."

"You were supposed to be sleeping."

"Well, I was vomiting, so I'd lost track of time just the same."

"If you're not mad and you're not going to kick me out, maybe we could keep this between us?"

She wasn't listening, deep in thought. "Oh my God, all that social media. The horrible things they said about you. That's so shitty," she said and winced.

"It's fine."

"It's really not, though. All those things. They call you 'Superbitch'! Now that I know you, I can't even imagine."

"It's just part of the job, Evie."

"It shouldn't be."

I pulled out my best Thompson impression. "With great power comes great responsibility."

She gave me a death glare. "To help when called upon, when you are able, not to silently put up with bullshit. Not to be harassed!"

Her agitation at my predicament made me smile. "Don't worry about it. It's nothing I can't handle. Besides, this summer is for me to push all that aside."

Her gaze said this conversation wasn't over, but she seemed to leave that part of it for now. "I have so many questions."

I took a deep breath, having anticipated this. "Okay, shoot."

"Did you go to one of those government places after you developed abilities?"

I nodded.

Her face twisted. "Was it terrible?"

"Sometimes," I said, thinking back. "The worst part was before, actually. When I came home after my first semester in college and told my mother and my ex-fiancé about what was happening to me, they totally freaked."

"Wait, ex-fiancé?"

"That's another story for another day," I said, and she nodded. "Anyway, my mother and Nick acted like it was some kind of curse, which made me more afraid than I already was. At first, they told me to just ignore it, and it would go away." I laughed uncomfortably.

Evie didn't laugh. "I'm so sorry that happened to you."

"I didn't go back to school after that, because I was afraid of being found out. I hid in my room, going outside just at night to run. My relationship with my mother grew even more strained than it already was. She barely spoke to me, only asking about wedding plans, which were 100 percent on hold. Or asking if I was better yet."

"How about your fiancé? Nick?"

I nodded. "He never even mentioned the wedding after I told him about the abilities. He'd just come visit from school every few weeks, and we'd watch a movie or something, and then he'd ask if I was better yet. Both of them were just waiting for it to be over, and there seemed like no point in moving forward until it was. I didn't talk to my friends, and they simply forgot about me."

"Birdie, that must have been horrible. All this stuff happening to you without any explanation or support. So, how did you end up in the facility?"

"The only thing I ever asked of my mother was that she wouldn't send me away. She'd promised because she didn't want anyone else to know about me any more than I did. But eventually, she got sick of dealing with me and made the call."

"You needed help," Evie said, sounding as through she sympathized with my mother.

"That's not the way I saw it," I said, my resentment showing.

Evie, clearly sensing I'd talked enough about the past, sat up straight and looked at me gravely. "Next question: Super speed doesn't translate to peeing? You pee like the rest of us?"

"What?" I laughed.

"Can you pee super fast? I just think about how much time we waste sitting on the toilet. If you are speeding throughout your day, do you have to slow down to pee?"

"Okay, a question no one has asked before. I'm impressed. And no, I guess I do pee like anyone else."

Eyes wide on me, she nodded sagely. "I never thought I'd be privy to such inside info." She let out a cackle and put her hand over her mouth. "Privy," she repeated through her laughter.

"Wow. That was . . ." I laughed with her.

"Hey, Birdie?"

"Yeah?"

"Why do you keep it a secret? It's amazing! You're amazing. If it were me, I'd be shouting from the rooftops—"

"It can make things difficult. It's better to just keep it to myself."

"You mean keep *you* to yourself."

I shrugged; I couldn't disagree. "Please, Evie. I need to keep this for myself. For the summer at least."

She grabbed my hand. "Your secret is safe with me."

"Not even Yash? Or Aiden?" I pressed.

She sucked air through her teeth. "It's going to come out, you know. These things always do."

I was hoping I'd be gone by then, that I'd be able to keep the secret until the summer was over.

"But it won't be from my lips," Evie said. "I promise."

—

NOW THAT EVIE KNEW THE TRUTH, I felt lighter, as though a weight had been lifted. I was afraid she'd change, be mad or embarrassed, or ask me to go. But Evie didn't miss a beat, and something about her reaction gave me hope for the future.

"Birdie?" Evie appeared at my bedroom door later that afternoon somewhat out of breath, like she'd just run a mile.

"What's wrong?" I stood up quickly from lying on my bed, where I'd spent the last hour staring out at the sand, trying not to wonder what my neighbor was doing.

She caught her breath. "There's a perfect specimen of a man outside!"

"What? Who?"

"Well," she heaved, "I'm not 100 percent sure, but he's gorgeous, like Statue-of-David-gorgeous. Also, he's very familiar. He asked for you."

"Jace is here?" I jumped up.

"Wait, Jace. The super from NYC. Your old hook-up?"

Oh yeah, I'd told her about Jace.

"No. No, no, no, no. That man is not a hook-up. *That* is a man you marry and make perfect, gorgeous babies with and screw his brains out every day for the rest of your life."

I wanted to laugh as she followed me out of my room, her jaw dragging behind her.

"Wait . . . he's lacking upstairs, is that it?"

"What? No, Jace is like the smartest guy I know. He's perfect, just like you said. He's just not *my* perfect."

"That man is everyone's perfect. How have you been holding out on me?"

"Evie," I said and grabbed her upper arms. "You've gotta chill. He's a friend only, and I'd actually like to go speak with him, so you have to manage your mania."

"Right." Her head lolled back and forth a little like a boxer between rounds. "I'm good."

I nodded and opened the door to find Jace lounging in one of Aiden's oversized porch chairs. He was at home there, as he seemed to be everywhere.

He stood as I stepped outside. "Bertha," he drawled as he swept me up in a bear hug. "You've been kissed by the sun gods." Setting me down in front of him, he perused me. "Look at you, legs on display, a little color in the cheeks. This strange place suits you."

I instinctually touched my cheek, not realizing I'd gotten so much color. "Thanks, I guess. Jace, what are you doing here? How did you find this place?"

He looked at me with his *I'm a fucking superhero* face.

"Never mind the last question, then. Why are you here?"

"You're not happy to see me?" He covered his chest in mock hurt.

"Of course I am. I just . . . I hadn't expected to see you *here*. Spill." The look of disappointment on his face wasn't familiar.

"What happened?" I sat down, inviting him to do the same.

He sat and let his head fall into his hands. "I met someone. End of story."

"You mean . . . ?"

"Like maybe *the* someone. We went out a few times. He's perfect. Crazy smart, funny, quirky. A total nerd."

"Super?"

"Nope," he said with a smile.

"And?"

"And when I told him I didn't plan to date publicly, he said it was a deal-breaker. He wouldn't hide who he was or who he loved. Not for anyone."

"Good for him," I said, and Jace looked offended. "Shit. I'm so sorry, Jace."

"No, you're right. I mean, I can't blame him."

"You won't consider dating publicly? Don't you think it's time?" Jace was very public with himself, but he feared, as many of us do, that loving someone in public puts them at risk.

"Look who's talking. You understand better than anyone. It's hard to be anything other than a super in this job. And I don't want to endanger anyone. Dating me does exactly that."

"Your city adores you," I said quietly.

"It will still change things. For him, more than anyone."

"Some, but maybe that's okay. Have you talked to him about it?"

"B, I'm not sure I can let this one go. He's fucking brilliant. He kind of makes everything better when I'm with him, you know? It's a trip."

I kind of did know. "Jace, this is great for you," I said and gripped his hand.

"It sucks."

I gave him a sympathetic smile. "That too."

He shook his head. "Enough about me. I want to know how you're doing. So, what's the verdict? Are you on the verge of a nervous breakdown?"

"Thanks for the vote of confidence—you could have just called."

"Look," he said, smiling and squeezing my hand. "This is a big deal for you, getting out of town, taking a break. I wanted to make sure you were doing okay in person."

"And hide from your own situation."

"Yes, and maybe that," he admitted with a roll of his green eyes.

"Things are fine. I'm enjoying my time here, actually."

A throat cleared, and Evie emerged from the front door. Let the gushing begin.

"Evie, Jace. Jace, this is Evie."

Evie confidently put her hand out to shake, and said, "Hi. I'm Birdie's best friend."

"Really?" Jace glanced at me, then back to Evie. "I kinda thought I was her best friend."

Without missing a beat, she said, "Well, she's allowed to have more than one, as long as we are different genders, of course."

"Could she have a third best friend?" Jace asked.

Evie shrugged. "Maybe, but only if we both approve of said third person. But who has three best friends, really? There's always only one or two," she said, pointing between her and Jace, "who are really the favorites."

"I know a person who could be up for the job of third. Could I bring 'em by for an interview?" Jace replied with a straight face, making it hard to tell if he was actually serious.

"Don't you think we have more pressing issues to deal with right now? I mean, as best friends, we are both failing."

He stood, appearing affronted. "Tell me what I'm slacking on."

"Duh—the love life that is nonexistent, of course."

I could tell Evie was charming his socks off because the largest grin appeared on his face.

"I like you, Miss Evie. I think we are going to be good friends."

Evie beamed. "Awesome," she said, but then her face fell. "However, our allegiance is to the primary bestie. Our friendship will be secondary, of course."

"Of course," he agreed. "Sorry, I must have forgotten the rules." He looked her up and down.

"Don't worry about it. But you should know that I myself am involved."

Jace's face was alight.

"He's my ex, but we're still together. I mean, it's a long story that Birdie can tell you if she wants, because it's not a secret, but we're going to work things out as soon as I figure out the rest of my life. So that means we can't have a thing."

"A thing?"

"A fling. An affair."

His eyes came to mine, asking me if she was for real. I just shrugged.

"Sleep together. Sex," she clarified. "I was just sensing an attraction and wanted to put clarity to the situation. I mean, I'm aware you're not really into women, or at least that's what I hear, but I wanted to be clear just the same, up front, from my perspective, I mean, just in case. Besides, as best friends of Birdie, we could never have that kind of relationship."

He looked to me for help, and I tipped my head like it all made sense to me. He nodded, absorbing.

"Now, would you like a sweet tea, Jace?" Evie said.

He smiled and nodded. "I'd love one, Evie," he said, and she blushed a bit before disappearing inside. "She's a hoot."

"She talks a lot when she's nervous."

"This is going to be a fun visit. How do I get me one of these cottages for the night?"

"No rooms left." We both turned as Aiden appeared from behind the cabin, his jeans lower than usual under the weight of a tool belt. Yes, a freaking tool belt. *Come on*, I wanted to scream, *I'm trying to be better at not ogling you!* "All booked up."

"Aiden runs the place," I said, standing when Jace looked to me for an introduction. "Aiden, this is Jace."

Aiden's jaw ticked. "There's probably a room at the hotel in town. Or the hostel."

"Oh, no problem, man. I'm sure I can crash on my girl's couch. I can pretty much sleep anywhere." His arm came to rest around my shoulder.

Aiden grunted before his gaze came to me for the first time since he'd arrived. "I can come by tomorrow and fix that drawer for you."

"What's that?"

"Evie said your dresser drawer wouldn't close," he clarified with a hint of barely hidden hostility.

"You don't have to—"

"I'll be by at eleven. You should probably be gone," he stared at where Jace's hand hung over my shoulder.

"Yeah, okay." My stomach sank. "I'll stay out of your hair."

He stalled like he'd just realized he'd been rude, but then remembered he didn't care. He walked up to his own porch and disappeared behind the door without another glance back.

"What was that?" Jace said when Aiden was out of earshot.

"What?" I came out from under his arm.

"That man wanted to tear out my jugular."

"He's just brusque. He's like that with everyone."

"Beatrix, I know the face of a possessive man. I've seen it many times before."

"Why is it possessive for men and jealous for women? Why can't women be possessive?"

"They can," he said, not taking my bait to change the subject. "That man was both. I'm going to need to know what's going on there."

"You're delusional. Aiden can barely tolerate me."

"It's a fine line, sweetheart. Does he know about the job?"

"God no. Only Evie knows. I want to keep it that way."

"Maybe tell him. He might surprise you."

"Okay, Mr. Relationship Expert. Why are you here and not wooing 'the one'?"

He looked sheepish. "Sometimes the game plan needs to be altered. I'm reassessing."

"Uh-huh. In the meantime, you're going to mansplain *my* life?"

"It's not mansplaining if you're too dense to see it yourself. Mansplaining requires some self-awareness on your part."

"That's sexist."

He chuckled. "You can deflect all you want, but we'll talk about this eventually. Because that man is clearly threatened by my presence and wanted to rip my arm off." He sat down. "Or . . . he's into me."

I laughed out loud as I sat. "Clearly."

As we joked, I couldn't help but replay Aiden's every move, searching for signs of anything expressing interest in me. And it wasn't difficult to replay, because I seemed to memorize every move the man made.

"I'm glad you're here, Jace."

"Me too, Bernie."

"Please don't call me that."

He stretched his long arms wide, taking in the view of the lake. "I can see why you wanted to stay here. It's nice." His brows creased as in deep thought before a playful grin emerged. "Now, let's see what this little town has to offer, shall we?"

"You sure you can go out without getting recognized? That baseball cap doesn't hide much."

Then Evie was at the door again, saying, "I know the perfect place."

13

WE RETURNED TO THE BAR with the oddly sexualized dancing bear, the one I still hadn't bothered to learn the name of.

"Is this the town's hot spot?" Jace inquired sarcastically, looking around at the smattering of older locals, all a few drinks in.

Evie huffed and said, "I like this place, okay? The other places are too clubby. Too much skin and rubbing against one another."

"That's the best part," Jace quipped.

"It's fine, Evie," I said, interrupting her death glare aimed at Jace.

"It's fine," he relented.

She smiled and guided us though the dark bar to the same booth we'd occupied the day we'd met. Jace slid in next to me.

"What's good here?"

"Everything," Evie offered before getting closer and lowering her voice. "I heard the bartender used to work at some swanky Chicago bar with thirty-dollar cocktails. She moved here to be close to her sick mom." Her face was inappropriately gleeful. "Anyway, she'll make any cocktail you want"—her gaze landed on Jace—"if you ask nicely." Jace feigned offense. "They taste like thirty-dollar cocktails for ten bucks."

Jace's face morphed into one of approval as the server placed our waters down. "I might have protested prematurely," he said.

"Hey, Evie," the man I'd recognized as our axepert said. "You throwing today?"

"Throwing?" Jace asked at the same time Evie said, "No thanks, Cole."

"Axe throwing," Cole said, pointing to the back room. "This one's a natural." He gestured in my direction. "Should join a league."

"Maybe another time, Cole," Evie answered. "I have a feeling I'd be outmatched by my companions here."

"Okay, what can I get you guys?"

"Can you make a French 75?" Evie asked. "I read about them in a book—it sounded delicious."

"I think we can handle that. How about you two?"

"Pilsner," we responded in unison.

"And fried pickles," Jace added.

Cole winked at Evie before taking off.

"How often do you come here?" I asked Evie. "You're on a first-name basis."

"Just the once. Guess I'm memorable."

"That you are," Jace said, lifting his water glass.

"Don't go falling in love with me, Jace superhero. I'm not available, and you'll just end up heartbroken."

He laughed. "I'll try to contain myself."

"Good. Please do."

———

"ARE YOU INTERESTED IN JACE?" I asked Evie, when the man in question got up to use the restroom.

"What? No!"

"You're flirting." I placed a fried pickle in my mouth, washing it down with a pull of beer.

"So? Birdie, I got married after high school, had breast cancer, got divorced. My only real relationship since then has been with my shrink." I waited for more as she took a sip of her cocktail, clearly happy with her selection. "I'm just flirting. It's fun. Totally innocent. I mean, he's beautiful, but it's just fun. Besides, I'm in love with Yash. I'm feeling more confident lately. No harm in a little flirting."

Did people flirt if they weren't interested in each other, without any possibility of intimacy? Jeez, I was so ignorant of this stuff. Was that what Aiden and I did the other day? While a feeling of sadness came over me, so did relief at knowing I no longer had to agonize over it. He wasn't interested. Joking with each other was just a bit of fun.

"You should try it," Evie said.

"Flirting?"

"Yeah." She sipped her French 75. "You're hot and single. This dating assignment isn't working because you're too serious about it. You need to just relax and play. Without expectations. I've only ever had sex with two guys, and even I know how to flirt."

"Wait, two? I thought—"

"I was young and wild," she said with a wink as Jace slid back into the booth. "Jace," she said with mirth, elongating his name.

"Hmm?" he replied, throwing two fried pickles into his mouth.

"Birdie here is worried that I'm leading you on by flirting with you when my heart belongs to someone else."

"Really?" He looked at me. "Barbie, you worried about me?"

"No," I assured him.

Evie huffed. "Please reassure her your heart is not at risk."

He sat back, his eyes bouncing between us with humor. "I'm a little broken up, but I'll be happy knowing you're happy."

"See, Birdie," Evie said, gesturing to Jace, "innocent flirting."

"So where is this guy who's . . . ," he started but gave up when Evie pulled out her phone and smiled, her attention instantly stolen by the only person capable of doing so.

"You guys mind if I invite Yash to join us?" She didn't even look up as she typed out the invite and slid the phone back in her pocket before we could reply. "He's just next door at the vet clinic. He's going to love you, Jace."

"I doubt it."

"Why do you say that?"

He shrugged. "Boyfriends hate me."

She considered this. "Yep. That tracks."

"Don't ditch me when you get a boyfriend," Jace whispered to me with fake sadness.

Aiden's face popped in my brain. "I don't think there's any risk there," I replied, "but I promise."

Evie jumped up with a grin the size of Texas and shouted, "He's here!" and took off to the door.

"Is she always like this?" Jace said.

"Yes," I answered him.

"Good," he smiled. "So, which one of us is going to be your maid of honor?"

I laughed. "I'd say you, Jace, but it probably shouldn't be someone I've slept with."

"Good point."

Evie returned then, eager to introduce the two men. Jace stood to shake Yash's hand.

"Hey, man," he said as he took Yash's hand, "heard a lot about you. You're a lucky guy."

Yash beamed. "Don't I know it. You look familiar. Have we met before?"

"Nah," Jace replied. "I get that a lot. I look like . . ." He trailed off as his eyes went to the man suddenly standing next to Yash. "Aiden, right?"

"This is my brother," Evie offered.

"Yeah, heard a lot about you too," he said. "You've got your work cut out for you," he chuckled. I hit his back from my place in the booth, and he laughed some more.

Aiden's hand found Jace's, but his eyes found me, and my heart thumped wildly in my chest as Jace sat back down next to me and Yash next to Evie. Aiden pulled up a chair at the end of the booth.

"We were talking about Birdie's dating experiment," Evie said.

"No, we weren't," I argued.

Yash said, "Really? Again?"

"Right?" I replied. "Enough is enough."

"I was saying she needs to flirt more," Evie continued.

"It's true," Jace said. "You've never been much of a flirt."

I pinched his side for ganging up on me. "Why is that a bad thing?"

Jace chuckled and turned toward me. "It makes breaking the ice a little easier, that's all. And Elvira over here is right. It's fun."

"Forgive me if flirting doesn't come naturally. Besides, the dating thing is just an exercise. I thought we all understood that."

"Birdie, you can't go into it expecting to fail," Evie said. "That takes the joy out of it. Which I think is the whole point. Aiden, what do you think? Should we force her to practice?"

I could feel his eyes on me but didn't dare meet them with my own.

"No," Aiden answered. "She can flirt just fine when she wants to."

"She can?" Jace leaned in closer and looked at me.

"Sure," Aiden said, and I glanced over to find a smile directed at me.

"I can?" I echoed, feeling the blood rush to my cheeks.

"Flirting is subtle. If it's right, authentic, you don't even realize when you're doing it."

"So how do *you* know she can do it?" Evie asked.

Aiden smiled, a full-blown smile with dimples. I thought back to our interactions. *Had I been flirting with Aiden?*

"I just know," he said and winked at me.

All eyes were again on me, expecting a response. I didn't know how to react. What was happening right now?

Yash thankfully saved me by starting a story about something at the clinic, but I couldn't bring my heart rate down enough to pay attention. I might have been melting into this sticky booth.

After Cole brought a round for the guys and some more food, Aiden gestured between Jace and me with an onion ring. "How do you two know each other?"

"Work," I said. "We met at a work training"—which wasn't *completely* different than a government facility for superpowered humans.

Jace wrapped his arm around my shoulder. "Bonded over the cluster-fuck that it was. Instant friendship."

Aiden was staring at Jace's arm when Evie added, "More like fuck-buddies." She looked immediately apologetic, realizing her loose lips just shared my very personal information. She really had zero filter.

My face morphed into the color of the bright red booths and I snuck a glance at Aiden, whose eyes clung to me. I didn't know what to say. They were all staring at me. Again. Even Jace.

"What?"

"Nothing," they sang in unison and went back to their food, until Yash brought up the town festival that was taking place that weekend and the booth Aiden was going to have, selling his creations.

I kept stealing glances at Aiden, wondering if he cared about my past relationship with Jace. Then I remembered people can flirt because it's fun. It didn't have to mean anything.

I finally looked up at Jace when his foot met my ankle, his eyes asking if I was okay. I nodded and tried to forget about Aiden, about the secret I was keeping and how it would never let me have him, even if he were interested, which he wasn't. He wasn't even engaged in the conversation anymore; instead he was focused on the beer in front of him, deep in his own thoughts. He clearly, definitely, wasn't interested. I needed to figure out a way to crush this crush.

———

JACE AND EVIE CONVINCED US to brave one of the more club-like places down the street, all nude walls and dim lighting. We found a table in the corner, and Jace took the seat facing the wall to avoid drawing attention to himself.

Eventually, Yash and Evie found themselves on the dance floor, and Jace said that watching them made him want to make a call, so he stepped outside.

I was alone with Aiden. We sat quietly for a few minutes, as he stared at me while I avoided his gaze, seemingly enthralled with the basic decor of the club.

"You and Jace a thing?"

I looked at him. "No, we kind of had a thing once, but that's over."

"Is it?"

My mouth went dry. *Why is he asking me this?*

"Yes. Like eight or nine years ago. We were never really anything but friends. Anything more was just . . . I don't know . . . convenient."

"Convenient?"

Can he stop repeating my statements as questions?

"Neither of us was good at dating. We didn't have a lot of opportunity. So, we had an arrangement."

"But you're not in love with him."

"No, I'm—I'm not. I'm not in love with anyone."

"And you're not having sex with him currently?"

"No," I responded, wanting this conversation to be over. "He's seeing someone anyway."

"So, you would be if he wasn't seeing someone?"

"Jeez. No. I love Jace, but I'm not *in love* with him. We're friends, nothing more. Is that clear enough? Why do you care, anyway?"

He sat back in his chair, apparently also interested in the benign decor of the space, and said, "No reason."

"Who was the last person you dated?" I asked him, remembering Evie saying he had a date the first day I'd arrived.

"Are you asking about the last time I had sex, Birdie?"

My cheeks burned again, and I wiggled uncomfortably in my seat. "Sure."

He smiled. "It's been a while. I've had a few dates recently that went about as well as yours seem to be going."

"What's a while?"

"Few months."

"Was she a girlfriend?"

"It wasn't serious."

"Have you ever had a serious relationship?" I asked, knowing that he was once engaged and curious if he'd tell me about it.

"Once," he said and took a drink of his beer as I watched his lips and he watched me watching him. "Anyone ever told you that you wear your thoughts on your face?"

"No. The opposite in fact. Why would you say that?"

"Because it's true."

"It's not. I repress my feelings—Doctor Evans said so."

He laughed lightly. "Those aren't the thoughts I'm talking about, Bowden." He shrugged. "Maybe you only have them around me?"

My eyes widened. "What are . . . you're so full of shit, Anders."

He leaned forward and whispered, "I can tell you're hungry."

I sat there, unsure how to proceed while he examined my increasingly bright red complexion.

"Can I get you a snack?" He pulled back, a smirk on his face. "Pretzels?"

"Okay," I squeaked out as he walked to the bar. I took a fortifying breath. The way he'd been looking at me was discombobulating, and I took the time he was away to calm my nerves.

He was back a few minutes later, with a bowl of mixed nuts and a bag of pretzels, which he placed in front of me.

"How many more dates you got lined up?" he asked casually, sitting down.

"One. For now."

"And who is it this time?"

"A guy from Oak Park. He works in finance, DJs on the side. That's all I know."

He laughed, muttering something that sounded like *typical*.

"He said something about taking me dancing, but—"

"But what?"

"I don't dance. At least not in an extremely long time. Not like this." I gestured to the dance floor, where bodies moved to up-tempo music.

His head moved up and down, and he tried to hide his smile.

"What?"

"How long are you going to keep torturing yourself with these dates?"

"I'm not doing it on purpose. Doctor Evans is making me. I need to break out of my shell."

"Do you?"

I didn't know how to respond to that. Wasn't the whole point of this to get me to move into another stage of life and find a way to be happier with who I was?

"I'm just doing what I have to do."

"No, you're doing what other people are telling you. What do you want?"

I ripped open the pretzel bag, tossing one into my mouth and choosing to ignore the last question.

Aiden stood and stepped to the side of the table. He placed his hand in front of me, waiting in invitation. His eyebrow quirked when I didn't respond, so I lifted my hand slowly and placed it in his. He pulled me up, his other hand cradling my low back, guiding me into the moving bodies on the dance floor. I followed stiffly, half-excited about the idea of being in his arms, half-anticipating the end of this thing with him once he saw how bad of a dancer I was.

We reached the center of the dance floor, and he wrapped one arm around my waist, intertwining our fingers with his free hand. He pulled me close enough to feel his warm breath.

While the movement around us leaned toward sexual, he held me chastely as we swayed.

"Relax," he whispered at my forehead. I tried, but my heart was pounding so hard I'm sure he felt it. His mouth found my ear. "Let go, Bernadette. I've got you."

I slowed my breathing and released as much tension as I could, relaxing into his embrace.

"There we go," he cooed as we continued to move with the music. We must have looked like a pair of grandparents out there, the way we were moving. But it felt heavenly to me. He held me so tight my only option was to finally relent and move with the roll of his hard body against mine. So I did.

As the song continued, his chaste movements became exploratory, his hips moving in deep circles, his arm taking me with him. His hand on my back was hypnotic. I wanted it there always, helping me carry the heavy burden of my thoughts. I became almost limp, exerting only enough energy to stay upright, him taking my weight, moving my hips with his. He pulled back to see my face, and I didn't look away at the sight of his soft smile.

"You liar," he said, and before I could ask, he said, "you *can* dance."

I considered arguing that I could follow a lead, but I remained silent. I laid my head on his shoulder. He didn't loosen his grip when the song ended and another began, this one with even more rhythm. Instead, he took my hand and put it on his shoulder, then joined his together on my back, pulling me close so our bodies were flush. My hands clasped behind his neck and he gripped my hips as our frames fused together, finding a rhythm that told me he knew how to use his body. He pulled back to look at me once again, his eyes hooded and dark, and I felt the sudden need to press closer, to feel him where my body ached.

"You're fucking beautiful," he said as he placed a hand on my cheek, tracing a finger back behind my ear, down slowly over my neck and spine to the top of my jeans. He pulled me flush against him again, something growing hard and eager between us.

Suddenly I felt a panic emerge. Not over the hard and eager thing, but the situation itself. I loved how he held me. How he let me fall limp in his arms. His words. It couldn't be real. It couldn't last. And suddenly I wasn't sure I would survive this crush unbroken.

It felt too consuming. I was imagining things now, feeling things that weren't reality. I couldn't be what he wanted. He couldn't be what I required. No one could.

"You fit here perfectly," he whispered, his mouth close enough to my neck that I felt the featherlight touch of his lips. And I let myself dwell in the warmth of it for a moment. I let myself feel the truth in his words. I let myself imagine that all of this was more than a dance.

Then I remembered what would happen next, when he found out the truth about me. I'd lived this already. I couldn't let it happen again.

I pulled away, and he let me.

"Birdie," he said, a frown marring his features when he saw my face.

"I've gotta go," I said, because I couldn't think of anything else to explain. "Thanks for the dance."

I turned and walked past the table where Jace was sitting alone. He stood when he saw me. "What's wrong?"

"I'm ready to leave," I replied just before he followed me out the door. I didn't look back.

14

THE NEXT MORNING, I avoided coffee on the porch with Evie. I didn't want to discuss my disappearing act the night before and, yes, I was avoiding Aiden as well. *Give him a day and it will be forgotten*, I told myself. He'd probably thought nothing of it. It was probably just me that felt like my insides were going to combust at the feel of his breath in my hair, the sound of his voice in my ear. It was just me who lay awake most of the night, wondering if he could be different than everyone else. Because in many ways, he already was. But could I let myself take the risk?

I started the day's work in cottage ten after checkout. A nice couple in their forties had left little evidence of their visit aside from the rumpled bedsheets and a small red wine stain on the coffee table.

Evie arrived a few minutes after I'd started, and she got straight to work without mentioning my disappearance the night before.

"Did Jace leave already?" she asked.

"Yeah, early this morning. He told me to say goodbye until next time, that he'd miss you. And that you need to take over cleaning all bathrooms from now on."

She chuckled, then placed a box on the counter with a flourish. "I made you something."

I set down the two plates I'd just retrieved from the dishwasher. "Oh?"

"Yeppers," she said and slowly began to open the box that had an overnight delivery sticker attached. "It's just a prototype, but your *situation* inspired me, and I'm wondering if you wouldn't consider a different approach?"

Whatever was in the box stayed hidden under tissue paper. "Maybe when you go back to work, you don't have to be invisible."

"I don't have invisibility."

She smiled. "No, I mean you were just . . . ordinary, aside from being super. A silent hero with no personality. You never spoke publicly, never posed for pictures. The press labeled you as rude, a superbitch. But maybe if you—"

"Right. Well, that was the job."

"But it doesn't have to be. Not anymore."

I stepped out from behind the kitchen. "It kind of does. Look, I appreciate—"

"You are the strongest, fastest woman—person—on the planet. You can do things no one else can do. You save people, on the regular. How did that become *ordinary*?"

"Mostly I help out construction workers. They actually have an appreciation for my talents."

"No jokes. Whether it happens once a week or once a year, you save people. You're special. One of a kind. And they've made you the butt of their jokes. It's not that hard to spin this. I could—"

"Nobody made me anything, Evie," I interrupted her. "I am what I am. I've never been flashy. I've always preferred to be—"

"Because someone told you that you were a liability. Someone said that you weren't behaving the way you were supposed to and needed to stay in the shadows, that you shouldn't be seen. You're not the first woman to be told that."

I felt tears stinging, her words striking somewhere deep. Apparently I'd opened the floodgates that day I met Evie.

"I don't *want* to be seen," I said firmly, unsure if that was even true, or if it ever was.

She stepped closer and placed her hands on my shoulders. "I see you, Birdie, and I'm in awe. I remember when the press first covered you. It was amazing. Everyone was intrigued. But the focus turned quickly, and now they just cover the flubs, the bad attitude. You weren't giving them what they wanted—access to you. So they villainized you, made you a joke. The world needs to see you like I do—strong and fierce. Women and girls, men and senior citizens and politicians too. Those assholes that refuse to be saved by you especially need to see you. The whole damn world."

"I don't think that's a good idea." A tear leaked out, and I quickly swiped it away, steeling my posture. "I'm fine with the way things are."

She was clearly not buying it. *I* didn't even buy it. Because what she said, while scaring the absolute shit out of me, sparked a familiar feeling I'd let die long ago. But it was too late now. My path was set, wasn't it?

"I'm not wearing tights or a cape. Also, I'm not showing more skin. I won't do—"

"I don't want to change you—I love who you are. You've got that whole hard-boiled antihero, verbal diarrhea vibe going on. It's very cool. I just think you could demand the respect you deserve."

"Evie."

She stood up straighter. "It's a little shocking, but I think that's necessary at this point. You need to get your mojo back and give everyone else a little jolt in the process."

"That's not how this works, Evie." I felt bad. She'd obviously given this a lot of thought. She wasn't entirely wrong. What would I do, though, insist on a press conference, ask for better pay? Take out an ad in the paper asking for more respect?

But I couldn't just shut her down. She was my friend, and friends were in short supply. No one else even cared this much to push.

An evil little smile appeared on her pretty face, and her hand emerged from under the tissue paper with a rumple of black cotton. She held it across her chest and waited.

It was a black T-shirt, like the one I normally wore as part of my uniform. But my eyes widened as I read the big block letters across the front, right over the chest.

SUPERBITCH.

"Evie," I said with a heavy exhale. "You're kidding."

Her hopeful eyes said she wasn't.

"I can't wear that!" What would the mayor say, the people of Chicago? It was still a blue-collar city. A girl could walk the streets in such a shirt, but a super who represented the city? I was already suspended; I'd be fired in a second.

"You can!"

"Why? To shock? To make me a laughingstock?"

She dropped her hands, the shirt along with them, looking forlorn. "No, it's not about shock. It's about what it represents," she said, putting the shirt in my hands. "You are a strong woman. For years, they tried to hide you, control you, because they were afraid of you. They are still trying to control you, mold you in a controlled fashion—'Look at our lady super. Isn't she lovely and polite!' This," she said, pointing to the shirt in my hands, "is how you take back control of who you are and tell the world to fuck off at the same time . . . subtly. Embrace the bitch. Own your power. People will respond."

"You sound like Jace." I stepped back as though the conversation was over. "I'm allowed to work as long as I don't become a spectacle."

Her voice rose four octaves. "No! You're allowed to work as long as you don't become an *icon*!"

"What are you talking about?"

"Don't you see, they want you compliant—mentally weak if not physically. That's what this is all about, this 'vagina crush penis' shit. I did my research, Birdie. It's been years of this. 'Should she be allowed to work when she's menstruating?' You've had to deal with way more than the male supers. It's been nonstop, and you've run from it. Now it's time to own it. They push the message that you can't wield your power, the power that's uniquely yours. These words say you can, unapologetically. You, my friend, are powerful up here"—she pointed to her forehead—"and you need to own who you are, that you contribute to this world. Everyone should look up when they see you jet across the sky. They should think to themselves, 'That is one powerful broad, not some polite basic bitch.'"

I barked out a laugh.

"I'm not asking you to change who you are, I swear. In the short time we've been friends, I see you. I only want the world to see you as I do."

Her sincerity was a knock to the gut. I looked at the words on the shirt in front of me. I could see it, me stepping out of the shadow, no longer hidden. Was I brave enough to be something else? Could I do it without losing myself? Did I even know how to do that?

A long time ago, I'd thought I was brave enough. But I'd grown tired over the years, beaten down.

Evie was staring at me with such hope, such excitement. I sighed, then pulled off my own shirt and pulled the tee on over my head. It fit perfectly, and I laughed while I looked down at the letters, feeling the message she was trying to convey. I'd played down my own power. I'd pretended I was less than to let others be comfortable. But the comfort of others had led to my own complacency, my invisibility, my weakness.

I smiled at Evie. I didn't have to decide anything today. She'd given me something to chew on.

"So, is it true?" she asked sheepishly.

"Is what true?"

"Can your vag crush a penis? I only ask because you know . . . well, I just want to know."

"I have no fucking idea, actually. I've never . . . tried it."

Her eyes widened before her hands went to her mouth and she tried unsuccessfully to hide the force of her laughter. An instant later, we both fell on the couch in a fit of hysterics.

———

THAT NIGHT, LYING IN BED and trying to push Evie's words out of my mind, all I could think of was how I ended up here, in this place. It

wasn't anything clear or blatant. It was just one thing after another, starting before I even got the job in Chicago.

"*Birdie, how are you feeling today?*" Doctor Chilt greeted me as I sat
down for my weekly therapy sessions, or what Jace and I joked were weekly
"holy shit—what do we do with these people" sessions.

Seriously? *I thought as I stared at the doctor, conveying the message on
my face.* "*I feel antsy. I've been here for more than a year. I'm not a criminal.
I've followed all the rules. When do I get out?*"

The truth was, I hadn't hated the facility at first. My new abilities were as
terrifying to me as they were to the rest of the world. I hadn't known where
they came from or where all of it would lead. In this place, I felt cocooned,
like I could hide from that world. But I'd become more comfortable in my
skin now—I knew my body. I was in control and was ready to get back to
my life. I missed my fiancé. I didn't want this jail anymore.

"*You can leave at any time, you know that. But it's unlikely you'll get
along well if you do. You need this program for employment,*" Doctor Chilt
responded, his face impassive as always.

"*I'm ready now. Jace is already out, and we arrived at the same time.
He's got a job in New York. People have come and gone since I've been here.*"

"*You are different. You have things to work on.*"

"*The only difference I see is that I'm the strongest female.*"

He didn't respond, straight-faced as usual. "*Tell me about the incident in
the cafeteria the other day, Birdie.*"

I rolled my eyes. Of course this was a thing. "*It was nothing. Gupta
pissed me off.*" Everyone knew Raf Gupta was a privileged asshole who
walked around the place like he was some kind of gift to women. Someone
had to put him in his place.

"*You threw him across the room.*"

"*He's perfectly fine. I knew I couldn't hurt him.*"

"*Okay. But out in the real world, people don't have the abilities Gupta
does. And there are always bystanders who could be injured.*"

"*I don't plan to do that to people who aren't Gupta. He's a dick.*"

"People outside are also rude. They'll trigger you out there just as much as they do in here."

"He's a chauvinistic pig. Do you even care what he said to me?" When it was clear he didn't, that it only mattered that I didn't just sit back and take it from Gupta, I deflated. "I only did it because I knew he couldn't be hurt."

"You could be a real asset to the world, Birdie. You could be something special. We've been placing people like you in jobs around the US, jobs aligned with their skills. You'd have options, and we'd remove the ankle band after a few years. Someone like you, with your physical powers, could be incredibly impactful, helping people on a daily basis, just like Jace."

"I'm not going to hurt anyone," I insisted. "I never have. I never will."

"Birdie, I want to challenge you to try a new coping mechanism."

"Yay, another one," I muttered.

He broke a smile. He wasn't a total robot. "When you feel a strong emotion, an urge to act, let yourself go where your instincts take you, but only in your mind. Play it out. If after you've done that, you feel it's still the most appropriate course of action, then do it."

"Jesus, Doc, I'm not going to throw anyone."

He put his hand up. "Just work with me, please? Often we have instincts that stem from our emotions. That can be dangerous in the wrong hands. Let's work on ways to keep ourselves in check. Can you do that?"

"You mean keep me in check. My emotions," I said, stressing emotions with air quotes.

"That's right."

"Tell me, Doc, will you be having a conversation with Raf Gupta about what he said to me, about how I've been in here so long because a woman can't be trusted with any real power, given she's basically an open wound 20 percent of the time?"

It was clear on his face that this was my problem, not Gupta's. It was my behavior that needed adjustment.

And because I needed to get out of there, badly, before I lost my damn mind, I said, "Yeah, all right. I can do that."

Tossing and turning, I reminded myself that I didn't have to worry about all of that. Not right now. I wasn't the Chicago Bird this summer. I'd worry about it later, when and if I got my job back. Then I fell asleep and stayed that way until morning.

15

THE NEXT FAMILY DINNER I attended marked week three of eleven. What had three weeks gotten me? My secret revealed to Evie. A deep knowledge of surfactants and the value of vinegar as a cleaning solution. A handful of dates, all of which could be considered total disasters. A painfully powerful and unrequited crush. And finally, more confusion about my future than I started out with in the first place.

I'd considered passing on the family dinner. But I'd only get so many of them, and the idea of missing one was too much for me to consider.

Besides, I missed Aiden. Despite my pathetic exit the other day, I wanted to get back to where we were, seeing him nearly every day, volleying snark, flirting for the sake of flirting. Because, crush aside, I just really liked him.

"Okay, give us the deets on the dates," Yash urged after we'd entered Aiden's cottage. He greeted Evie with a kiss on the cheek.

"You are such a gossip," Evie chastised.

"You only say that because you already got the story," I told her, gaining a smug smile from Yash. I loved that he was interested in my life, that he was checking in on me, that there was friendship brewing. I loved how good he was to Evie.

"Well . . . ," I said. I grabbed a cheese-topped cracker from Aiden's counter and tossed it into my mouth.

"Bowden," Aiden said, handing me a glass of sweet tea. He gave me a friendly nod, but nothing more. My heart sank, but at the same time, I felt relief at the lack of awkwardness I'd anticipated.

I turned back to Yash. "I had one date yesterday with Kyle and one the day before with Craven." I'd scheduled the two dates to keep myself from running into Aiden in the evenings. "Kyle is a real estate agent, and he spent the first part of the night trying to get me to buy a home. He went into detail about at least six different places."

Aiden handed Evie something in a bowl along with a whisk without saying a word. She responded with a "yummy" and got to work mixing whatever it was.

"When I finally made it clear I wasn't buying a new place, he shifted to trying to get me to go back to his house."

"Tell them what he said," Evie encouraged.

Aiden glanced my way before resuming his position at the stove. My eyes had a hard time leaving him, the way his body moved in performing mundane tasks way more engrossing to me than it should have been.

"He went on and on about how women, meaning me, of course, should be okay with sexual freedom."

Aiden cursed at the stove.

"Good?" Yash looked over his shoulder at Aiden.

"Yep, fine," Aiden said dismissively.

"He's a feminist," I continued. "That's how he sold it to me. He was being supportive of my freedom to be as open and expressive as a man."

"Idiot," Yash scoffed. "What did you say?"

"I slept with him, of course."

Before I could laugh, a glass of water hit the floor and shattered.

"Fucking hell," Aiden muttered, storming out of the kitchen.

"What's his deal?" Evie said as we stared after him.

"I think he doesn't like this conversation," Yash said, eyeing me.

"It was a joke," I said as Aiden reappeared with a broom and dustpan. Yash took it from him. "I'll get it. You keep an eye on dinner."

"Thanks. Sorry about that. Slipped," he said as he found my face. His glare was so lethal, I wanted to laugh at his grumpiness. "Finish your story," he stated.

Oh my. "That's about it. I told him that he needed to work on his sales tactics. Then I said goodnight and left."

"I've seen his pic on benches in town. Slimy." Evie stood and took her mixed bowl to Aiden, whose back was turned again. "Aiden makes the best tacos, Birdie," she said, glowing with pride at her brother. "Gimme, gimme. I'm so hungry," she whined, grabbing something from the pan before he swatted her hand away.

"Brat," he chastised in the way only a sibling could make endearing.

"Hurry up, slowpoke," she tossed back.

"Hold your horses, woman."

I watched as Aiden plated everything, taking pride in his presentation. When Yash and Evie picked up their plates and retreated to the table, I stood to collect mine.

Aiden turned from the stove and leaned against the counter, his arms crossed as he watched me approach. He was blocking my plate.

I wanted to lighten things between us, get back to being easy.

"I told 'Kyle the feminist' that I was working here, and he begged me to pass along his card to you." Aiden's brow furrowed when I pulled the card from my pocket and held it out. "In case you want to list the place. Or, maybe, if you are up for freely expressing yourself sexually."

A hint of a dimple appeared as he ignored the card in my hand and stared at me. "He didn't try anything with you?" he asked, his voice deathly stern and sending a tickle of elation through my body that he'd care enough to ask.

"I can take care of myself," I replied, but his face didn't change, and he was still blocking my plate.

"I'm aware," he said, still waiting for an answer.

"No," I relented with a smile. "A verbal idiot, but harmless, like I already told you."

"You seem to attract a lot of those."

I shrugged. "You going to defend my honor?"

Aiden's lips quirked. "If you had any, I might."

"Ouch," I said, my hand on my chest, and his grin fully appeared.

Once settled at the table, everyone dug in, and silence filled the room. Evie had been very accurate in her anticipation of dinner.

"Tell them about the other one," Evie said.

"Right, my other date this week was with Craven. Thirty-five. Looks like a young Danny Glover, full stash and all. Very seventies and very . . . um . . . what's the word, proper, maybe? Nice guy. And who doesn't have a thing for Roger Murtaugh?"

Aiden nodded like he was fully on board with that assessment, and I grinned.

"Anyway, he pulled out my chair, opened my doors, and ordered my drinks. It was like he was following a dating manual from 1955."

"Sounds like—" Yash started.

"Overkill? Suffocating? Boring?" Evie finished for me.

"He was sweet," I said, recalling how nervous he was. "But he ordered all my food for me, saying he knew the best thing on the menu. I learned about his mother, Edna, who suffers from arthritis. He has an iguana and a chinchilla. He collects twentieth-century action figures. His favorite is Misty Knight. And he's doing the Lord of the Rings tour in New Zealand next summer."

Yash and Aiden were all smiles.

"He was a talker. Also, probably the sweetest date I've had yet. Then, at the end of dinner, he asked me to split the check, which is normally fine, but it seemed a little unfair since I didn't get to order any food for myself. But no big deal, right? I couldn't really fault him for anything. He tried. But then he said he didn't think it was a love match and he needed to get home to feed his pets, and he up and left me at the table to finish my dessert alone. Which I did."

They all chuckled.

"I never want to date again," Evie said, and Yash looked across the table at her.

"Me neither."

Something passed between them while Aiden and I waited patiently for it to be over.

"I literally think I said about five sentences the whole evening," I added. "I'm batting a big fat zero in the dating department."

"You know *craven* means 'cowardly,' right?" Yash interjected.

"Pretty sure he gave himself that name. He has a thing for Wes Craven movies."

"Ah." They all nodded in understanding.

"You're too good for these guys," Evie said.

Yash snagged a pickled onion off Evie's plate. "Do you even screen these guys?"

"I'm not really in a position to reject offers. I'm on assignment, so . . ."

"You intimidate them," Aiden interjected.

The words struck me in the gut. "I'm not intimidating."

"To men, you are."

Great. That was the story of my life—and I was tired of being intimidating, like it was my fault for how others reacted to my existence. This experiment was me trying to leave that behind. But maybe I'd never be able to leave it behind, super or not. Aiden didn't even know about me, and he still saw it.

"Any confident woman is intimidating to most men," he added.

I huffed, feeling that familiar need to lash out. "You mean all men."

Aiden didn't seem fazed by my attitude. "There are some of us who find confidence and strength attractive. It requires a certain level of confidence and strength on the part of the man as well. That's harder to find. It's more a reflection of men than it is of women."

Did he say "us"? Was he in that group?

"Keep looking," he added with a wink, and I gave him a weak smile. No one found my brand of strength attractive, but I appreciated the sentiment.

More small talk carried us through our dinner, thankfully away from my dating life, and I found myself retreating inward. I reminded myself of Nick, of why our relationship ended. He couldn't handle it. *You're emasculating*, he'd said. The words were on repeat in my mind.

The more I considered it, the more I wanted to finish my therapy and go home. Get out of Grove. Because the longer I was here, the more I wanted to stay. But that was impossible. I wasn't even being honest with them.

I excused myself to use the bathroom as the thoughts continued. I stared at myself in the mirror and tried to remember who I was, that I was here to get okay with my life, not to want another that didn't belong to me. I was the Chicago Bird, and my life wasn't meant for this. I was a super, and I had to figure out how to be a better one and go back to doing that. Plain and simple.

A knock on the door startled me out of my thoughts. I opened the bathroom door to see Aiden standing there, leaning casually against the wall.

"Sorry, all yours." I tried to pass him.

"You okay?" he said as he grasped my arm gently.

I stopped, not looking at him.

He stepped closer and brushed his thumb across my cheek, tipping my chin to meet his dark eyes as they bore into mine. "Tell me."

"Nothing. I had something in my eye. Allergies, I think." It wasn't a total lie. I did have allergies.

"Hmm," he said, and looked me over without releasing my chin. He didn't buy it, but he let it go. "You skipped out early the other night."

"Sorry about that. It was nice what you did. I'm just . . . I'm not good in social situations. I appreciated the dance. It was a good refresher. Maybe it'll come in handy at some point. A date with someone, I mean, for my assignment." I was so tongue-tied as he watched me, his eyes unwavering. His smile said he could see right through me—could see how much he got to me.

"Did I say something to upset you out there?"

I forced a grin. I needed to get away from him before I did something stupid. I steeled my voice. "Nothing that wasn't true. I'm fine, really."

"Bernadette," he said as he pushed the escaped hair from my ponytail behind my ear.

"Yes?" I said, breathless.

"You can relax."

"I am relaxed." I wasn't. My entire body was stiff from his simple touch on my face.

He stepped closer, and I was stuck between his hard warmth and the doorjamb of the bathroom, holding my breath, eyes wide.

"Breathe," he whispered, and I took an audible breath. His mouth was so close that I thought for a second he was going to kiss me, that his lips would finally touch my own. But his mouth moved to my ear. "You are a puzzle, Bernadette Bowden." His breath spread goose bumps in its path on my neck before he pulled away. "One I very much want to—"

Suddenly Yash appeared in the hallway behind us, but I couldn't take my eyes from Aiden. How did he always manage to take my words and thoughts from me, rendering me stupid each time he got close?

"Oh, sorry," Yash said tentatively. "Evie asked me to come get you. She's in the living room."

"Right," I said and pulled myself away, finding my mental balance the further I got from Aiden. I returned to the living room, my face warm, my hands shaking slightly.

I stopped next to Evie in front of the TV, and my attention shifted as Jimmy stood in front of City Hall, with my jet pack on his back, accepting some big golden key to the city. Thompson stood there, presenting it, spouting something about bravery and heroism, his mayoral smile conveying he wasn't too eager about it. My hands clenched, and I felt a fury rise inside me.

I wanted to be happy for Jimmy. After all, it mattered what he did. And he was popular. If Jimmy had an impact on kids in Chicago, I was glad. It was what the city needed. But I'd done similar things. I'd suggested programs and school visits, but I'd been told it wasn't my role. And maybe it wasn't. Jimmy knew these kids better than I ever would. I grew up with privilege. He didn't. Maybe he was better than I was for the job. Better for the city. It was clear as day. That's why he got the key. That's why I was out and he was in.

"Fucking piss," I muttered and walked out the door. I was done with family night. I was done with Thompson and Jimmy. I was done with everything.

"**YOU DISAPPEARED AGAIN**," Aiden said as he placed a warm cup of tea in my hands. "You keep doing that. How are you feeling?"

"Fine. Why?"

"Evie said your stomach wasn't well."

"Oh. Right." An excuse for my disappearance. "A bit better, yes."

"If I didn't know any better, I'd think it was me you are always trying to get away from."

I stared at him. "It *is* you. I totally can't stand you, like at all. You're absolutely the worst. You just won't take the hint."

He smirked. "Scoot up a sec," he said and placed a flannel blanket around my back, tugging it close at my chest before taking a seat in the open porch chair next to mine.

I watched him settle in, not saying a word, feeling the warmth of the blanket sink into my skin and the smell of woodshop in my nose. I closed my eyes, already mourning what would soon be lost. This man who, if I were someone else, I'd have already fallen head over heels for.

We sat quietly as he waited for me to talk first.

"Ever feel like you're being replaced before you ever got a chance to have an impact? Like you're being sidelined?"

Aiden looked up at the sky. "No."

I laughed. "Of course you don't."

He grinned, but then looked thoughtful. "But maybe I know what it's like to be discarded."

I glanced over, a bit surprised.

"When I came here in the summers, I was mostly on my own. My father wasn't around. He didn't notice that I was even here most of the time. He was out drinking or with random women, and I managed the place with the help of the maintenance guy, Harold. Harold was more a father to me those summers than my father ever was. There was one summer . . . I never saw my father once. He never showed. Harold said he'd gone to California with a woman. But it was no matter if he was here or not. I had everything I needed, building things with Harold in the shed. So, while I'm not sure I can relate to whatever it is you're feeling, I think I understand the notion of feeling obsolete to the people who should care the most."

"That must have sucked," I whispered, in awe that he had shared a part of himself, something real.

"It did. And it took me a while to realize that it was my father's loss. I wasn't going to become obsolete just because to him I was."

"What happened to Harold?"

Aiden smiled fondly. "He retired, moved to Florida with his wife. I visited him a few years back." Aiden's gaze was mesmerizing. His small smile made me forget I was sad, if only just for a minute.

"Evie says I need to own my identity."

"And what do you think? What do you want?"

"I guess I just want to be important to someone." The words were out of my mouth before I could think too much. "I want to not think about how I come off. I simply want to be. No expectations, no rules. No overthinking."

We locked eyes. "Want to talk about it?"

"Do you believe there is one person out there for everyone?"

After a few seconds of silence, he said, "No."

"Me neither. I think some people are just meant to be on their own."

"Maybe," he said before drinking the last of his tea. "Maybe not." Then he stood up and stepped toward me, leaning down to drop a kiss to my forehead. "Goodnight, Bernadette."

I sat there a while longer, the feel of his lips warming my whole body.

16

"**EVIE IS TRYING TO GET ME** to wear dresses. Wants me to wear one to the festival today."

Doctor Evans nodded, waiting for me to continue.

"I haven't worn a dress in a decade. I know it shouldn't be a big deal, but it feels like it is. It feels like I'm pretending to be something I'm not."

"Something you don't want to be?"

"No. Just something I'm not. Not anymore."

"Okay, let's unpack this a bit. What does wearing traditionally feminine clothes represent to you?"

"Come on, Doc, that's too easy. The clothes represent my mother. My mother, who ingrained in me what it was to be a woman. Yet my abilities are all masculine in nature, causing my mother and fiancé to reject me, which left me grappling with my own gender identity. I've left any semblance of femininity behind because I can't reconcile it with the super stuff. The feminine stuff feels fake now. It feels futile. It feels like *they* are always there, disapproving."

"How's the dating going?"

"Um, well, it kind of sucks. A total waste of time. Did you hear anything I just said?"

"I did."

"And?"

"And what? You have a good handle on the past and how it continues to impact your present."

"That's it? You don't have anything to add? My mother's disapproval has crippled me. The rejection of my ex. Not to mention the world thinks my vagina will crush any penis that comes near it."

Doctor Evans's brows rose in question. "Can or will?"

"What?"

"*Will* crush a penis is different than *can* crush a penis."

"What difference does it make?"

"A lot. Is it true?"

"Jesus. No. Or at least I've never tried to crush anything with my vag. I mean, maybe I could if I tried. But why would I? Good vibrators are expensive, and I'm on a union salary. Anyway, people are capable of all kinds of things that they choose not to do."

"Why are you so bothered by it? I'm sure there have been other things said about you. Why does this bother you so much?"

"It's fucking insulting! Not to mention archaic. My damn cunt is what makes me a liability? You've seen the memes. This bullshit has been around since the beginning of time in one form or another. Now Evie wants me to plaster Superbitch over my chest for the world to see."

Doctor Evans shrugged. "It's not a bad idea, actually."

"Seriously? Come on, Doc, it's batshit! And you know what else is batshit? Me with all this baggage, all these issues to face, and all you care about is me dating." I took a breath and sat back, happy to finally have said it.

"Birdie," she replied, placing her notebook in her lap, "you are highly intelligent and incredibly self-aware. You clearly know who you are and have a pretty good understanding of what's going on around you with your employment situation, your issues with rejection. And yet, you allow your mother, your ex, and some idiots on social media to have this debilitating hold over you. You filter everything you are through their eyes. *That's* what's batshit. What *I* think is that you need to let those people go. You need *new* people. People who see you for who you are, not as an accessory or entertainment. We all need support to live our lives authentically, to make us brave enough to be ourselves. So, yes, I'm focused on getting you to a place where you can accept friendship and maybe even love."

"Oh."

"And regarding the vagina stuff, it's amazing the power a little thing like an auxiliary verb can have."

—

THE GROVE SUMMER FESTIVAL was a big deal. The whole town was involved, and the festivities lasted well into the night apparently. My next attempt at a date would take place at the festival. I'd set it up over a week ago and wanted more than anything to cancel and instead join Aiden and Evie selling Aiden's pieces in the booth. But knowing I needed to report back to Doctor Evans that I was making the effort, I'd go through with it.

I put on a pair of denim shorts and a fitted T-shirt I'd picked up in town. I let Evie force a new pair of sandals on my feet because my boots were "absolutely not date-appropriate."

My date and I had agreed to meet at the festival entrance at noon. The band had already started, and the booths were lined up for blocks, full of meat on sticks, vegan delights, baked treats, and local artisan goods. It reminded me of the Chicago festivals but with a small-town, ice-cream-social feel. Everything was a bit more spread out, with room for kids to play and tables where people could sit and relax. There was even a small midway showcasing a long line for the Ferris wheel, a fun house with a slide that ended in a crocodile's mouth, and a few other kiddie rides—including a massive bounce house emanating cheerful, high-pitched screams as mingling parents conversed in a large circle around the outside.

"Birdie?" A voice came from behind me as I stood awkwardly at the entrance. I turned to find a man about four inches shorter than me. He must have weighed a buck-twenty soaking wet. Looking closer, I guess I could see the resemblance to the image he'd shared online—a black-and-white close-up of his face. He was not what I'd expected, but no matter, I wasn't there to marry the guy.

"Hi. Simon?"

"That's me," he said, his hands up as though conceding the fact he'd misrepresented himself and hoping I'd let it slide. And I would. Anything else would make me a hypocrite, since I was holding back who I was as well.

"You look very pretty," he said robotically as he stared at my chest. I wasn't sure if he was interested in my breasts or just didn't feel like looking up at my face from below.

Chalking it up to the height difference, I said, "Thanks. You look nice as well."

He nodded and straightened his tie.

Yeah, a tie, for a daytime date at a fair. In his chinos and button-down shirt, his attire looked . . . well, warm.

"I think I overdressed," he said with a shy smile. "Guess I was nervous."

"I hear you. It's never an easy decision," I said with a relaxed smile. "And you look fine."

"Would you like to get a lemonade?" he asked.

"That sounds nice."

The man in front of the stand wore a bright yellow lemon atop his head and a pained smile. "What can I get you?"

Simon ordered, and we stepped aside to wait for someone to prepare our drinks.

"Are you from the Chicago area?"

"I'm from Evanston. I'm a doctoral candidate in genetics," he said with a puff of his chest.

"That's interesting. I went to college for a bit, but I dropped out."

"Really—why?"

"I realized my future profession didn't really require a degree."

"That makes sense, I suppose."

I looked at him, surprised by his words. "Does it?"

"Well—you said in your bio that you work for the city. Most of those jobs don't require higher education."

The statement and the way he said it didn't sit well, and my instinct was to lash out. But I paused and made an effort to not assume the worst. I wouldn't let my inner saboteur take over already. See, I was learning.

Simon picked up two cups chock-full of freshly cut lemon and sugar, handing me one and taking a sip of his own. We walked for a while, commenting on the booths but without much else to converse about. The only thing we had in common seemed to be our dismal ability to make small talk.

Eventually we came upon Aiden's booth.

"You mind if we stop here?" he asked. "I heard this guy is really good."

"Oh, I'd prefer not—" but he was already inside the booth examining the coat rack at the entrance.

I followed slowly, scanning for Aiden, wanting to avoid the conversation where I needed to explain that I was on a date. I didn't know what was going on with us, but it was enough to make this interaction awkward. I made eye contact with Evie as she talked with a customer. She smiled but kept her attention on the sale.

I didn't immediately spot Aiden, so I took the opportunity to look around. It was the first time I was able to see his work presented so professionally. He had such variety in the booth—several tables of different sizes, bookshelves, a rocking chair that belonged in someone's nursery. There was also a jewelry box, a massive wall clock, and a bed frame that instantly made me blush at the thought of Aiden in it.

The work was amazing in its simplicity. Some of the items were solid wood. Others used multiple wood species, while others had colors like the chair I'd fallen in love with. I wondered if he'd sold it. The thought that I wouldn't see it again made me a little sad.

While Simon looked around, I examined a table, mahogany with a series of three long gouges running down the center, leaving a blood-red color behind. It was beautifully dark. Next to it was a small end table colored with blues and whites resembling waves crashing on the beach.

"In the market for an end table?"

I felt him behind me as I continued to examine the intricacies of the piece. An instant thrill ran up my spine. "What is it made of, the color?"

"It's a resin. Epoxy." His voice was deep and warm, suddenly very close to my ear, and I felt the hairs on my neck rise.

"It's amazing. You've captured a force of nature, a moment in time." I turned and Aiden stepped back. His gray T-shirt was tight at the shoulders, and his dark jeans hung low on his lean hips. His hair, usually left a bit wild, was combed to the side, his stubble neat and tight.

"You look different," I said.

"Oh yeah?"

"Yeah, but it's nice," I offered quickly. "Your Sunday best."

He smirked. "Do you want to watch?"

My face scrunched, turning red. "Watch what?"

He laughed. "I'm asking if you want to see me trap the moment in time. You mentioned—"

"Yes," I said immediately, because I did want to see him work. I imagined him in such a state of concentration that his movements were precise and organized as something amazing was made from something ordinary. He smiled knowingly, and I felt an overwhelming desire to kiss him.

"Do you do custom work?"

The interruption slowly drew Aiden's attention away from me to none other than Simon. "I do. Functional items."

"Display carvings?"

"No."

I followed Simon's gaze to the figure of a female, tall and lean, the lines of the wood following her smooth curves. Her face was without detail, her body exuding force. It was spectacular, done with an obvious level of care.

"What about that piece?"

"When did you do that one?" I interrupted, drawn to its beauty.

His eyes found mine before returning to Simon, and he said, "This week."

"I was thinking more detailed carvings of deer or elk," Simon said.

I laughed out loud; I couldn't help it. Aiden grinned at my reaction.

"Like I said, I don't make nonfunctional items."

"What about that one?" Simon persisted in asking, pointing to the figure of the woman.

Aiden glanced in my direction once again. "Spontaneous inspiration." Then he looked back to Simon. "Anyway, that's not for sale—it's personal. I take commissions for certain projects, but I don't do the detail work you're talking about. There's a booth further down that has some of what you might be looking for."

Simon nodded, then put his hand out. "Shall we?" he asked.

For a second I forgot I was supposed to go with him.

"Oh. Sure."

"You guys are together?" Aiden asked with a mix of surprise and amusement.

"We are," Simon responded, puffing out his chest.

"Right. Good luck with the search," Aiden said, holding my gaze with a *why are you doing this to yourself / I told you so* smirk. I bit my tongue and followed Simon, waving to Evie, who was already engaged with another eager customer. As we walked away, I glanced back to find Aiden speaking with two young women whom I'd observed were clearly more interested in the artist than the art. But I couldn't blame them. The work was extraordinary, but the artist was . . . something else entirely.

We walked around the festival for another hour, making more conversation about the booths. I bought a local artist's picture of the beach, one with Aiden's cottages in the foreground. I'd put it on one of the many empty walls in my apartment and remember the people I'd met here.

Feeling satisfied that I'd given the date my best effort, I was about to thank Simon for a nice time when he asked me if I wanted to get food.

"Sure," I replied, my stomach growling at the thought. But before we could pick a place, a group of early twentysomethings stopped in front of us.

A young woman spoke first, Southwestern Illinois University printed across her T-shirt, her dark hair tied into a low ponytail over her left side. "Oh my God! Are you who I think you are?"

"I doubt it," I said, moving to step around her, but a man blocked my path.

"You so are. You're the Chicago Bird," he said, his mouth forming a grin. "We did a class on supers at the U." He looked back at his friends. "A whole section on the Superbitch," he said, overly enunciating the last word.

The sound of their laughter made my neck heat, emotion boiling up. I needed my jet pack. My legs itched to run, to get out of there and be alone. I suddenly resented the fact that I was surrounded by people, powerless.

"That's real nice. You have me confused, I think," I said through gritted teeth. I turned swiftly to find Simon staring wide-eyed at me. "Let's get something to eat."

"You her boyfriend?" another guy said, this one in a manbun and leather sandals. "Aren't you worried, man?" He placed his hand between his legs, wincing. "Isn't it like a death trap down there?" His friends all laughed.

Simon didn't say a word, just stared at me with his mouth hanging open.

They wanted a rise out of me. Clearly, they knew I was short-tempered— my inability to control my words, my temper . . . they'd studied it, in fact. I envisioned taking the guy's manbun and tossing him into the air with it. He would bounce off the bounce house and fly into the sky, landing somewhere in town, right into Doctor Evans's perfect thorny rosebushes, his scream trailing him, while little kids squealed in joy as they were flung high into the air before returning safely to the bounce house.

"Don't you have anything to say?" The woman stood behind him with her phone out, clearly recording, eagerly waiting for my reaction.

I instantly turned, and latching on to Simon's hand with my own, started walking away, their childish laughter dying out behind us.

Simon paused a minute later. "Wait a second," he said.

I stopped walking, forgetting I was dragging him along with me in my eagerness to get away. I let go of his hand, and he stepped back.

"Tha—thanks for the date," he stuttered, running his hand over his mouth and tracing his tie down to his stomach. "I gotta go, actually." His eyes darted around, anywhere but at my face. "I got a thing. I forgot. So . . . see you around."

He couldn't get away from me fast enough.

———

I TOOK THE LONG WAY out of the fairgrounds, keeping a wide berth from Aiden's booth. I needed to get out of there. Be alone. I needed to run.

"Birdie!" My head turned instinctively at the sound of my name. Evie was walking away from the bathroom area in front of me. I stopped, and she approached with a smile. "Done with your date?"

"Yep, I'm going to head out. Tired," I said, hoping she'd not question it, but I knew Evie better than that.

"No way. Come have some food with us. We're just closing up the booth for the day—almost sold out." It was midafternoon, and the festival was morphing from a shopping event to a dinner, drinks, and socializing event.

"Evie, I don't feel well."

"Nonsense. You had another stupid date. Come hang with people you like now." Evie, from day one, could read me. There was no point in arguing.

I couldn't do what I needed anyway, which was burn energy, exhaust myself. "Yeah, okay."

"Want to tell me about it?" she asked as we walked toward the booth, her eyes looking up at me in concern. "Was he another asshole?"

"No, I just forgot who I was for a while. He reminded me," I confessed, as I thought about telling Aiden about me. Seeing him pull away.

"Let's go somewhere, talk it out?"

"No," I replied, and she almost looked hurt. "Nothing to talk about."

"Back so soon?" Aiden said as we entered the booth. "I take it you didn't make a love connection, then?" His face said he was still quite amused with my date.

I narrowed my eyes, willing him to understand the thoughts behind them. "Shut up."

Aiden laughed a little, and it was a welcome, deep rumble. "Well, you're just in time to help us close up. Hungry?"

"Famished."

I helped them for the next hour, finishing up about five o'clock. Evie and I rejected Aiden's offer to pay us for the time. Instead, we accepted his offer to treat us to dinner and drinks. We snagged a four-top in the middle of the closed street, knowing Yash would join us later.

Ordering wine and ceviche, we watched a local Girl Scout troop do an Irish dance followed by a trio singing oldies. Evie talked through most of it, telling us about all the sales they made and how many jobs they had to follow up on. Aiden could only take on so many; he had the luxury of picking what he wanted. I showed them the photograph I'd bought of the beach with their cottage in the foreground.

"I'll do a trade," Aiden said as he admired it. "Anything in the shop for the picture."

"Really?" The picture cost fifty dollars, and nothing in Aiden's store was worth less than ten times that. "Anything?"

He nodded once, confident.

"What if I pick the chair?" I joked.

Evie scoffed. "Aiden spoke too soon. He won't even let me have that chair. How long did that take to make?"

"Done."

Evie choked on her wine, and I laughed. "Yeah, right."

"You drive a hard bargain, Miss Bowden."

"No," I whispered, "not really?"

He sipped his wine and grimaced. It wasn't good, probably turned. I'd already figured that out but didn't want to be rude because it was a local wine. "Deal's a deal. Maybe we put the picture at the front desk. Evie?" Aiden looked back at the band while Evie and I gawked.

"Sure," she muttered, still in shock, her gaze curious as she stared at her brother.

"You can get another photo," I said. "I bet the artist has more. If not this one, then one very similar. I won't take the chair."

"Sure you will. Consider it a trade as well as a thanks for your help today."

"You don't owe me anything." I wasn't sure why he felt he had to give me this under the pretense of a trade. I was suddenly angry. I didn't want to fall for him any more than I already had. Ultimately, I didn't even want the chair because it would be a constant reminder of what I could never have, a reminder of him, of him in this place, when I went back to my shithole studio. "It would never fit in my apartment anyway. Maybe I'll pick something else."

He brandished me with a hard stare, meeting my frustration level. He was looking at me as though he knew my every thought. He always looked at me that way. It was unnerving. "You don't want something else. You want the chair. Take what you want, Bernadette. I'm giving it to you."

What? Was this even about the chair anymore? "I don't want it," I assured him, feeling caged by his stare, needing to escape.

He shook his head, exasperated. "Fucking hell."

Why was he frustrated? He had no right.

"I was just joking. You can have the photo, but I don't want the trade. I don't . . . I was kidding around. I . . . never mind." I scrambled for my bag and picked up the photo. "I'm gonna head out. It's been a long day, and I'll just leave this at Evie's, and you two can decide later where to put it."

Aiden stood and placed his hand on my elbow. I kept my eyes on Evie, who was watching with her wine held in front of her lips like we were some epic play unfolding before her.

"Don't go," Aiden said. "Let's forget it. I just wanted to repay you, because I . . . we appreciated your help today. Every day, really. You keep your photo."

Clearly I had overreacted. There was an annoying lump in the back of my throat, but I swallowed it and sat down, and we all gave our attention to the trio finishing their rendition of "Just My Imagination."

As they scrambled off the stage, the mayor of Grove was introduced. I turned back to Evie and Aiden. "They were really good," I said, trying to recover from my earlier outburst.

Evie smiled weakly, and Aiden nodded, setting his wine to the side. "Let's get something else, shall we?" He flagged down the server and ordered.

I turned back to the mayor, who was announcing a guest. "We're lucky today to have with us a very special new arrival to the Chicago area. He's just come to the city a few weeks ago, and you've probably seen him across the news outlets. He'll be on call to support smaller communities in the metro area, like our little Grove. He's *super* excited to be here today. Everyone, please welcome . . . Jimmy the Juggernaut!!"

Then it happened. I heard that familiar sound that always brought me a sense of purpose and calm, a feeling of freedom and independence that made the crappy pay and often daily humiliation almost worth it. My jet pack, the feeling of soaring through the sky, the world miniscule below me. Except the sound wasn't behind my ear. It was softer, distant, and growing louder as it descended onto the stage.

Jimmy landed with a thud, almost falling backward, righting himself as the crowd clapped and a few little kids rushed the stage. He waved brightly, his smile friendly and open, a useless ability at the end of the day, but more important than skill and experience, according to the city council.

Jimmy was fit, a beefcake like my first date, Sarge, wearing a spandex top and a pair of some kind of special green trousers. He was strong—not as strong as me, because only Jace was as physically strong as me—but strong nonetheless. He wasn't particularly fast either. But what he had was a true asset of another form. Jimmy was a little bit telepathic, and that came in handy more often than you'd think.

Unfortunately, he was also very young and possessed an inflated ego. He flaunted his abilities as though he were Superman. But he wasn't Superman. He was a novice who possessed a charming smile and was happy to kiss the city council's ass.

"Hello, Grove. How is everyone doing? I'm *super*!" He winked and waved. Why did people keep saying *super* like it was clever? It was a fucking word. "I'm so happy to be here with you all today. I thought I'd pop in to say hello and tell you I'm thrilled to . . ."

His words blurred in my head, and I felt a rolling in my chest. I was going to lose it. Since when does a Chicago super do press tours? What happened to silent stoicism? Power in the shadows? What happened to not making a spectacle? And why the fuck did Jimmy get my goddamn jet pack?

A series of images appeared in my head, like a comic strip. Me tearing my jet pack from his weak body and strapping it on. Me tossing Jimmy into the fun house. Me taking off into the sky, away from this ridiculous display, away from Evie, who was staring at me like I was going to combust, and away from Aiden, who would never see me as anything but a liability once he found out that I was a super-powered freak.

"Birdie?"

I turned to Evie, her mouth twisted in concern, her eyes anxious to see my reaction.

"Everything okay?"

I was beet red. I had to be. It took every ounce of self-control I possessed and some I didn't to keep from running up there or going back to Chicago to demand answers from Thompson.

But any reaction from me would serve to prove the point they were trying to make in the first place: I couldn't control my emotions. I wasn't fit for the role.

And maybe I wasn't. Not anymore. I didn't need this crap.

In the beginning, I could have been Jimmy. I could have been happy and excited and done press tours and kissed babies. But I was strong and fast and a woman. The world had never been good about accepting women with power. It never did believe we could wield the power we possessed.

I told myself I was better, more stoic than the others because I'd kept out of the limelight and let my work speak for itself. But in the end, I'd sunk further into solitude.

I turned into exactly what they'd always thought of me—a sour, angry, people-hating superbitch who wasn't fit for the job, couldn't handle all the aspects of it, and was ruled by emotion. I didn't even recognize who I'd become. It wasn't until I'd come to Grove that I'd even started to find Birdie again.

But my past life was here now, staring back at me. Smiling and embracing his power, while I continued to hide mine from the public and from myself most of all.

I'd reached my limit. I pushed my chair back so hard it skidded along the pavement and drew eyes. I mumbled an apology to Evie, who was looking at me like I was a ticking time bomb. I didn't dare look at Aiden.

I stalked off as I heard Evie say, "Let her go," behind me and quickly got out of view of any other living soul. Then I ran as fast and as far as I could, needing to feel the power in my legs. I needed to feel exhaustion and release. I ran and ran, with absolutely no place to run to.

17

I'D BROKEN THE RULES. Again. But it was the only way I knew to expel the tension that had built up in my body. It was all I'd ever known. I thought about why I'd gotten angry at Jimmy. But it wasn't him I was angry at. I was an outdated super who would never reach her potential.

I'd dedicated my life to the job, and now there wasn't much of a life left. Somehow I'd fallen into this box, and now I wasn't sure how to get out.

"Birdie," Evie called.

"Back here," I replied from my room, fresh from a shower.

She came to my door. "You okay?"

"Yeah. Sorry about earlier. I just—"

"Don't apologize, I get it. And Aiden would, too, if you'd tell him."

"No," I replied adamantly from my bed, looking at the wall.

She stepped inside, and I felt her staring at me, though I didn't dare turn to look at her. "I think there's something there. He cares for you. He wanted to follow you—"

"Don't even go there."

She sat on the bed. "Are you wearing a dress tonight?"

I grunted. "Pass."

"You know I don't wear pretty things for other people. I wear them for myself. I like the way I look and feel in something nice. You feel boring and plain, Birdie, so that's what you reflect to the world."

"Thanks a lot," I muttered.

"But you're the furthest thing from either. I see through your facade. My brother sees through it too."

My head came up to look at her. "I understand what you're trying to do. Don't bother."

"Birdie. Please, for me."

I planted my face in the blankets. I just wanted to go to sleep, exhausted after my run. Doctor Evans's words played in my head. What the fuck did I want? Did I want to go back to Chicago at all? Could I just give it all up? I needed to get over the past. Move on.

"Whatever."

"Really?" she gasped.

I turned to my side, picking at a loose piece of string in the comforter. "Why not? I used to actually wear dresses. Fancy ones."

She didn't reply as she walked into my closet, finding the shorts and tees I'd purchased in town along with a few things she'd lent to me. Then she moved to my drawers.

"You're not going to find anything pretty in there."

Then she paused, staring into the open drawer. "Oh my gosh. Is this it?"

I sat up. She was examining my neatly folded uniform, complete with my mask lying on top. "Yep."

"It's strange to see it. Like I knew you were a super," she said, holding up my shirt, "but this uniform is iconic."

"Hah! This from the woman who wants me to ditch it."

She turned to me and let the shirt fall. "It's iconic. You should be proud! That's really what the other shirt is all about."

"Right now, I'm a series of memes and TikToks. I'm a joke—and probably soon unemployed."

"They'd be crazy to let you go. You just have to show them who you are. Make yourself un-fireable."

"I thought I'd done that with my save record," I muttered, falling backward, staring at the ceiling lines I'd memorized over the weeks.

She grabbed my hand and pulled me to a sitting position. "No talk of work tonight. We are going to the festival party. We are going to dance with handsome strangers."

I eyed her, and she smiled.

"Okay, you are going to dance with handsome strangers, and I'm going to dance with Yash." With a wink, she said, "Let's find you something from my closet."

She left the room as I called after her, "I won't fit in any of your clothes. I'm a behemoth compared to you."

"Shut up. You're fucking fit," she called from her room.

"But I've got like six inches on you," I yelled back.

"I'm sure I've got a dress that will . . . yes, this will work quite nicely!"

She reappeared, holding up a cream-colored linen dress that looked long enough to hit my ankles. "I kept meaning to hem it. I must have been saving it for you!"

It was quite pretty, and simple and outdoor-festival-appropriate. More importantly, I didn't have any fight left in me. I groaned. "Fine. I'll try it."

She squealed, and I put my fingers in my ears.

I replaced my sports bra with a dainty little thing that gave me a significantly more feminine shape. Evie had ordered it online after she'd "properly measured" me. I slipped the dress on and stood in front of the bathroom mirror. It was pretty, and it made me look like someone I used to be—someone who believed she was attractive but didn't care that much about it. Someone who was happy to show the world that she was feminine and strong. I missed that girl.

Evie opened the bathroom door, her eyes wide. "Yes, queen!"

I examined the thin straps supporting the material that dipped low between my breasts. My chest was still milky white because my tees always covered me. The dress came in at the waist, then flowed over my hips, hitting my ankles with a light ruffle. "I think it's too much."

"No. It's perfect. It's elegant, and it suits you."

I turned away from the mirror. "I don't want to look at myself anymore."

Evie completed the look with a swipe of mascara and a braid that was significantly more whimsical than my typical utilitarian one. She handed me the only pair of sandals I had left. I'd destroyed the last pair during my little jog.

"Don't ruin these," she warned me.

As we walked back into town, it wasn't lost on me that I was a thirty-one-year-old woman who hadn't worn a dress in more than a decade. And while that wasn't anything by itself—plenty of women didn't subscribe to traditional feminine styles—I used to. And I'd given it up. My mind wandered to my mother.

It was the loveliest dress I'd ever put on. Like a bluebell. I watched myself in the mirror, the taffeta and tulle giving it a princess appearance, making me look much younger than my nearly sixteen years. I walked down the hall in my bare feet to show Mother. Me in pretty dresses always cheered her up.

I slid into the living room, where she stood with a woman looking at an oversized book with carpet samples.

"Darling," she called. "Come help me pick out a color for my wardrobe."

I walked closer, slowly swinging my hips so the dress would move and she'd notice.

"You have a lovely daughter," the woman said, sipping the wine my mother had poured for them.

Mother beamed. "Yes, I think so." Her warm smile made me proud. "Which one, sweetie?"

She flipped the thick pages, and I ran my hands along the softness of the samples. "The cream one. It's like your skin and won't clash with the clothes you try on."

She laughed. "Of course, what was I thinking?" she said, her voice slurred with a tone of pretend cheer.

The woman smiled and closed the book. "I'll get it ordered right away."

"Thanks, Janette."

Janette looked at me. "That's about the prettiest dress I've ever seen."

Mother took notice, and I curtsied.

After the woman left, Mother braided my hair, and our conversation returned to the same topic that had dominated in recent weeks, my sweet sixteen party. I closed my eyes at the lull of her soft hands in my hair.

"Should I wear this dress?"

She tied my braid and turned me around, her eyes taking mine in, never fully satisfied by what she saw.

"You should cut your hair—I see the damage at the ends. The swimming maybe."

I nodded and she examined the dress.

"This is a dress for a child, Bernadette. You are becoming a woman. You'll wear a dress fit for a woman. I remember I was wearing a deep gray silk evening gown when I met your father. He said I was the most—" She swallowed and turned away.

"We'll go shopping for the perfect dress," I assured her, eager to distract her, to keep her mind on something, anything but my father. But she stood and went into the kitchen. She refilled her wine, a glass of which seemed ever present since my father had died months before. She took a generous sip and disappeared into her room.

The party was in full swing when we arrived, the sun setting in the distance. Locals and tourists danced in the street, and the band was decent, playing their own version of some classics. Evie and I sipped our drinks as we watched the revelry.

Suddenly, a man stood in front of me. He couldn't have been more than twenty-five, with smooth dark skin and short hair with perfect lines. His smile was dominant on his face, both eager and timid.

"I'd love to dance with the most beautiful girl at the party," he said.

I started to laugh, but stopped when I realized he wasn't joking. "Oh, I'm not planning to dance tonight."

"Yes, she is." Evie pushed me forward, and the guy gripped my hand gently.

I gave him a tentative smile, reluctantly following him to the dance floor as a slow song began. He stopped at the center of the floor and placed a hand at my waist, looked me in the eye, and started to count.

It had been a while, but this kind of dancing is like riding a bike. I recalled the simple steps that my mother had drilled into my head before my sweet sixteen party. It all came rushing back as he counted out his steps. He was concentrating hard, staring at his feet with his hand limp at my side.

"Sorry, I'm not a great dancer," he said.

I smiled. "It's fine. Thanks for asking me to dance. I'm Birdie."

He glanced at my face and beamed. "You're the prettiest girl here, Birdie. I'm Byron."

"I'm a little old to classify as a girl, Byron, but I'll take it as a compliment. Thank you."

We fell quiet as he continued to count in a whisper. I let him lead as he stared down, and I found myself looking at the other dancers, some fluid, some as awkward as we were. I anxiously surveyed the crowd for the idiots from the afternoon. I wouldn't let them chase me away, but I really didn't want a scene either.

Byron chanced looking up and stepped on my foot. "Sorry."

"No problem. Do you want to call it?"

"No," he insisted.

I nodded, and we continued to waltz.

I felt eyes on me, a heavy gaze. Aiden stood next to Evie and Yash, his body turned toward them, his eyes fixed on me. He didn't bother to look away when I caught him watching me. I gave a self-deprecating eye roll as a hello, hoping he'd forget about my outburst earlier. But he didn't respond. He simply stared intently. I creased my brow, asking silently if there was a problem, but still he didn't respond to me, didn't look away . . . until he did. And then he sauntered off and didn't look back.

When the song ended, I thanked Byron for the dance and declined another. He was disappointed, though he accepted politely.

I found my way back to Evie, who was wrapped in Yash's embrace.

"Our friend Birdie, the cougar," Yash teased.

"He wasn't that young. And more importantly, I'm not that old!"

"He's twenty."

"No!"

"Yep. I work with his grandfather at the clinic."

"Jeez, I guess I am that old."

Yash laughed, then stopped as his gaze landed on something. "Uh-oh. Incoming."

I followed his attention to find Aiden talking to a woman. A very tall, thin, beautiful woman who looked to be hanging on his every word. He leaned in to say something, and she laughed a lovely feminine laugh, and I suddenly felt like an imposter in my pretty cream linen dress. Then I felt angry at myself for letting the presence of her make me feel that way.

When they moved onto the dance floor, my stomach sank. I forced myself to perk up and pushed aside the silly notion that I ever had a chance with Aiden Anders.

"She's just a friend," Evie whispered in my ear.

I turned to glare at her for the implication, her face telling me not to bother.

"I don't care, really."

"Okay," she said, her face saying the opposite was true.

"They are a nice-looking couple," I offered, unable to hide the hint of bitterness.

"She wants to be a couple. But he's always kept it strictly friendly."

"It's none of my business." I turned away. "I'm tired. I think I'm going to head home."

Evie's face fell. "Stay and have some fun," she pleaded. "Come dance with me."

"I'm really tired."

"You are not!" She grabbed my hand and we headed to the dance floor and began moving to the up-tempo song. Yash joined us after a bit, dancing with both of us. We jumped around and laughed out loud as they began a rendition of OutKast's "Roses." I found myself letting go, falling into the musical chaos, Evie's lightness contagious as ever.

And I wasn't alone. I had two people with me, as ridiculous as I was. Yash was doing some version of a robot and Evie the running man. As the song neared the end, Yash disappeared and returned with three bottles of water as a slow song began to play. I recognized the lyrics. The band's singer was no Adele, but she wasn't too shabby either.

Yash looked over my shoulder, then grabbed Evie with his free hand and pulled her into an embrace. I nodded, letting them have this one, but they were both looking over my shoulder. Just as I turned to go find a table, I ran smack-dab into Aiden's hard chest.

"Bernadette," he crooned as his hand snaked around my waist, holding me firmly in place. I looked up as he grabbed my water and downed it before passing the empty bottle to someone walking by. The guy gave Aiden a funny look but took it anyway.

"I don't think he's a server," I said.

"Don't care," he replied, placing my hands against his shoulders, keeping me close as he wrapped his hands around my waist.

"Aiden," I whispered, as his fresh shower scent reached my nose. He always smelled so good. "You don't have to ask me to dance, just because—"

"I didn't ask," he said, guiding my movement. I meant to protest, but I couldn't find the will. We danced awhile in silence before he whispered close to my ear, "You look like a wet dream, Bernadette."

I grinned as my body reacted to the statement, my nipples pebbling against his chest, my cheeks glowing red. "This old thing?"

He chuckled. "You were keeping it hidden and brought it out to impress that kid over there?"

I pinched the shoulder my hand rested on, getting nothing but hard muscle. "I didn't know he was twenty."

"Is he that old?"

"Shut up."

He leaned back to meet my eyes and said, "I kind of wanted to punch that kid for getting to you first. That's what you do to me."

"You snooze, you lose. I'm taken now, officially."

His grip on my waist tightened for a moment, before relaxing. "I don't think so."

Dancing with Aiden wasn't anything like dancing with Byron. Aiden's grip was confident, powerful. He could dance without thought. His strong hands led me where he wanted me. It was too easy to just relax into it. The smell of clean laundry and sawdust filled my nostrils as I laid my head against his chest.

"The dress isn't really me," I said. "I don't feel like I can curse in it."

"You can definitely curse in this dress. It's positively sinful. Try it."

I smiled against his shoulder and uttered, "Cum-licking fuckwad."

I felt his grin as he pressed his chin against my forehead. "See, still you."

I laughed, pressing closer to him. His hand descended along my back, caressing the rim of my panties with his pinky. It was really getting warm out.

"You're making the rounds tonight, I see."

I felt his quiet chuckle against my body. "You're jealous."

"You wish," I replied unconvincingly.

"It's okay; you don't have to admit it."

I pulled back, putting on my defensive mask. "There's nothing to admit other than you have an ego that needs a reality check."

"Baby." I may have broken a sweat the way he said it. "I see you. I see the way you look at me. You're half in love already."

I wanted to run, because his words were meant to tease, but I also felt the truth of them, and fuck if that didn't confuse me. Was I that transparent?

"Did you wear this dress for me? So I could imagine removing it later when we're alone?"

The thought went straight to my penis-crushing vag. "Wow, you are delusional. It's not an attractive trait, you know. You'll never get a girl if you can't grasp reality."

He laughed and cinched my waist back into his embrace, continuing to move with me. I followed his steps, my mind fighting my libido. I loved being lost in him, letting him pull me under, to a place I didn't need to pretend, to think. I loved being wrapped inside him, away from everything else.

"You like me," he whispered. "I like that you do."

"I don't." My words lacked sincerity.

His hand gripped my neck gently, pulling our bodies flush, his breath at my ear and his large fingers moving softly along the back of my neck.

"I think you do."

My body lit up everywhere he touched as dancers moved around us, oblivious to my pounding chest.

"I like you back. In fact, I'd like very much to fuck you tonight, Bernadette." He whispered the words directly into my ear, without chance that anyone would overhear. "I'd like to fuck you the way you deserve to be fucked."

I may have had a mini orgasm at his words.

Part of me felt ridiculous, like I should push him away and slap his face for speaking that way. The other half? The *winning* half wanted to melt into him, grip his shirt, and drag him out of there. Something about Aiden made me trust him, want him. Who knew grumpy, kind Aiden had such a vulgar side? He was right. I liked him. Everything about him, obviously. I liked him saying that to me. I liked what it promised, the way it made me feel, the way my base instincts emerged. I believed he was very capable of what he promised, and I wanted very much to be wanted by this man.

When he looked down at me, waiting for a response, his eyes holding a fraction of self-doubt as I stared back up at him, something inside me slipped. This was something I'd let myself fantasize about. But it wasn't real life. Because I was the Chicago Bird. I was always in control; lives depended on it. Could I give in to this for a night and regain my control tomorrow? Could I keep my secret from him long enough to have a fling? How mad would he be when he inevitably found out about me? Would the perfect, raspy sound of lust in his voice turn into disgust, to words of regret? Would I see familiar relief in his face when I walked away? Was that inevitability worth the fun we could have until then? Was I a terrible person for letting it happen, knowing he'd regret it later?

Yes.

I pushed away and looked him in the eye, my face clear of any indecision. "I can't."

His face twisted, disappointed, maybe hurt, a little confused. I couldn't tell exactly because I walked away—again.

———

THE MOON WAS BRIGHT as I meandered back to the cottage, embarrassment and regret warring for their proper place in the forefront of my mind. Ultimately, I settled on simply wishing my life was different, wishing *I* was different, or the world was, and remembering why, for me, it wasn't.

I rubbed the skin beneath the ankle monitor for the millionth time, wondering if it would be there forever. Nick watched me from across the room.

I smiled, and he smiled back. But none of his smiles felt real anymore, and it made me wonder if they ever had been. More than a year apart was a long time, and the weeks since had been, to put it lightly, strained.

"I have a dress fitting tomorrow."

He nodded as he stared at his phone.

"Want to come? I don't care if you see the dress before. I'm not that traditional. It'll be fun."

He glanced at me, but too quickly his attention returned to the phone. "You'll care the day of. Besides, I have work."

"Okay." I glanced down at the monitor again, wondering if he was just over the wedding planning. I rubbed my ankle. "I really hope I'm not wearing this on our wedding day."

He set his phone down, annoyed. It seemed no matter what I did these days, I annoyed Nick. He used to think that I was charming, that things I said were amusing. But I couldn't do anything right anymore. I even tried not to use my abilities in front of him. It seemed to throw off his mood. I figured it would just take time.

"Not everything in the world is about you, Birdie."

"I'm sorry?"

"Ugh, never mind," he said as he picked up his phone.

"I wasn't aware I made everything about me. I . . . I know I talk a lot about the powers and the monitoring, but I—it's kind of a big fucking deal, what has happened to my life."

"That's another thing." Phone down. "Since when do you curse like a sailor? You used to be sweet, and now it's like fucking this and fucking that. It's jarring."

"Seriously?"

"It's not feminine."

"You're kidding, right? You know I spent a year in a government facility that was just a little bit too much like prison, right?"

He huffed and shook his head in frustration. "It's not just the cursing. It's all of it. It's a lot to take."

"What exactly are you referring to?"

Nick and I had been together four years, including the year I'd been away. I'd never asked him how he'd spent his time while we'd been sepa-rated. Something told me I didn't want to know.

"Listen, Birdie," Nick started, his hand in his hair, his face pained. "I wonder if getting married right now is what's best for us."

"What? Why?" I said, not feeling the surprise my words conveyed.

"Maybe we should wait until all of this calms down, until you are back to normal, and we both finish college."

I'd considered going back to college, but I also had an internship of sorts waiting for me in Chicago.

"Oh my God. You don't want to marry me."

"That's not what I said. I just . . ."

"I'm never going to go back to normal, Nick. This is my normal. I can't go backward. I'm not sure there won't be even more changes." I paused and saw he had his head in his hands, pulling his hair, letting out a groan. "Do you not want to go forward with me?"

His face said it all. "Birdie, I feel . . . I don't know. I'm not feeling it with you lately. Maybe it's a rough patch, but I don't know."

"You aren't attracted to me anymore."

"Oh for God's sake, Birdie."

"It's true, isn't it? So what is it? Is it the monitor? Is it all the attention supers are getting? Are you jealous?"

"Come on, Birdie, don't be ridiculous. I'm not jealous. I just can't bring myself—" He stopped. Whatever he was going to say was bad, because his face made his intention clear. He wanted out.

I'd seen it coming. I'd thought it might pass, that maybe it was us getting used to a new normal. But I wasn't surprised.

"You're a coward."

He stood up. "That's rich. Is it cowardly that I've stayed with you through all of this? Everyone around me wonders why I'm even with you anymore, asks me what it's like to be engaged to a freak. Asks if you're now the one wearing the pants. It's fucking emasculating. I stayed because I care about you. But I'm sorry, Birdie, I can't . . ."

"Say it. Let's just put all our cards on the table. Say it. Just say it!"

"I'm not attracted to you, okay?" he burst forth. "You used to be sweet. But you've turned into a . . . something else. And the cursing and . . . it's like you're just not feminine anymore."

I'd known the changes had been difficult for him, but this hadn't occurred to me, not in this context. His words lodged in my brain and set up residence.

"I didn't mean it like it sounded."

"I didn't ask for any of this. It happened to me. And from the time you realized I'd be stronger than you, that I'd have these abilities you don't have, you checked out. You loved the idea of a woman to stand beside you, but you *never loved me. I can't change back, and I'm not even sure I want to. You've felt this way for well over a year, and now you're making this my fault. I'm not feminine? Well, seems to me you're not much of a man."*

Anger was written all over his face. "It takes a real woman to know one. And I'll move on and find just that. No man wants what you are now, whatever that is."

Silence descended, and I felt tears welling up, but I shoved them back. Permanently. Nick saw my face, his anger quickly fading. He reached out, saying my name, and I pushed his hand away.

Four years with someone, and this was what was left. He was disgusted with me.

"I can't change how I feel," he said, "but I am sorry."

He didn't look sorry, though. He looked relieved to have finally gotten the words out. It was the same look of relief my mother had on her face when the feds had escorted me from her home.

And what was there to say to that?

There was nothing left. I was on my own. I'd always be on my own. The realization settled into my chest like a winter's cold that constricted the lungs. And when I walked out the door, I left behind everything I was before.

18

TWO MORE DAYS OF AVOIDING the life I'd left behind. And two more days not trying to salvage the one in front of me. Two more days of avoiding Aiden.

I'd ditched a lunch with Evie, Yash, and Aiden, saying I didn't feel well. And I didn't. I felt embarrassed. I felt confused. I felt like a coward.

Instead, I went on a date. A simple way to pretend I was moving on, getting happy, working on myself. It was another disaster.

"Don't you think strong women can be feminine?"

"Of course."

"I mean, it shouldn't be that complicated. I'm just a woman, a person same as you. Just because I can lift a car and you can't—is that reason enough to crush attraction? What is it with men anyway?"

"I'm not sure I . . ."

"Never mind. You don't want to get mixed up with me. I'm not a good influence. I have a sailor's vocabulary. Wait. Does a sailor have a bad vocabulary? Why did they get that reputation? Does every sailor curse? I doubt it. We should really be more sensitive to sailors."

Poor, unassuming single dad.

Okay, I'd had a few drinks. In my defense, I had been trying to drown out the sound of Aiden in my ear. The way he'd said he wanted to fuck me. I'd been strung high and tight since then, and I hated that I wanted to take back what I'd said and climb him like a tree and ask him to take me home and keep me there until I couldn't walk.

At some point, my poor date who hadn't gotten a word in had simply disappeared. Good for him. Right choice.

I took my slightly inebriated ass to the street and headed home.

I pouted as I walked along the beach back to the cottage, avoiding onlookers and feeling ridiculous in a dress I'd picked up the day before on a shopping trip with Evie.

Why do I bother with these dates? I thought as I trudged through the sand. I was who I was. I was all I needed.

Right then and there, I decided I wouldn't do it anymore. I was done. Doctor Evans could think of something else for me to do, some other way to get to know myself. This wasn't working. I didn't want to date. I didn't want to be reminded time and time again that I wasn't woman enough for anyone.

I needed to drink myself into oblivion and wake up tomorrow and go back to Chicago, get back to where I was comfortable, where I belonged. If Doctor Evans wouldn't let me go back to work, I'd drive back and forth for my sessions, avoiding the Grove Cottages.

But the idea of leaving made my stomach turn. Picturing Friday nights without family dinners, not waking up to the lake or seeing Aiden gather trash in the mornings, not having breakfast with Evie and cleaning the cottages listening to nineties rock. What would I do without it? Go back to my apartment, wander the city looking for trouble?

"Bernadette?"

I stalked toward the front door, ignoring the sound of my name coming from next door.

"Bowden!" he said firmly as he stepped onto the porch behind me. I kept my head turned, fumbling with the key. The last thing I needed was for Aiden to see me cry.

"Dammit, Bernadette, hold on."

Just as I unlocked the door, his hand landed on my elbow and he turned me toward him.

"Hey. What . . ." He saw the tears and his brows drew in. "What happened?"

"Nothing," I mumbled.

"Tell me," he demanded in a low tone. "You had a date?"

I nodded, refusing to look him in the eye.

"Tell. Me," he said through gritted teeth.

"Forget it. It was nothing. It's me. It's always me. I just can't do this anymore. It's too hard."

"So don't do it. Quit," he said, his hands on either side of my face, his thumbs trailing over my cheeks, taking my stupid tears with them. I looked up at his perfectly chiseled jaw.

"I can't just quit. My job depends on it."

"You don't have to keep dating to keep your job. It's just an exercise. You can say no. Take some time for yourself. Or . . ."

"Or what?"

"Or date me."

I grew still, my tears forgetting to fall. "What?"

He shrugged, his eyes on mine, his hands keeping me inches from him. "Date me."

My eyes crinkled, "Are you asking me out?"

"No. You made it clear the other night that you're not interested. I can take a hint."

All of a sudden, I wanted to cry harder.

"What I am saying is you can date me so you don't have to date anyone else. Just for Evans."

"Oh." I let my breath out. For a minute, with his rough hands on my face, I'd let myself think maybe I could. "You don't have to do that. I'll tell Evans I need to slow down on the dating thing. I'm sure she'll give me something else to do. She's very reasonable," I insisted without conviction.

His hands were warm, his thumbs still stroking my cheeks. His gaze moved to my lips, and my breath was stolen again.

"Aiden?"

"Yes."

"What are you doing?"

"Did you mean what you said? That you don't want anything with me? This is the last time I'll ask, Bernadette. So you'd better tell me the truth this time."

"No." It came out in a rush, before I could think about it and inevitably say something else. I was fucking tired of thinking everything over, arriving at the worst possible outcome to every situation.

He smiled knowingly. "You look beautiful, Bernadette." His body was warm, and I leaned in.

"Okay," I whispered without thought, our lips a hair apart, my legs weak.

"But I still like your ass better in jeans."

"Okay." His lips met mine ever so lightly and my body stilled, his touch the only sensation registering as my mind fell quiet.

Then headlights were shining on us. A car pulled into the reserved spots next to the reception booth. The lights dimmed, and the car doors opened.

Aiden pulled away slowly, his eyes on me. Then he dropped my face and stepped back, our gazes turning to find Evie and Yash heading toward us.

"Birdie!" she called, seemingly oblivious to what they'd happened upon.

She stepped onto the porch. "How was the date?" A frown emerged. "You're home early. What happened?"

"Nothing, I'm fine."

"You were crying. Your mascara's all mussed."

I wiped my face with my forearm. "Really, it's all good. It just wasn't a love connection, and I—" I didn't say more because Aiden was still there, and his gaze was intent on me. I turned to Yash, who, from the look on his face, had clearly seen more than Evie had, before returning my attention to Evie.

"Let's watch romcoms and curse men for the rest of the night." Evie rubbed my shoulder.

"Hey," Yash objected.

"Sorry, babe," Evie replied, giving him a sympathetic glance before turning back to me. "We'll curse all men but Yash."

Aiden cleared his throat.

"Geez, sensitive," Evie said. "All men but Yash and Aiden."

I couldn't keep my eyes from Aiden. As Evie's gaze followed my eyes to her brother, her curiosity piqued. I tried to push him from my mind, my lips still feeling the soft pressure of his. It had absolutely been the most perfect almost-kiss.

"Earth to Birdie!" Evie finally said.

"That sounds perfect!" I said too eagerly as I fled into the house, tearing my eyes from the lips that had just been on mine.

———

"YASH WANTS TO HAVE SEX," Evie said as she sat across from me on the sofa, sipping tea.

"What? You're not having . . . I just assumed." I tucked my feet up under me.

"I know, I talk a good game. And we're together all the time. We act like a married couple. But we haven't crossed that line, not since before we divorced, not since before my surgery."

"Wow. And Yash?"

"He hasn't, since the woman."

"You believe him?"

"Yes, of course; he's never lied to me. Not that it should matter if he did. But he's been more than patient, and I want to as much as he does."

"So what's holding you back?"

"That's just it. There's nothing. Except . . ."

I didn't reply, letting her find her words.

"The image of him with another woman pops into my head every time we get close," she spat out, then recoiled.

"Oh."

"What kind of fucked up mess is that? When I'm with him, and we're getting close, I'm imagining him with another woman. And not in the sexy way, but in the . . ."

"What way, Evie?" I didn't need the answer, but she needed to say it.

"In the she's a whole woman kind of way. In the I'm not good enough anymore kind of way." Her eyes filled with tears. "I thought I'd gotten over this."

"Oh, Evie," I said, leaning forward and grabbing her ankle in my hand. "You must know that's ridiculous. Not that you feel it, but that he would ever want someone else. I've never seen a man so engrossed in a woman."

"I know! And I know he loves me. I mean, how could he not—I've got perfect fake boobs now."

We both laughed.

"But I still feel less than. He's seen me when I had no breasts, when I was riddled with cancer and never felt less like a whole person. I think that's what plagues me, that he might still see me that way when we're together."

Suddenly, bright, fun, brave Evie wasn't so different than me. She was fighting an internal battle of what being female meant. "Maybe don't fight it. Maybe let the thoughts and images come, and maybe tell him the truth. Then see that he isn't there with her—and never was in the way he is with you. You don't need to chase her away—you need to see yourself the way you are. Strong and beautiful. Fierce."

She nodded, deep in thought. "If the whole super thing doesn't work out, you have a lot of promise as a headshrinker."

I sat up straighter. "I'll bill you."

She smiled. "What about you? The dates are still duds?"

"I'm not meant to date, I think."

"That's stupid. How are you going to find a mate if you don't date?"

"Evie. Not everyone is meant to have a mate."

"True. But you're not one of those people."

"How do you know?"

"Because . . ." She paused to pick up a handful of popcorn, filling her mouth full while the TV played in the background. "I just know."

I smiled with a shake of my head, wondering if Evie truly saw something I didn't. "I'm glad I met you, Evie. I'm not sure where I'd be this summer if I hadn't. I probably would have adopted forty-two cats, given up on showering, and slipped into a diet of HoHos and vodka in my studio apartment."

She nodded and said, "That sounds about right."

"You're the first person I've ever met who's accepted every part of me and stuck around. The first person to—"

"Love you?" she asked, her eyes welling with tears when I nodded. "That's the saddest and most wonderful thing I've ever heard."

I laughed in an effort not to cry. "I love you, too, Evie."

"And I can't remember having so much fun with anyone."

"Wow, okay," I replied. "I've never been described as fun, even before the powers."

"Well, maybe you just hadn't found your pack."

"Is that what we are?"

"Obviously. Me and Yash. You and Aiden. They are besties; we are besties."

"Wait. Me and Aiden?"

"Oh come on, Birdie—I'm not blind. There's something there."

"Yeah, a pissing contest," I insisted.

She beamed, her face full of mischief. "It's the best kind of foreplay."

"No, no. No. There can't be anything." Was I trying to convince myself? "He doesn't know about me."

"Your abilities? So what? It's not that big a deal."

"It is," I assured her. "It changes things."

"So you admit something is going on, then?"

"We flirt," I said dismissively.

"You can lie to yourself, but I know the truth. You like him. He likes you."

I stuffed my mouth with a large handful of popcorn, a few kernels falling in my lap.

"I've never seen him look at anyone the way he looks at you."

"Like what?" I couldn't resist asking.

"Like he wants to eat you alive."

"Yes. I'm incredibly sexy," I said, popcorn falling from my over-full mouth.

"Ha-ha. A sister knows these things," she said, eyebrows wiggling.

I swallowed. "It's just flirting," I said. I knew it was turning into more for me, wanting it to be more for him—but I was terrified to voice it. "It would end," I told her. "And when it did, I'd be all weird, and I don't want to risk our friendship. Please, let's drop it."

She wanted to probe; it was clear by the look on her face. But the look on mine told her to drop it.

"Okay, Birdie. For now."

19

DAY HAD YET TO BREAK as I lay in bed, tossing and turning, wanting to sleep, unable to shut my brain off—the lingering presence of Aiden's body close to mine, his breath on my cheek, his lips a whisper away. I was a live wire. I could have reached my hand down and taken care of it, but that wasn't what my body craved, so I didn't bother. With a frustrated sigh, I threw my covers off, brushed my teeth, and went to the kitchen to start the coffee. I situated myself at the counter as I stared out the window at the beach, the soft rumble of the coffee maker a welcome sound as dawn shimmered over the waters of Lake Michigan.

As though my mind conjured him up, Aiden appeared on the beach, walking with his trash bag and poke stick. I couldn't help but smile at the sight of him, so intent on his morning ritual, alone on the beach before the guests woke up.

I didn't give it another thought. I filled two mugs and stepped outside in my sleep shorts and tank top. I caught up with him a ways down the beach, a hesitant smile on my face as he turned in my direction.

"You shouldn't sneak up on people in the near dark. You're likely to get poked like a piece of trash," he said thrusting his stick in my general direction.

"Aiden, I didn't know you cared," I retorted as I offered him the coffee.

"Smart-ass." He took the cup and sipped. "Thanks for this, but you're going to have to walk with me and hold on to it so I can finish the job." He lifted the trash bag.

"That was the plan," I replied with a grin, happy he wanted me to stay.

His eyes were soft as he handed the mug back to me. He poked a chip bag from the sand.

"How is it today?"

"Not too bad," he said, nodding at his nearly empty trash bag, "but anything is too much."

"Fucking savages," we said in unison. I laughed, and he smiled. I once again committed the sight to memory. Maybe I *was* a morning person if this was what the morning brought.

"I wanted to talk about yesterday," I said.

"Figured that was why you were out here," he said and grabbed a bottle cap, tossing it in the bag, glancing at my bare legs before returning his eyes to the beach.

This was going to be harder than I thought.

"I'm not sure if you were feeling sorry for me, or being nice for Evie's sake, but I wanted to say thanks for your . . . kindness yesterday. But you really don't have to date me."

When he didn't respond, I stupidly filled the silence. "I appreciate the offer. And part of me likes the prospect of it, but we don't really know each other that well, and I'll be leaving by the end of the summer, and a pity date, while kind, isn't going to fix my problems."

We continued in silence. With my bare feet sinking into the sand and two coffees in hand, I fell in behind him, unable to see his face. I wondered if I should turn back. But even if he didn't speak to me, I didn't want to be anywhere else but walking with Aiden on the beach, picking up trash as the sun rose on a new day.

When we reached the end of the cottages, he set the bag on the sand and the poke stick on top of it to keep it from blowing in the breeze. He turned and looked at me for the first time since I'd rattled on. His bare feet took a step toward me, his body humming with energy, imposing even in board shorts and a T-shirt that hugged his broad shoulders. Then he took another step, and I moved backward with the force of his stare. His hand reached behind his shoulder and pulled his shirt over his head, displaying a perfectly sculpted bronzed chest.

"What are you doing?" I asked as he took yet another step.

Then he smiled, the kind of smile that promised something, but I had no clue what. He dropped the T-shirt on the sand and took the last few strides toward me. He suddenly took the mugs from my hand and dropped them as well. Before I could react, I was over his shoulder, my face staring at his lower back as he strode into the waves of Lake Michigan's cool July water.

"Aiden!" I screamed once, too shocked to find additional words. Then his hands were at my waist, and I was in the air for a split second before I hit the waves.

My feet flailed for the bottom, but before I found it, I was drawn up into his warm chest, my arms instinctively wrapping around his neck as he continued walking deeper into the water, settling in around mid-chest. I clung to him as one hand pressed into my low back, the other on my ass, encouraging my legs around his waist. When he had me where he wanted me, he dipped himself under the water, taking me with him. Emerging, he brushed his hair from his face before doing the same to mine.

"I don't think—" I started when he interrupted me.

"Don't think. You'll ruin it."

Before I could say a word, he leaned down and pressed his mouth to mine. He held it there, warm and soft, before his lips began to move, encouraging mine to do the same. Shock made me slow to respond, but my body clearly wanted what he was offering because a moment later his tongue was in my mouth, dancing perfectly with my own, and I was pulling myself up, climbing him like the wall of a man he was. His hands ran up and down the outside of my tank top and over my ass. Our mouths sparred for control, out in the cold water of Lake Michigan before the rest of the world woke for the day.

But too quickly, he pulled away from me. "I don't do pity dates," he growled before he returned to my mouth with a guttural groan that had me pressing closer for warmth of all kinds. We got lost in each other out there as the rest of the world floated away, unable to touch us. Where we were weightless and the strength of the waves was the only force that mattered, and it pushed us together. No thinking.

"Let's get you warm," he said when I shivered, breaking our kiss. But I'm not sure it was the cold that made me shiver. Nonetheless, he started back toward shore with me still wrapped around his midsection. I'd never in my adult life felt more cared for than I did with that one simple gesture. I could have stayed in that water with Aiden forever.

As the water dipped below his knees, I unwrapped my legs and let them drop to the rocky sand below, wondering what would happen next. Was he going to go home now? Back to his cottage and me to mine? What did the kiss mean?

But he didn't let me get far, because he grabbed my hand as we walked up the sand into the cool morning air. This time I did shiver with the absence of him. He picked up his dry shirt from the sand and told me to remove my wet tank top.

When I hesitated, he turned me so my back was to him. He lifted the drenched tank top, exposing a thin bralette I'd slept in, one that left nothing to the imagination, and pulled his dry shirt over my head.

I turned around to see him twisting the water from my tank before he handed it back to me. He picked up the mugs, dumping any remaining coffee and sand. He retrieved his trash bag and poke stick and maneuvered it all with one arm, leaving a hand free to grab hold of mine as we walked purposefully back to our cottages.

I prepared myself for the worst, his silence leaving too many unanswered questions. I felt helpless in this scenario, knowing he had all the power with his next words. Because the truth was I had a massive crush on Aiden Anders, the kind of crush that turned into more, and I had no idea how to handle such a thing because I'd never felt so helpless against this kind of desire.

Then my wispy feelings of romance fell into a well of anguish and flowed into a sea of resentment. How dare he make me feel so powerless, so open to the whims of how someone else felt about me. No, I couldn't let this happen. Aiden wasn't interested in dating me long term. Not really. Maybe he wanted a fling, and with someone else that could have been fun. But already I knew I'd be left demolished by his affection when it eventually was taken away.

Escorting me to my cottage, he opened the door and nudged me inside.

"Go warm up," he said softly as he handed me the mugs and placed his hand on my arm, rubbing it up and down as though to warm me. I realized he was leaving me with his T-shirt. "I'll be back in fifteen for fresh coffee, and we'll talk."

I stood there dumbfounded. He dropped his hand, but his eyes didn't leave me. "I'm not a whim kind of person, Bernadette."

I loved how he said my full name, like a dirty secret.

"I've thought about this," he said as he leaned against my door jamb, "a lot. Since that day in Evans's office when you manhandled me with your eyes."

"I never."

Then he kissed me again, pressing his lips to the side of my mouth, his body a whisper away from mine. "I won't hurt you, Birdie. But you're gonna have to let me in. You think you can do that?"

His eyes were intent, waiting for something from me. But I needed a minute. "I . . . I don't know what's going on."

"You're cute when you're turned on." He was still smiling at me.

My eyes went wide as he reached behind me and pulled the door shut, leaving me alone inside the cottage door.

But my terrified euphoria was cut short at the shrill sound coming behind me.

"Holy shit buckets! What did I just witness?" followed by a deeper familiar tone that held a hint of a smile. "Well, it's about damn time."

—

I KNEW I NEEDED to tell Aiden the truth if anything was going to happen between us. But I also knew the truth would end anything before it began. That would be it. So maybe there was no point in telling him.

Aiden was a little bit comfortable, a little bit sweet, and a whole lot dangerous. He made me feel like I was someone completely different than who I was, and I didn't want it to stop. I still had more than seven weeks left of my hiatus from life. Seven weeks where I wasn't the Chicago Bird, just Birdie.

Evie, after squealing in excitement about how we could really be sisters, finally, at the behest of Yash, went to town for breakfast, leaving me alone to talk to Aiden. True to his word, Aiden returned fifteen minutes later, and I had fresh coffee brewing.

His knock at the door had me checking myself. I'd put on dry clothes—jeans and a fresh tank top I'd picked up in town because Evie had told me my farmer's tan was out of control. I opened the door to an already smirking Aiden.

"Hi there," he said.

"Hello," I responded, nervous as hell, yet very happy to see him standing on my doorstep.

"You look like you're going to puke."

Suddenly I wasn't nervous. This was just Aiden. "And you look like a prick."

His smirk turned to a full grin, and I wanted to kiss him again. Instead, I turned around with a huff, and he followed me inside. I sat at the counter and picked up my coffee, taking a sip.

"Got one for me?"

"I'm off duty."

He chuckled, and I waited until his back was turned before I smiled. I leaned forward onto the counter, watching intently as Aiden poured his coffee.

He took a drink, then stalked around the counter. I kept my face expressionless until he stood towering over me, taking the coffee from my hands and placing it on the counter. "We've spilled enough coffee, I think." Then his calloused hands were on my face, his touch gentle and warm. "We need to talk."

No talking, please. "Okay."

"But," he said and pressed into me, my lower back hitting the counter, "maybe we should do this first." His hands gripped my waist and easily lifted me to the counter. One hand returned to my neck as the other wrapped around my waist, bringing us flush when he kissed me. It was slow and exploring, and I let him go where he wanted, completely open to him, falling deep into a place I feared I couldn't emerge from even if I wanted to. He kissed me like he knew everything about me, like he had all the time in the world, working me over with his perfect mouth.

"There. That should do it," he said, stepping back.

I wanted to whimper at his release. "Do what?"

"Get you relaxed enough for this conversation."

I tensed, though not on purpose.

He shook his head with a slight smile before his mouth was back, and I melted into him again. "I'd like to date you, Bernadette Bowden. Not because of my sister or doing you any favors. My reasons are purely selfish."

"I don't—"

"I wasn't finished."

I closed my mouth.

"I'd like us to date because you interest me in every way a woman can interest a man. I like you. I like your mouth. The way it sounds and the way it tastes and even the ridiculous words that come out of it. I'd like a chance to explore the other parts of you. I have a feeling I'll like those as well."

"I'm only here for a few more weeks." I'd said the words because they were what I'd practiced, but my brain was still soaking in his words about my mouth and exploring other parts.

"Well, let's take it one day at a time, shall we?"

"I can't."

His face turned darker. "Why?"

"We don't really know each other."

"That's what dating is—getting to know someone."

"In seven weeks, I'm going back to Chicago. I can't have any loose ends here. I can't do a relationship."

His brows cinched together and he looked behind me. "Fine. Seven weeks, then."

"Then we go our separate ways?" I knew it was a bad idea. No way I'd be able to spend nearly two months dating Aiden without falling for him. But right then, I didn't care. This was my excuse not to tell him the truth, because it was temporary. I just wanted to be who he thought I was. I wanted to have a fling with Aiden and forget that he'd regret it later when he inevitably found out the truth about me.

"If that's how you want it."

"That's how it *has* to be." The words tasted sour.

"Right. Well, let's not waste any time, then."

Before I could reply, his tongue was in my mouth again, and I moaned at the sudden intrusion as goose bumps broke out on my body. I wrapped my legs around him, and he pressed his pelvis between my legs, another moan escaping as I felt his arousal. At this, his kiss got dirty, sloppy, but in the best out-of-control way before he stepped back, pulling my shirt over my head. His mouth returned as he gripped the back of my bra and tugged desperately before he unclasped it. His kiss slowed as he pushed my bra from my shoulders. He pulled back to look at me.

He pinched my nipple between his fingers gently and pulled until it slipped from his grip and bounced. It was delicious, and I felt the ache between my legs grow.

"Fuck, your tits are even more perfect than I expected. I'm going to have fun with them."

I battled the instinct to withdraw, the notion of being desired so distant a memory, one I'd long buried. I found the counter behind me and leaned back on my hands, pressing my chest out in a display of pretend confidence. His smile was dark, and I instinctively knew Aiden Anders was a boob guy, and I couldn't wait to see how that would play out. He pinched both of my nipples and pulled until my body moved closer to him, the pleasure bordering on pain, and his mouth found mine as his fingers fondled me. His mouth slid to my ear and neck, then across my collarbone and to my left breast as he laid his tongue flat and licked from bottom to top. He did the same on the other side, and I ached for more, hungry for his touch. Pressure from his hands had me lying back on the counter, the cold quartz a welcome sensation on my overheating body. He looked down at me. "Bernadette, I've wanted to do this since I first saw you in these tight jeans."

He popped the button of my jeans and pulled the zipper down, sliding them down my legs as I lifted my butt, my undies following until I was completely naked in front of him. Feeling exposed, I pressed my knees together.

He smiled darkly and said, "Nuh-uh, filthy girl. I want to see if that pussy is also as pretty as I've imagined. Open."

His words were jarring, but I welcomed the shock to get out of my own head—his utter disregard for decorum turning me on more than anything else.

He pulled off his own shirt and started on his jeans as I let my legs fall open, feeling in that moment, the way he was looking at me, like I couldn't disappoint Aiden if I tried. His eyes were unmoving and his teeth were clenched under his hard mouth.

"Fuck, this clean little cunt is going to get very, very dirty."

Then he slid his fingers through my folds, bottom to top, before sucking his fingers dry. I was so close already. He could just touch me, and I'd fall apart.

Then he pulled up a bar stool and sat down, my legs spread before him. He stared at me. My face, lips, breasts, and below.

"What the fuck are you doing?" I asked him, as my self-consciousness resurfaced.

"Memorizing," he replied. Then he stood, pulling his jeans down, revealing he'd gone commando.

He slid his cock along me before he swiftly put on a condom and slipped inside. I didn't get a good look, but I felt myself stretch and fill as he whispered in my ear, "Where's that sarcastic mouth now, baby?"

Unable to find any words, I moaned or groaned or made what to my ears was a terribly unappealing sound.

"Nothing to say when you're filled up with me?" He smiled. "I like you like this. Desperate. Totally exposed for me. Taking all of me, your pussy gripping so tight."

The words and sensations made my brain fuzzy with desire. I don't know why, exactly. His dirty mouth didn't seem like something I should like or ever had before, but with Aiden . . .

But I'd not let his ego get too big. "Are you going to wax bullshit all day or are you going to fuck me?"

He laughed out loud and did just that.

20

ONE GLORIOUS ORGASM LATER, both of us breathing heavily, Aiden helped me down from the counter.

"Why don't you go get cleaned up?" he said, motioning toward the bathroom. I nodded and walked away, turning to see him in the same spot, watching me with a strange, almost content look on his face, before I closed the door behind me.

Five minutes later, I came out of the bathroom in a towel to find him waiting, one arm holding the clothes we'd been wearing. He had on his jeans and a lazy grin, but nothing else. I was relieved at the sight, having feared he'd be gone when I came out.

He leaned in to kiss my cheek and guided me into my bedroom. Placing our clothes on the chair, he stepped in front of me and slowly unrolled the towel from my chest, letting it drop to the floor, leaving me once again completely exposed to him. He reached around me and pulled open the covers in invitation. Without hesitation I jumped in and turned to watch him remove his jeans, giving me a view I'd not soon forget, before he jumped in next to me. He situated himself and pulled me close, and I found myself snuggled into his big, broad body. I closed my eyes in contentment.

Instead of examining the ways this could go bad, I let myself think of how nice it was to feel the little hairs on his chest against my cheek, the sound of his heartbeat below my ear, the smell of clean soap and sex, the feel of his arms around me. I just let myself enjoy the man next to me.

"You have the cutest orgasm sounds I've ever heard."

"What?" I shot up on my elbow, looking down at him.

"Your sounds. Part kitten, part howler monkey."

"Do you suppose it's good manners to comment on the sounds a woman makes when she's orgasming?"

He shrugged, pushing my hair back over my shoulder. "I thought we had no expectations."

I narrowed my eyes. "Well, if I had to comment on *your* sounds, I'd say it's a mix of whale and blowhard."

He pinched my naked side. "Those seem awful similar. Anyway, I like your sounds. It's you, and it's fucking sexy."

"Too late; I'm already self-conscious about it."

He growled and flipped me so I was on my back, and he crawled on top of me. Hovering, he said, "I'd like to hear them again."

"Nope, you killed the mood."

"Hmm, well," he said and positioned himself on his side next to me, his head propped on his hand. "I guess we'll just talk, then."

"Meh," I said, hiding my disappointment, but not too well apparently, judging by the wicked smile on his face.

"Tell me about your job."

"Oh." *Shit.* "I work for the city, I told you."

"In what capacity?" He pulled the covers down so my bare breasts were exposed to him, but his eyes stayed on my face, waiting for my answer.

"I coordinate on high-risk situations."

His tongue barely touched the tip of my breast before he pulled back. "Can I have an example?"

I didn't want to lie. I wanted him to keep doing what he was doing. "When there are people in trouble, I go to the site and then work to help them out."

This time his mouth closed over my nipple and he suckled lightly before he pulled back with a pop and returned his attention to my face, his eyes darker. "So you're not police or fire, but you help them help people in trouble by coordinating?"

"Yep."

"No offense, but isn't it somewhat inefficient to have a middle-woman? Why don't they just talk to each other?" Lick.

Fuck, fuck, fuck. I should have said I was at a desk.

"That's the exciting part, but that rarely happens. Mostly I'm on call, working on the boring situations. Just a regular old municipal employee."

He was back to suckling my nipple, and it was draining my concentration, sending signals straight between my legs.

"Oh God," I muttered.

He popped up, leaving my breast aching for more. "We're just talking. No sexy sounds, remember?"

I closed my mouth tightly, and he smirked as he returned to my breast and blew lightly on the nipple. My hips arched.

"Tell me about your life in Chicago."

"Nothing to tell. I work all the time and pretty much keep to myself," I said quickly, my skin tingling for more of him.

He looked at me with sad curiosity. "Why?"

"What about you, in Texas?" I asked, not wanting to get too deep into this topic, but wanting him to get deep into something entirely different.

"I guess it was mostly work, too. I like this better." His tongue found my nipple again, and the soft touches to just that one single part of my body were driving me insane. I needed his hands and his full mouth and all of him.

"You are very responsive, Bernadette. Even if you continue to evade my questions, your body responds to me in the most delicious ways, as instructed."

"As instructed?"

He nodded. "I want you on edge, ready for me. I want you wet. And all it takes is a little nipple play to get you there."

"I guess I like nipple play."

He grinned. "That makes two of us." Then he disappeared below the covers. "Tell me about one of these instances at work," he said before I felt his tongue on my clit. Soft and barely there. He groaned, and my eyes might have rolled back into my head for a second.

"Ah. I just do what I'm told . . . go places and help out." I pressed my hips up.

"All in good time, my eager girl. Keep talking." His mouth made full contact.

"Right, I, um, I can't remember. I . . . oh fuck, Aiden. I'm gonna. Ohh."

"No wonder you got suspended," he quipped, and I pushed my core into his mouth to shut him up. He bit my clit gently, and I fell over the edge, taken under by the most intense orgasm I could recall, with just his tongue and teeth.

He stayed there until I was sated. Then he dragged his tongue from my clit over my hip, stomach, breast, nipple, and neck to end up at my mouth, kissing it the same way he'd kissed me to orgasm, before sliding inside me. He pumped slowly until I came apart, him following quickly before collapsing onto his side, his face in my neck.

"God, there is no part of you I don't want to fuck. Cunt, mouth, tits, ass."

"Jeez, Aiden, you really do say the sweetest things."

He bit me gently on the neck and settled in. "I say what I want. And I can't remember ever wanting anything this much," he whispered.

"Oh," I said, letting the word hang in the air a while before I said, "me too," just as the sound of soft snores filled the room.

I sprawled out, taking my time to replay everything that happened that morning, to relish in Aiden next to me. I was happy. I wasn't going to think about anything but that. I was going to dwell in this feeling for as long as possible.

When I finally moved my arm, Aiden stirred, saying good morning to various parts of my body.

"I have to get to work," I said, laughing as he growled into my neck. "It's past checkout."

"Is it?" He pulled back. "Shit. I'm late to meet a buyer," he said, releasing me and standing. He dressed quickly, and I stayed under the covers a while, watching him, unsuccessfully trying to hold back my grin. Then he leaned in to kiss my lips. "Worth it," he said, and left.

I cleaned up and met Evie in cottage nine.

Yash was standing at the island, and Evie was scrubbing out the microwave when I arrived. "I think a small animal exploded in here. It's always the freaking microwave."

"Gross," I replied from the door.

"Yes, it is gross," she replied pulling her head out. "Birdie, tell Yash he's allowed to help me out when my partner is late." She stared at him, mentally tapping her foot.

"I'm only here because it pays my rent," I said. "You have a job that pays your rent, right, Yash?"

He laughed. "I do indeed."

We both looked at Evie, and she huffed, returning to the microwave.

I went to start on the bathroom. Twenty minutes later, Evie showed up at the bathroom door just as I was finishing up.

"So?"

I threw my rag in the bucket. "So what?"

She narrowed her eyes at me. "Don't play coy with me, missy. You and my brother. Spill."

I didn't answer, but she must have read the answer all over my face because she screeched—and then thought better of it and said, "Ick," but then screeched again.

"So, is this like a friends-with-benefits thing or like an actual relationship?"

I moved past her to get out of the bathroom, where the cleaning fumes were getting to my head.

"I don't know. I'm still leaving in under two months, so if you need a definition, I'd call it a fling."

"But maybe it could turn into like a real relationship?" She was too excited.

"No. You said yourself, Aiden isn't interested in long-term relationships. And I'm not either."

"Did you tell him?"

I stopped in the kitchen and filled a glass of water from the sink, downing the whole thing before I replied. "No."

"Birdie."

"Why should I? It doesn't make any difference because in a few weeks I'll be gone, and it will be over, and there's nothing else to consider."

"It matters because it's part of who you are. Just tell him—he won't care. I don't understand why you need to keep it a secret."

"No, Evie, you don't. This is my vacation from that life, and I want to enjoy it fully. Everyone, and I mean *everyone*, looks at me differently after they know. I don't want that with Aiden. With him, I am just a woman, and I want to feel that way for just a little bit. We have an agreement that this is temporary. We don't owe each other anything."

"What if it turns into more?" she asked, her hands on her hips, her eyes hopeful.

"No one will get their heart broken, if that's what you're worried about." Except me. Definitely me. "No one is falling for anyone, so we don't have to put our baggage on each other. So please, let it be. In the end, it won't even matter."

She was quiet, and I was afraid she'd send me home. I'd go, too. The last thing I wanted was to put her in a difficult spot, but I couldn't tell Aiden. I knew that much. Because Aiden was close to perfect, and I wanted a little perfect in my life.

"I won't tell. I think you're wrong about most of what you said. But I won't say anything."

Then she turned around and walked out the front door, and I eventually followed.

———

AFTER CLEANING TWO MORE COTTAGES, I put on my ten-year-old bathing suit that should have been thrown out years ago and went for an evening swim in the cool water. It was the first time I'd swam, aside from my dip with Aiden, since arriving here, and it felt right to finally do it. I swam long and hard, but not enough to draw attention or break rules.

The sandy beach in front of the cottage was clean and beautiful, but the bottom could be rocky and got deep very quickly unless you knew the good spots; the surf often was rougher than other areas as well. There were better swimming beaches on the other side of town, which left the cottage beach sparsely populated most days—usually just a few cottage guests or sunbathing locals.

I found a spot where I could lie down and watch the sunset. But mostly, I thought of Aiden. I wondered if he'd thought about me after he left my bed this morning. I wanted to know if he was happy or regretful. Would it be weird between us?

I felt like he held all the cards now. Where was he now anyway? If I went to find him, would he think I was clingy? Did he need time alone? Maybe I'd just find him and we'd talk and it wouldn't be weird. I just wanted to see him.

I stood and threw on my linen cover-up. I dropped my towel and e-reader on the front porch of Evie's cottage and meandered over to Aiden's shop, my heart racing as I got closer. I told myself I was the fucking Chicago Bird; I could talk to a guy I'd slept with hours before. How difficult could it be?

The door was open when I arrived, so I knocked lightly on the outside of the building. The sound of a buzzing saw welcomed me as I entered slowly. The area was lit with a skylight and additional spotlights targeting whatever project Aiden was working on. There he was, standing over his work, the sound of the saw drowning out the sound of my intrusion. I greeted my favorite chair, my hand running over the smooth lines of it.

Aiden retracted a table saw and removed whatever he'd cut from it, placing it on the next table. He was a sight, with his low-slung jeans and tight T-shirt showing off the lines of his lean physique, his body sprinkled with sweat and sawdust. His hair was slicked back and held down with a pair of safety goggles.

When he finally looked up and saw me standing several yards away in the shadows of his shop, he stopped, observing me.

He removed the goggles, placing them on the table, and wiped his hands on a rag before tossing it aside. He walked around the table, straight toward me, his eyes finding me on the way. I held my breath until he was standing in front of me.

"Flip-flops are not shop-appropriate," he said, his eyes cast down, taking in the length of my cover-up, which covered very little. "I'll let it slide this one time."

"Your mouth isn't socially appropriate," I replied, my nerves subsiding. "I'll let it slide this—"

"I missed you," he interrupted.

"You did?" My voice came out hopeful.

His lips touched my cheek. "I did."

"Me too." After a few seconds of staring at each other stupidly, I said, "I'd like to watch you work. Is that okay?"

He nodded and moved to pull my favorite chair closer, then handed me a pair of safety glasses. I put them on and sat down.

"You're just in time for the pour."

I watched as Aiden completed a frame, a large piece of natural wood inside it. He mixed buckets of acrylic resin and then lifted and poured the contents slowly into the crevices of the natural wood laid out on the table. It flowed like a slow river, moving into every nook and cranny, all held in by the wood frame he'd just created around it.

He turned briefly to see my face and nodded his head for me to come closer.

"It's amazing," I said, standing next to him.

He smiled, keeping his concentration on what he was doing.

We didn't say much after that. I wandered around his shop, looking at the projects, not a little woodland creature among them. Then I made my way back to the chair and took a seat, closing my eyes, feeling the welcome ache of the sexy morning workout and afternoon swim in my bones.

My eyes opened at the feel of his hands on my bare legs.

"Hey, babe."

Yep, I wasn't going to survive this. "Hi," I said.

"Sorry if I bored you. I'm not used to people in my workspace."

"I like watching you work."

"I like seeing you here." He was squatting in front of me, his hands lightly stroking my legs. "It's also a little distracting."

I grinned. "Good."

He pressed my legs open an inch, pressing a kiss on the inside of my thigh, just above the knee. "I like you in my space."

"I like me in your space, too."

"I need a shower," he said, eyes intent on the space between my legs as I spread them wider.

"Me too."

His hand caressed my inner thighs, stopping short of the line of my bathing suit. Then his eyes narrowed. "What the fuck are you wearing under this thing?"

Shit. "It's the only bathing suit I have."

"It's hideous."

"Thanks a lot, a-hole," I threw back without much venom as his fingers moved to caress me outside of said hideous swimsuit. It really was an awful suit, full-coverage elastic losing its grip and sagging in various places on my body.

"Good thing I like what's underneath so much."

"Well, I'm not sure I like you much anymore."

"Can I kiss it and make it better?" He slipped his thumb underneath the fabric and slid it into my wet folds. "Fuck. I need to taste you." He pulled me down in the chair, my legs spread wider, my see-through linen cover-up riding up my back.

"I probably taste like the lake."

He gripped the suit in his two hands and pulled. The fabric tore easily, like it was more than ready to welcome its own demise, and it hung from my body as he slowly brought me to orgasm with his lips and tongue.

Then he stood and pulled me up with him. His mouth was on mine and his tongue almost in my throat as I gripped his shirt, the feel of sweat and sawdust on his skin making me desperate for him. He walked me to a beautiful table in the corner, ready to be sold, or maybe already sold. He turned me around, pressing my back so I was face down on the cool acrylic. He pulled up my linen cover-up, and I barely heard the zipper of his jeans before he was inside me, filling me gloriously. His hand slapped against my ass, and I moaned in appreciation, not realizing how welcome the feeling was as he lifted my leg over the side of the table, pressing my pubic bone down, furiously pushing in and out, his balls colliding with my clit upon each thrust.

I came quickly and loudly, and he followed with a grunting moan as he fell forward, kissing down my spine.

"You okay?"

I moaned in the affirmative, and he stood and pulled me up with him. He turned me and kissed my mouth gently and held the sides of my face.

"You make me lose my mind. I'm sorry if that was a bit rough."

I shook my head. "No, you're not."

He grinned. "I am if you didn't like it."

"It was perfect."

He smiled and kissed me like I was precious to him.

"You owe me a swimsuit, you brute."

"Whatever you say, Bowden."

———

I SNUCK BACK TO MY COTTAGE with at least half of my butt cheek exposed under the white cover-up. I showered and changed into shorts and a T-shirt before knocking on Aiden's door. He opened it and smiled. "Just in time—food should be here in a minute."

"I'm starved."

"Good." He wrapped his hand around my waist and kissed me, then returned to the kitchen, gathering plates. "Table or couch?"

"What are we eating?"

"Indian."

"Definitely couch, then."

"Agreed," he said and laid out the settings on the coffee table. The doorbell rang, and he told me to pick something to watch.

I went to Netflix and meandered.

"Have you seen *The Witcher*?" I asked when he returned.

"Nope."

"You up for a series?"

He set the food down and sat next to me. "A series, huh?"

"Or a movie."

"Which would you prefer, Bernadette? A movie or a series?"

It felt like the answer to this question had nothing to do with the content.

"Well, it's eight episodes. I think I can do eight episodes."

"Is there a second season?"

I nodded.

"Good. Series it is, then."

After an enormous amount of Indian food was consumed, we pushed out the coffee table and lay back for episode two. Aiden pulled me close and ran his fingers through my hair. It's possible I purred.

"You're kind of like him, don't you think? The Witcher?"

Aiden laughed and asked, "How's that?"

"Smart and quiet. Brutish. Grunting. Sexy."

He laughed again. "You have an interesting perspective."

I sat up and looked at him. "You don't think so?"

He shrugged. "I think I'm whatever you want me to be, as long as I get to kiss you."

I leaned in to do exactly that, realizing it was the first time I'd kissed him. "But then you go and say sweet things like that and I wonder where my asshole went." I kissed him again.

"Ouch," I screeched at the hard smack on my ass, followed by a hard kiss.

"Also, you probably have lots of girlfriends who you leave wanting more as you meander through life. A caveman."

"Meander through life?"

I shrugged and said, "Sure."

"Are you digging, Ms. Bowden?"

"No!" I defended. "I'm assessing." I was totally digging.

"Hmm."

"See, you grunted. Lots of ladies?"

"I've dated. But I haven't had much in the way of relationships. And I would not have fucked you bare in my shop if I'd been with anyone else recently."

"You did fuck me bare. You're not concerned you'll get me pregnant?"

"Evie told me you were on the pill."

"Seriously? Why?"

"She was on one of her tangents about how women were the dominant sex, how much pain you all have but never complain about. She mentioned not even you were immune from terrible cramps, so you were on the pill."

Dammit, Evie. She'd out me eventually. I shifted the conversation. "Why no relationships?"

He kept his eyes on the TV. "I'm not against it. I've just never met someone I liked enough to spend that much time with."

"Not even your fiancée?"

He pulled me closer and looked at me, almost chest to chest, our breath intermingling. "I didn't understand what a relationship was supposed to be back then. She left me because I didn't initiate enough time together." My eyes watched him closely, and he leaned in to kiss my nose. "What about you? No serious relationships?"

"One. A long time ago. Though it seems more like complacency now."

"Now?"

"Just so long after."

"Hmm." Aiden purred, his hand on my face, his attention fully on me. It filled me up so completely. "I like you," he said. "Very much."

"You do?" I eked out, warmth cascading to every part of me.

"Hmm," he affirmed, his lips barely touching mine. "Now watch your show before I throw you over my shoulder and take you back to bed."

"See, a caveman," I said against his lips, before I curled up in his lap, my eyes on the TV. He caressed my hair, lulling me to sleep before the show was over. I woke the next morning, wrapped in his arms in his bed. I had never wanted to stop the passage of time so much, or to stay stuck in a place forever.

21

WE GOT A SIDEWALK TABLE at a place called Lila's Cafe the next evening. Evie and Yash on one side, me on the other, next to an empty chair that would soon be filled by Aiden. I hadn't seen him since the morning. Hadn't talked to him. Hadn't discussed what we were to each other outside of the closed doors of the bedroom. We didn't even have each other's phone numbers. My anxiety rose as we waited. The server dropped off our drinks, mine a light pink thing that looked tasty. I was wearing shorts and a wide-neck tee exposing a shoulder. My boots were tucked in my closet and Evie's gift of sandals adorned my feet. My hair was tied in a loose knot at the base of my neck and a few locks spilled out, tickling my exposed neck. I wore mascara and a clear lip gloss. I felt pretty, and for the first time in a long time, I liked the way that felt. I liked the way Aiden made me feel.

Yash was talking about a pit bull puppy delivered to the vet clinic the day before. Someone had found it thrown out with the trash. His distaste for anyone who was anything but kind to an animal was palpable, and Evie gazed at him with stars in her eyes as he spoke. It made me happy for him, knowing he wasn't the only one completely smitten.

I'd almost forgotten about my anxiety at seeing Aiden when I felt a warm hand on my naked shoulder. I shifted as the scent of the woodshop reached my nose. His lips touched the side of my neck, and he whispered in my ear, "You look edible."

His touch left goose bumps in its wake as he came to sit next to me, giving his greetings to the stunned faces across from us. I'd thought all day about how this would go. Would we keep things casual? Pretend we hadn't had amazing sex like five times in the last forty-eight hours? Would he be awkward in front of other people? Would I? I didn't know how to navigate this, so I figured I'd take my cue from him.

His hand found my thigh as he leaned forward to take a sip of the beer Yash had ordered for him. The contact put to bed any lingering insecurities. It was clear we were something.

The light squeeze of his large fingers just above my knee sent a wave of warmth straight between my legs, and I finally looked directly at him. He smiled back, his eyes dark and hungry.

"Okay?" he said quietly.

I had no words, distracted by his hands and eyes and the smug grin that emerged on his face. I nodded.

"Good," he said.

What was wrong with me? I was never tongue-tied. Never at a loss for words.

Evie was holding back a smile as she stared at her brother, who was choosing to ignore her impatient gaze.

"Got a rescue in yesterday, I was telling the ladies," Yash spoke up, breaking the stares all around. He continued to tell us about how all the little guy needed was a good bath and flea treatment and he'd perked right up. Lucky dog.

Aiden's hand left my leg when our food arrived, but I still felt its imprint there. The conversation was light as we all ate, and when our dishes were cleared, I nearly choked on my cocktail at Evie's next statement.

"Mom wants to come out," she informed Aiden. "Did she tell you? She's looking at her calendar."

"Good. Whenever," Aiden said as his hand returned to my leg, absently stroking my skin with his fingers.

"You'll love her, Birdie," Yash said, bringing me back into the conversation. "She's a hoot. She just retired, so she's eager to be near her kids."

"Eager for grandkids is more like it," Evie added.

Yash shrugged. "Sounds good to me."

Evie gave him a chastising look, but then smiled.

"Is she coming soon?" I asked, trying to keep my voice carefree. Hopefully it would be after I left, but if before, I'd take a few days back in Chicago while she was here.

"Who knows," Aiden said. "She's not a huge planner. Acts on a whim. She'll come when she comes."

"Like someone else I know," Yash said, looking at Evie.

"It's an endearing quality. Isn't it, Aiden?" Evie stated.

"Whatever you say, sis," he replied as his hand squeezed my leg, maybe sensing my trepidation.

"What are your parents like, Birdie?" Yash asked.

I sat up a bit, considering my words. "My dad died when I was young. Mom lives in Georgia. She loves it there. She doesn't like it up north much, more of a warm weather person. What about you, Yash?" I said, attempting to steer the conversation elsewhere.

Evie groaned, while Yash and Aiden chuckled.

"Well," Yash began, "Mom—"

"Hates me," Evie interjected.

"No, she doesn't," he scolded. "My folks are very traditional. They are both doctors from India. I guess you could say they wanted me to be a doctor and marry an Indian doctor, or lawyer. They would have been happy with a dentist."

"So they got 50 percent. That's not bad," I said.

"A vet is not a doctor in their eyes. But they're fine about it now."

"They still hate me," Evie whisper-yelled.

"My mother just isn't used to your energy. She doesn't understand our past. But it doesn't matter. She's not with you. I am," he assured her with a kiss on her head. "Anyway, she does like you. She just doesn't really relate to you. But she tries."

"I try too," Evie said.

"I know you do. I love you for it."

"She probably really hates me now that you're away from Texas."

Yash flattened his lips. "Probably."

"Yash," Evie whined, and he leaned over to whisper to her. I took the opportunity to look at Aiden, who was looking at me as through no one else was around. Hidden under the table, his hand slowly made its way up my leg, tickling the skin under my shorts. I pushed it back closer to my knee. He smiled in mirth as he linked his fingers with mine before returning his attention to the conversation.

"If you could have any superpower, what one would it be?" The question—coming from the obvious source—startled me and, in that moment, I imagined how quickly I could provide this source with the world's most unforgettable wedgie. I could do it so fast no one would probably even notice. She'd be stunned silent, and the incredibly inappropriate question she'd just asked would evaporate into the drone of voices that carried down the table-lined street.

"I think I'd be super strong," she went on. "Like I could lift a whole building if I wanted."

Yash smiled and Aiden laughed, and I realized he'd been doing that a lot more in the last few days.

"Even if you're strong enough to lift a building," I spat out, staring daggers at her, "you'd destroy it if you tried. Physics and all."

"Huh," she replied, as though nothing was amiss. "Interesting. What about you guys?" She knew exactly what she was doing. I was going to kill her later.

"Maybe I'd have the power to heal," Yash said. "It'd come in handy on the job."

There were no known recorded cases of any super with any kind of healing ability, not medically anyway, but it fit that he'd say that considering his job and Evie's past. She leaned over and grazed his cheek with her lips.

"What about you, Aiden?" she said.

"Never given it any thought," he said as he played with the coaster in one hand, his thumb caressing the inside of my wrist with the other.

"That's why I asked—give it thought now."

He took a sip of his water and smiled. "X-ray vision."

She threw her napkin at his face, and he chuckled. "Perv. It was a serious question."

"Oh. Well then, let me give it *serious* consideration," he joked.

"Would you still love me if I was super strong?" Evie asked Yash. "Like . . . stronger than you?"

"Of course," he said without thinking. And she smiled like it was a real answer, like it would hold up in real life. It wouldn't. It never did. And instead of making me feel like telling more, it reminded me I should end this thing with Aiden now before he had a chance to find out the truth about me and end it himself.

"What about you, Birdie?" Evie asked with all the innocence in the world, a tiny evil smile playing at her lips.

"Like Aiden, I've never given it much thought, I guess."

And as though I had willed it, the server appeared with our check. Yash threw in his card, and as I reached into my pocket for my card, Aiden leaned over and said, "I'd like to, please."

I nodded.

I'm pretty sure he could get away with anything with that one word: *please.* He said it with his mouth and eyes and his big hand cradling mine. A simple thing that I absorbed into my skin like the first beams of warm sunlight in the spring. My hormones were going wild, so it's possible I was imagining everything—his longing looks, his affection. I was feeling overwhelmed by it all when I was pretty sure any other woman would just take it in stride.

Men didn't hold my door open or grip my hand when exiting a car. They certainly didn't pay for my dinner or look at me the way Aiden did. I'd been the Chicago Bird for the last decade, and today I felt like Birdie Bowden again. Was it that simple? Just become someone I'd never had the chance to grow into? Someone I wouldn't be again after the summer was over?

"Walk with me?" Aiden asked as we stepped away from the table.

"See you back at the cottage, Birdie," Evie said, before I could answer. She giggled as Yash pulled her out of the chair and toward wherever they were heading.

I looked back at Aiden, who was watching his sister and his best friend with a quiet smile, and I suddenly felt timid, unsure what to say, what to do with myself. I knew I wanted to tuck my hand in his and maybe curl up into his hard chest forever. Instead, I stood silently. My mouth may have been open, and Aiden's gaze turned curious, then amused.

"Still thinking about this morning, are you? I do have that effect on women."

"The only effect you're having is on my gag reflex," I responded, breaking free of the haze he'd put me in.

He chuckled. "There she is." His lips touched the space below my ear, his hand gripping my waist before he stepped back. "I'd like to have an effect on your gag reflex."

"You're a pig," I said, and he chuckled.

"And you're too easy. Shall we?"

He didn't attempt to touch me as we walked, and I was relieved, needing the space to breathe and think.

"What about your superpower?" he said, and my heart stopped, as did my feet. "What would it be?"

"Oh," I said and forced myself to walk while taking a moment as if to think it over, though I already knew the answer. "Flying."

"Really?"

"I know it's the generic answer, but it would be so amazing, so . . . freeing." And it was. Without my jet pack, I felt like my wings were clipped. So many times I'd wanted to escape into the sky, feel far away from the earth below, where we fought for space and resources. In the sky, everything below felt so little, so useless, so unnecessary. It was an honest answer—I would have picked it over my real powers any day.

"I imagine so."

"What would you want to see?" I asked him with a roll of my eyes. "With your X-ray vision?"

We passed a tiki restaurant playing Jimmy Buffett, a large group of twentysomethings singing along as they danced on the sidewalk. One of the guys was about to run into me but quickly grabbed my hand and moved to twirl me under his arm. I laughed because he was happy and harmless. He twirled me a few more times but then took my smile as invitation to bring me in closer. Aiden's hand on the man's arm stalled his movement, his loaded smile communicating there was a line he didn't want to cross. The guy released me with a quick bow and returned to his rowdy group.

"It wasn't a serious answer. Not really," Aiden said, and it took me a second to realize he was answering my question, not feeling the need to address the incident that had just occurred. An incident that caused my heart to trip over itself, one I knew I would later replay over and over in my head to decipher what his intentions were, and if what had happened was chivalry, possession, or one man simply reminding another to keep his decorum.

Either way, I reveled in the feel of it. The feeling of belonging to someone, of being important to them, in the simplest of ways.

"I'm not sure a superpower would be much use to me. A convenience maybe, but I guess I'm fine with the world the way I experience it."

"You think the supers are freaks?"

"No. Why would I think that?"

I shrugged. "Some people do."

"I have respect for anyone with talent if they work hard."

I wanted his words to be true, and in many instances, they probably were. Aiden wasn't the type to judge. But acceptance of something and a romantic relationship were two very different things. "So no superpower?"

He clasped my hand and continued walking. "Nothing in my life is missing. Maybe I'm just too old to want to change."

"How old are you?"

"Thirty-four."

"That's not old."

"Oldest I've ever been."

We walked in silence a few beats before he turned, continuing to walk backward. "You still dating?"

"I—" Was I? After everything that had happened in the last two days, I hadn't had time to consider it. "Would you be jealous if I said yes?" I laughed, not wanting to give the wrong answer.

"Damn right. I don't share."

"That's not what I hear."

"And what did you hear?"

"Just that you're not really into monogamy or relationships in general. You said it yourself." My body was getting warm, anxious about his response, whatever it would be.

He stopped walking, and we stood inches from each other. "I said monogamy is for relationships. I haven't been interested in a relationship. Never seemed necessary."

"Okay." My stomach plummeted with the idea that he'd move on from this much easier than I would, unlikely to think of me again after a few romps.

"But I'm interested in *you*. And I'm interested in seeing how this plays out, even if just for the summer . . . monogamously," he said the word with a growl. "So, Bernadette, let me ask you again, are you still dating?"

I smiled, letting my brain fill up on Aiden's attention, not dwelling on the future. "Well," I began flippantly, "the assignment is to date, but Doctor Evans didn't specify how many people I had to date, so if you can make the time to fill all my date nights, I suppose I don't need—"

His lips collided with mine before his tongue ran along the seam of my lips and I opened. He growled as he entered my mouth, filling my senses, tasting of beer and warmth. I pouted a little when he pulled away.

"If I promise to try to be a little bit less of an asshole, could I convince you to come back to my place?"

I squinted my eyes and said, "Do I have to sleep on the couch again?"

He grinned darkly. "You mean, if you pass out drunk on my front porch, will I carry you to the couch and tuck you in fully clothed, again? No, I'll take you to my bed where I can wake up next to you, my dick sliding into your pretty little cunt, warm and wet for me."

My brain was absorbing his crass words as well as the knowledge that he had been the one to take care of me even though he'd hated me that first day. It elicited an ache in said pretty—

"I'd strip you first, of course, so I could feel your perfect tits and long legs up against me while you slept it off. Easy access in the morning. But I don't plan to ply you with alcohol. It wouldn't be very gentlemanly."

"And you're nothing if not a gentleman," I quipped.

"Exactly." His hands squeezed my waist, tension in his grip. "Is that a yes?"

"Yes," I said without thought. I could try to play hard to get, be coy. But it was useless. He'd see right through me. I wanted this man, and he said he'd date me so I didn't have to date anyone else and kill two birds, right? We walked with a little pep as we headed back to his cottage in silence.

—

AIDEN WAS QUITE DOMESTICATED. He knew his way around a kitchen as well as he knew his way around me. His place was tidy, and he had a system about things, lots of order, everything in its place. His closet held T-shirts folded neatly alongside his jeans, next to a rack full of suits and ties I'd never seen him wear. I wondered if Grove Aiden was different than Texas Aiden, the environmental engineer. Was he like me, taking a break from that life? Was I a brief distraction before he returned?

His home had plants and a few pictures of his sister and their mom and one of Aiden with his stepdad, whom Evie resembled. Aiden's darker coloring must have resembled his father. But I saw no pictures to prove my theory.

While he'd planned to sell the cottages, it was clear that Aiden had also been making himself at home here in Grove. He'd planted perennials in the yard and set up his woodshop, made commitments for his custom furniture, and taught classes. He hosted family dinners every Friday and had built himself a fancy headboard that had recently left a series of scuffs against his wall.

Aiden and I eased into a routine in the weeks that followed. When, at one point, I jokingly asked if he was getting tired of me yet, he reasoned that since we had such a short time together, we may as well get the most out of it.

And he made it easy. There was no discomfort. When he wanted to see me, he saw me. He never second-guessed if he was too eager, not eager enough, or what the implications would be when he dropped by midday just to give me a kiss in the middle of vacuuming. He never avoided me. He never seemed turned off by anything I did. He never made me feel like I was too much or not enough. Eventually, I forgot to even consider the fears that lived inside me, falling into a level of comfort that carried me through every day.

"Do you miss Texas? Your job?"

Aiden finished chewing—he'd made risotto for us. He sat next to me at his kitchen island in shorts and a T-shirt, with a few days of stubble that was quite glorious on him. "Sometimes. I miss the work, but not the lifestyle so much. What about you? You miss your job?"

"Same, I think."

"Hmm. How so?" he asked, and I chewed without answering. He shook his head at my silence. "Well, since you don't want to talk about your job, tell me about your family. You never talk about them either."

"Not much to tell. No siblings. I'm not close with my mother."

"Why?"

"You are very inquisitive this evening," I said with a smile.

"You started it. And you are deflecting, as per usual."

I took a bite and chewed as he waited for my response. "My mother was very specific about the daughter she wanted, and I didn't fit the mold, so we don't have much of a relationship. We talk on the phone occasionally."

"Tell me about her."

"Why?"

He shrugged. "Curious."

Aiden had told me a bit about his father, and they seemed to have had a similar strained, bordering on nonexistent, relationship.

"She's very southern, a socialite, and maybe a high-functioning alcoholic."

"What did she want you to be?"

Not a super. "Polite. Polished. Feminine. Married to the man of her choosing, giving her lots of perfect grandchildren who would eventually replace her on her charity boards." *Someone I could never be.*

He took a drink of water, then set it down and leaned in. "I guess your mouth wouldn't qualify as especially polite. Though I quite like it." He kissed my lips with my mouth full of food. "Polished is a terrible adjective for a human. And feminine? I think your mother and I have a different understanding of the word, because to me, you are the very definition."

I finished chewing slowly while my brain malfunctioned on the sentiment.

"And the rest is just bullshit." Another kiss.

I struggled to comprehend his words. I understood what he was saying, but I couldn't believe he knew my innermost insecurities and was arguing the opposite.

"When was the last time you talked?" he asked.

"A few weeks ago," I replied before adding absently, "she suggested coming to see me."

Aiden swallowed the last of his risotto. "Invite her."

"What?" I set my fork down and wiped my mouth with my napkin, shocked by his suggestion. "Here?"

"Sure."

"God, no. That would be horrible for everyone. Did you not hear what I just said about us not having a relationship? Where would she even stay? I mean, no. That's just a terrible idea. Disaster. Hard pass."

Aiden watched me, his face pensive, before he said without judgment, "She's still your mom." He stood and kissed my forehead, and then holding my chin to meet his eye, said, "Besides, she must have done something right." He went to the sink to refill his water.

I smiled in spite of myself. Then, eager to move away from the mother conversation, I said the first thing that popped into my head.

"Aiden. What do you want? From life, I mean?"

He laughed at my obvious avoidance and leaned against the counter by the sink, setting his glass down.

"Tell me," I urged, suddenly more than curious.

"Well. If you would have asked me a year ago, my answer would have been different than a month ago, and that answer is different from today."

"Okay, what did you want a year ago?"

"A good job, a healthy sister, time to make things with my hands."

"And a month ago?"

"Same. But also for my foul-mouthed, annoying new neighbor to leave me alone so I could stop picturing her naked and get my shit done."

I swallowed. "And now?"

"Now I really only want one thing." He paused longer than necessary to consider his next words. He started toward me, rounding the counter to join me on the other side. "I want you . . ."

I turned on the stool to face him, his hand brushing against my cheek, and he continued, ". . . to clean my cabin like you clean the rest of them. I fucking hate dusting."

I rolled my eyes. "In your dreams, asshole."

"Come on, I'm sleeping with you. Isn't cleaning my place kind of your job now?"

My jaw fell open, and he kept a straight face. "No wonder you're single. You're everything that is wrong with men."

He laughed. "Am I single?"

"After that comment? Yes. You definitely are."

He smiled. "Don't worry about it. I can clean better than you can anyway."

I shook my head. "Are you better at giving yourself blow jobs, too?"

He stopped laughing. "I've never tried it, but probably."

"I hope so, cause you've gotten your last one from me."

He wrapped his arms around me, looking down into my eyes. "I love working you over."

"Don't even. I hate you," I said without conviction.

"No, you don't."

"I do. You're not funny." But it was annoyingly charming that he often joked about gender roles. In a weird, demented way, it made me feel better about my own hang-ups.

"Have you ever wanted a family of your own?"

"Not really," he replied without thought.

Why had no woman begged to be his wife and mother of his children? "Really? Why? You should have a perfect little domestic wife with—"

"I don't really want a perfect little anything," he interrupted. "Clearly, I like my women a little bit feral."

I slapped his chest from where my hands lay against him. "Did you just call me feral?"

"I said 'a little bit.'" He smiled. "But I'm no cup of tea. As you may have realized, I'm a bit of an introvert. I can barely tolerate Yash, and he's my best friend."

"Whatever, you two are so in love with each other."

He laughed as his hands held my face looking up at him. "Jealous?"

"Maybe a little," I mumbled as he pressed on my cheeks.

"Don't worry, your blow jobs are way superior."

"I am quite talented." I beamed up at him, and as he smiled down at me, there was something in his face I'd never seen, something that didn't say casual to me. It caused my stomach to clench thinking anyone would get his attention like this after I was gone.

"Care to show me how talented you are again?" He said the words as his fingers caressed my neck.

"Not a chance."

But the memory of him completely vulnerable to me, desperate for my mouth and his own release, his body so tight with the desire of something only I could give him—I really did want to show him again.

So I did.

22

THE FAN ABOVE MY HEAD churned the early morning air that drifted in through the open windows, the sound of the waves lulling me into a state of half-asleep, half-awake. I knew Aiden was awake because he was caressing my shoulder, but we hadn't yet said a word. My face rested on his bare chest, my leg over his waist, my bare breasts pressed to his side.

Just as I was drifting off again, Aiden moved, pulling his arm from behind me and sitting up.

"Stay," I whined.

"You need to stop it," he said, looking down at me.

"Stop what?"

"Every time you move, I feel your hard nipples, your smooth legs, your little breaths against my chest. It's driving me crazy."

I held back my smile, tucking my lips inside my mouth, not moving anything but my leg, bending my knee and running my toes up along the side of his naked thigh until my leg wrapped around his back and pressed down. He let me guide his front to mine until the evidence of his crazy was pressed to my naked center.

"You are such a cock tease."

My smile broke through, and I couldn't help it. I moved against him, plenty of wetness inviting him in.

He gripped my chin. "You're not too sore? I worked you hard yesterday."

He had. And I'd loved every second of it. I shook my head and his eyes dilated.

"Good."

Then he flipped us again, and I was on top as he guided himself inside me. "I want to watch these perfect breasts bounce as you squeeze my dick."

I obliged without hesitation, moving slowly at first. I smiled to myself when I noted that I was squeezing him inside me without any screams of agony from the suspected crushing of his phallus.

"What's so funny?" he said as I moved above him, working us both up.

"Nothing. Just happy."

"More secrets, Bowden?" he said, slipping his fingers between my legs as I set the pace. His other hand was on my hip, his eyes passing between my eyes, breasts, and where our bodies came together. "You'll have to tell me all your secrets eventually, you know."

When I found the perfect angle, I moved faster and bounced harder. He cursed and his grip on my hips grew tight. The tension in his face and his curses spurred me on and my speed was venturing on the edge of superhuman. The banging of the bed against the wall was growing louder. He grew harder, and I knew he was holding himself back, waiting for me.

"Fuck," he said on a grunt. "Your body is perfection. Come for me."

And I did. And he did. I leaned above him, his hands pulling me down to his chest. He gripped my hair, stroking my scalp. But the banging of the headboard continued until we both realized it was actually coming from outside the room. The front door.

"Fucking guests," he mumbled. He moved me to his side and stood, throwing on the jeans he'd worn yesterday and a T-shirt lying on a chair. He stopped to kiss my shoulder before he left the room. "You're going to be the end of me," he called from the hallway.

I lay there thinking the same thing about him. And what a glorious end it would be, I thought, a hard lump forming in my chest.

—

I THREW ON MY SHORTS and T-shirt and snuck into the bathroom. The voice I heard as I crossed the hallway to the bathroom wasn't one I recognized, but it sounded at home in Aiden's cottage.

I closed the bathroom door and peed. I tried to tame my hair, pulling it into a pile on my head. I wanted to shower, but for some reason it felt weird to have the shower running, like that was a clear signal of what Aiden and I had done in his bedroom while this person had banged on the door.

I cleaned up as best I could from the sink, brushed my teeth, and made my way into the living room, not knowing how long this guest was staying and not wanting to hide in the bedroom.

The idea that this visitor was a woman from Aiden's past, or present, had crossed my mind, but I wouldn't dwell on it.

I stopped at the threshold of the kitchen. Aiden was starting the coffee while the woman messed about the kitchen, searching for something.

"It's under the silverware drawer," Aiden said as he turned to see me standing there.

His smile grew wide, and my anxiety vanished. In that moment, I knew his face was all I needed to see in the morning to make it a good day. He flipped a switch on the coffee machine and started toward me.

He placed a kiss on my cheek and whispered, "I was going to bribe you out of bed with coffee."

"Well, what do we have here?" the woman said from behind Aiden and he turned, his hand holding mine.

"Mom, this is Bernadette Bowden. Bernadette, this is my mother, Darlene. She's come up from Texas for a visit."

"Aiden, I didn't know you had company," she scolded. "Well, look at you. Aren't you just lovely. It's nice to finally meet you, Bernadette," she said with a kind of sincerity and curiosity I wasn't used to. "I've heard quite a bit about you."

"Hello, Darlene. I'm very happy to meet the woman who birthed the most wonderful woman in the world, and also this ogre." I pointed at Aiden.

She laughed hard and long and then said, "Oh, I think we will get along fine. Evie was right about you."

Not needing to ask what Evie had said, I asked, "Can I help you with anything?"

"I was going to make my children their favorite breakfast, but I'd rather make whatever you want. What will it be?"

She was a breath of fresh air, and I never even got the chance to feel anxious about her.

"I'm happy with anything. Let me help," I said as I stepped forward.

"All right then, I hope you know your way around this kitchen better than I do."

"I think I can locate a few things," I offered, "but I'm not much of a chef."

"Me either—I just make breakfast. My late husband made the kids dinner when they were growing up. He taught Aiden how to cook."

"Well, he did an amazing job," I said, looking at Aiden. He was standing there, watching us with a grin.

When Evie and Yash arrived, we sat down to eat breakfast burritos, and the perfection of it all had me groaning as I bit into the eggs, bacon, and melted cheese wrapped in a thin tortilla. Evie and Aiden fought over the last of the orange juice, but I ignored them as I savored breakfast.

"How long have you been making my grumpy boy less grumpy?" Darlene whispered next to me with a knowing smile.

"Oh . . . I . . . I'm staying with Evie in her spare room for the summer. I mean, I work here, in exchange for a place to live," I rambled, unsure how to answer her question and not wanting to say the wrong thing to this woman, who was so much like Evie in her desire to see Aiden in love and happy. I liked her immediately and didn't want her to hate me. Aiden and I were temporary. She didn't need the specifics.

"Oh? I thought I was staying in Evie's spare room for the next few days. Evie? You didn't mention you already had a guest in the spare room."

"I don't. Birdie hasn't slept there in weeks. She's been staying at her boyfriend's house." She said boyfriend like a teasing twelve-year-old.

"I'll stay wherever there's room," Darlene offered with a smile.

"I'll just go back to my place for a few days," I said, hating the idea.

"Why?" Evie asked, setting her fork down. "No, don't do that. Please."

"Okay, but you guys will want some family time, and I don't want to interfere. In fact, I'll do all the cleaning for the next few days to give you all some time together."

I smiled at Darlene, wanting her to get to spend time with her children, whom she clearly adored. I was a squatter at Evie's and a booty call at Aiden's. What must she think of me? Aiden just watched me with humor as I fumbled through this uncomfortable situation.

"That's silly. Please, no one change anything for me. And you, my dear"—she placed her hand on my elbow—"are the most interesting person here, so you won't be going anywhere. Or spending the entire time working. When I visit, it's a *holiday*."

"Okay. But I must insist that you stay at the table and visit while I clean up."

"If we absolutely must," Evie said, and I was happy to step aside and give them time as Darlene told them about the drama of her retirement community.

Aiden snuck up behind me as I was washing the pans. He grabbed the pan from me and dried it.

"You didn't tell me your mother was coming *today*," I whispered.

"I didn't know," he responded, his voice low. "She likes to surprise visit, to see us in our natural environment."

"She's used to showing up to women coming from her son's bedroom, then?"

Aiden grinned. "You're digging again."

"No," I argued. I was totally digging.

"It's been a long time since my mother has seen a woman in my home."

"Your fiancée?"

He nodded.

"I could go away for a few days. I don't want to intrude."

He grabbed the next pan from me. "You are not intruding, Bernadette."

"I'm not family."

He sighed. "What's bothering you?"

When I didn't immediately reply, his voice turned firm. "Bowden, what's happening in that head of yours?"

"I . . . I'm just not used to this family thing. What if she hates me?"

"Why would she hate you?"

My track record. "Because I'm just here for the summer. She'll think I'm . . . loose." My mother would.

He laughed out loud. "Did you just say that? My mother is a modern woman. She doesn't think anything like that. You're fine. She's fine. Don't worry about it."

Before I could respond, Yash was standing at the counter, pouring a fresh cup of coffee for his mother-in-law, ex-mother-in-law, future . . . whatever she was.

"Yash, how is your mother?" Darlene called from the table.

"She and my dad are both well. Aside from the fact she'd prefer that I were in Texas."

"Oh dear, I would imagine so. It's difficult for a mother to be so far from her children. Where are you from, Bernadette?"

"I'm from Chicago. But call me Birdie, please."

"Birdie, then," she said with a smile. She made her way to the counter where Yash handed her the coffee. "Are you close with your family?"

"It's just me and my mother, though we aren't really close."

"Why is that, sweetie?"

"Mom, that's personal," Evie chastised.

"I'm only here for a few days, and I have every intention of getting to know the woman who has my son bewitched." Her voice dropped low, and she grinned. "And just may provide me with a grandchild. I'm not getting any younger."

I reddened and didn't dare to look at Aiden, afraid of his reaction. Was he bewitched? Did he want children? It was something I'd long ago decided I'd never have. Was this still a summer fling? Suddenly I was in a spot I didn't want to be in. Darlene was another person to disappoint. Another mother to see I wasn't good enough for her son, in the end.

The room was silent.

"I'd better get ready for work. Darlene, it was truly wonderful to meet you."

"Okay, dear. I'll see you later on, then," she said, her eyes wide in concern.

I nodded and left them in the kitchen to get to work.

———

WHEN EVIE JOINED ME an hour later, I told her I had it covered and insisted she spend the day with her mother. She relented, and they all went into town for shopping and lunch.

When they returned a few hours later, I watched them from the cottages as I finished. They set up beach chairs and an umbrella in the sand. Aiden and Yash brought out a football and were tossing it back and forth. Evie and her mom sat in the chairs and chatted. They looked happy, like a family. I'd had a family once, before my father died and my mother fell apart. The thought of it made my heart ache.

"How are my girls today?"

Mother and I looked up, mid-giggle, from our place at the kitchen counter, where we were smearing homemade icing in our mouths as much as on the cake in front of us.

"Daddy! You're not supposed to be home yet," I said accusingly as I jumped down from the counter and ran over to him. "Close your eyes," I said, pushing him backward into the living room.

He laughed and covered his eyes. "All right, kiddo, why don't you take me to your momma, and I'll keep my eyes closed tight so I can't see anything."

I huffed, but relented as I took his big hand in both of mine and walked

him into the kitchen, his other hand still over his eyes. When we stood in
front of my mother, she set aside her spatula, the biggest smile on her face as
she walked into his arms, which immediately wrapped her up.

"You smell like cake," he said to her neck as he kissed her there.

"Dad!" I chastised. "It's supposed to be a surprise."

"Sorry, little bird," he laughed, then placed a big kiss on my mother's lips.
"Taste like cake too."

"Happy birthday, darling," my mother said, wrapping her arms around
his waist.

"Dad!" I grumbled, pushing them apart.

He relented, pulling away from my mother and kissed my cheek before
he left us alone.

"Dessert first tonight!" he called out behind him.

Evie screamed as Yash leaned his lake-soaked body into hers and
Aiden crouched down next to his mom to talk. I watched them with
a hint of a smile as I considered what to do with myself now that I'd
finished cleaning. Darlene had my room at Evie's, so I went where my
clothes were. Stepping into Aiden's bedroom, I realized how comfortable
I'd gotten there. My clothes were strewn about, invading his previously
tidy space. My underwear took up residence next to his in the drawer, my
clothes in his hamper, sharing a cycle in the wash.

I'd all but moved in, and he'd never said a word about it. I'd chosen not
to think about how intertwined my life was becoming with the Anderses.
I'd invaded their family dinners, their homes, Aiden's bed.

I showered and considered putting on a bathing suit but remembered
that Aiden had destroyed the only one I had. Aiden and I had gone for a
few night swims in the last few weeks, but I hadn't needed a suit for that.
I put on a pair of shorts and a T-shirt. I grabbed my e-reader and aimed
for the little patio outside the guest room.

"Birdie!" Darlene called from the front door as I headed down the
hallway. "Come to the beach with us. It's such a perfect day."

"I don't want to intrude. I've got some reading to catch up on."

"Fiddlesticks. You'll come out."

"Oh no, really. Thank you, but I'm good here." I hadn't seen Aiden since this morning, and I felt like such a fool for leaving the way I had.

"Please. Come entertain me. Sometimes family runs out of things to talk about. A new person helps spice things up. Besides, after all the work you put in today, you'll need a swim."

She wasn't giving me a choice, it seemed. "I don't have a swimsuit."

She looked at me quizzically. It was strange to live on the beach without a swimsuit. I figured I wouldn't share the reason I didn't have one.

"Underwear covers more than a suit anyway. Go on, put something on."

I retreated into the bedroom and found a pair of high-cut black underpants and a gray sports bra. I threw my clothes on top and returned to the living room.

"I'm sorry about this morning," Darlene started as I stepped into the kitchen. "I didn't mean to pry or make assumptions. It's just that Aiden has talked about wanting to be a father, and I—" she stalled upon seeing my surprise.

"He has?"

"Oh, I'm getting ahead of myself. Ignore me. Forget I even said anything."

"It's fine," I said with a forced smile, my mind whirling and finding myself again feeling unworthy, wishing I was a person who wanted what he wanted, who could give him the life he wanted. But I wasn't.

"I'm just excited to see my son in love. Evie told me about you, and I had to see for myself. And it is something, the way he looks at you."

I started to argue, but she wouldn't let me. "You don't see it, but I do. It's not something I've seen before, ever. I wasn't sure he was built to fall in love. Clearly, I was wrong. And I'm happy for it."

"Darlene, it's not like that with us. I'm just here for the summer. I mean, I don't think either of us is looking for a forever kind of relationship."

"No? Why is that?" She seemed truly interested.

"I'm just not built for that kind of thing. Relationships and family, I mean."

With a sigh and a sly smile, she said, "That's fiddlesticks. Whoever told you you're not good enough was an idiot. Parent, lover, friend. Doesn't matter. They got it wrong." She took hold of my chin the way a mother does. "I see the effect you've had on my children, *both* of them. And already I see that you are perfectly you. Perfect for my boy."

My eyes were wide, filling with something I pushed back. Why was this woman I'd just met this morning drawing this out of me? Why did I care so much what she thought? But I knew why. I knew exactly why.

"I also like to unpack my things when I visit," she said nonchalantly, her eyebrow up.

What was she talking about? Oh, she'd seen what I left in the drawer of Evie's guest room—my uniform.

She almost whispered her next words, but I heard her clearly. "Aiden was such a loner. Yash was his first real friend. He was happy making things, building things. He never needed people around. He loved his family in his own way, has such a protective instinct with Evie. He just always struggled with affection. When he got engaged, he was trying to be what he thought I wanted. It didn't make him happy. He grew increasingly temperamental over the years. But I knew he just needed the right person. He's very particular."

I listened, eager to soak up any new insights.

"I saw it when he opened the door this morning. He was different. And not only because he'd just left you in his bed," she said with a wink, "but he was brighter. All day I've seen it. He talks about you. His expression belongs to someone I barely recognize—someone I've been waiting my whole life to meet."

I was stunned. I wanted to hug her. And I wanted to run away.

"My point is, you may not be like everyone else. But neither is my son. Give it a chance."

I launched myself at her, holding her tight. Partly because she was so freaking kind and partly because I wanted to thank her for being who she was, for loving Aiden through his strange ways. For never thinking he was less than perfect just as he was.

"All right now," she said pulling back, her eyes glossy with affection. "Let's see if we can't find something with some bubbles from the kitchen, shall we?"

We gathered champagne and some plastic cups and walked to the beach together.

Aiden met us as we made our way down.

"Ladies," he said, taking the supplies from his mother before we continued on. Then he looked at me. "Okay?" he asked, and I nodded.

"You told your mother you wanted to have a kid."

"No," he said with a sigh, pausing in the sand. "After she asked me a hundred times, I told her I could *see* being a father, but not so much the lifelong partner part. She hears what she wants to hear. And that was way before I met you, so don't worry about it. Besides, people change their minds all the time."

I could have asked him which part he'd changed his mind about, but either way, the answer wasn't something I was ready to hear. Besides, I wouldn't be around after a few more weeks. This was a discussion for couples with a future. So, I didn't say more. Instead, I just stepped closer and sank into him, wanting to be surrounded by his smell, his warm body. He obliged and held me tight, a bowl of ice in his hand. Then he kissed my head, my nose, my lips. He kissed me like no one in the world was watching.

But his mother was. And she smiled.

23

DARLENE LEFT AFTER A FEW DAYS. She hugged me goodbye, holding me as long as she did her own children. I held her just as tightly, wishing I could keep her.

Aiden and I never discussed how weird I was when she arrived. We didn't discuss our relationship or the future. He stopped asking me about my job or why I was suspended.

"You can keep your secrets," he'd said. "For now."

We just got lost in each other for the time we had. I'd grown used to being in his space and didn't for a minute miss the solitude of my apartment. I loved that I usually woke to his mouth on me, his body holding mine. But a few days after Darlene left, I woke to an empty bed.

I found breakfast in the kitchen along with a note telling me to stay and rest because the only checkout today was a late one. It also said he wanted me well rested when he got back in a few hours.

I couldn't think of any better way to spend the day than lazing around waiting for him to come back and do whatever he wanted to me. Because it seemed everything he wanted was for me to have as many orgasms as possible. And who was I to argue with that?

I showered and found a pair of his boxers and a tank top, sans bra, to wear as I lay on the couch with his TV remote, finding an old episode of *Drag Race* to pass the time. I quickly drifted off and woke up to two voices in the kitchen.

Sitting up, I saw Aiden and Yash hunched over the kitchen table mumbling quietly. Aiden, upon seeing me awake, was up and on his way over.

"Morning, Birdie," Yash called mirthfully as Aiden sat next to me.

"I didn't want to wake you," he whispered. "Hungry?"

"Yes." Wasn't I always?

"We're going to make chickpea fritters for lunch."

"Sounds perfect. Can I help?"

"Why don't you get dressed and grab Evie at her place."

"But I'm well rested," I pouted.

Aiden smiled and kissed my hand. "Is my girl greedy?"

I nodded, still feigning disappointment. He gripped my chin, his thumb mushing my pout. "Be good. Or I'll take you over my knee later."

My eyes widened, but his words again settled within me, lighting a fire.

He leaned in close and whispered, "I'm glad to know a little spanking isn't out of the question." He stood, returning to Yash at the kitchen table.

I moved to stand with the blanket wrapped around me, Aiden and Yash watching as I stumbled back to the bedroom, Aiden's eyes perusing me and Yash's alight with humor. I tripped over the blanket, but righted myself. They both laughed as their attention returned to their work.

—

"WHAT ARE YOU GUYS WORKING on anyway?" I joined them at the table. Evie and I had decided to work on the fritters while they continued with whatever it was that had them so engrossed. A new shop project, I'd assumed.

"Expanding a few of the cottages," Yash said.

"Really?" I leaned in to see the plans laid out across the table.

"Expanding up mostly, into the attics," Aiden added as he gripped my waist, my butt landing in his lap. "More bedrooms to accommodate larger families and groups. See here, we add a staircase by removing this nook."

He moved his hand to the other sheet and said, "And upstairs we'll have three small bedrooms and a full bath here."

"Wow. Is this a long-term or short-term investment?" I asked, again fishing for information on his future plans without offering any of my own.

He shrugged. "Either way, it's the right move. These small cottages are pretty limiting in terms of clientele and profit. It would be good to get more usable space out of a couple of them."

"This is very cool," I said as I examined the plans, enjoying the closeness to Aiden's warm chest, his hand on my waist.

Yash and Evie stepped outside to set up lunch at the picnic table, and when it was just Aiden and me, he whispered, "You smell amazing."

I twisted in his lap to face him. "Do I smell like chickpeas?"

"Hmm. Chickpeas. Vanilla. And you." He playfully bit my arm. "Yum."

"Ouch," I teased, pulling away.

He came back chomping and growling, and I stood up to get away. He followed me as I escaped into the kitchen, and he cornered me at the counter.

"I like you," he said, veering closer, "very much."

The words washed over me, and I grinned like an idiot. "I like you, too."

"Good. We'll tell each other if there is anything we don't like, yes?"

"Yes. I'll go first."

He face turned grim. "What is it?"

"I don't like that you are not kissing me right now."

His smile was half-angel, half-devil as he stared into my eyes. "I'm going to get you for that."

"You better."

His smirk was more satisfaction than humor before he kissed me properly, and that was how Yash and Evie found us, with a loud clearing of throats.

Lunch was ready.

———

YASH PLOPPED DOWN ACROSS the picnic table from me after lunch while Evie and Aiden were cleaning up inside.

"All of a sudden, he's ready to move forward with the plans."

"What's that?"

"Aiden. Imagine my surprise when I got a call early this morning that he's ready to expand the cottages and wants my input. He made these plans months ago, and he's been sitting on them since then. Suddenly, he wants to renovate this spring so we're ready for rental by next summer. I just . . . I've never seen him like this."

I didn't respond. What did one say to that?

"You're good for him." He waited for me to meet his eyes. "Evie didn't believe I could love her. Not when she was sick. Not when she couldn't stomach the idea of sex, or when she lost her breasts, and not when she didn't care if she lived or died. But I did love her. Always. Just as I always will. I let things fall apart. *We* let them fall apart. Because she couldn't let me love her, and I couldn't let her heal the way she needed. We're still working on it."

I brushed a piece of food from the table to the ground. "Why are you telling me this?"

"We have to trust people when they tell us how they feel. When they tell us what they need. We have to let them love us even when we can't see how they could. And we need to be honest."

"Okay?" This conversation had taken a turn.

Yash smiled and stood up when Evie called out, telling him to get into the kitchen where he belonged.

"It's a good thing, I think, the expansion," he said, disappearing inside. I stood to gather the rest of the glasses when it dawned on me. Evie had spilled the beans to Yash about me.

—

"**SHE TOLD YASH.** She promised she wouldn't, and she told him anyway. It's only a matter of time before Aiden knows."

Doctor Evans watched me from across the little table with water and tissues, waiting.

"I mean, I'm not mad. I knew she couldn't keep it a secret." I caught Doctor Evans's brow draw up slightly. "Fine. It's on me to ask her to keep a secret like that. It's just . . ."

"Time to come clean?" she offered.

I looked away, then back at her, then away again. "Thompson called me this morning."

She stayed silent.

"To check in and inform me how well Jimmy was doing. Have you talked to him?"

"I haven't spoken to him regarding you, if that's what you are asking."

"Maybe they don't need me anymore."

Doctor Evans tapped her notepad with her pen. "When you arrived here, all you cared about was getting the job back, returning to work. What makes you say that now?"

I sat back in the chair and flexed my hands in front of me. "Maybe I'll stay here. Maybe I don't want to be the Chicago Bird anymore. Maybe I'll give up the powers."

"I wasn't aware that it worked that way. That you could just give up your abilities."

"I don't mean the abilities, just the practical use of them."

"It's fair to consider a change of career. But you're talking about what . . . hiding a part of you? What brought this on?"

"Maybe staying here."

"With Aiden?"

I nodded, my anxiety growing as I waited for her response.

"You still won't tell him."

I bent forward with my head in my hands before sitting up again. I was fully aware I was in the wrong here. I was lying.

"I can't. I mean, I physically can't. I keep telling myself I will, and then I chicken out, telling myself I'll tell him tomorrow. He knows I'm keeping something from him. His patience is wearing thin."

"When was the last time you spoke to your mother?"

I shook my head. "Jeez, you switch topics a lot."

She smiled unapologetically. "I know. When was the last time you spoke?"

"We chatted a few weeks ago on the phone."

"When was the last time you saw her?"

"Years."

"Have you spoken about the nature of your falling out?"

"Yes."

"And?"

"And she's apologized. Said she loves me and was afraid and didn't know what to say, so she said nothing. She's admitted to falling apart. She was still grieving my father."

"Have you forgiven her?"

I thought about that. Did I forgive her for pushing me away when I needed her most? "Yes."

Again with the silence on her part.

"She lost her way when my dad died. He was her touchstone, and she could barely function when he was gone. That's probably why I ended up engaged at eighteen. Anyway, I'm not angry at her anymore. And I know I played a part in all of it; I certainly didn't make things easy for her. But I just don't want her in my life."

"Why is that?"

"Because if I invite her back in, I'm not sure I could take it if she chose to stay away or leave again later on."

"Just like with Aiden."

"Ugh," I groaned. "Fine, yes. Just like with Aiden."

Doctor Evans smiled, almost proudly. "How do you think your father would have reacted to your abilities?"

A powerful surge of emotion engulfed my body, and my eyes teared up immediately.

"Fuck," I muttered, taken aback by my body's reaction to the question. I took the tissue she held out to me.

"Birdie?"

I wiped my tears and wadded up the tissue as I pushed the emotion down long enough to answer her question.

"He would have loved it. He would have been proud. He would have made it all okay."

Doctor Evans didn't respond, but she looked quite satisfied as she handed me another tissue.

"I used to imagine him still here, after the powers, I mean. I'd hear him telling me he was proud, that I was still his little bird. That being this new person didn't change that." I laughed lightly and shook my head. "I know my issues," I said. "And yes, maybe I'm just too chickenshit to do anything about them."

She allowed me a few moments to collect myself, then set her notebook down next to the box of tissues on the table between us. She did this when she wanted me to hear—really hear—something.

"You won't know the answer to your question until you tell him. What happens when he finds out from someone else? Will that make this situation better or worse? How will he feel when he realizes everyone knew but him?"

"I know," I said, exhausted at the thought of it. "I just want to keep what we have a bit longer. I'm not ready to let go. I know that makes me awful, but I don't care."

I thought of Nick. I thought of the way he let me go. Our relationship had lasted years. He loved me. I know he did. But this thing—this one *big* thing—was enough to make him fall out of love with me. It was enough to make Simon run from our date. It was enough to make my mother walk away from her daughter.

"I'm just not ready yet."

AS THE WEEKS PASSED, Aiden threw himself into his shop and planning the attic remodels. When he wasn't immersed in that, it was me he chose to immerse himself in, and I him. We fell into a happy pretend life, where he wasn't planning to return to his job in Texas and I wasn't a super.

We still didn't speak of our other lives. We just worked and cooked meals, swam naked at night in the warming, late-summer water. It wasn't until I was alone or lying in Aiden's arms as he slept that I worried myself sick about the future, wondering how much he'd hate me when he realized how long I'd kept this from him. If he'd even stick around long enough to hate me.

But when I wasn't thinking about the future, I was good. Better than I'd ever been. I was finding out who Birdie was, and I liked her. I liked her *here*, in this place, with these people. I'd ditched the jeans altogether, opting for shorts and a few summer dresses. I wore my hair down sometimes, pulling it up when the warm sun was too intense. I joked. I played. I had more patience. I had family. I even imagined calling my mother and letting her come see me here, knowing she'd be happy for me, and knowing Aiden would give her a bit of a shock.

Sometimes I found myself forgetting about my abilities. At other times I felt the urge to run, to search for trouble, the need to have an impact. I missed the rush, the responsibility, and the feeling of being something, being someone. But I didn't miss them like I had in the beginning. I felt content to leave them on the shelf for now. And I thought maybe I could do it permanently.

Evie and I had taken over running the cottages almost entirely. Aiden often would find reasons to stop in while I cleaned, whispering in my ear the crass things he was going to do to me that night. He or Yash made dinner most nights, and we'd eat together, the four of us, then we'd watch an hour of TV before he'd take me to bed and I'd fall asleep in his arms.

When I caught a slight cold and offered to go back to Evie's, Aiden scoffed, telling me that he wasn't going several nights without me in his bed. And when menstrual cramps kept me up one night, he'd brought me painkillers and ran me a hot bath before he lulled me to sleep with his hands in my hair. He took care of me. And I wanted nothing more than to take care of him. I found ways to be close, refilling his coffee in the mornings when he worked. I ogled him in his shop in the hot afternoons, and he smirked at me and laughed, then came over from where he was sawing or measuring and kissed me.

Things were perfect, and I'd almost forgotten about my other life, one I couldn't imagine going back to now. I'd forget I was keeping something from him because I was terrified it would change the way he looked at me. And in those moments when I remembered, I was hit with a strong sense of dread. Because I was desperately in love with Aiden Anders.

My mind was consumed by these thoughts as Evie and I strolled through town on a mission of finding her some new lingerie.

"I'm ready to ramp up our activity in the bedroom," she said. "I finally have a sex drive. I'm not wasting any more time. We're as bad as you and Aiden now." She smiled.

"Evie, do we have to get into the details again? I'm happy for you. But I couldn't look Yash in the eye after our last discussion of your renewed sex drive."

She wiggled her eyebrows. "Whatever, we're going to be talking about our sex lives for the rest of our lives. That and everything else. We have to keep each other in check, you know? We need a sounding board when we fight with our guys, someone to tell us when we're 100 percent right and when we're only 90 percent."

I laughed. I liked the idea of Evie being my sounding board.

"Speaking of sounding boards, I've got some more ideas about your return to the job."

"Hmm," I said dismissively, my eyes on a rack of lacy underthings.

"We need to look at all the past shit that's been out there. All the memes and headlines, and we need to turn it on its head. We need to embrace all the bullshit. Embrace the Superbitch, you know."

"How about this one?" I said, holding up a black corset with lace detailing at the bodice and straps crisscrossing the abdomen.

She tilted her head and touched the garter strap. "That's perfect. For you."

"We're here for you."

I placed it back on the hanger, and she came from behind to pick it up.

"We're here for fun. This will be fun for you and Aiden. OMG, can you imagine his face when he sees you in it, Miss White-Cotton Briefs?"

The image of it made me smile, and I picked up a deep red panty and bra set.

"I don't have it all worked out exactly, but we can print up some merchandise."

"What?"

"Your return to work. Your image." She said it like it was obvious to me. "You'll need some press training, which I can do, but again, we don't want to change things too much. You should still be fully yourself, just a little less," she stopped to consider her wording, "pissed off. And maybe tone down the cursing like 50 percent."

"What kind of merchandise?" I asked, horrified at the thought of more attention.

"Just a few T-shirts or lunchboxes," she said, putting a light-pink teddy to her chest and raising her brow. She put it back with a huff, misinterpreting my frown. "They could have your current logo or some of the new ones on it."

"Wait, new ones?"

"Yeah. We need to branch out. Make it fun. Let people relate to you. We'll start with *Superbitch*. It's like a rally call for your return, and you get to define what it means—you'll be an inspiration to women around the world! But don't worry, I've got other ideas as well."

Evie continued to rattle on about her plans, and my mind went blank. I needed to tell her that I wasn't sure I was going back—that I might not be the Superbitch any longer.

24

IT WAS A PERFECT AUGUST afternoon. My skin had bronzed to a color not seen in all my thirty-one years. I didn't have a care in the world as I dozed in and out of consciousness on a lazy Thursday afternoon, the waters of Lake Michigan lapping around me.

Evie had stormed inside Aiden's cabin early that morning, with Yash hot on her tail. She'd rented a boat for the afternoon, and we were all going out because we didn't have any checkouts that day and she was going to live it up. Aiden had kissed my neck, removing his arms that had me wrapped up as we lay in bed. He got up and stepped out of the room in his sweatpants to discuss plans with his sister, who was going on about a forecasted storm that never showed, leaving cheap last-minute boat rentals.

A few minutes later, Aiden had returned to where I'd waited in his bed and tossed me the tiniest black and white bikini I'd ever seen. I picked it up and laughed. "You can't be serious."

"Deadly."

"I'm not wearing this."

"Why?"

"Because it's obscene—that's why, you brute. Where did you even get it?"

"It's not that bad. Besides, we're going to be on a boat, and Yash is so gone over my sister, he's not capable of appreciating anything else. It's for my eyes only."

"You see me naked. Right now, you can see me naked. I don't think . . ."

Suddenly, the covers were pulled back, and I clamored for the sheet to cover myself.

Aiden prowled up the bed until he hovered above me. "Wear whatever you want. You are perfect in nothing and everything. But know this, Bernadette Bowden, greatest sex of my life."

Wait, what?

"I know for a fact that you would rock that bikini. I'm getting lightheaded just thinking about it. But that's the last I'll speak of it." Then he kissed me hard and jumped up. "Get up, woman, we have boating to do!" he'd said, and walked out of the bedroom, my brain working overtime to unpack all his words.

That's how I ended up on a sailboat in a tiny black bikini consisting of some thin white straps connecting the triangles.

I'd stripped off my cover-up thirty minutes into the trip while Aiden had smiled smugly behind the tiller. His gaze shared time between the open waters and me. A bit later, he finally found a perfect spot and dropped anchor. He climbed up to where I lounged and casually sat next to me, pretending he was unfazed. But I could feel the tension rolling off of him.

"Mr. Anders, to what do I owe this gracious visit?" I turned to expose my backside to the sun and Aiden's eyes.

"Do you have sunscreen on?"

"I couldn't reach my back," I whined, pulling the tube of sunscreen out of my bag and handing it over.

"You'll be the death of me," he muttered as he began spreading it over my backside while I laid my face on my hands and smiled. A few minutes later, his hands disappeared, and I sat up at the sound and feel of water splashing. His head popped above the water several yards away, and now it was his turn to look like a wet dream.

He swam back to the boat and gave me a little splash. "Come on, beautiful. Let's get you wet."

I dove in, emerging in front of him, my legs easily keeping my head above water. We stared at each other, both treading water. Then I leaned back and let myself float, the water carrying me while I stared at the sky, feeling like maybe I could give up the open sky for this. I could just be Birdie, and it would be worth it.

———

AIDEN AND I RETURNED to the boat shortly after our dip, drying ourselves in the hot sun.

"We ran into Mr. Real Estate the other day," Yash said as he and Evie sat curled together in the boat's bench, "the guy Birdie went out with."

"Oh? Did he ask about me?" It was one date, but I played along, wagging my brows as I lay on my belly, snacking on potato chips.

Aiden provided a light slap on my very exposed bottom.

Evie snickered, and Yash smiled and said, "He's a very persuasive man. Knows his shit, too."

"Right?" I laughed. "I hope you didn't blow all your savings on an overpriced bungalow with a two-car garage, zoned heating, and a den that can also be used as a nursery."

When no reply came, I turned to sit up, giving the conversation my full attention now. Upon seeing their grinning faces, I screamed, "You didn't!"

Evie squealed as Yash shrugged. "Guilty."

"So you're settling here, then?" Aiden asked stoically.

"We are. It's the perfect place. We're good here, we love the town and the vet clinic. You guys are here."

"Wow. Congrats!" I uttered, happy for my friend, ignoring the insinuation that Aiden and I were here indefinitely, something we hadn't discussed, something I'd been avoiding.

"We'll have more space now," Evie said. "Aiden, you can rent out my cabin. And I'm officially giving my notice. Once the summer season is over, you'll have to find a new cleaning crew."

"What will you do?" he asked as he pulled on a T-shirt.

"I've got a few ideas I'm exploring." She gave me a look, and I realized her plan included me returning to the life that seemed so far from who I was now.

"That's very cool. I'm so happy for you," I said, injecting all the cheer into my voice I could while pushing aside the knowledge that I was now keeping secrets from Evie as well. "Where is the house?"

Evie started in on the house's best attributes, and I was hyperaware of the fact that the summer was coming to an end. I was losing Evie to her new life. My time with Aiden was closing in. I was due back in Chicago in a few weeks. I felt Aiden's presence behind me, close enough to touch, but neither of us reached out. The plans of our friends made evident our lack of any kind of plans together.

"What about you guys?" Evie said, and it took a minute to realize that she went there, knowing exactly where we stood, in limbo.

Neither of us said a word. The silence was overwhelming. I forced myself to speak, regretting what came out.

"I'll definitely come visit," I said, implying I'd be in Chicago, despite it being the last place I wanted to be.

Evie's face fell, but she forced a smile, the discussion not going the way she wanted.

I heard a grunt from behind me. "I also saw Mr. Park Bench in town a few weeks ago. He's coming by to talk about a listing."

I froze, unable to turn around.

"Really?" Evie said. "You're selling? I thought maybe you'd stay."

I heard nothing from him, imagining his head shaking in reply.

I stood and cleared my throat. "Celebratory swim?" I asked and held my hand out to Evie. Her eyes said she saw right through me, but she stood and followed me into the water.

We splashed around for a few minutes while the guys talked, and when we got back on the boat, Aiden pulled anchor. We sailed for a while longer, but unlike every time I'd been with Aiden since the first time, his eyes didn't find me again. I found my cover-up, suddenly wishing I'd worn much more than this tiny little bikini.

Evie and Yash carried our things and what was left of lunch back to the car while Aiden tied off the boat and returned everything to its idle state. I stood on the dock, watching him as he ignored my presence.

"Suddenly I'm invisible," I said, my hands stubbornly on my hips.

He stopped what he was doing and looked at me. "Do you have a question, Bowden?" His tone lacked all the warmth he usually held for me, and it felt like a slap in the face.

What did one do in this situation? It felt foreign and created a deep ache in my chest. So, I did what I knew. I walked away.

I heard footsteps behind me, and then felt his hand on my arm, slowing me and turning me to face him.

"Look at me," he said. "What do you want, Bernadette?"

The question encompassed everything unsettled between us.

I want you to want me. I want you to fall for me the way I have completely fallen for you. I want you to never know the truth. I want you to know and love me anyway.

"Nothing," I said, because what was there to say? It wasn't fair for me to ask anything of him. I wasn't even telling him the truth about who I was.

"Dammit, Bowden," he muttered, dropping his hand from my arm. He was letting me go, and my heart fell. "You're a terrible fucking liar."

"**ENOUGH SULKING.**" Evie's voice penetrated my hiding place beneath the covers in her guest room.

"I'm not sulking. Anyway, it's your fault. What was that today? You knew exactly what you were doing."

"Yes, I did. The two of you need to get your shit together. But mostly you."

"Thanks," I mumbled as I threw my head back into my pillow, hoping that was the end of this conversation.

The dip of the bed told me it wasn't.

"Go away."

"No."

I groaned.

"I need you to see something."

"What?"

"Get your sad-sack face out of the pillow and look at it."

"Ugh. You're a jerk." I sat up.

"No, you're the jerk. You're a jerk to my best friend who is amazing. You continue to tear her down, telling her she isn't enough, or too much, or whatever. When the truth is she's just her, and there is no such thing as too much or not enough. I've been told my whole life I'm too much, and I got cancer and let parts of me die. I'm getting those parts back now and I like me, and anyone who doesn't can suck it, including me. So you, too, you can suck it."

I laughed, and she joined in.

"You should not be a motivational speaker."

"Whatever, you got it."

"I did," I assured her. "And you're right. You are very right. Doctor Evans is right; Aiden is right. And I've been such a shit. I've been a shit for so damn long."

"Because you were alone. You didn't have me to tell you when you were being an ass."

I smiled sadly, wishing it were that simple.

She placed her hand over mine and squeezed. "But you are not alone anymore, Birdie."

My eyes filled with tears. "You are still too much. More than ever, I reckon."

She beamed. "Thanks."

Then she pulled her phone out and placed it in my hand. It was open to a webpage titled *Where Is Our Bird?*

"It's had close to a hundred thousand hits. An endless list of comments in just a few weeks."

I started reading through the comments. People were speculating where I had gone, wanting me back. It was line after line of people sharing their experiences of me, asking where I was, saying the city wasn't the same without me. There were even sightings of me reported, too many to read—some real, most not.

"I've read most of it. It's 90 percent positive, which is surprising for any kind of internet comments. The other 10 percent get great responses your foul brain would be proud of. Most are women, but there is a nice supply of supportive men as well. A lot of young women are wondering where their foul-mouthed hero went, the one who won't take shit from douchebags on roofs. See, Birdie, they noticed you. And they notice your absence."

Evie put the phone down and leaned forward. She got into my space and made an intense level of eye contact that made me want to turn away.

"You are valuable. You are seen."

I looked at the phone again, scrolling through the statements and calls for my return. Maybe for the first time, I felt a little bit seen by the city I thought had completely forgotten me.

"It's not getting much mainstream press, but the press is a joke nowadays anyway. What matters is what the city is saying, and they want you back. Your boss can't ignore that forever."

It was everything I wanted that I didn't want to admit. I wanted to be their Bird. I wanted to clear icicles from skyscrapers in the winter before they fell. I wanted to lift fallen trees from metro tracks after storms. And most of all, I wanted to save lives on the rare occasion I was afforded the opportunity. I wanted to work with Jimmy, let him teach me how to connect to the whole city while I taught him to better hone his abilities. I wanted to show girls that there was power in being physically strong. There was greatness in being one of a kind.

I wanted my job back. Somewhere between the obligation and anger, I still loved my work. I'd always said I didn't want accolades, but seeing my city missing me, wondering where I was, giving even a little bit of a shit . . . it was enough.

"Birdie, you have to tell him. This has gone on long enough. You're making it worse the longer you wait."

"I know." There it was, the first step in getting it all squared, in getting back to myself. But it was also going to be the most difficult because I wasn't ready to let him go. "I'm so in love with him, Evie."

"I know," she said, placing her hand on mine. "It's clear as day."

"He's going to be mad."

"Maybe."

"He'll end things."

"Maybe. But Birdie, you have to give him the space to do it. You can't make this decision for him. It's not all about you. It's time to be a grown-up," she added with a motherly glare.

"Jesus. Asshole must run in the family," I quipped, knowing she was right.

"Just tell him the truth."

"Fine. Yes. I know. I'll tell him."

"Now."

"Not now. I just . . . I need to think. Tomorrow. I'll tell him tomorrow."

She shook her head. "It's your last 'tomorrow.' Otherwise, I'm telling him."

"Jesus, Evie, I said I'd do it."

She walked to the door and stopped. "You were my assignment, you know."

"What?"

She played with her fingernails. "The day I met you, I had been to see Doctor Evans. I was nervous because I knew I'd let things get bad, stagnant. I wasn't feeling my life. I was letting Aiden mother me; I wasn't moving forward with Yash even though I missed him like crazy. I'd lost my spark. I'd needed to check in with her. Anyway, she told me to get a life. I wasn't dying anymore, and I needed to stop acting like it."

"Harsh."

"It was what I needed. I was alone because I'd made it that way. I'd worked through so much with her, but for some reason, I'd gotten lazy with getting my life back. I didn't want the same life as before, and I wasn't sure how to get a new one. She gave me an assignment, kind of like your dating thing." She paused, examining the fan blades that turned above us. "She said I needed to befriend one person before our next meeting. I could fail, but I needed to try. To trust someone and let someone in, a girlfriend."

"That's why you kidnapped me?"

She laughed. "I never would have approached you that day if I hadn't been forced. You were so clearly broken, but you also exuded a strength and confidence I'd never seen before. You were so easily you. Intimidating a little. And I wanted that in my life. I wanted you to be my friend because you were strong, and I don't mean physically. You are the strongest person I know. You know exactly who you are, but you won't tell anyone because you're afraid."

"Evie, I—"

"You changed my life. You don't know it because you didn't see me before, but everything changed for me that day. You're the best thing that has happened to me in a very long time." She finished with moisture brimming her eyes.

"Evie, I don't know what to say."

"I love you, Birdie. I'm not going anywhere. If this friendship dies when you go back to Chicago, it will be because of you. And if it does, and then you need me back in the days or months or years from now, I'll still be here, because you are the best friend I've ever had, no matter what happens with Aiden. I need you to know that."

I stood and hugged her. "Shit, Eves. I love you too." It was the first time I'd said the words in so long, and the first time I ever heard them spoken to me with sincerity. And I felt a little bit more like I was ready to face the future, whatever it was.

—

AS MUCH AS I TRIED to ignore it, the guilt of my secret ate at me every time I thought of Aiden. My mood matched the storms that had arrived after a day of warmth and blue skies. The thunder and wind came up, keeping everyone inside, peeking through the windows for a glimpse of the night sky lighting up.

Evie and I had gathered the things in from outside while Aiden and Yash secured the outdoor furniture. But I didn't talk to Aiden again that day, and he hadn't seemed interested in talking to me.

Every one of our experiences now seemed tainted with *what if he'd known?* None of this would have happened. We never would have been together. I went from feeling guilty to being on the verge of tears to feeling angry at Aiden for not having wanted me if he'd known the truth about me.

I might have been losing my mind.

One moment I was ready to come clean . . . the next I couldn't find the strength.

It was my fault that Evie was keeping a secret from her brother. I didn't want to put a wedge between them now or later. I lay in Evie's spare bed, feeling it better to give Aiden some space. I was going over and over our future conversation at the same time I was wondering why I hadn't heard from him since I'd stormed off.

Maybe it was already over. I was so lost, wondering how to act in this relationship; this non-dating, friends with benefits, maybe dating, but only temporary, world.

"FUUUCK." I groaned in the dark.

"I was just going to sneak in to say goodnight, but if you want to, I'm happy to oblige."

I shot up to see Aiden peeking through my door.

"Hey."

"Hey yourself. What's with the nighttime cursing?"

He came closer, sitting at my bedside as I switched the lamp on, casting a soft glow across the room. Now that he was here, I felt myself breathe deeply for the first time that day. He was looking at me the way I craved, like he cared what happened inside my nutty brain.

"Couldn't sleep."

"You were thinking about my mouth, weren't you?"

I laughed. "You are seriously an egomaniac. You need help."

"I think I just need a kiss goodnight. I think maybe you need the same thing."

"Maybe. I'm sorry about today."

"Me too." He grabbed my hand. "I wanted something from the situation. I didn't get it, and I reacted poorly. It won't happen again."

"Me too." I wanted to ask him to stay, but I didn't want to push my luck, didn't want to risk him saying no. "Are you really selling?"

He shrugged and said, "That depends."

"On what?"

"On you, dummy."

My head fell forward, and I struggled with how to respond. I could tell him. Now was the perfect time, right? But I hadn't worked out the best words yet.

"I don't want you to make any decisions based on me."

He looked away from me, shaking his head. For a second, I thought he was going to leave. But then he turned back, like his mind was made up. "Please, just say it."

"Say what?" I was such a coward.

He pressed his lips into a tight line. "Whatever it is you're keeping from me. We can manage it. But we can't continue like this."

"I—I can't say it. Not yet."

He sighed, his frustration clear.

"We'll talk tomorrow," I assured him.

He nodded and stood up, poised to walk away. I reached for his arm. "You're leaving?"

"I can't stay tonight."

It was the first night we would spend apart in weeks, and I realized that my last morning waking up in Aiden's embrace was behind me. I dropped my grip. "I understand."

Aiden sagged as he watched me. I laid the pout on pretty thick. He groaned as he returned to my bed. He placed a kiss on my nose, and my chest fluttered like a schoolgirl's.

"God, you're beautiful and infuriating," he said just before his lips found mine, and it went from schoolgirl to dirty teacher in an instant. He licked my tongue and pulled me closer until I was straddling his lap without realizing I'd moved. He gripped my ass as we mauled each other's mouths, and when I pressed against him, he growled like a bear. Eventually, he set me back on the bed and moved away. I mewed, and he smiled.

"I've been thinking about you naked since I saw you in that bikini."

"What a coincidence," I admitted. The truth was, Aiden Anders consumed way too much of my thought processes on a daily basis. I found myself watching him cook, watching him create beautiful pieces of furniture. I thought about him when we weren't together and when we were. I wanted in on every thought he had. I wanted to know everything about his past, be part of his future. I wanted to know all the strange things that passed through his head that so many people never voiced. I wanted him just as he was, always. I wanted all of him.

Aiden leaned over, gently kissing my lips. "Goodnight, Bernadette."

"Please stay," I begged, and he eventually relented, removing his shirt in a swift pull, followed by his shorts. He slid in next to me in just his boxers, pulling me into his chest without a word. He was asleep minutes later, and I was left to wonder if this was the last time I'd fall asleep in Aiden's arms.

25

HIS WARM BREATH RELEASED into my hair. His skin was hot against my own, and I tucked myself closer, the dusting of his chest hair tickling my nose as I breathed deeply, taking in his smell. Just in case this was the last of it.

He stirred. "Hey, gorgeous."

I smiled, pushing away thoughts of the future. "Hey yourself."

He chuckled and pulled me on top of him, palming my ass. "Hmmm. I was dreaming about this beautiful ass. The day I met you, I knew I wanted to get underneath those tight jeans."

"I thought you were a boob guy."

"Like any loyal bird watcher, I enjoy the view from all angles."

"You're ridiculous," I laughed.

"And you are making this very hard for me."

"What's that?" I said as I gave a little wiggle.

"My decision to stay away from you until you spill the beans."

"So don't. Stay away, I mean."

I kissed his chest and lightly bit his nipple. He groaned. My mouth traveled down his body to where his cock was eagerly waiting. I pulled down his boxer briefs, and I licked. He let out a string of curses as I wrapped my mouth around him.

"You feel like heaven." Then he pulled me up and underneath him. He wasted no time sliding inside me—moving in and out slowly. I tried to keep the weight of my lie from encroaching on the perfect feeling of being stretched to the brim by him, but it was there, in the daylight—because

I was sure I was in love with Aiden, and that made keeping this secret unforgivable.

Just a little longer, I said to myself. *I'll keep him just a little longer, just until . . .*

He pushed himself up on his arms and looked at me as his lower half took me in hard thrusts.

"Fuck, Bowden, your pussy is fucking milking me," he rasped, "so goddamn good."

"Your mouth is a fucking liability," I chastised him.

"Only for you." He was losing control as one hand held both of mine above my head. His other hand was on my neck with just the slightest pressure. I was so close.

"Fuck, Bernadette," he groaned as he came inside me, then collapsed on top of me. He moved to my side and rested his chin on my shoulder, his dick against my thigh. His hand slowly stroked my stomach.

"What was that?"

"Sorry, babe, I couldn't hold back."

"Yeah, right, since when?"

His head popped up so he could look into my eyes. Then he smiled. "Just a little encouragement and . . ." He kissed me hard on the mouth, then chin and neck, moving down until he sucked my nipple, and I felt him twitch. "I might be convinced to go round two."

"You're evil," I said, my body on edge, needing release.

"You can end it all right now." His hand snaked down my body to where I was left bereft. "Say it. Tell me what's holding you back."

He thought this was something I could just spit out during sex.

"Please, Aiden," I begged as he tormented me.

"I could do this all day. Just say it."

I closed my legs and turned away from him, angry and wired with no release in sight.

He groaned behind me. But then his hand snaked around my thigh. "I'm sorry, love," he said as he found the space that ached. "That wasn't nice."

I pushed his hand away. "Forget it."

"Birdie."

I pouted.

He turned me over and kissed my nose. "I'm sorry, Bernadette. It was a bastard idea." Another kiss. "Will you forgive me?"

I nodded because he was adorable when he apologized.

He smiled and pushed my hair back. Then he whispered, "You are amazing, Bernadette Bowden. Nothing you tell me is going to change that simple fact."

I tucked my head into him, willing the courage to speak. He stroked my hair and kissed my head. His palm eventually found my ass, and I climbed on top of him, knowing he was ready for me. This time, he waited for me before he found his own release.

Just as we found our breath, I heard two sets of hands slow clapping outside my room.

"Bravo," and "Well done," came through the door, followed by retreating laughter.

"Oh my God, I forgot where we were." Horrified, I dropped my face to his chest.

Aiden chuckled. "What can I say? I can't get enough of you. Someday we'll be old and gray and won't have the energy for this. We need to take advantage now, don't you think?" He turned to his side, taking me with him. "Okay, maybe a little rest, now."

I forced a laugh while my mind was stuck on his words *someday we'll be old and gray*. It was the first time he'd ever mentioned a future. And while it may have been just a joke, it hit me hard in the gut, because I wanted that more than anything—maybe more than the job, more than the powers.

He brought my hand to his mouth. "You did a fantastic job distracting me this morning. Now we're going to dress and go about our day. But tonight, we talk. No more waiting."

"Tonight," I replied. No matter what happened with my job, I had to say the words.

A shrill sound invaded our reverie. I ignored the first blasts, but Aiden's head shot up. "What the hell is that?"

I pulled myself together as it sounded again. "Oh shit. Shit, shit, shit." I reached over to find my jeans on the floor and pulled out my phone as Aiden let me go. Just as the ring tone promised, the screen lit up: Thompson.

"I gotta get this." I glanced back to see a slight look of confusion on Aiden's face before I hit answer.

"Yeah," I said, breathless.

"Birdie," his voice rang out. "How are you enjoying your vacation?"

"Ah, it's good. Why are you calling me?"

"Wow, okay. Cutting to the chase. I respect that. We need to talk about your return to work."

"Okay," I said tentatively, turning back to Aiden and mouthing, *It's my boss. Sorry.*

He rolled over and grumbled as he stood up, completely aware how distracting his naked body was.

"Hello? Birdie?"

"Uh. Yes." I pulled my eyes from Aiden as he dressed and gave my attention to the call. "What's up?"

"I'll cut through the bullshit. I met with council last night."

Aiden bent down to kiss my lips, then left the room, closing the door behind him.

"Okay."

"They're happy with Jimmy."

My blood boiled. "And? Why are you telling me that?"

"Look, you still have a job here. But they want to go with Jimmy as the official Chicago super."

I sat up in bed, my head hanging between my sheet-covered knees. "And I'm what, a fill-in?"

"The job doesn't change for you. You never liked the press aspect anyway. You'll continue to do the work you do, and he'll be more of the face of the team."

"You told me to avoid the press! This isn't about my job performance. It's about suddenly changing my job description without telling me. Without offering any support for the change. This is about the city's image, not mine!"

"I know you're upset now, but the other cities are capitalizing on their supers, and we need to be out there. We need a face."

"This is bullshit," I said, shaking my head.

"Look, I'm pissed off too. And truth be told, you were right about him. He's green and not 100 percent reliable. But I'm not sure what I can do about it. I did try."

"You're the mayor, aren't you? How is this not your call?"

"You'd think that, wouldn't you? But the aldermen have always been involved in this one. It's an issue of city perception, and they don't want the super changing as often as the mayor. The city needs a reliable long-term super."

"I've been there ten years!"

"They like his persona. They like that he's from Chicago."

"I'm from Chicago!"

"You have media baggage."

"This is final?"

"They're making the announcement tomorrow."

Of course they are. This is what I wanted, anyway, isn't it? To stay with Aiden, if I give it all up.

The next word I uttered was painful. "Fine."

"Fine?"

"What do you want me to do, boss? Beg for my job back? I don't want to be anywhere I'm not wanted."

"Birdie, I'm sorry. The truth is this city needs you, but they don't know it. And that's my fault. I let it happen under my watch."

I pinched the bridge of my nose. "It is what it is."

"What will you do? Will you come back?"

I lay back down in the bed, the smell of Aiden making my heart hurt. The plan to tell him I was the Chicago Bird tonight was now shaky because, in truth, maybe I wasn't anymore. The city had made their decision: demotion. Maybe this meant I could have a future with Aiden. If he never saw me that way, maybe we'd make it.

"I don't know. It feels like you're affirming everything that's been said about me. I think I'm better than that. I want more than that." I imagined telling Evie the situation and could see her colorful reaction in my mind. "I deserve better."

"I agree," he replied. I stared at my boots that sat in the corner of my room. "The day will come when they see what they lost today. Your day will come. I hope I get to be there to see it. I'm fucking in awe of you, kid. Look, I gotta go. I'll call later."

"Yeah, okay. Bye, Thompson." I hung up before he could say more.

I lay there for a time, naked and potentially jobless. I stared at the ceiling, my mind blank. Thompson's words swirled around in my head: *Your day will come . . .*

I finally rolled out of bed and shuffled into the shower, still in a bit of shock, not knowing what the next days or years of my life would be.

———

I STEPPED OUT OF A CLEAN cottage later that afternoon, my mind preoccupied with letting Aiden know he'd need to remove the handcuffs the guests had left on the headboard and a paint job was needed on the wall behind said handcuffs.

Then, maybe after I told him that, I'd slip in that I'd been demoted today from my job as the Chicago Bird, that I was thinking about not going back, that I was technically a superhero, and hoping maybe he'd fall in love with me anyway.

My preoccupation had me and my cleaning gear nearly mowing down the guests exiting the next cottage with a beach bag and little boy in tow.

"Excuse me," I said on reflex. "Sorry about the—" The words died on my lips as I stared into the face of the man in front of me.

"Birdie?" He said my name like an old chum. "Wow, what a surprise!"

"Nick," I whispered the name.

"How are you?" He picked up the kid, who couldn't have been older than three or four. "Just a minute, Sammy. Daddy's talking to an old acquaintance."

An acquaintance? We were engaged for years before he fell out of love with me. "I'm great," I said in a daze, staring at the boy who kept pointing to the beach, saying "sand castle" over and over. "How are you?"

He looked at the woman standing next to him. "Excellent. This is my wife and my son." He cleared his throat. "Do you work here?" He was looking at my basket with cleaning supplies.

"I do."

"I thought you were in Chicago. I saw that news story of yours. Guess the city wasn't happy with it. Tough break."

I told myself that he wasn't gloating, that I wouldn't overreact. "I still work for the city. I'm just taking a long vacation and helping my friends with their business." Wanting to sound confident and strong, my words instead came out sounding defensive and maybe a bit childish.

"Well, good for you."

"Hello, I'm Caroline," Nick's wife said as she reached out her hand, the beach bag hanging from her elbow. She was beautiful, of course, tall and lithe.

I found my manners and shook her hand. It wasn't her fault her husband was a dick. "Hello, I'm Birdie."

"How do you two know each other?" Caroline asked.

My eyes flew to Nick. "She doesn't know?"

He took a heavy breath and said, "Caroline, Birdie and I used to date, many years ago."

"We were engaged," I added, sure that his wife should know and letting my desire to get in a jab overwhelm any measure of tact.

But the look on her face had me instantly regretting it. She looked stricken, obviously unaware her husband had had a fiancée before her.

"I'm sorry," I muttered, unsure of what else to say.

Sammy stared to wiggle and point toward the beach.

"Just a minute, buddy," Nick said, setting him down and holding on to his hand. "You can't go without Dad."

I needed to get out of this situation. "Be careful today. It stormed last night, and the undertow is strong." I pointed awkwardly to the beach. "Red flags are out."

"You a lifeguard now too?" he asked, his eyes on his wife, who was already marching away toward the beach.

"I do it all, I guess." I felt the sourness on my face, regret. His son started crying, and we stood there, watching him melt down because he wanted to go with his mom. His blond hair was lighter than his parents', but he had Nick's face.

When I looked back at my relationship with Nick, I wondered if I had ever really loved him. I racked my brain but couldn't remember feeling about him the way I felt about Aiden. Aiden was consuming. He was a deep well—everything I wanted and a lot I never knew I needed.

I tried to tap into the anger I'd carried for so long but found there was none left. Because maybe when Nick broke up with me, he did us both a favor—something I hadn't had the courage to do. It wasn't his fault he didn't love me. He couldn't control who he fell for.

"Nice to see you, Birdie," Nick finally said, dismissing me, his eyes still on his wife, who stood at the beach now, watching us. She looked like she was about to cry, and I swallowed hard. It wasn't my fault he'd kept secrets. Besides, she had him now. They had a kid. A cute one.

"Okay, then. Enjoy." I walked quickly toward Evie's cottage, glancing back to see them talking on the beach.

I wanted to feel good about outing him, but I just felt gutted. Because I was no better than Nick. Worse, actually, for calling someone out on my own issues—I was doing the same thing to Aiden, keeping a part of me from him. But my lie was a lot worse. It wasn't in the past. It was a living, breathing lie, not one I could push into the closet and forget about. It would permeate everything we were. Suddenly I knew that lying to Aiden was worse than the secret ever could be.

———

FAMILY DINNER IN AIDEN'S little backyard was quiet. I was quiet. Distracted. The others tried to carry on a conversation that included me but quickly gave up on my participation. I knew I was making it weird, but I was stuck in my own head. I needed to tell Aiden the truth. And I needed to do it *now*.

Evie's glances were getting into my head. The closer it got, the more anxious I became, playing out every kind of reaction—most of them ending with me going home alone.

"Hey." Aiden's hand was on my knee, and he craned his head so he was in my line of vision as I fixated on the sea-glass table centerpiece Evie found on the beach. "Tell me what's up." Evie and Yash had gone into the house, leaving us alone.

I finally gave him my attention, his face shining with what looked like . . . like something I desperately wanted, and I cringed inside. Would this be the last time I saw that look from him?

"I'm just preoccupied."

"About what you're going to tell me?" He turned his body to fully face mine, his knee on the bench between us.

I did the same. "Yes. Also, the family in cottage four."

"What about them?"

"The guy is my ex-fiancé."

Aiden didn't react. He did nothing but watch me, looking for something. "The relationship you mentioned? You were engaged?"

"It was a decade ago. But now he's here with his wife and kid."

His voice was a bit strained when he spoke. "How do you feel about seeing him?"

"I don't feel anything, I guess."

He swallowed and asked, "Do you still have feelings for—"

"God, no. I mean, I can't even hate him. Yes, I was shocked at the time, but now it just feels like nothing."

"Okay, that's good, right?" His legs moved and he straddled the bench, scooting closer, his hand rubbing my calf. "What are you thinking about?"

I gazed into Aiden's dark eyes, manifesting courage. I needed to tell him. I knew that. But the idea of him looking at me any other way than the way he was currently looking at me filled me with such dread.

"I'm thinking about how things ended between us, how things turned ugly. He fell out of love with me. And I'm not saying you're in love with me or anything, but . . . there's something I need to tell you. It's going to change the way you feel about me. And not for the better."

He gave me what was intended to be a reassuring smile and grasped my shaking hands in his. He leaned forward and let his lips linger on mine, then at my ear. "Tell me your secret so that I can finally tell you how I feel about you."

Tears welled up then. "Shit," I said, not sure I could get the words out. "Aiden."

"Yes, Bernadette." He kissed my neck, my nose, and pulled back to look at me, but not getting too far away.

"I'm not who you think I am."

He kissed my palm.

"Stop doing that," I scolded.

"Doing what?"

"Being sweet and perfect."

He chuckled. "Okay. How would you prefer me to be?"

"I don't know. Just, I can't think when you kiss me."

His eyes turned dark. "I'm aware. It's one of my favorite pastimes."

"Kissing me?"

"Yes, and getting you out of your own head."

"Oh."

"Babe, most things are simpler than we work them up to be."

"Not this thing."

He moved my leg to the side and pulled me close. "Just say it," he encouraged, his beautiful eyes inches from mine.

"I'm scared," I replied.

"Why is that?"

"I can't change who I am. I don't even want to. I've realized I like who I am."

He grinned. "As do I."

"You won't much longer."

"Well, why don't you let me be the judge of that?"

I nodded, knowing that once I said the words, it might be months before he fully grasped the implications of who I was and what it meant for him. I'd agonized over this, looked at it from all angles. If this didn't end immediately, it would die slowly. I thought about what the press would do to me, what those kids said to Simon at the festival. The press would rip him apart, the comments historically directed at me falling to him. Even if he stayed with me, could I do that to him? I needed to make a choice—Aiden or the job. But first, I needed to say the words.

"Aiden, I'm not like other people. I'm the Chicago—"

"Birdie! Birdie!" the sound of a woman's cries filtered through our cocoon. Screams came from the front of the cabin.

"What the—" Aiden said, letting go of me and standing up. I was up as fast as he was, and we walked quickly toward the sound of the cries.

As we got to the front of the house, I could see Evie and Yash hurrying out of Aiden's front door. They too had heard the cries.

I stalled at the sight of Nick's wife in hysterics at Evie's front door, where she stood banging on it with her fist.

"Caroline?"

She whipped around. "Sammy! We turned our backs for a second. Nick went in after him. Please, Birdie. Please!" She stepped off the porch, pleading.

"Where are they, Caroline?" I asked, already knowing the answer.

She stared out over the unforgiving waves of Lake Michigan, and pointed.

26

LAKE MICHIGAN IS THE SECOND-LARGEST body of fresh water in the United States. With over fourteen hundred miles of shoreline, there was good reason it was dubbed the deadliest lake in the country. Each year, the lake claimed dozens of lives, and the number one reason was rip currents.

We all ran with Caroline to the beach, where she obviously hoped to see her husband and child emerging from the water. When we saw nothing, she began screaming and frantically pointing at the water. The waves looked particularly brutal in the late summer evening, the sun setting too quickly. No one should have been in the water. Caroline was muttering how they'd taken their eyes off him, just for a second. Then she looked directly at me in terror.

"Please," she begged.

Aiden was removing his shoes, asking where the boy was when she last saw them.

"I don't know!" she screamed. "They were right in front of me. Then they disappeared. Oh my God, this can't be happening. We were having an argument and turned away for just a second. He was gone."

Aiden and Yash started into the water and after one last look out, I didn't hesitate. Tossing off my flip-flops and throwing my phone on the sand, I was in the water, swimming past them a second later. I swam hard, diving deep. The water was murky from the waves, and my vision was limited. Surfacing past the breaking of the waves, I found Nick treading water, panic stricken, yelling at the top of his lungs, "SAMMY!"

I swam toward him. "You okay?" I called.

"Birdie! I can't find him. I had . . . I had him, and the water ripped him away. SAMMY!"

"Go back," I called to him. "You need to go back. I'll find him, I promise."

"I can't, not without him!" he yelled, his voice quaking with a kind of fear I'd heard before from parents.

"Go back," I said again as sternly as I could. But I wasted no more time with him. Just before I dove back in, I saw Aiden and Yash still making their way out against the crashing waves.

I swam faster and longer, covering as much territory as possible, hoping that what I couldn't see, I'd make up for with territory covered. I wouldn't leave until I found him, but time was passing, and I needed to be faster. Better.

My superior lung capacity was tested, and I emerged for another breath before returning to the murky water. How long had this kid been in here? Was it going to be too late by the time I found him? I couldn't let Nick's kid drown. No matter how much I'd thought I hated him, I could never see him in that kind of pain. They were fighting about me no doubt, about what I'd told Caroline. That's why they took their eyes off Sammy.

I always carried a sense of urgency during a save, but this felt more personal, and I wouldn't come out of this water empty-handed, or worse. I went deeper, kicked harder, my lungs straining for air to feed the level of effort I was exerting. I'd been idle for weeks, and now my lungs were paying for it. I'm sure I was creating even more turbulence above me, making it harder for anyone to help. But I knew I was the only one who could find him in these conditions.

Then I saw him—I practically ran right into him. My legs and arms spread wide to stop my momentum, and there he was behind me, submerged and unconscious. Without thought, I pulled the little boy close and surfaced. I put his face in front of mine and felt no air. He wasn't breathing. Kicking with my legs, I was able to keep our heads above water as I pulled his little face below mine and blew into his open mouth. Once, twice, a third time.

"Come on, little guy," I urged as I tried again.

He coughed, water spewing from his blue lips, and I almost submerged us again as relief swept through me. I turned his face over my shoulder, allowing him to continue coughing as I started back to land from about a hundred yards out, riding the waves slowly, doing my best to keep his head above water.

His little arms were tight around my neck and soon his coughing morphed into whimpering, which I took as a good sign. When I was close enough to see everyone on shore, I spotted Nick sitting on the beach, rising to his feet when I came into view, his hands in his hair. Aiden stood next to him, his face unreadable, watching us. He was soaking wet. Evie called my name in relief, while Yash held Caroline back from running out to me.

I finally found the ground beneath me and stood, pulling Sammy away from my neck to get a good look at him. He was shell-shocked but otherwise breathing relatively normally, and his whimpering turned to a full-blown cry upon seeing my unfamiliar face.

I handed him off to his mother when she tore free from Yash, reaching me knee-high in the water. I stopped to let her embrace him, but stayed to make sure they kept their footing as the breaking waves pummeled our lower bodies.

I glanced up to see Nick standing back, the guilt and relief warring on his face. Aiden gave him a pat on the back, encouraging him to go to his family, and he did, joining his wife and child as I guided them to the shore.

As we walked toward their cottage, Nick cradled his little boy, and Caroline held my hand tightly, telling me how amazing I was, how grateful she was, how I was a gift from heaven. This reaction wasn't new to me. People like her were the reason I'd had a job in the first place; their letters to the mayor and city council had kept them from replacing me. Except now those letters apparently weren't reason enough.

Arriving at the cottage porch, Nick threw himself into one of Aiden's chairs, his son in his arms, tears running down his face as his wife fell to her knees, her face in her husband's lap next to their child. They were everything to each other, and I'd almost ruined that with my hang-ups, my insecurities. My heart ached as I watched them, realizing I wanted what they had, all of it. I wanted that with Aiden—a life, a future, maybe even a little boy or girl who looked just like him, and a little like me too. But mostly, I wanted to keep everything that I'd found here in Grove.

"I've called emergency to come by and check him over," Evie said and Nick nodded silently, before looking at me.

He stood, passing his son to his wife. The look on his face was one I'd seen before but never from someone familiar. He stepped close, his hands in his drenched pockets. "Birdie," he said.

"You don't have to say anything, Nick."

"I'm sorry. I'm so sorry."

"Don't. It's not worth it. It's fine, I promise."

"Please," he interrupted. "I'd like to say this. It's long overdue."

I nodded.

"I'm the luckiest man in the world to have this family." He glanced at them with love before turning back to me, his expression that of a man realizing how close he came to losing it all. "I'm sorry about the past. Truth is, I was never going to be what you needed. You were heading into a life where I couldn't follow. I resented you for it, and I handled things poorly. I'm sorry about how things ended with us."

"Nick—"

"And look at you now. I'm in awe of you. The world is in awe of you. I'm sorry about a lot, but I'm not sorry I knew you. I'm not sorry to have been a part of your life for a little while." He wiped his eyes. "I can't even begin to thank you for what you did today. You saved my whole world."

There was sincerity there, and I appreciated the words. He was right. We'd grown apart, and while it didn't have to end with ugly words, it had needed to end. I couldn't hate him for not loving me, and I could forgive his words. It was me who'd held on to them the way I had.

I snuck a glance at Aiden, who was watching Evie as she answered a phone call, a look of concern on his face.

"Thank you, Nick. I'm glad everything is okay."

"Birdie!" Evie called as she came closer. "There's an emergency. You need to go back to the city."

I took the phone she held out to me.

"Birdie, we need you."

"Thompson?"

His voice was firm with what sounded like dread. "Wells Street at the river. Get here."

The line went dead.

I looked at Aiden, his face concerned. "What's wrong?"

I took a moment to memorize him perfectly as he was. Because as much as I wanted to stay in his bed forever, forget about the rest of the world, the job, and be only his, I couldn't. I had a job to do, and I always would. Even if I wasn't paid to be. Even if I was a joke to some, I was the Chicago Bird.

"I'm so sorry, Aiden. Goodbye."

"Goodbye?"

It was the last word I heard before I was gone, not caring that he'd just seen me use my speed. I gathered my uniform from Evie's cottage and stood next to Thompson not a minute after the call ended.

"WHAT HAPPENED?" I mouthed to no one as I absorbed the scene in front of me. The "L" train had derailed, and two train cars were hanging precariously from the platform over the Chicago River, another having detached and fallen in, filling quickly with water. First responders were arriving as I did. A few civilians were already in the river, trying to reach the car but having no way to get inside it.

I assessed the situation. The sinking car was my first priority. I ran along the bridge and jumped down, landing on top of the train car as it disappeared beneath the water. The river wasn't all that deep, but it was enough for the car to be fully submerged. My fist went through the layers of metal, and I ripped back the roof. Inside, there appeared to be about twenty-five people, children and adults alike, their heads barely above the water as it rose around them.

I reached down and grabbed the hand of the first person I saw and pulled them up, setting them behind me as a tourist ferry pulled up alongside the sinking car. I pulled out another, and another, and another, each second the car filling faster as water started pouring through the opening I'd created. I was losing sight of the people beneath me.

Suddenly a few rescue divers with small oxygen bottles attached to their mouths dropped inside the hole I'd created.

"We'll bring them to you," one said just before disappearing under the water. In and out my hand went, one after another. Several people were unconscious or bloodied; my body barely felt the weight of them as I placed them behind me into the capable hands of the first responders getting them onto the waiting ferry. Then the train car was submerged completely. Just as I was about to jump inside, an oxygen mask popped up, followed by a diver who confirmed they'd gotten everyone.

I looked up at the bridge as the train car dangled above it, swaying with an awful moan of metal on metal. I leaped back up to the bridge where responders were evacuating the train cars that weren't hanging over the side.

"What can I do?" I asked a woman I recognized as the deputy fire chief. She was directing her team and working with the police to form a game plan.

"Thank God you're back. Can you lift this thing back to the bridge?"

"I don't have my jet pack," I said, not sure even the jet pack would have enough juice to lift the weight of the train car. "I could try to pull it back up, but I'd need to get a good handle, and I don't want to rip through the steel and risk it falling."

She looked at me, waiting for my answer.

"I'll give it a shot."

Two train cars were off the tracks, one staying mostly on the bridge, the other dangling from its end. I pulled the first train car back ever so slowly, and the one below it swung. I stopped as screams pierced the air, the squealing of the straining metal rising above the chaos.

I stepped into the car already cleared of passengers and made my way slowly to the other end that hovered over the river. I moved outside onto the tiny platform between the cars for a better view below. I could see people huddled on the opposite end of the passenger car—too many people, scared and bloody. Others were clinging to seats and poles along the sides. I wasn't sure how my strength or speed could immediately help, not with the specifics of the situation. Not without possibly making things worse.

"Bird!" I heard my name from the opening of the train car behind me and turned to see Mayor Thompson standing there. "I thought you might need this."

My jet pack. I moved back through the car and took it from him greedily. "Where's Jimmy? I could use a hand here."

"Not sure. The brakes malfunctioned. He tried to stop it, but . . . he said he just made it worse. He dropped this with me and took off. You're on your own with this."

I'd deal with Jimmy later. I strapped the pack to my back, relishing the feel of it shooting me with adrenaline. I'd missed this. This was who I was, who I was meant to be. I'd never give it up. Not for anyone.

Then I was hovering in the air next to the train car and forcing the doors open as people scrambled toward me with terror in their eyes. They moved calmly, though, carefully working together to get the injured to me first. One man, wearing a suit jacket over what likely started the day as a crisp white shirt, was covered in blood coming from a gash in his head, turning his gray hair a shade of deep red. He was clearly in pain as I flew him to shore, but as I placed him on a stretcher, he touched my elbow, and I turned momentarily to catch the words "Glad you're back" before he was enveloped by medical personnel.

I carried two people at a time when possible, going back and forth from the train to the ambulances on land. One woman clutched a small barking dog in her arms as she cried; a young boy just stared in part awe, part fear as we flew; a few were unconscious; and yet another woman wailed about a lawsuit. Most breathed a clear sigh of relief as I took them in my arms. I moved with singular focus until the train car was empty.

Returning to the bridge, I slowly pulled the dangling car back, the sound of scraping metal filling the air until it was close enough to lift it, with the help of my jet pack, back to the bridge.

Once everyone was out of immediate danger, I left the mess of the trains to the professionals, letting them know I could help with whatever they thought best to minimize damage during the cleanup. I told them I would call in Jace for additional support once the time came to move the cars.

I thoughtlessly made my way past the camera flashes and clamoring reporters to Thompson, who stood just south of the bridge. I unhitched my jet pack and held it out to him.

"Keep it," he said with his hands up. "It's yours. Always was. See you back at work when you're ready, Bird."

Jimmy appeared next to us in a bit of a panic. "It's my fault. I tried to stop the train, but I fucked up. I think I did this." He gestured wildly toward the train. "I freaked out. I'm so sorry."

Thompson stopped to talk with him. But I needed to decompress before I dealt with that.

I was going to take off, but hesitated. I usually left the scene to go home, but I suddenly couldn't quite visualize where exactly that was. The idea of returning to my apartment was draining. I wanted, with everything inside me, to return to Aiden's arms, have him carry me to bed and kiss my forehead and tell me I'd earned the right to sleep all the way through the day tomorrow. I wanted him to tell me he was proud of me and mean it, without any shame or embarrassment in his eyes. I wanted Evie and Yash to come wake me hours later, unable to stand not hearing all about it any longer. I wanted to go home and finish dinner with my family, because it was still Friday.

But they weren't my family. And I wasn't theirs. I wasn't anyone's. I was the Chicago Bird, and I was no one's girlfriend. I was the superhero, not the heroine. Any feelings Aiden may have had for me would be quickly swept away with that realization. It was better this way, because at least I'd have this perfect, unspoiled memory of Aiden and my time in Grove.

"Bird! Bird! Do you have time for questions?" In my hesitation to leave, I'd let myself be surrounded by the paparazzi, all of them thrusting microphones and cameras into my face.

"Tell us how you feel after saving all those people today!"

"Are you coming back to your job?"

"Where was Jimmy today?"

"How did this all happen?"

"Birdie, what are you wearing?"

A young woman stepped up in front. "What do you have to say to all the kids watching today, Bird?"

I met her eyes and smiled, suddenly ready to speak, not caring how it was received. Evie's endless instruction about speaking to the press came to mind.

"Today this city came together, the police and fire, the doctors and nurses, the ferry operators and civilians of this amazing city. We came together to help our own, Chicagoans and our visitors, who are always welcome as Chicagoans for the day. We did our best, and that's all we can do, but it was a good day to be a part of this city. I'm honored to lend a hand, always."

They'd fallen silent as I spoke with a level of authority I'd never allowed myself, and then they erupted into questions again. I kept my attention on the young woman up front.

"Why did you decide to leave the mask at home today, Bird?"

I furrowed my brow and my hand touched my face before realizing I didn't have my mask on. It wasn't there when I'd grabbed my uniform. My identity was on full display; everyone was seeing *me*.

"Don't need it." The words came without thought.

She smiled. "And the T-shirt? Is this a message for anyone in particular?"

Again confused, I looked down to see my wet T-shirt, black cotton with white letters reading *Yeah, My Vagina Can Crush Your Penis.*

Oh my God—Evie! She'd switched out my shirts. I'd kill her—if I ever saw her again. I'd surely kill her.

But then I considered what she said when she'd given it to me. *Own it, who you are, what you are.* I looked right into the camera before returning my attention to the woman who'd asked the question. What did I have to lose?

"No, no one in particular." I flattened my mouth and pulled my shoulders back, so everyone could read the words. I gave her a confident smile and said, "Just the truth."

Her mouth curved into a huge grin. "Bad. Ass."

I laughed, and the interview came to an end as I stepped back and shot into the sky, a satisfied smile on my face.

27

A SAVE ALWAYS GAVE ME A RESTLESS high with the pure adrenaline coursing through me, and I felt on top of the world. This save had been one of my best, and I rode that high for the next . . . oh, fifteen minutes or so before I stood inside my apartment, staring at the sterile white walls and twin bed.

"What kind of adult has a twin bed?" I said aloud as I realized I was once again alone. And my post-save high took a dive when there was no one to talk about it with, no one to come home to.

I sat on the bed and realized that Aiden and Evie and Yash were in my past, like a dream. A really, really good dream that I didn't want to wake from.

Maybe I could go back? Maybe Evie could still be my friend when her brother hated me. But I could never face him. I reminded myself once again that it would kill me to see the affection fall from his eyes the way it had from Nick's, the same disappointment emerge over time, the same relief on his face when it inevitably ended. No, I'd take my last memory of him the way it was, kind and perfect and maybe a little bit crazy about me. I had two weeks left to my suspension, and while Thompson had made it clear I could go back to work, I wasn't ready. I couldn't fall back into old routines. I could handle my life, my solitary life, but Evie was right, I couldn't hide from myself or the city I served. If I was going to give them my life, my dedication at the sacrifice of everything else, they'd have to take all of me. I wouldn't hide any longer.

I'd have to prepare myself, plan.

That is, if I still had a job after my fiasco with the press. I looked down at myself. *Jeez, Evie, this shirt.* The aldermen would certainly have something to say about this. But for the first time, I didn't care. They could fire me if they wanted. I'd still be me. I'd still show up when I was needed. I'd still help, even without the paycheck and the jet pack.

My phone buzzed in my pocket, and I pulled it out to see Evie's name lit up on the screen, a picture of her in her best runway pose. I declined the call.

It was better this way. Better to make a clean break.

I removed my uniform and took a scalding shower before hiding under the covers, imagining a kiss from Aiden as he climbed in next to me. I could almost hear his words as I drifted off to sleep.

"You did all right today, Bowden."

———

"YOU UPPED THE ANTE WITH that T-shirt." Doctor Evans smiled across from me. I knew that look. I'd never seen it on her before, but there was a hint of admiration on her face now.

"It was an accident."

"Oh? Well, how are you feeling about it now?"

"I'm not sure." I shrugged. "I guess I don't really care. I'm indifferent." I was feeling indifferent about a lot of things today. "I'm not fired yet."

Her lips pressed together. "One might say that's progress. And did you have a chance to tell Aiden before all this happened?"

"Let's just say he knows now."

Her eyebrows went up. "And how did that conversation go?"

"It didn't."

She closed her eyes briefly, though her face gave nothing away. "Birdie. How many times have we discussed this? There is really nothing else I can help you with if you aren't willing to put yourself out there."

"I won't saddle them with all my baggage. Maybe Evie could handle it, but Aiden . . . he didn't sign on for this version of me."

"What version is that?"

"I lied to him. I'm not—"

"Don't. Just don't finish that sentence." Doctor Evans set her notepad aside and stood up. She paced to the window and back, then sat again. "People in your past—the people who left—didn't choose you. They chose the easy way out. They chose to give up." She picked up her notepad and pen, settling into her lap, sitting back in a relaxed fashion, before adding, "But then again, maybe you did too."

She let that one settle for a moment, then said, "You have this delusion that there's no perfect people out there just for you, that you are meant to be alone. But let me tell you a little secret. There are no perfect people, period. There are no soulmates. No one's *meant* to be in a relationship or *meant* to be alone. This life is about choices. You choose to be a friend. You choose loyalty. You choose to do right by people. You choose to be brave. And love is also a choice. If it gets hard, you choose to keep trying or choose to call it quits."

She leaned forward and spoke slowly, a sliver of frustration showing through. "Consider what choices you are making now, Birdie. What are *you* choosing? *Who* are you choosing? Think about it."

I didn't immediately respond. and Doctor Evans returned to her poised position in her chair, her voice back to normal. "I've already sent my assessment to Thompson. I see no reason for you not to work. The rest is up to you." She looked up at the clock. "Our time is up."

—

FOR THE NEXT FEW DAYS, the question stayed in my head. What was I choosing? It wasn't that simple, was it?

Uncertain, I wallowed in my apartment, staring up at the ceiling and thinking of Grove. I thought of Evie and Yash moving into a new house. I thought about Aiden, about how his feelings for me felt so simple, so easy, and how I made it all so difficult. I thought about his reluctant smile, his deep laughter, his calloused hands. I imagined him in his kitchen, in his shop, in our bed.

In an effort to break myself of the downward spiral, I decided I'd go see Jace in New York and pretend I had everything figured out, that I didn't miss Grove more than I'd ever thought capable.

I met Jace's guy. Well, not quite his yet. But Jace was diligently working on it. Just as he'd described, Claudio was handsome, a little shy, and very nerdy. And by nerdy, I mean very into pop culture, comic books, and role-playing games.

Claudio wasn't exactly what I would have pictured for Jace, but he was also exactly right. They were clearly head over heels. It was fun to watch the most confident man in the world struggle with falling in love for the first time.

When he wasn't wooing Claudio, Jace took me to his usual haunts where people knew him but didn't care too much about his celebrity status. We raced each other around the island of Manhattan. He said he let me win because I looked so damn miserable; he was a liar. On several occasions, when he asked me to talk about the life I was avoiding, I told him to leave it alone. And he did, doing his best to cheer me up.

The night before it was time to go home, I met Jace and Claudio for dinner. I'd arrived a few minutes early and was waiting at the bar in my summer dress, my hair down, light makeup, and wearing a pair of glasses. My best disguise yet. It seemed the most recent save had made the national news and, while I refused to pay attention to the media frenzy, I had been recognized a few times since being there. I wanted to be anonymous tonight.

As I started in on my martini, Jace entered. I knew it because of the muted commotion that followed him everywhere in this city.

He leaned in to kiss my cheek and said, "Hey, Blanche, you look great. What's the occasion?"

I shrugged. "Just wanted a change."

"Change is good."

"Where's Claudio?"

He picked the olives out of my martini and slid them from the tooth-pick into his mouth. "He's parking the car."

"Really?"

"No. Who has a car in this city? He's finishing a phone call with his mom outside."

"Right."

Just then, Claudio walked in. "Birdie," he said with a tone of sadness, "I can't believe this is your last night here. What am I going to do without you running interference with this guy?"

"Hey." Jace pouted before Claudio went in for a brief kiss. My heart thumped as I thought of Aiden.

I tried to push the thoughts away, but it seemed the more days that passed, the more of Evie's phone calls I declined, the more I missed them. So many times a day, I thought of things I'd wanted to share with Evie only to sag at the realization that I'd pushed her away with the lies I'd told her brother. I'd never wanted to put a wedge between them.

"Check out what I bought online," Claudio said in a singsong voice. "Just arrived today." He unbuttoned his dress shirt and pulled it off, giving it to Jace, who tucked it into his lap.

I spit my martini across him and his T-shirt. Because it wasn't his tee. It was mine—or Evie's. What was important is that the shirt said in block letters, "Yeah, My Vagina Can Crush Your Penis," followed by a cute little superhero emoji with a braid and mask.

"Where did you get that?" I said, sounding almost accusatory.

"Online, like I said. I barely got my order in before they went on back-order. They're selling like hotcakes."

"No!"

"Yeah, they are. Where have you been the last two weeks? Check it out, you're trending." He pulled up his phone to the video of me on the news with like a gazillion hits, Evie's shirt on full display as I said with a visible confidence, "Just the truth."

"There are shirts that say that too." He leaned in, whispering, "My elderly neighbor got one that says *Yes, My Vagina Can Crush Your Penis, But I'm Too Old to Bother*."

"Oh my God," I screeched, and heads turned.

"Oh, Birdie, don't be such a prude." Claudio put his phone away. "I saw one the other day that said, *Yeah, My Asshole Can Crush—*"

"Stop. Please. This is bad." I glanced at Jace, who was enjoying the conversation, having never said a word to me about this. "I'm supposed to be a wholesome municipal employee. Clean and universal, approachable."

"Oh, Bea, there's no such thing," Jace finally interjected. "We're all a little dirty, and if we're not, we're repressed and angry."

"Even Jace's nieces have them. That's who I saw them on first—they're all over Insta."

My face was stricken. "The asshole one?" I whispered.

Jace laughed out loud, then showed me the picture of his niece, and sure enough, her shirt said *Yes, My Vagina Could Crush Your Penis, But I'm Not Old Enough to Date Yet.*

"How is this a thing?"

"Girl, your tees are all over the country."

"But it was just ten days ago."

"I know. I thought maybe it would burn out, but it keeps going. Good for you, marketing yourself."

"But I'm not, Jace. I didn't market myself. It's not me doing the shirts."

"Well, someone is making money off this endeavor."

This was bad. I'd be sacked for sure. Thompson didn't like a commotion, at least not historically. And I wasn't sure this was the "face of the city" they'd asked for. I pulled out my phone, finding a long string of texts from Evie.

I typed out **Are you selling T-shirts?**

The reply came in seconds. **Don't be mad.**

Then a few minutes later: **Birdie. Don't be mad.**

I'm not mad.

I wasn't mad. I was in shock. I looked up at Jace, who was watching me intently.

"You okay?"

"Yeah, I just think I need to go home and get everything sorted."

"Now?"

"Yeah. I . . . this might be bad."

Jace stood and picked me up in a bear hug. "Call him," he whispered in my ear. "Let him be the one to end it. It's not right for you to make this decision for him. It will only bring regret."

I pulled away and looked up. It was the first time in ten days he'd specifically mentioned Aiden.

"I'll think about it."

"Bye, Beatrice."

"Goodbye, Jace. Good luck with this one," I said, leaning in to give Claudio a kiss on the cheek.

"I don't need luck," Jace called out after me as I walked to the door. "I've got a super penis that can't be crushed!"

I stopped just as those around us did, taking in his words. I didn't turn back, but I had a smile on my face as his chuckle followed me out the door.

28

ARRIVING BACK IN CHICAGO on foot, I slowed as I made my way through the city. The thing about physical speed like mine was that it often rivaled mental speed, faster than reaction time, so I rarely moved at top speed in the city.

Coming up through downtown, my feet came to a nearly immediate halt, my shoes smoking against the pavement. Suddenly, I was standing in front of . . . well, myself. There I was, blown up to the size of the Stay-Puft Marshmallow Man—okay, not quite, but it was a huge vertical banner of me, standing in a Superbitch T-shirt and classic braid, maskless. It was an image that eliminated any option of returning to the shadows. My face, for the world to see in downtown Chicago. In big letters it said "Welcome to Chicago—Home of the Chicago Bird."

For ten years, I'd managed not a single recognizable picture in the paper. No glowing reviews on the evening news. Suddenly, I was visible, exposed. I took in the image, the unfamiliar look of confidence on my face. A surge of anxiety rushed through me. *Am I ready for this?* But there was something else there too, something that brought a hint of a smile to my face. I felt a rush at the image of a powerful female being celebrated; of *me* being a source of pride as opposed to embarrassment. Things had turned around overnight, it seemed.

There were two people in that moment I wanted to speak with, two people I wanted to share this with. Two people I wanted to let reinforce what I knew deep down but had a hard time accepting—that it's okay to be celebrated once in a while. It's okay to feel pride.

I took out my phone and opened the text messages from Evie. Her first messages were of support and encouragement, telling me how badass I'd looked on TV, how she'd branded the T-shirts. Her messages got increasingly confused and worried, then a little angry.

You know, I need you as much as you need me. It's not fair of you to forget us when you get all popular.

Her last message just said, **We'll be here when you're ready.**

Wait—*we?* Did she mean she and Yash? Was Aiden part of the proverbial *we?*

After all, seeing this banner in front of me now had been seemingly impossible three weeks ago. And apparently I still had a job. What else was possible for me?

Then my belly hurt for an altogether different reason. Hope sprang inside me like a geyser, and while my brain tried to squash it, as it had done so many times before, that shot of pride I felt wouldn't let it. Now that I'd had a taste of something else, a taste of the impossible, the feeling of falling in love and an understanding of friendship and family, I wasn't sure I could accept the loss of any of it without a fight. I switched to Aiden's text stream and saw nothing.

But why would there be anything? I'd disappeared without explanation after lying for weeks. I'd pushed him away.

Suddenly, every decision I'd made in the last few weeks wasn't a choice I could see myself making anymore. I wanted more. And I needed to be brave enough to take the chance.

I finally responded to Evie. **I'm ready to come home.**

Dots appeared. **Where is that, exactly?**

I hesitated, going with blatant and vulnerable honesty. **With Aiden in Grove. And with you.**

When no dots appeared, I started to panic. **Does he hate me?**

Where are you?

I just got back to Chicago, why?

Go home to your apartment for now, Birdie. I'll call you tonight.

I deflated. He didn't want to see me, and she was going to break it to me gently. My throat constricted as I started home.

I stepped into my apartment, the barrenness of it engulfing me in a sour mood. By going to New York, I'd only been delaying the inevitable. Now it was time to face the music, even if the music was the same lonely tune I'd been listening to for a decade.

I set down my bag at the door and walked in the direction of the kitchen as I stared at my phone, willing Aiden to call. I decided to finally look through all the texts I'd been ignoring since I'd gone to New York. I started with the ones from Thompson.

> Give me a call
>
> Let's discuss your return date
>
> Need to set up some press for your return—nothing too big, I promise
>
> Why are you not answering my calls?
>
> You are coming back, right?
>
> My wife is wearing your T-shirt. Thanks for that btw
>
> Apparently, it's the new "I drink and I know things"

Standing in front of my open refrigerator, I responded.

> How much blowback? On a scale of 1 to 10?

His response started, and I blankly watched the dots as I retrieved a Fanta from the fridge.

> It's not exactly how I would have handled it. But you saved fifty lives two weeks ago. Nick and Caroline Wolff have been all over the news singing your praises for saving their son. And apparently you are bringing positive female empowerment to our city, in a sort of offbeat, vulgar way. It's the age of the woman, and council has no choice but to embrace it. Most of them are eager to do it.

I sighed in relief.

But . . .

I was happy about all that age-of-the-woman stuff, of course. But that didn't fix me personally. I didn't automatically know how to exist in this new world where expectations had changed, even if in my favor. It didn't change my life. But maybe it could. Giving up on Aiden and Evie had been a mistake. One I could try to right, a first step. I just hoped they hadn't given up on me yet.

I turned toward the living room and jumped with a screech when, dropping my unopened Fanta to the floor, I found someone sitting quietly in a familiar chair—one that didn't belong in my apartment.

"Evie!"

"Hey there," she said, utterly relaxed like the evil genius she was.

My tears emerged with the relief I felt. I walked directly over to her, and she stood and embraced me. She let me cry into her shoulder, let me fall apart a little.

"Hey, you should be happy. You are fucking killing it," she said.

"No, *you* are killing it. This is all because of your shirt."

"*No*," she scoffed. "This is because of who you are and what you do every day. This is because of the commitment you've made to this city and what you've sacrificed for it. This is because you are embracing your power. I'm just doing your PR."

I laughed through my tears. "Well, you are extremely good at it. Even if it's a little bit over the top."

"Thanks," she beamed. "I don't come cheap, either. But I think the money we are making with the shirts will cover it for now, with plenty left over for whatever charitable causes you pick out."

"You're amazing. Thanks for being here."

"Where else would I be?" she said, grinning like the world was her oyster. "So, I know this is all about you today, but I have to tell you."

"Tell me what?"

"I'm engaged!" she shrieked.

I smiled, knowing this was perfect for her.

"I love that. Yash is—"

"We talked about everything. About what I need, what he needs. We're going to have a long engagement, but we know we want to be together always. He's my family."

"I'm so happy for you, Evie. You both deserve it."

"What about you, Birdie?"

"What about me?"

"Do you want a family?"

"You've been my family since that day you kidnapped me and forced me to be your best friend. It just took me a while to realize it. You are, without a doubt, the best person I've ever met, the best thing that ever happened to me," I whispered as my eyes watered. "You changed my life."

"Damn right," she said, wiping her eyes as tears spilled. "Does that mean you want to come home?"

I wiped my eyes as well, pushing back the emotion. "More than anything," I admitted. "Do you think . . . I don't know. Have you talked to him?"

"Yes, but he doesn't say much. When I said I was coming to see you, he made me bring this chair."

I looked down to see my chair. The one I'd claimed from Aiden so long ago. The one he'd claimed *me* in.

"Is it a goodbye gift?" My heart tugged at the words.

She shrugged. "He said it belonged to you the moment he saw you in it."

I scrunched my eyes, my heart aching for the man who crafted it.

"He made it for you, before he even knew you."

I laughed. "Aiden would never say something so sappy."

She tipped her head. "I believe in love. I always have."

Trying to get a grip on my emotional overload, I asked, "How'd you know where I live anyway? That I'd be here?"

"Jace. And it seems you never lock your door." She looked around and said, "I can see why."

"Hey!" I protested, knowing she was right.

I sat in the chair, the smell of it bringing Aiden into my home. But it didn't feel right. It was too bright for this place. It belonged at his cottage on the lake, the same place I wanted to belong. I rubbed my hands along the arms of the chair, my eyes following the river that flowed through the wood.

I looked up at Evie, who was sending a text with a happy smile. I was happy for my friend. She was getting what she wanted, love and a pretty stellar new job, it seemed. "You carried this thing from Grove all alone?"

"God, no. I have no upper-body strength."

"Who carried it?"

"Well . . ." She finished up on her phone and shoved it in her pocket. "I didn't exactly come alone."

My blood surged in anticipation, but I didn't speak. Evie just grinned. She reached down next to the chair and grabbed her purse.

"I'll be back in a few hours. I'll text before I come barging in."

"What?" I stood and followed her to my door. "Where are you—" but my words died as she opened the front door. Aiden was standing there, his gaze finding mine, his face blank of any emotion I could pinpoint.

"Later, kids," she said and leaned in to kiss my cheek, then did the same to Aiden before he stepped into my apartment and closed the door behind him.

"Hi," I squeaked out.

He said nothing as he passed me on his way to the bar stool at my kitchen counter. He took a seat before locking eyes with me. I stood unmoving, barely able to think. I knew I should say something. I needed to apologize. I thought I'd have time to work all this out in my head. But he was here now in all his handsomeness, and all I could think of was how much I loved him and how I wanted to spend my life trying to make him laugh and hearing the filthy things he'd say on a daily basis.

"Two-ninety," he finally said.

"Two-ninety? What is that?"

"Two-ninety is how much I can bench. I didn't want to tell you earlier because, well, I didn't want to brag."

I scrunched my face. "Okay?"

"I can run about a six-minute mile, though I haven't tracked it in a few years. Pretty fast, right?"

Then it dawned on me. I smiled as my heart lifted and filled with hope. I wanted to cry, but I held back and timidly asked, "Why are you telling me this?"

He pursed his lips as he thought it over, finally releasing my gaze to stand up and take in his surroundings, my sad apartment. He shrugged. "I thought it was time."

"Oh," I replied, taking a deep breath as he slowly walked toward me.

I was frozen, anticipating his words, his touch. When his hand landed softly on my cheek, I closed my eyes and a tear fell.

"Why did you run away?"

When I didn't immediately answer, both his hands were on my face. "Because I'm afraid . . . I didn't think you'd want me."

"Listen to me." He lifted my face, my eyes locking on his. "I want you, only you. You have to know that. I'm fucking in love with you."

I braced myself. "How? Now that you know everything . . ."

"Because you're mine, Bernadette. Because you—"

"You think that now," I interrupted. "You think you still feel the same way as before. But give it time. After a while, it will get to you, what I am, my powers, the life and the media attention that isn't always as good as it is right now. Apparently I can be quite emasculating."

He barked out a laugh. "That's the stupidest thing I've ever heard."

"I couldn't take it, watching you fall out of love with me," I said, my voice cracking.

"Bowden," he interrupted, pressing his forehead to mine. "What am I going to do with you?" Then he pulled away and guided me back to the bar stool. He sat, pulling me to stand between his thighs, his hands around my waist. He looked up at me, waiting for me to look at him, and spoke softly. "Did you hear me when I said that I love you?"

"I've been here before," I started again, "and you'll feel less powerful, less like 'the man.'"

He cut me off. "Fucking hell, babe. Give me some credit here. I know who I am. I know who you are. I'm not one to feel emasculated, whatever that even means. Let's let me decide who I fall in love with. You don't get to decide how I feel about you, now or later."

I wanted to believe his words, wanted what he was offering. I wanted it all.

"You want to know what makes me feel powerful?" He pulled me in closer. "How you look at me, like I hung the fucking moon, like you're head over heels for me."

I rolled my eyes.

"Don't do that—I know you are," he said, as he smirked and gave me a squeeze. "How you let me be me, how you challenge me with your words and ideas. How you make me laugh every day. How you love my sister, how good you've been to her. How strong you are," placing his hand on my heart, "in here." His eyes grew dark. "How I can make you wet with just my words. How you can't help but let me take you anytime, anyplace. I feel most powerful when you fall apart in my arms."

I blushed, because his words were true. I was putty in his hands. I'd never felt that way with my ex-fiancé. With the supers I'd dated. With anyone.

"It makes me feel powerful that you choose me. Because you are the fiercest and most beautiful woman I've ever known. Every part of you. Your power isn't a threat to my ego. It's part of what makes me know that I'm the shit. That you, a woman who is independent and amazing, and perfect, are mine. I don't need you to need me, baby. I need you to choose me. And the only thing that could break me of this is if you send me away."

I wrapped my arms around his neck and drew myself closer still, smelling his clean scent, trusting every word he said, knowing he was genuine.

"You say that like you've known about me from the beginning. But you just found out, and what if you change your mind? You didn't know when you fell in love with me . . ."

He stiffened and cleared his throat. "I did, actually."

I drew back. "What!"

He had the gall to smile sheepishly. "I've known for a while."

"When did you know?"

"A while."

"No."

"Yes."

"*No.*"

He quirked his brows, "Ahh, yes."

"How?"

He chuckled. "Birdie, I'm not completely dense. No offense, but you and Evie couldn't keep a secret if your lives depended on it." He rubbed my low back. "I was hoping you'd tell me yourself. It was clear you had a history and were struggling to tell me. You needed to take a break from it, and I wanted to give you that. But I fell in love with you with a pretty full understanding of who you are."

"Oh my God. All this time, I've been agonizing over telling you this, and you knew. You knew the whole time!"

He smiled. "It was pretty adorable."

I pulled back and pushed his shoulder, but he held me tight.

"Come home with me, Bernadette. Please. Let yourself trust me."

Yes. Yes. Yes. I wanted that. "You don't have a problem with what I do for a living, then?"

He shook his head. "Bowden, you can do whatever the hell you want during the day, as long as you come home to me at the end of it. Also, I was prepared to have the discussion about where we wanted to live, but this place seals the deal. Let's go home to the cottage."

"It's not that bad."

"Yes. It is."

"Fine." I kissed him, and he kissed me back. "You sure you want me there? 'Cause I can totally kick your ass."

He grinned and wiggled his eyebrows adorably. "I'm looking forward to it."

This man. He didn't make me anything I wasn't before, didn't change me, but he gave me such comfort so I could emerge into the world as myself. I knew now that I could give my whole self over to that full and complete love with total trust. The truth was, I was proud to know Aiden Anders, proud that he'd chosen me, with all his strength and vulnerability. He made me so freaking happy. My sexy, smart, brooding boyfriend, egotistical enough to love me.

"Do you love me, Bernadette Bowden?" he whispered as he looked in my eyes.

I hadn't said it yet. But I knew it without question. "I do love you, Aiden Anders. I choose you, always."

29

Four months later

"IT IS MY GREAT PRIVILEGE to present this honor to someone who embodies what it represents. Someone who's dedicated many years to this city and its citizens. Someone we hope will stay with us despite the efforts of other cities to lure her away."

Standing in Daley Plaza in downtown Chicago on a blustery December morning, Mayor Thompson cleared his throat. "She is someone who has been a role model, a valued citizen, and an asset to our great city. She needs no introduction. Birdie, please accept our appreciation, esteem, and sincere gratitude for your years of dedicated service. You are the person we call upon when we need a hero—whether it's to save lives or to save taxpayer dollars." Thompson laughed at his own joke along with a group of folks that must have been from the budget office. "She is someone I'm honored to call a friend. Birdie Bowden, get up here and take this key to your great city."

Cheers and eager applause carried through the massive crowd that had gathered in front of city hall.

"We love you, Birdie!" came from a group of young women in various fan T-shirts, all designed by Evie. Some dirty. Others downright vulgar.

I stepped forward from behind Thompson and accepted the key to the city.

"It's about damn time," he whispered, shaking my hand.

Then I stepped to his side, shaking Jimmy the Juggernaut's hand.

"Congrats, boss. Long overdue," he said with a comical grin, knowing how ridiculous I thought all this was.

I pasted on the most sincere smile I could muster, before looking down at the oversized plastic key, frowning. "What the fuck am I even supposed to do with this thing? It's the size of a four-year-old child. About as useful as one too."

A round of laughter rumbled behind me when my words were picked up by the hot mic on Thompson's lapel.

I cringed, and Jimmy smiled, leaning into the mic. "That's our Bird. Best save record in the country and no regard for public decorum."

I turned just as a piercing whistle rang from the beautiful asshole in the front row. I met his handsome face, shining with pride. I rolled my eyes, which just made his smile bigger.

Next to him, Evie was throwing me double thumbs-up, encouraging me to say the words we'd practiced. I stepped up to the microphone at the front of the erected platform, a massive Picasso sculpture looming to my left, my smile firmly in place.

"I want to thank the mayor for this honor." I looked at the hundreds who stared back at me. "But the true honor is serving the great people of this city alongside our police, fire, first responders, construction workers, and the like." I glanced at Evie, who was still giving me the thumbs-up. But that was all I had to say. As everyone stared at me, a few hoots and hollers rang out.

"We fucking love you, Birdie!" a man yelled. "You're the shit!"

"Thanks," I laughed. "I fucking love you guys too."

Laughter and applause carried forward. I looked at the cameras that were on me. "Hope you guys aren't broadcasting this live."

A man's face popped out from behind the camera. "We always give you a three-second delay," he said and winked.

More laughter. "Good to know."

I glanced at my people, all standing front and center. Jace and Claudio,

Evie and Yash, and Aiden. My eyes found his again, borrowing courage. His smile was all I needed. "And thanks to you, the people of Chicago, my friends, for embracing me and letting me get away with all the verbal cock-ups." I quickly stepped down as cheers continued. I handed Claudio my key, knowing he'd hock it on some website for a pretty penny and donate the proceeds to the free training institute Jace and I were establishing for kids and young adults who were developing powers.

The two of them, Claudio and Evie, had banded together in the past few months to manage my public relations and marketing along with Jace's and a few other supers around the country. The income was more than they needed, so the rest went to the program.

Evie gave me a hug. "Great job," she said. "Only two or three curses."

"Too much?"

"Never."

Jace patted me on the back. "I think this qualifies you as fodder for Snatch Game. RuPaul would be proud."

Before I could reply, I was enveloped in the warmth of Aiden as he held me close and whispered, "Never let them tame you."

I settled into his arms as any remaining tension released, fully aware the cameras were still on me. I was getting better with public events, but I'd been avoiding any events that "honored" me, because, well, I was still a work in progress.

"Can we go home now?" I asked, staring into his warm eyes that lit up just for me.

"As you wish."

All seven of us huddled into the back of Yash's newly purchased full-size SUV. He'd bought it in preparation for their planned brood of children, the first one of which was currently cooking inside Evie's growing belly.

"So, Captain America," Aiden said, breaking the silence from the second row where I was curled into his side, "when are you going to follow in my fiancée's footsteps and embrace your man on national television?"

I pinched him.

"Ow! You wound me, woman," he said, flinching.

"Don't rush him," I said, then looked back at Jace. "Sorry."

"It's in the works," Claudio offered.

"Soon," Jace said with a smile. "The super-duo are working it all out." He glanced at Claudio and Evie with affection, then looked back at me. "Besides, we can't all just wing everything with perfection like some foul-mouth super lady I know."

"It'll be hard to beat the Superbitch coming out, but we've got a few ideas," Claudio said with excitement.

"Like what?" Jimmy asked, smashed between Jace and Claudio in the third row.

"Ball drop," Evie squealed from the passenger seat. "It's going to be so perfect! So romantic!"

"This woman couldn't keep a secret if her life depended on it," Claudio groaned.

"Speaking of romance," Jace interjected, "Jimmy the Juice, how's the love life, kiddo?"

Jimmy huffed. "Don't call me that, man. And what love life? This one," he said, nodding at me, "has got me training during all my off hours. Of which there are very few."

"And it's paying off!" I argued.

"It is," he admitted.

"What about the woman down at the community center?" I asked him, raising my eyebrows.

"Caanndice," Evie and I said in unison.

"Are you guys, like, five?" Jimmy blushed, and we laughed.

After some additional chatter, we pulled into the parking lot that said *Anders Family Beach Cottages* and piled out of the behemoth vehicle.

We gathered in Aiden's kitchen—*our* kitchen—where Darlene and my mother had been turkey-sitting and prepping some sides for the celebratory lunch they insisted on.

"Birdie!" my mother called as I entered. She gave me a hug. "I watched it streaming—I'm . . . I'm very proud."

"It's not a big deal. It's just a novelty for the city, the key and everything. It really means nothing."

"I don't care about the stupid key. I'm very proud of *you*," she said with a timid smile. "Though I'm especially happy to see you get a bit of long overdue recognition." At this, she looked down at the floor. "I should have done better in that department."

I waited until she looked up again. "Thanks, Mom. I'm glad you're here."

She let a heavy breath out, as though she'd been holding on to it for a decade, and kissed my cheek before heading back to the kitchen to help Darlene. As she walked away, I smiled at the small logo on the back of her T-shirt—*Superbitch* written between her shoulder blades. When she turned again, I saw the other side, a little emoji of me in my jet pack flipping the bird.

I found my way to the bedroom, where I changed out of my uniform and into some loose jeans and a baggy sweater that hung off one shoulder. I unraveled my braid and let my hair fall. I slipped on some warm socks and glanced outside at the snow-covered beach. My life had taken an amazing turn, and I had to sometimes stop and take it all in.

When I returned to the party, they'd turned on the music. Evie and Yash were dancing in the living room, and Jace and Claudio were dancing with Darlene and my mom in the kitchen.

Aiden met me at the kitchen counter with a glass of wine.

"How's my city girl doing?"

"I'm good. A little overwhelmed."

"Big crowd today."

"Yes."

"You were perfect, Bowden," he said and kissed me just below my ear.

"Shall we dance?" I whispered.

"Hmm. Promise you won't run away this time?"

I tipped my head to the side. "Can't make any promises." I smiled. "What will you do if I run?"

Aiden wrapped his arm around my waist and pulled me in. "I'll come get you, again. Always."

"No need for that. I'm smitten," I said wiggling my finger in front of his face, showcasing my engagement ring.

We all sat down for a meal together, told stories, and teased one another. I soaked it all in, relishing the life I'd almost let slip away because I'd let myself think there were prerequisites to deserving love and family.

Once the last guest departed for the evening, I grabbed a blanket and found my favorite spot on my favorite chair on my favorite porch of my favorite place in the world. Home.

When Aiden joined me, he pulled me up and sat in my spot, settling me into his lap.

"I found something interesting in cottage seven yesterday."

"Oh?" I snuggled closer.

"You wouldn't happen to know anything about a broken bathroom tile under the tub, would you?"

I tensed. "Uh. I plead the fifth," I choked out, having totally forgotten about the broken tile.

"Hmm. Figured so. Drop the tub, did you?" he said, trying not to laugh.

"I'll help you fix it," I said, feeling a little bad.

"Yeah, you will," he said, nuzzling my neck.

"It was your fault anyway. You scared the crap out of me."

"I made you hot and bothered, you mean?"

"Hmm. True," I admitted, loving the warmth of Aiden.

We sat for a while, enjoying the brisk night with all the Christmas lights twinkling around us.

"What's going on in that head of yours?" he asked.

I pulled the blanket up. "Nothing—I'm just happy."

"Good," he said and placed his lips on my exposed shoulder. "Warm enough?"

"Enough for now."

"You were amazing today," he said, nuzzling my cheek, then quietly whispered, "I fucking love you."

I looked up to see his face. "Don't you mean you love fucking me?"

He raised his eyebrows. "That's not what I said? It's obviously what I meant."

I extracted myself from his embrace and turned fully to face him.

"What is it?" he asked.

"Thank you for being there today. Every day, really."

"Don't thank me for that," he said. "Beyond my control. You bewitched me, remember?"

"No, I mean thank you for being *with* me, supporting me. You make me less grumpy and that makes me better at my job."

He gripped my hands and brought them to his mouth. "Just don't let them change you. I kind of like you as is."

"I won't. As long as you stay part asshole."

"Oh, you can count on that." Then he stood up, forcing me to do the same. He grabbed my hand and guided me back inside. "I'd like your help with the construction project tomorrow if you can swing it." We walked through the cottage, heading to the bedroom.

"What's up?"

"We already walled in the new stairs on cottage ten. But then we decided to get a larger tub than originally planned, which won't fit up said stairs. I need it brought in through the Juliet balcony."

"*Okaaay.* And what do I get in return?"

"I'm going to give it to you right now. I think you are going to like it." We entered the bedroom.

"Does it involve me being naked?"

He dropped my hand and wrapped me up, flush with his body. "That is step number one, yes."

"Oh, there are multiple steps, then?"

He kissed my lips. "I can guarantee multiple."

I pulled back, turning serious. "Aiden."

"Uh-oh. Lay it on me."

I paused and took a heavy breath because I wanted to get this part right. He waited patiently, and I thought maybe a little wave of anxiety crossed his face.

"There is a possibility . . ." I was doing my best to keep a straight face. "It's possible my vag could eventually crush your manhood. Does that worry you?"

"Fucking hell, woman," he growled, then grabbed me and tossed me into bed, pulling my sweater over my head in a rush. "I can't think of a better way to go."

I laughed out loud. "I'll take that as a no."

Acknowledgments

THANK YOU TO MY EARLY READERS and supporters, including Margaret Lara (who gifts me all her physical books whether I want them or not), Keely G (from our first book club together, I knew yours was an opinion I valued), Elizabeth (aka "Bert aka Lucille," aka "Booth"), Marianne H.W. (who always reminds me that we are writers), and Jennifer Trethewey (the fastest beta reader of all time).

Thanks to my amazing editor Ava Coibion and the rest of the editing and design team at Greenleaf. Thank you for existing!

And to Jeremy, thank you for your unwavering support and encouragement from the first word written to the last, for reading everything I throw at you, and for saving me from a life subsisting only on peanut butter Cap'n Crunch and Raisin Bran.

About the Author

S.L. WOEPPEL gets antsy being in one place too long, so she's lived in various places across the United States, most recently moving from Chicago farther north for even more cold and snow. She has five great loves—family, writing, reading, travel, and municipal bonds. She has an embarrassingly large supply of those tacky souvenir spoons (like more than two hundred) that she keeps in a box in her closet. She can't help it; she just keeps buying them every new place she goes. And she believes there's a little bit of superhero in all of us.